A FINE SCOTTISH TIME

A SCOTTISH ROMANTASY

THE MAGICAL MATCHMAKERS OF SEVEN CAIRNS

BOOK ONE

MAEVE GREYSON

This is a work of fiction. Names, characters, places, and incidents either are the product of the author's imagination or are used fictitiously, and any resemblance to actual persons living or dead, business establishments, events, or locales, is entirely coincidental.

A Fine Scottish Time

COPYRIGHT © 2025 by Maeve Greyson

All rights reserved. No part of this book may be used or reproduced in any manner whatsoever without written permission of the author or Author Maeve Greyson LLC except in the case of brief quotations embodied in critical articles or reviews.

NO AI TRAINING: Without in any way limiting the author's [and publisher's] exclusive rights under copyright, any use of this publication to "train" generative artificial intelligence (AI) technologies to generate text is expressly prohibited. The author reserves all rights to license uses of this work for generative AI training and development of machine learning language models.

Contact Information: maeve@maevegreyson.com

Author Maeve Greyson LLC

55 W. 14th Street

Suite 101

Helena, MT 59601

https://maevegreyson.com/

Published in the United States of America

PROLOGUE

Good day to you. I am Mairwen, Master Time Weaver. In truth, I am Master of all the Divine Weavers, ordained by the goddesses Bride and Cerridwen to ensure the blessed Highland Veil remains intact and that the many worlds and planes of time that it separates remain separated, except for a few friendly visits here and there to unite fated mates.

Ye see, fated mates experience the strongest love bonds, and that strengthens the weave of the Veil, protecting it against those who would destroy it to spread chaos through every known reality. The darkness always seeks to take control. It must be kept at bay.

My apprentice, Keeva, assists me in keeping up with this particular plane's latest temptations. Things that catch a mortal's eye and lure them—beg pardon, I mean, *entice* them to visit Seven Cairns in the Highlands of Scotland, change throughout the centuries. At first glance, Seven Cairns appears to be a quaint Scottish town known for its healing waters, but the Council of Weavers and I know differently.

So if ye find yerself compelled to visit a wee quiet village in the

Highlands, dinna ignore yer intuition. The blessed Highland Veil could require yer help and be calling to ye.

CHAPTER 1

Modern Day
Early summer
New Jersey, USA

"See it? Right there. It's back again." Jessa Tamson angled her cell phone so Emily Mithers, her best friend since they were toddlers, could see it. "I deleted that app fifteen minutes ago, and it's already back. Check and see if yours came back, too."

Emily rolled her eyes. "We're already here, Jess, waiting to board." She patted her fluorescent lime green tote, securely tucked under her arm. "We have our tickets, our cottage booked, our rental reserved. What difference does it make now? It's just some silly dating app that keeps reinstalling itself. Ignore it."

"Some silly dating app?" Jessa couldn't believe her ears. Here they sat at Newark Liberty International Airport, Gate Nine, about to fly off to Scotland because that *silly dating app* had intrigued both of them for over a month now. "You didn't think it was so silly when the same tarot cards kept popping up for a visit to Scotland, and that one guy always shows up behind them no matter how many times I swipe left to see other options." She bumped shoulders with Emily as if they were still children. "And who was it that talked me into spending a good chunk of my shrinking savings on this trip because of that *silly app*?" She felt a little guilty, blaming *all* her irresponsibility on her friend, but dear old Em had been the deciding vote that had teetered her over the edge, head first into this lunacy that couldn't possibly end well. "What if—"

Emily shushed her with a familiar scowl that bordered on the demonic. "Just shut it, Jess. All right? The tickets are non-refundable, and you're way overdue for some good *juju*. Besides, there was no way you were going to be able to afford your landlord's latest rent hike, no matter how much you scrimped and saved, so why worry about it? Mama's sending Papa and the boys over to box up your stuff and get you out of the apartment before the end of the month. You know they love you, Jess, and the loft over their garage is yours as long as you need it. It's nice. You'll love it."

"Then why don't you live there?"

"Because my parents drive me batty. I love them, but their *helpfulness*—and the interference of the fearsome five who are always around looking for a free meal—is unbearable." She grinned. "With you living above the garage, I'm hoping to aim my annoying brothers your way. Maybe then I'll finally have some peace from them. At least, for a little while."

"I'll just tell them you're dating...uhm...crap...I can't remember his name." Jessa picked at the lint on her black leggings that were not only comfortable but helped visually slenderize and elongate her short, thick legs. She wasn't overweight. She was under tall. Clocking in at not quite five feet and on the curvier side of the spectrum, she needed all the help she could get to look taller and slimmer. Therefore, black was her color of choice when selecting garments. "What was his name? The one they hated so much that they showed up at his workplace? That'll get the furious five back on your scent. You know they take whatever I say as gospel."

"You are so ungrateful." Emily shook her head, making the many strands of her long black braids sway with a gentle grace that Jessa's thick mass of coppery curls could never mimic. Emily tapped on the screen of her phone, then showed it to Jessa. "It says here that Seven Cairns is known for its healing waters. Reckon that includes healing bad luck?" She winked. "Maybe we should dip you an extra time or two."

"Wouldn't that be nice?" Jessa shifted in the uncomfortable seat at the boarding gate. Why did decorators never think of short people when designing waiting area chairs? "If those magical healing waters replace bad luck with good, I'll need at least three dips by my figuring." She counted off on her fingers. "Once for either a new job or help with my freelancing as a digital creator. One for a reasonably priced vehicle since my paid-off one didn't survive the neighborhood carjacking, and then one last time for an affordable yet safe place to rent." She wrinkled her nose. "I don't like sponging off your parents."

"It's not sponging off them. You know you're one of us." Emily glanced up from her phone with a compassionate yet somehow pained look. "Mama and Papa love you, Jess. Just like me. Especially after—"

Jessa stopped her with a curt upward flick of her hand, then looked away. The last thing she needed right now was a revisit to the memory of her parents cutting all ties with her by *loudly* announcing in the middle of a crowded restaurant they wished they'd never adopted her. It had happened over five years ago, but that day was still a raw, open wound. "I love your mom and dad, too. Let's leave it at that, okay?"

Emily nodded, then frowned at the vacant airline counter and the closed door behind it. "They're waiting till the last minute to board. I hope nothing's wrong with the plane."

"Do not plant that seed in my head." Fidgety and almost nauseous from nerves, Jessa tapped on the impossible-to-delete app, then tapped again on its tarot deck that always appeared on the home screen. The cards fluttered off the main deck and flipped over to reveal themselves on the vibrant green background that reminded her of a card table at a casino. She released a heavy sigh. Those were the same three cards the app had dealt her for the past month, no matter how many times she tried it. At first, she'd blown it off as an error in the creator's coding. But that was before Emily had tried and gotten different results, and Emily's parents and brothers had all received wide-ranging outcomes every time they tapped on it.

But Jessa always got the same three cards. The ace of wands that the app said represented the beginning of a journey, the birth of new ideas, and the start of creative projects. The fool, supposedly representing wonder, anticipation, excitement, and the need to go your own way, and the unicorn from the oracle deck, said to bring messages of hope and attract love, light, and healing, and beneath all three cards were the same three words: Seven Cairns, Scotland. She shook her head. That app was one hell of an advertisement for Seven Cairns, Scotland's tourism board.

With her finger hovering over the triquetra symbol flickering from green to gold between the cards displayed on the app, she tried to ignore the urge to tap it and see if the mysterious Mr. MacSexy, as she and Emily had dubbed him, appeared yet again.

"Might as well," she muttered and touched it.

There he was, a dark-haired, broody male with fierce gray eyes that flashed like lightning in a stormy sky. He had a square jaw dusted with a day's growth of beard and an aquiline nose crooked enough to make him even more handsome. Full lips. A cutting glare. He was so unbelievably gorgeous that Jessa had enlarged the picture as much as possible to see if it was real or AI generated. He seemed real enough, but it was hard to tell these days. With no profile name or personal details, she had finally decided he was a character programmed into the app. But if that were the case, why did Emily and her family retrieve pictures and data on all sorts of individuals whenever they tried to help Jessa prove that the stupid thing was malfunctioning?

"Leave it alone, Jess," Emily told her without looking up from her own phone. "You're just winding yourself up."

"I can't help myself." Jessa powered down the device and shoved it into the faded denim backpack she'd carried since college.

Emily also put hers away and scowled at the vacant airline counter again. "You applied your patch, right? And brought the plastic barf bag we got from Papa's office?"

"Yes, to both, and I haven't had anything to eat or drink, so if I do get sick, it'll just be the dry heaves." Nobody knew her as well as Emily. Jessa touched the motion sickness disk stuck behind her ear and sent a silent *thank you* to Dr. Mithers, Emily's dad. He'd recommended the patch because he knew she hated taking any sort of medication that made her feel *disconnected*. The patch might make her a little drowsy, but it wouldn't turn her into a glassy-eyed zombie.

She scooted forward in the uncomfortable chair and nervously tapped her toes on the floor. "Come on," she said with a quiet groan. "Let's do this."

"Here he comes," Emily said.

A harried man loped toward the waiting area, dodging passengers and their luggage as he shrugged on the official blazer that told everyone his untimeliness was the reason they hadn't boarded yet. When he reached the counter, he flipped on the microphone, making it squeal so loudly that everyone cringed. "Sorry about the last minute boarding, folks, and the noise too. Nothing wrong with the plane, mind you. Everything tickety-boo there."

"*Tickety-boo?*" Jessa gave Emily a hard side-eye. "I think I've changed my mind."

"Non-refundable, Jess." Emily grabbed her by the arm and tugged her to her feet. "Come on. We're going. This trip'll do you good. Especially when Jeremy sees all the fun you're having without him."

Jessa swung her backpack onto her shoulder, purposely whacking her friend with it in the process. Of all the people for Em to bring up right now: lying, two-timing Jeremy. She clenched her boarding pass even tighter as they lined up and slowly made their way to the jittery and quite possibly overly caffeinated airline worker scanning the passes. "I've blocked that jerk on every site," she told Emily. "My doings are no longer available for his viewing pleasure."

"Yeah, well, I haven't blocked him, and I'm tagging him in everything." Emily hugged her cheek against Jessa's and held up the phone for a selfie. "Smile, Jess. Big smile that tells the world you're loving life without that loser."

Jessa faked a wide smile that made her cheeks ache while second-guessing this trip to Scotland for the thousandth time. But as Emily had said, the tickets were non-refundable. "No more selfies for a while, okay?"

"Whatever you say." Emily showed her boarding pass to the attendant, went through the door, and disappeared around the turn.

Jessa held out her pass, but when the man tried to take it, she couldn't seem to let it go.

"Madam?" He tugged on it again while giving her a fake *please, lady, can we just get on with it* smile. "I need to scan it, and then you may have it back. I promise."

"She's just a little nervous about flying," Emily told him as she rushed back, yanked the pass out of Jessa's grip, then gave it back to her once he'd finished with it.

"I'm just a little nervous about life right now," Jessa muttered as she plodded down the ramp behind Emily and stepped onto the plane. This last year had sucked the life out of her. The breakup with Jeremy right when she'd thought they were about to make things permanent. Laid off from her dream job. The carjacking. An unexpected hike in her rent, or, to be more accurate, losing her apartment and having to accept Emily's parents' charity. She almost gagged at the thought of being so desperate and needy. She had always been independent and adventurous, but this harsh run of bad luck had her ducking for cover over the slightest things.

They found their seats and stowed their bags under the seats in front of them. The rest of their luggage was in the belly of the plane. Or, at least, Jessa hoped it was there since they planned to stay in Scotland for a month. As a popular influencer, Emily could run her business from anywhere, and as a freelance digital creator, Jessa could as well. The lady from the cottage they'd rented in Seven Cairns had assured them of passable cellphone reception and marginally better wireless connectivity. If all else failed, they were within an hour's drive from Inverness and several reliable possibilities they could access for little or no additional cost.

"Our adventure is set." Emily excitedly patted her on the arm and winked. "Maybe we'll even find your Mr. MacSexy."

Jessa closed her eyes, pulled in a deep breath, then eased it out while concentrating on relaxing. "I'm sure all we'll have to do is look up *MacSexy* in the phone book, and it'll lead us right to him."

"It's going to be all right, Jess," Emily said with rare but genuine seriousness. "I feel it."

"I hope you're right, Em." Jessa kept her eyes tightly closed. If she opened them, tears brought on by anxiety and worry might escape. She faked a yawn. "This patch is making me sleepy. If I snore, nudge me. Okay?"

Emily pressed a tissue into her hand, then gave her arm another squeeze. "I promise it's going to be all right."

With all her heart and soul, Jessa hoped her friend was right.

MAIRWEN SHUFFLED the tarot deck while waiting for the rest of the Council. She idly dealt them in her favorite layout and slowly turned them face up. The familiar smoothness of the cards with their worn, faded edges felt like a chat with an old friend. Ah, but old friends were rarely so cryptic when they offered advice. The somewhat confusing symbolism of the cards could be troubling to those who took them too seriously. Some mortals were afraid to sneeze without the colorful cards' permission. She laughed and re-dealt them. Those mortals should focus on looking within and connecting with the higher energies. That thought made her slowly shake her head. It seldom worked that way. Mortals rarely took the wisest path. Guiding them was much like herding cats. Of course, not all of them possessed the ability to embrace the powers, and more often than not, those blessed with the auld ways shied away because they feared what others might think.

A wry snort hissed free of her. Then there were those who couldn't connect with the energies if their lives depended on it. Yet they conned the world into thinking they were the ultimate mystics and seers. The wealth and fame they attained by manipulating the fears and beliefs of others were lowly and without honor. Little did they realize that everything they sent out into this world would eventually return to them times three. Retribution would come and not be pleasant when it did. Karma never forgot or overlooked anyone.

She picked up the cards and shuffled them again, finding their quiet shushing between her hands pleasant and calming. This era's ever-increasing fascination with the mystical made her apprentice Keeva's *app* most effective. Mairwen paused and made a face. Was that the correct word? *App?* After a moment of study and sorting through her memories, she nodded with certainty. Yes. That was it. *App is short for application,* Keeva had told her. Mairwen often wondered where her wily apprentice came up with such things, but the dear girl did spend a great deal of time among the mortals studying their interests to gain more clarity about joining them with their fated mates.

Keeva's zeal and devotion made Mairwen hum a prideful little tune. She had been wise to select that particular young one for training. Few would devote so much energy to understanding the complicated yet treasured mortals. The apprentice had quickly discovered that evolution among those they sought to match seemed to follow an uneven pattern, much like raindrops spilling down a glass. Some raced along, advancing, learning, and readily accepting that which the energies offered. But then others stubbornly clung to the same spot as if fearing to move in any direction. Odd yet exquisite creatures, they were, and it was a Divine Weaver's honor to guide them while protecting the strength of the ancient Veil.

"They're coming," Keeva announced from the doorway of the meeting hall. "Most are, anyway."

"Most?" Mairwen tidied her stack of cards and set them aside. "*All* are needed to prepare. Our guests are due to arrive this evening. Where is Killian? He can help ye bring them along."

Keeva wrinkled her nose and tucked a strand of long hair that was currently dyed a deep purple behind one of her ever so slightly pointed ears. "He's fetching the dark ones. I passed the word amongst the light."

Mairwen folded her hands on the table and gave her apprentice a sharp look she knew the lass would take to heart. For Keeva to become a Master Time Weaver, she needed to overcome her insecurities about dealing with the Weavers of the Dark, those who guided mortals with conflict, curses, nightmares, emptiness, and hate. "Next time, I want ye to be the one to fetch the dark and Killian to fetch the light, ye ken?"

"Aye, Mairwen. I will." Keeva chewed on her bottom lip and glumly stared at the floor. "Shall I make sure the tea is ready for the meeting?"

"Aye." Mairwen hated making the young one feel *less*, but the apprentice had to learn that unpleasant tasks should not be shirked or bartered off to others. It was far better to complete them and get them over with. She leaned back in the ornately carved, high-backed chair at the head of the table and fixed her gaze on the doorway, watching for the nine who completed the Council of Weavers and reported directly to the goddesses Bride and Cerridwen.

As per usual, Ishbel, Master of the Spell Weavers, arrived first with her favorite grimoire tucked in the crook of her arm. She swept off her bright purple and red cloak, giving a friendly nod as she draped it over her chair, then took her seat at the table. The Council's long wooden table had served them well for untold ages under the protective magic of Seven Cairns. The amiable witch patted and smoothed her messy curls, but only made her rather unwieldy gray bun wilder rather than tamer. "Will we be matching both the lasses with their mates, then? A two for one binding this time?"

"That has yet to be decided," Mairwen said. "The second one does not appear destined for the same place in time as the first."

"More's the pity, then. They are more sisters than friends. Reckon we can work out something to enable them to remain connected? The Veil's weave thrives on many forms of love, ye ken?"

"We shall see." Mairwen refused to get into particulars until the others arrived.

Shona, Master of the Tranquility Weavers, and Glennis, Master of the Dream Weavers, arrived next, chattering and talking over one another like a pair of cackling hens. Bedelia, Master of the Love Weavers, followed close behind, herding them along like a loving shepherdess. The three took their seats on Mairwen's right. From this position, those of the light faced the tall arched windows on the eastern wall of the stone building that resembled an ancient seat of power more than a sleepy village's meeting center. Most in Seven Cairns couldn't recall when the goddesses had erected the structure. It had simply always been there. Mairwen had an inkling of when it came to be, but that was one of the many secrets the Master of all the Divine Weavers kept to themselves.

"It is my understanding that Killian is gathering the rest of our group," she said in answer to the pointed looks at the empty seats on the other side of the table. Those chairs faced the wall of the room, which always found itself in shadows, no matter the time of day.

Ishbel rolled her eyes. "It is always the same."

"It is always the same because our invitations are always extended last." Malcolm, Master of the Conflict Weavers, scowled at them from the doorway with his twin sister, Darina, at his side, looking ready to defend him.

"That has been addressed," Mairwen told him. "Please join us.

There is much to discuss about this particular bonding. Darina, this meeting is restricted to those of the Council."

Darina offered a sly grin. "I know. I simply wished to make ye say it." She spun around and left the building, her smug chortling floating back to them through the open windows.

"Ye always say there is much to discuss," said Taskill, Master of the Curse Weavers, as he entered the room and took his seat. "Shall we cut the theatrics and stick to the facts? There are presently many in need of cursing."

"Once Flanna, Sadbha, and Graine arrive, we shall begin." Mairwen focused on the doorway, ignoring Taskill's fidgeting. It was always the same, Taskill in a hurry to go, and the last three dark ones late.

He drummed his fingers on the table. "Do we really need the Nightmare, Emptiness, and Hate Weavers this time?"

"Together, we make a whole, Taskill. Ye know that as well as I." Mairwen smiled at those around the table. "We balance each other. Without the darkness, we cannot appreciate the light. Without the light, the darkness becomes nothing more than a void."

"We are here," Flanna, Master of the Nightmare Weavers, said as she swept into the room. Sadbha, Master of the Emptiness Weavers, and Graine, Master of the Hate Weavers, accompanied her. The three women took their seats at the table, all appearing less than interested in being there.

"I have visited the one called Jessa for several months now," Flanna said. "Her strength against my nightmares is impressive."

"Sadbha and I were also unable to maintain a suitable presence within her because of her friend," Graine reported.

"The friend, the one called Emily, allowed you to manifest hatred for a while," Sadbha told Graine, then shook her head, making her gleaming white braids sway from side to side. "But neither of them tolerated my emptiness. The skills of my Weavers will be of no use in this bonding. We could put ourselves to better use instead of sitting at this table and twiddling our thumbs."

"Nevertheless," Mairwen said, "yer perspective is valued and needed for balance—so says Bride and Cerridwen."

"So says Bride and Cerridwen," all at the table echoed.

Mairwen nodded for Keeva and Killian to bring in the tea, then smiled and patted the tarot deck. "As I already shared with Ishbel, the lasses due to arrive this evening are not destined to reside in the same age, which could prove troublesome since the two are more like sisters than friends. Ishbel asked if a special circumstance might be settled upon. I, too, would like to discuss that possibility since close friendship is a form of love and might help the Veil."

"The male that the first one is to be matched with is due a curse," Taskill said with a curt tip of his dark head. "Had he been more patient with his first wife and her addiction to the laudanum—"

"His first wife was not his fated mate," Bedelia said. "The Love Weavers cannot foster that which is not meant to be. He was kind to her and did not set her aside. She left him. The woman completed her destiny as it was written."

"All mortals are to be valued. He placed little value on her and the time they shared. If he had, she might have stayed and overcome her weakness." Taskill glared at the Master Love Weaver, squaring his shoulders as if ready to brawl.

"That is enough." Mairwen waited for them both to cede without protest, knowing they would, because out of all the Weavers in existence, she possessed the most power and the closest relationship with the goddesses. Some even believed her to be a direct descendant of both Bride and Cerridwen, but she never confirmed or denied that rumor, preferring to earn their respect by her actions rather than her bloodline. "Grant MacAlester has endured curses enough by surviving eighteenth century Scotland after the Jacobite uprising. The war nearly decimated his clan before he was even born, and now he fights against the start of the clearances. Starvation and want have walked with him like a brother. Only now do his kith and kin flourish under his leadership and a smuggling operation he has honed to the sharpest efficiency I have ever seen. Is that not curses enough for ye, Taskill?"

"Many endured those bloody times," Taskill said with a defiant scowl. "Because the Fates deemed it so. Not because of my Weavers' curses."

"He refuses the love of a wife or family. All he concerns himself with is the survival of his clan." Bedelia's eyes twinkled as she peered at the Master Curse Weaver over the rim of her teacup. She took a slow sip before continuing. "Could those things not be considered curses as well, depending upon one's perspective?"

Mairwen watched Taskill, waiting as the Weaver came to his own conclusion. As one of the youngest masters, he tended to overthink things and took his time about doing so. But even her infinite patience had its limits, and she didn't wish this meeting to last the entire day. "What say you, Taskill? Will you allow it and leave Laird MacAlester to his fated mate and the other Weavers?"

Nostrils flaring like a bull about to charge, Taskill snorted and threw up a hand, shooing away the unpleasantness of relinquishing power. "I will allow it—but only this once."

Mairwen nodded at Killian, Keeva's brother. "So note it, if ye will."

With a strange short stick, a sleek, black *stylus pen*, or so Keeva had called it, Killian recorded the decision on the thin device he balanced in the palm of his hand. To Mairwen, it looked like a rectangular plate that glowed with a soft white light. Keeva had explained that the mortals would think it was one of their *tablets*, even though she had created it to record decisions of the Council into the goddesses' Ledger of Infinity. Such an inventive apprentice, that Keeva. Mairwen allowed herself another moment of pride for choosing her.

"Since there are two," Malcolm said, his pale blue eyes gleaming with their usual appetite for conflict. "Could some of my younger Weavers train with the *friend?*"

"I will not grace that with a response." Mairwen allowed her displeasure at the devaluation of their soon-to-arrive guests to be mere practice subjects to alter the vibration and hue of her aura. It was a subtle warning all the Weavers recognized.

"I was merely asking." Malcolm looked aside and shifted in his chair, obviously insulted, but wise enough not to push the issue.

"As we have done in the past, we will warmly welcome our visitors and treat them as the valued individuals they are." She narrowed her eyes at Malcolm. "Which means we will not refer to them as annoying tourists or rude Americans. Is that understood?"

Malcolm pointed at Taskill. "That was him. Not me."

"The last three *were* annoying and rude." Taskill bared his teeth in disgust. "Fated mates or not. I canna stomach the rude ones." He rubbed his fingers together. "Makes me itch to curse them, whether 'tis warranted or not."

"I am sure they'll find our little village and its healing waters enchanting and a balm to their souls," Shona said.

Graine snorted. "Spoken like a true Tranquility Weaver. The lot of ye are so deluded."

"At least hatred doesn't eat us alive," Shona replied sweetly.

Mairwen thumped the table with her fist. She knew exactly who was behind the unrest at the table. "Malcolm! Ye will cease this verra minute. If ye continue sewing discord during meetings, there will be consequences. That is a blatant misuse of power and ye know it as well as I."

The Conflict Master tried to stifle a wicked grin and failed. "Forgive me, Mairwen. I thought a bit of levity might move things along."

"Yer definition of levity needs adjusting," Mairwen told him, while allowing a mystical *sting* that was much like a frustrated mother's pinch of an unruly son's arm to touch him. "Ye're well past a thousand years old, and ye behave as if ye're barely a hundred. Act yer age or I'll be sending ye straight to Cerridwen so fast yer head will spin off yer neck."

Malcolm sat straighter and bowed his head. "Forgive me. It will nay happen again."

She glared at him a moment longer before turning to the others. "Graine and Shona, in future, before ye *react* one against the other, consider what might be triggering the urge for that reaction. Ye may be opposites, but that doesn't mean ye canna work together and attempt to get along for the good of the Veil. Do ye wish to face the chaos that would come were it to fall?"

Graine bowed her head and held out her hand to Shona. "Forgive me, Master of Tranquility."

Shona took it and bowed her head as well. "Only if ye will forgive me, Master of Hate."

Mairwen forced herself to find the calm needed to maintain the balance among the powerful Weavers. "Thank you. I appreciate robust discussions and opinions from everyone here, but I canna tolerate that which does not benefit the Veil. Now, as I said earlier, the ladies are coming to Seven Cairns not only because of Keeva's app but also to find respite from their troubles. We are a quaint, *friendly* village in the Highlands known for our healing waters, and that is all we shall be to them until time to send Jessa Tamson back in time to join with Laird Grant MacAlester."

"And the friend?" Ishbel asked. "I sensed powerful magic in Emily Mithers as well."

"As well?"

"Aye, both lasses have the gift. They just don't know it yet."

"Interesting." Mairwen looked to Bedelia. "Did ye know of this when ye discovered Miss Tamson belonged with the laird?"

Bedelia shook her head. "My Weavers and I search out mate bonds, not magic."

"As I said, interesting." Mairwen picked up her tarot deck and started shuffling. "These guests might prove even more enjoyable than expected."

CHAPTER 2

Jessa shifted her weight from one foot to the other and noticed Emily was doing the same. "Do you think it would offend them if I offered to help?" She tipped a subtle nod at the elderly couple in front of them.

"Go for it. Offended or not, I'm ready to find the quickest way to the train station so we don't miss our connection. The lady at the gate said this guy could help us better than anyone."

Jessa eased up beside the frazzled pair of seniors whose same questions repeated over and over had become more like roaring shouts pelted at the employee behind the rental car counter. "Hi there," she interrupted, doing her best to sound harmless and helpful. "I'm Jessa. Is there a problem?"

The young man behind the counter threw up his hands. "I ken they're fair scunnered, but there's no reason for that old roaster to threaten a square go. I offered them a stoater of a ker."

The older gentleman growled and shook his fist, but the grandmotherly woman at his side caught hold of his arm and gave a sharp shake of her head. "Enough, Leonard," she said overly loud, which made Jessa wonder if the fuming senior had trouble hearing. "Perhaps this nice young lady can translate for us." The poor woman's imploring look told Jessa everything she needed to know. The pair were exhausted and struggling with the Glaswegian employee's slang.

Thankfully, she and Emily had come across this very topic on social media and researched it further since they were landing in Glasgow and then taking the train to Inverness where they intended to rent a car and drive to Seven Cairns. She picked up the keys and jingled them at the equally frustrated Scot behind the counter. "Which one?"

"Red. Far side. Third row. It'll make'm look right minted, it will."

She had a fair idea that the guy was very proud of the car and guaranteed it would make the weary couple look like they were rich. Jessa doubted if the oldsters cared about that particular point, but she would pass it on to them. "Have they signed everything? Can they take it and go?"

The cute in an overgrown puppy sort of way Glaswegian grinned. "Aye."

She turned and waved Emily forward. "While I get Mr. and Mrs. —?"

"Reedsbee," the scowling gentleman said with a growl, his shaggy white mustache twitching as if he wanted to bite the next person who dared to speak to him.

"While I get Mr. and Mrs. Reedsbee into their car, you find out about the train." She smiled at the pair who could be anywhere from their sixties to their nineties. It was hard to tell because it wasn't the years that aged a person but their experiences. "Let's find this pretty red car that he guarantees will make you look like the richest couple in Glasgow."

"Great. We'll get mugged," the old man said as he hitched the strap of his suitcase higher on his shoulder.

"Stop it, Leonard." His wife gave Jessa a relieved smile. "Thank you so very much for your help."

Once they found the car and Jessa had helped them stow their bags, Mr. Reedsbee tried to press some money into her hand. "Here. For your trouble."

She shook her head and backed away. "No. None of that now. You and Mrs. Reedsbee enjoy Scotland, okay?"

Still grumbling under his breath, he shook the wad of cash at her again. "You helped us out. Take it."

"Goodbye, Mr. Reedsbee," she said as she turned and walked away. "Don't forget to drive on the left side of the road."

"I know that," he said with another snarl, then muttered more that she couldn't hear.

Jessa smiled to herself as she headed back to the rental car center of the terminal, hoping the couple got some rest and enjoyed their trip. Good deeds always made her feel warm and fuzzy, but had this one really been all that good? She'd done it to get access to the guy behind the counter and his knowledge about the train. So did that mean it wasn't good after all, because she'd done it for her own benefit? The thought wiped away her smile and made her sigh. Seems like there was always a dark side to everything.

Emily met her at the door and pointed at a sleek black limousine pulling up to the curb. "Guess what? We get a free ride in style to Glasgow Central as a hearty thank you for bailing out that guy so he could call his girlfriend about their date tonight. At least, I think that's what he said. Anyway—we're all set."

The much happier Glaswegian brought their luggage out on the trolley and helped the limo driver load everything into the trunk.

"Hope yer stay's a right peach!" he called out as he headed back inside.

"The last time I rode in a limo was senior prom, I think." Jessa slid across the sumptuous leather seat, hugging her backpack and trying not to touch anything. She was grubby from travel, and the child seated in front of them on the plane had thrown his sippy cup at his mother and showered them all with a sticky substance that was some sort of fruit juice.

"This is nice," Emily said, touching everything she could reach.

"You're as bad as that toddler on the plane."

"What is this?" Emily pulled open a door and gasped. "Look! All kinds of drinks and snackies."

"Traffic's no' bad this time of day, ladies," the driver said. "Should have ye there in no time at all."

"I think that's code for *leave stuff alone*," Jessa whispered to Emily while snatching away the soda and crisps Emily had taken from the minibar. She returned the items to where they belonged, then threatened her friend with a stern shake of her head. "We'll eat when we get there. The lady said she'd stocked the cottage with enough essentials to get us started."

"It's a little over three hours to Inverness," Emily said. "I'm starving."

"We'll grab something at the station. Surely, there'll be vending machines there. If not, I've got a nutrition bar you can eat on the train." Jessa hugged her backpack tighter, her anxiousness ratcheting even higher than before they'd boarded the plane back in Jersey. They were in Scotland—men in kilts, bagpipes, and adorably hairy cows freaking Scotland. She had spent most of her hard-earned savings to spend a month here because...Well, because she was a lunatic, she guessed. What in blue blazes had she been thinking? She shifted in the seat and happened to meet the driver's amused gaze in the rearview mirror. The connection with him squeezed the air out of her lungs, making her choke and gasp. His uniform had somehow disappeared, replaced with clothing that made him look like he belonged in some historical reenactment.

"Jess! What the hell?" Emily pounded her on the back. "Are you all right?

"It's him," she wheezed while nodding at the driver.

Emily glanced at the man, then frowned and leaned closer. "Who?" she whispered.

"Mr. MacSexy." Jessa thumped her chest, fighting to calm down.

How could she have missed it when he'd held the door for them while they climbed into the limo? How could she not recognize that face she'd studied for the past month on the app? And how in blue blazes had he changed clothes while driving? Was he some sort of freaking magician? "It's him. And he changed clothes. It's him from the tarot dating app."

"I think that motion sickness patch is making you hallucinate." Emily took out her phone and started texting. "I'm going to wake up Papa and ask if that's a side effect."

Jessa risked looking at the driver again and shuddered with an eerie chill. He was back in his uniform and unquestionably handsome, but old enough to be her grandfather and most definitely *not* the Mr. MacSexy who always glowered at her from the app on her phone.

"Yeah," she weakly mumbled as she sagged back into the buttery soft seat. "Find out if hallucinations are a side effect."

"Papa says, *possibly,* but it's more likely due to anxiety and travel fatigue." Emily texted a reply, her thumbs flying as she messaged her parent again. She stared at the phone, waiting. When it softly dinged with another message, her eyes narrowed, and she nodded, then reached over and peeled the patch off Jessa's neck. "Just to be on the safe side, he said."

"What if I puke on the train?" Jessa rubbed the spot where the patch had been stuck behind her ear.

"Then you puke on the train." Emily fixed her with a stern look. "Or would you rather choke until you pass out because of a hallucination?"

"Puking sounds the better of the two."

"You need to try to relax, Jess. I'm worried about you." Emily rubbed her back, making Jessa wince as she thumped her between the shoulder blades. "Everything is going to be all right. We're here for a glorious month, and when we get home, you'll be safely nested in the loft above the garage. That's not so bad now, is it?"

"Almost there, ladies," the driver said. "Is yer friend there all right, miss? She's gone a bit peely-wally."

"I'm fine, thank you," Jessa hurried to say before Emily could answer. "I think the long flight's catching up with me."

The driver responded with a polite nod, but Jessa noticed he kept glancing at her in the rearview mirror. Poor man. He probably thought she was about to throw up all over the expensive leather interior or pass out, and he'd have to deal with getting her medical assistance or clean up her mess.

She sat straighter, forced a smile, and pulled in a deep breath to put his mind at ease. Emily was right. She needed to relax and tackle —no—*enjoy* each moment as it came. This free ride was very nice, much better than a taxi or an Uber. It was like floating on a cloud as the vibrant buildings and busy sidewalks of Glasgow slipped by beyond the tinted windows.

Just as she was breathing easier, they arrived at Central Station. After unloading their luggage, the driver tipped his hat, then eyed Jessa a moment longer and winked before getting back inside the limo and driving away.

His *wink* sent a tingle through her that lasted far longer than it should have. She stared after the car with the definite feeling that something important—she had no idea what—was dangling just beyond her reach. "I think I'm losing my mind."

"Anxiety and travel fatigue, remember?" Emily nudged her along. "Come on. This place is huge. We better get a move on and find where we're supposed to be."

Jessa brought up the ticket information on her phone. "According to this, we're going to have to change trains at Glasgow Queen Street. Looks like we should've gone through there instead of starting here at Glasgow Central."

"Yeah, well, live and learn." Emily squinted up at the boards. "What number was it again?"

"Four zero five. They estimated it would be Platform Four."

"It is." Emily pointed. "That way."

After stopping at a shop and loading up on snacks and energy drinks, they scanned their tickets at the platform and discovered that, somehow, they had been upgraded to first class. A smiling attendant confirmed it and pointed them in the right direction.

"See?" Emily said. "Scotland is already bringing us good *juju*."

Jessa settled into the roomy seat in front of a wide window and patted the table in front of her. "This is nice. Shame we have to lose it when we switch to Glasgow Queen Street."

"Didn't you catch what he said? We're first class all the way to Inverness." Emily set her energy drink on the table and tore into her bag of chips. "I wonder why they call them crisps?" she said while studying the package and crunching *loudly*.

"From the sound of it, probably because that's what they are. You don't find it strange that we mysteriously won the railway ticket lottery and got upgraded to first-class seats?" Jessa welcomed good luck whenever it came, but lately, anytime something good happened, something bad quickly followed.

Emily shook the bag and held it out to her. "Eat some crisps and be thankful."

"I think I'd better hold off on eating until we get to the cottage." She jumped and grabbed hold of the table as the train slid into motion.

"Papa should've prescribed you something stronger than motion sickness patches," Emily said. "You're a wreck."

"Sorry." Jessa felt guilty about casting a pall over the trip that would surely give them memories that lasted a lifetime. She pulled in a deep breath, then let it ease out while assuming a pose of serenity. "My calm is coming. Sometimes, it's just a little late to the party."

"Wow, by the time we get comfortable, it'll be time to switch trains." Emily stuffed the half-eaten bag of chips into her carry-on and gulped down her energy drink.

"Your heart is going to explode if you keep chugging those like that," Jessa said as she read the label of her unopened can. "You should've gotten one of these. Mine's healthier."

"There is a time to be healthy and a time to be awake." Emily held up her phone and grinned. "Selfie to show we've arrived in bonnie Scotland? You refused at the airport."

"Fine, but better make it quick. Looks like we're pulling into the station to make our switch." Jessa rose and leaned across the table so she and Emily would be cheek to cheek in front of the window. She held the smile until Emily plopped back down into her seat and started tapping on her phone with blinding speed.

"All posted," she said as the train slid to a smooth stop. "Just in time."

Jessa rose and secured her denim backpack onto the handle of her rolling suitcase. As she wheeled it out into the aisle, she halted and stared at a man up ahead who scowled back at her. It was *him* again. Mr. MacSexy. Dressed in those clothes that had to be from a historical reenactment, a travel agency ad, or a movie set. Unable to move, barely able to breathe, at least she didn't crumble into a gasping mess this time. She closed her eyes tightly, then slowly opened them. The man was gone. She stretched to see around the passengers getting off the train, trying to find him again, but he was nowhere to be found. She raced to catch up with him.

"Jess! Wait up," Emily called out.

As they stepped onto the platform, Jessa debated laying her hard-sided suitcase on its side and standing on it so she could see farther.

"Jessa!" Emily sounded like a frustrated mother trying to keep track of her overactive child. "What is going on with you?"

Jessa hurried to shake her head. "Nothing. Just thought I saw someone we knew."

Emily frowned. "Who?" Suspicion dripped from that one word.

"Josh from the internet cafe," she said, knowing that if she told Emily the truth, it would throw her into a panic and cause a ripple effect through the entire Mithers family. "He mentioned planning a trip to Scotland the last time he worked on my laptop."

"Liar." Emily narrowed her eyes, fueling the accusation with concern. "You thought you saw Mr. MacSexy again, didn't you?"

"Come on." Jessa ignored the question and threaded her way through the crowd. "We don't want to miss our connection. The other platform's just up ahead, and people are already loading." A hard tug on the strap of her backpack pulled her to a stop.

"We're not going a step farther until you fess up."

"I'm just tired. Once I've napped and adjusted to the time difference, I'll be fine." She forced a reassuring grin that would've done any award-winning actress proud. "If I'm not, you can dunk me in those healing waters until I come up giddy for an adventure."

"Don't think I won't."

Jessa didn't doubt for a minute that Emily would take great joy in sousing her under until she gave in and embraced all the good *juju* that Scotland had to offer.

***

MacAlester Keep
Scottish Highlands
Year of our Lord 1785

"Old Mairwen is here. Wants a word with ye."

"Dinna call her old, lest ye want yer willy cursed to shrivel and fall off." Grant MacAlester leaned back in his chair and rubbed his tired, gritty eyes. He'd stared at the logbooks for hours, making certain he and the clan had not been cheated on the latest haul of tea, tobacco, and brandy.

"Ye ken why she's come, then?" Henry Skelper, more a brother than a friend, shifted in place until the floorboards groaned under his massive weight. He was such a bear of a man that he could toss Ben Nevis over his shoulder as if it were naught but a pebble rather than the mightiest peak in all the Highlands.

"If I were the bettin' sort…" Grant stopped scrubbing his weary eyes and let his hands drop to the arms of his chair, "and I've been known to place a wager or two. I'd say the clan has nettled her into speaking with me about taking another wife. Some seem overly concerned about an heir for the earldom." He jabbed a finger at Henry. "And if ye call me *Lord Suddie*, I'll skin ye."

"But ye are Lord Suddie," Mairwen said from the doorway.

An eerie shiver raced through him. It was always the same whenever the white witch, as Grant always thought of her, appeared on his doorstep. "Be that as it may," he said as he stood out of respect, "I prefer not to be addressed as such."

The petite, silvery-haired matron had eyes such a startling shade of blue that they made the clearest of skies seem dim. She narrowed them at him long enough to set his teeth on edge, then made her way into his office, moving with such effortless grace she seemed to float across the floor. "And the clan has not nettled me into coming here. I came of my own accord."

"Ye have the hearing of a wee owl." Grant motioned to the chair in front of his desk and gave a nod for Henry to leave. He couldn't resist chuckling as the massive man, who feared nothing except Mairwen, almost tripped over his own feet in his hurry to get out the door. "What did ye do to poor ol' Henry this time?"

"Do?"

"Aye. Did ye not just see him run as if his tail was on fire?"

She rippled a dismissive shrug. "I merely asked after his health. He seems a bit *less* of late."

"I see." Grant hadn't seen a change in the man, but he refused to waste time arguing the point. There was only one matter he wished to make clear. "I'll no' be taking another wife, Mairwen."

"Why not?"

"How many times have we talked about this?" He ambled over to the cabinet in the corner and poured two glasses of whisky. She was the only woman he had ever met who could drink him into a blethering fool while she remained as sober as if she'd had nothing stronger than tea. He offered her the glass. "From one of the older barrels. Tell me what ye think of it, m'lady."

She took a sip, then grew thoughtful while holding it on her tongue. Raising the drink closer to the oil lamp on his desk, she swirled the golden liquid to catch the light of the flame. "Verra nice. Fine color and smooth on the tongue. 'Twill fetch a good price should ye decide to offer it to yer customers." She took another sip, then slid the glass onto his desk and relaxed back into her chair. "I would move it among the elite with the caveat that it was made exclusively for them, ye ken? Play to their bloated sense of self-importance. Greater profit that way." Her infuriating calmness as she studied him warned she was not done with him yet. "Now tell me, why will ye not consider taking another wife? A love match this time."

"Mairwen."

"Rumbling my name in that warning tone neither frightens nor convinces me to leave ye be." She barely tilted her head to one side and smiled. "And I remember all yer prior arguments, so let's not waste our time by repeating them, ye ken?"

"I dinna believe in love. Therefore, why bother?" And that was the truth of it. He had never loved. Well, he had. But that was a different sort of love, love for his clan, for his friends, for kith and kin. "And ye ken as well as I how my first marriage, the arranged one, ended. We will not travel that path again. 'Twas far more trouble than pleasure."

"Ye are a stubborn man, Grant MacAlester."

That made him smile. "Aye. So ye tell me at every opportunity."

Her expression daunting, she rose and leaned over his desk, making him itch to push his chair back to escape her. He tightened his fists and forced himself to hold fast and hide his leeriness.

She spoke quietly, as if knowing her words always thundered through him. "What if I told ye Seven Cairns has found that part of yer heart ye've been missing all these years?"

He swallowed hard and sucked in a deep breath, suddenly starving for air. Nothing chilled him more than the mention of Seven Cairns. 'Twas an unholy place in the eyes of the church, and Grant knew why. It wasn't a simple weaver's village, and neither was Mairwen a harmless weaver. Seven Cairns was one of the holiest of places in the Highlands to those who still followed the auld ways. He'd heard the tales of the place told around the fires on long winter evenings, and somewhere, deep in his soul, he knew those tales were not just stories.

"My heart is whole," he said. "It beats in my chest just fine."

She pushed away from his desk and meandered around the cluttered room, idly touching a book here or a bauble there as though committing the place to memory. "And what of her from yer dreams?" she asked with a slyness that made him swallow hard again. "Do ye not wish to meet her?"

"I dinna ken of whom ye speak."

Without even glancing at him, she huffed a snort of amusement. "Dinna lie to me, my fine laird. 'Tis insulting." She pulled a book from its shelf, opened it, and slowly paged through it. "Only the truth between us, remember? I have never lied to ye or any of yer clan." She thumped the book shut and returned it to its place among the others. "I have seen her and think her a lovely lass. Tiny but mighty, what with that coppery hair of hers that shines as though newly minted. Reminds me of the Goddess Bride herself."

The woman he had dreamed of for the past few months appeared in his mind as if commanded to do so by Mairwen. "She is not tiny," he said, shifting in place at the hard rising that the vision of the enticing lass always gave him.

Mairwen ceded with a nod. "True. Her shape is bountiful for one so short in stature." The witch's smile became all too knowing. "She would keep ye warm on the coldest of nights and be a fine mother to yer many sons."

"She is naught but a dream." He refilled his glass and downed it, welcoming the burn in his gullet. "If ye need more supplies at Seven Cairns, ye have but to send a messenger, ye ken? There is no need to risk coming here yerself."

"Our supplies are ample for now." Mischief flashed in Mairwen's eyes. "I came about the missing piece of yer heart *and* to have a bit of amusement by stirring the priest's blood. He canna cause me harm."

Of that, Grant had no doubt. "Aye, but the man can be a verra large pain in my arse."

Mairwen threw back her head and laughed. "Ye always bring me such joy, MacAlester. 'Tis why I am determined to see ye settled and happy."

"My happiness is my own concern." He didn't wish to be rude, but she needed to understand that on this, he refused to change his mind.

"So ye mean to stand there and tell me that if I brought ye this lady, ye would refuse to make her feel welcome here at yer keep? Ye would deny her yer clan's hospitality?"

He found himself tightening his buttocks as if he was a lad and his grandmam was about to smack his arse for him. The ridiculous reaction unsettled him. Bloody hell, he was a laird and a Scottish earl—not to mention one of the most successful smugglers in the Highlands. "If that be all, Mairwen?"

She offered him a graceful nod. "That will be all once ye find the bollocks to answer my question."

He bowed his head to keep from baring his teeth and bellowing something disrespectful at the woman whom he had no doubt could turn him into a feckin' toad if she so wished. After struggling to rein himself in, he lifted his head and squared his shoulders. "My clan is hospitable enough. They and I always make our guests feel welcome."

"My, my, when did ye become such an expert in diplomatic cowardice?"

Jaw-clenching pride burned its way up his spine. "I am not now nor ever have been a coward."

"Except when it comes to women." She angled her chin higher, daring him to deny it.

And deny it, he would. "I am not afraid of women."

"It pleases me to hear that." She meandered back to where she'd placed her unfinished whisky on his desk and downed it. "Then ye'll have no trouble preparing to receive the most important guest of yer lifetime, aye?"

He tensed to keep from groaning aloud.

"Aye?" she asked again, the sheer enjoyment of his misery gleaming in her eyes.

"When?"

Her smile widened. "Soon, my laird. Verra soon."

CHAPTER 3

The bubbly young woman with the gorgeous streaks of purple running through her long black hair bounced around the cottage with enviable energy, pointing out all its amenities. She opened a tall, narrow cabinet in the tiny but pristine bathroom. "And here ye will find plenty of sheets and towels. As many as ye will ever need. Just place the soiled ones in the hamper beside the door that lets out to the garden. Laundry's picked up on Mondays, and that's when the cabinet gets filled with fresh." She closed the cabinet and patted the door. "But if ye find yerself needing more, or needing anything for that matter, dinna hesitate to call or text me. We want yer stay here at Seven Cairns to be as perfect as can be."

Jessa tried to remember the different storefronts she'd seen in the small village on the way in. "Is there a laundromat near here? For when we need to wash our personal things?"

"A laundrette?" The girl who had introduced herself as Keeva but never mentioned a last name turned and frowned at their two large bags and backpacks sitting just inside the front door. "Ye nay brought much, did ye? Just the one big suitcase for the each of ye and then yer small bags? I wish I could pack like that. Mairwen said ye paid for the full month. Ye've nay changed yer minds, have ye?"

"We travel light," Emily said, then tipped a nod at Jessa. "And all she ever wears is black, so it's good for more than one wearing."

"Are ye in mourning, then?" Keeva eyed Jessa as if trying to decide what sort of creature she might be.

"No. Black is just easier. Is there a laundrette here in Seven Cairns?"

"Sorry, no." Keeva shifted in place, suddenly seeming uneasy. "But I'll speak with Mairwen. I'm sure we can figure something out for when ye need to wash yer things."

"Or we could drive back to Inverness for a wash. It's not like we're restricted to Seven Cairns," Emily said.

At the moment, the prospect of an hour-long drive, one way, to wash clothes sounded exhausting. Jessa forced herself to unclench her jaws and not take out her weariness on those around her. Maybe she should've drunk one of Emily's energy drinks with all its dyes and additives. "I'm sure that'll be fine. Excuse me. I need some fresh air to perk me up." She crossed the small, cozy cottage, opened the back door, and stepped out into the warm sunshine. Scotland's mild early summer was much nicer than Jersey's sweltering humidity.

A waist-high fence of flat stones stacked and woven with amazing artfulness surrounded a surprisingly sizeable backyard that was an eclectic mix of colorful statuary, haphazard pots of greenery, large patches of moss, and clusters of wildflowers. Stone and ceramic cats, in a variety of colors, lounged in various poses around the yard. Brightly painted chickens with comical expressions joined them. Most noticeable and largest of all were the statues of hot pink sows with such joyful faces that Jessa couldn't help but smile.

She ran her hand along the back of the nearest concrete pig that the sun had warmed enough to give the impression that the creature lived and breathed. For some silly reason, touching the happy sow loosened the tightness in her chest and made it easier to breathe. "If all else fails, I can wash my clothes in the bathtub and drape them out here to dry. There are plenty of places to hang them." She'd done that before when low on money, and it had worked out just fine.

Lifting her face to the sun, she closed her eyes and pulled in another deep breath. The air even smelled sweeter in Scotland, cleaner, somehow, and full of promise. On impulse, she kicked off her shoes and walked barefoot across the soft moss, wiggling her toes in its cool sponginess. Maybe this place was a little bit of heaven after all. Stepping stones created a trail around the yard, and there was even a peacefully gurgling water fountain in the back corner. A plump little brown bird splashed and fluttered in it, enjoying its bath while completely ignoring Jessa.

Her tension and weariness drained away, leaving her feeling boneless and ready to drop into a slumbering pile of carefree nothingness. She was half tempted to stretch out under the tree in the corner opposite the fountain and take the welcoming backyard up on its silent offer of a nap. "Why not?" she asked the bird flitting in the fountain's water. "Em said to chill, right?"

Since she could still hear Keeva through the open windows, happily chattering to Emily, Jessa decided not to stretch out flat on her back. Instead, she settled down at the base of the tree and leaned back against it. Its sprawling roots with their knobby knuckles protruding up from the ground and the concave shape of the enormous trunk cradling her as if she were a part of the garden rather than a visitor. The wind sighing through its leaves relaxed her even more, making her eyelids heavy. She relinquished the battle and let them flutter shut.

"There she is," Keeva called out. "Miss Jessa—wake up, lass. Ye canna sleep at the base of that oak. The fairies might steal ye away."

"They would return me when they got to know me," Jessa said through a grumbling yawn. "And call me Jessa. I can't be that much older than you."

Keeva offered her a mysterious grin. "I promise I am a good bit older than yerself, miss. Looks can be deceiving." She held out a hand to help her up. "Come, yer friend wants to see the path to the healing springs."

"Tell her I'm relaxing, and we can find the path tomorrow. What is she doing, anyway? Unpacking?" Jessa had no desire or intention of moving from the tree's comfortable embrace. It was as though she was melting into it, and all that was wrong with the world was slowly ebbing away.

Keeva caught hold of her hand and tugged while scowling up into the tree's branches. "Stop it. It's nay time yet, and ye know it. Besides, she is not for ye."

"What are you talking about?" Jessa yanked her hand out of Keeva's. Why would the friendly Scot abruptly turn rude?

The lass backed up a step and seemed almost startled. "No, no—not yerself, miss. Forgive me. I was scolding the oak."

"Scolding the tree?" Jessa stared at her, the back of her neck tingling and the hairs standing on end. She scrubbed her arms and suddenly noticed a cloying dampness seeping up from the ground as though it was trying to repel her. She hopped to her feet and brushed off her behind. "That's odd. The ground wasn't wet earlier."

"Sometimes it takes a while for the earth to send its tears up to ye," Keeva said. She looped her arm through Jessa's and smiled. "Come on, lass. Yer Emily's waiting inside for ye."

Jessa halted and fisted her hands against her middle. A breathtaking eeriness paralyzed her, locking her in place. Every yard ornament had moved. And not just a few inches, but drastically. The largest of the pigs was now on a different side of the fenced-in area. Some of the cats had disappeared, and all the chickens now surrounded the fountain as though gathering for a drink of water. "Keeva."

"Aye?"

"What time is it?"

Keeva glanced at her watch. "Half past two. Why?"

"That means I can't have been out here any longer than fifteen minutes or so, right?"

The girl recoiled, squinting as if Jessa had lifted a hand to strike her. "I really couldn't say, since I didn't look at the time ye arrived."

Keeva was lying. Jessa could almost taste it. She marched over to the pig that had moved the greatest distance and tried to lift it, straining to shift the heavy thing until she was left trembling with the effort.

"Miss Jessa, if ye dinna want the pig there, I can call my brother and one of his mates. They'll put it wherever ye want it to be."

"The pig already moved, Keeva. Stop acting as if you don't know that." Heart pounding, Jessa turned in a slow circle, pointing out all the differences. "Those chickens weren't over there, and some of the cats are gone too."

"I better fetch Miss Emily."

Before Jessa could stop her, Keeva disappeared into the cottage.

"I am losing my mind." Rubbing her eyes with a shaking hand, she stumbled over to the bench against the side of the house and dropped onto it. She bent forward, pulling in deep breaths as she put her head between her knees.

"Jess, come inside." Emily rubbed her shoulders, then gently pulled. "Come on. You need rest. I've already turned down your bed. All you have to do is climb into it."

"I need to go home, Em. I should never have come here." Jessa remained locked in place with her head between her knees. "Get out my laptop and see if you can switch our return tickets to, like, right now. Or as soon as we can get back to Glasgow."

"You're just tired. Once you've rested and settled in, you'll be fine."

"I will not be fine." Jessa jerked away from her. "Since we've arrived in Scotland, I've seen Mr. MacSexy everywhere, but it always turns out he's not really there. Our hostess scolded the tree for making me feel so comfortable, then said the earth wept for me, and every one of those freaking yard ornaments was in a different spot twenty minutes ago, and I was the only one out here." She thumped herself on the chest. "I didn't move them, and neither did Keeva. Did you sneak out here and move that pig that weighs more than our rental car?"

Frowning, Emily sat on the bench and wrapped an arm around Jessa's shoulders. "It's going to be all right, Jess. Let's just sit here for a while and catch our breath, okay? It's kind of nice out here." She pointed at a plump little stone dragon peeping out from behind a planter of geraniums. "That little guy is kind of cute. You like dragons. Did he move too?"

Rattled to the point of pure despondency, Jessa shrugged. "I don't know. Probably."

"Probably," Emily repeated. "It would be cool if he did. Maybe we could take him home as a pet."

"Humoring the insane can be a dangerous thing, you know." Jessa glared at her, wishing she could be as calm and put together as Emily.

Her friend grinned. "I've always loved living on the edge."

"Ho to the house," a deep voice called out from beyond the fence and out of sight from around the corner of the cottage.

"Maybe that's Mr. MacSexy!" Emily whispered excitedly. "Come on. Let's see."

With her heart not pounding nearly so hard and able to breathe again, Jessa rolled her eyes, then pushed up from the bench and followed Emily to the side of the yard where a set of wooden steps, complete with handrails that she'd not noticed before, leaned up against the fence. The step-stool-like thing reached the top of the stone barrier, enabling a person to exit the backyard by using the steps to climb over it. Jessa couldn't remember for certain, but she thought they called it a *stile*. Having had her fill of surprises for the day, she lagged back, tightly hugging herself to keep from shattering into bits. Emily could handle their visitor.

"Keeva sent me," said the man Jessa couldn't see. "Said ye needed a pig moved?"

Emily turned and looked at Jessa as though they were asked that question every day. "You need a pig moved, Jess?"

"No. The pig moved itself." She refused to deny it. "While I was under the tree, that biggest hot pink pig moved itself clear across the yard." She knew it sounded ridiculous, but it was the truth.

"You saw the pig come to life and walk across the yard?" Emily asked, still infuriatingly calm.

"No. My eyes were shut."

A man so striking that he could star in a superhero movie cleared the fence with ease by resting his hands atop it and leaping over. Silvery blond hair, smiling blue eyes, and a neatly clipped mustache and beard perfectly set off the muscular vision dressed in a faded blue tee, a kilt, and hiking boots. With his hands on his hips, he fixed the yard animals with a fierce scowl. "Which of these beasties is causing ye all the trouble, miss?"

Jessa glared at him. "Did no one ever tell you it's rude to make fun of the tourists?"

"Who's making fun of ye, lass?"

She narrowed her eyes at him, waiting for him to catch on and stop being a jerk.

He grinned. "I'm Evan, by the way, and ye are?"

"Jessa." Apparently, last names were never used around here, so she decided not to share hers.

"What a glorious name, and I wasn't making fun of ye." He tipped a nod toward the largest pig. "I know they move. Seen it myself, though usually, 'tis only at night during a full moon. Yer arrival must've made them so happy they couldn't wait till then." He winked. "Scotland is filled with magic, lass. Ye'll be hard pressed to find those who dinna believe in it."

She wasn't buying any of that malarky, no matter how handsome the salesman. "Then why did Keeva panic?"

He shifted his broad shoulders in a dismissive shrug. "Keeva does that sometimes. It's cause she's afraid she'll stir Mairwen's anger."

"And you're not afraid of Mairwen?"

He backed up a step and lifted both hands in surrender. "I have a healthy respect for Mairwen. She's reasonable enough unless she gets her back up. *Then* is when I fear her." He aimed a smile guaranteed to break hearts at Emily. "And yer name?"

Emily sauntered toward him, ignoring his question. "You cleared that fence with ease and did it silently. Admit it. You moved the yard animals to play a trick on the unsuspecting tourists."

Evan shook his head and looked as if he was about to deny it, then offered them both a dramatic, apologetic bow. "Aye, ladies, I did it. 'Twas just meant as a bit of fun. Surely, ye'll grant a man a bit of leeway. How else was I to meet ye?"

While it was irritating, Jessa grudgingly admitted it was flattering too, and it made her feel a great deal better about the whole yard statues coming to life situation. "I suppose Keeva was in on it, too?"

"Aye, cost me a promise to work on that wreck of a car of hers." He crossed his arms over his chest, making his already huge biceps bulge even larger. "So do the two of ye grant me forgiveness?"

"Only if you promise not to do it again," Emily said, "and you bring us dinner tonight."

"Done!" He gave her a victorious smile and another lavish bow. "I'll bring ye the finest Seven Cairns has to offer. Around eight or so. That'll give ye time to get good and settled in. And now, if ye will excuse me, ladies, I need to get back to the shop afore old Drummond wakes up and misses me."

"Your boss wouldn't appreciate your taking time off to pick on the tourists?" Jessa asked, storing that bit of information away in case she or Emily needed it for future reference.

Evan laughed as he hopped back over the fence. "Drummond's not my boss. Although he likes to think so. He's my cat." He threw up a hand as he jogged away. "See ye at eight."

"His cat," Emily repeated, still staring after him. "A guy like that toeing the line for his cat. You believe that?"

Jessa eyed the expression on the nearest concrete pig. The thing looked even happier than before—almost as if it were about to burst out laughing. She shook her head. It had to be travel fatigue and anxiety. As she headed for the door, she threw up her hands. "I don't know what to believe anymore."

～

"Did no one tell the watchers to behave themselves?" Evan, the Tranquility Weaver almost as powerful as the Master Tranquility Weaver Shona, burst into Mairwen's sanctuary without knocking. "Neither woman believed the lie I told them. I saw it in their eyes. Their magic looked right through me. Ishbel is right. Both have a touch of the gift."

"Keeva?" Mairwen didn't bother pausing in the study of her writings. A ripple in the energies had already whispered there was trouble in the air. She had hoped her apprentice had it well in hand. Apparently, her hope was not to be. When the girl didn't answer, Mairwen set down her quill and fixed Keeva with a look guaranteed to make her confess.

"I told the watchers to behave," Keeva said, "but they're drawn to Jessa. They like her better than most of the fated mates we've brought here." She carried another ream of parchment over to the stack on Mairwen's table and placed it with the others. "And it's not just them. The earth and oak embraced her as well. So I panicked and fetched Evan." She caught her bottom lip between her teeth and bowed her head. "I am sorry. It seems I have failed ye yet again."

Mairwen folded her hands atop her papers. "Ye did right to fetch Evan. The lass needs some tranquility. The Conflict Weavers pushed her to the edge of reason with the discord they unleashed in her life to bring her here. I must speak with Malcolm about teaching his Weavers to use more restraint and finesse." She eyed Evan, studying the shifting colors of his aura. "Ye are not meant for Jessa or her friend. Go with caution in this task, Evan."

"I know my boundaries, honored one. I did what I could to calm them and will ensure there are no misunderstandings when I take them their supper later."

His scowl surprised her, making her wonder if he had sensed more than he was telling. "What else have ye to share?"

"It is not only the Weavers and watchers meddling with Jessa Tamsen. There is another. An uninvited another."

"She is here? In Seven Cairns?" Mairwen rose and hurried to the window, opening it wider to breathe in the wind and search for that which she hoped not to find.

"Not her but one of her own." Evan joined her at the window. "In the garden. Near Jessa while she slept." He turned and shot a disappointed look back at Keeva. "The oak was protecting her. As was the earth. Did ye not feel that?"

"I sensed nothing," Keeva said, her voice shaded with panic. "And thrice I swept the cottage and the grounds for evil and sensed nothing."

"This is not just yer failing, Keeva, but mine as well." Mairwen frowned at the view before her, a quiet, peaceful Scottish village, because that was how the Divine Weavers intended to portray Seven Cairns to the world. One main street lined with the sorts of shops and pubs tourists would expect in a sleepy Highland town. Quaint, white-washed cottages and dwellings with colorful gardens and even brighter doors and shutters dotted the landscape on the fringes of the village. Most of those who lived in Seven Cairns were not twenty-first century humans but Divine Weavers from across the realms. A few from this world did live there, but they were far from average mortals. Descended from generations of the loyal Defenders of the Veil and sworn members of the Order, the Weavers considered them treasured allies even though they were only humans with sadly brief lives. She sent her senses into the wind once again, spiritually touching everything she crossed, like a worried gardener searching for invasive insects. Had they all grown overly complacent here within the boundaries of their carefully constructed sphere?

"Why would she be so interested in this particular mate bond?" Mairwen asked, speaking more to herself than Evan or Keeva.

"Could be because the last bond snatched one from her clutches that she had decided should die by war," Keeva said. "Perhaps she plotted to take Grant MacAlester in his stead."

"The Mor—"

Mairwen whirled and silenced Evan with a look. "Her name is not to be uttered on our holiest of grounds. It could give her the very toehold she seeks."

He dropped to a knee and bowed his head. "Forgive me."

"What should we do?" Keeva asked softly, moving to stand beside Evan.

Mairwen had no idea what to do. All she knew for certain was that she would protect Seven Cairns and the Highland Veil at any cost. She nodded at the door and shooed them away as if they were children. "Out wi' ye. I've much to stew over. Be more vigilant and share this with all, so they might be vigilant as well."

∽

"What will ye do when she brings her?"

Grant shifted in the saddle and resettled the worn leather reins in his hands, ignoring Henry's question as they waited on their mounts atop the rise overlooking the mouth of Cromarty Firth. A ship with a fair-sized cargo of tea, spirits, and lace was due in this evening. The infernal man, who was nosier than an old woman, should concentrate on securing the goods and moving them to their next stop rather than worrying about Mairwen's return.

"MacAlester? Did ye hear me?"

"I've not gone deaf yet, unfortunately."

"Dinna be red-arsed with me," Henry said in a low voice in case enemies lurked in the shadows. "'Tis best to be prepared. At least Mairwen warned us this time that she would return rather than just appear all unexpected like as is her usual."

The man had a point, but Grant wasn't about to agree with him. Not here in the dead of night while watching for those who might cause his men difficulties with the business at hand. "If ye wish to go down and help Gordon and Lachie with the wagons, dinna let me be stopping ye."

Henry snorted. "Thank ye kindly, but I would much rather stay right here and nettle yer arse. Me father was a Defender, as am I, and ye might as well be for all ye've done to help us. All that's missing from it being official is ye've never taken the oath to defend the Highland Veil." His gruffness dropped to a more hushed tone of reverence. "Mairwen wants that for ye, ye ken? And they say she carries the blood of both Bride and Cerridwen. If ye've the least bit of sense about ye, ye'll not cross her."

Grant decided to goad the man just to see what he would say. "I have no intention of crossing her—other than refusing to allow her back inside my keep with some woman she's found for me to marry." He eased his horse back into the shadows to remain hidden from the nearly full moon's light. "And I believe in doing that which is right for the sake of rightness, not because I belong to some secretive, exclusive order. So there will be no vow-taking either. What would ye do if ye were me?"

Even though the shadows concealed Henry's expression, Grant could tell the man stared at him in open-mouthed disbelief. Henry sputtered and hissed like a boiling teakettle before regaining control and quieting himself. "If I were ye, I would accept the mantle of the Order and marry the feckin' woman Mairwen told me to marry."

"Ye've no imagination, Henry. Or backbone when it comes to Mairwen."

"And ye've no sense of survival," Henry spat back at him. "I've plenty of backbone when it comes to her. I respect and honor the woman as the descendant of the goddesses that she is."

"Henry is a wise man," Mairwen said quietly from deeper in the shadows. "Ye would do well to heed his advice."

"Dammit, woman." Grant struggled to calm his poor horse. He'd alarmed the beast when he'd startled and yanked on its reins. "Ye once said ye wished for my clan to believe ye nothing more than an old woman gifted in the ways of herbs and healing. Appearing like this, out here in the dead of night, square in the middle of an important endeavor, is not the way of a harmless old woman."

"I came to warn ye," she said, as if he had not said a word.

"Warn me?"

"Ye've Defender blood in yer veins, MacAlester, and there are those who would drain ye of it."

"What the devil is that supposed to mean?"

"Stay vigilant, listen to Henry, and when I return, keep your heart and mind open about the woman I bring with me. I shall also send a few Weavers to watch over ye."

A disturbing sense of compliance washed across him, one that he knew had not been of his own doing. It was not his nature to yield to anything—not even when it was in his best interest. "Stop with yer spells, witch."

Henry gasped like a wee lassie startled by a mouse. "He means no disrespect, Mairwen."

"Aye, he does," she said with a weary sigh. "But it is his way, and I accepted that about him long ago. I still mean to protect him." She pointed at Grant, making a chill ripple through his flesh. "Do as ye are told or regret it, ye ken? I canna snatch ye back once Death wraps his bony fingers around ye and pulls ye from the living."

Then, the surrounding shadows darkened with an eerie murkiness, swallowing Mairwen from view as a heavy fog rolled in and covered the firth and its port.

"This is her doing." Grant bared his teeth and nudged his horse into motion, trotting down the hillside toward the shoreline. Past experience with the witch told him she was long gone. If anything happened to Lachie and Gordon while he couldn't see them, he would hold her personally accountable and somehow make her pay.

The steady thunder of wagon wheels and horses' hooves came toward him through the fog. He slowed his mount and took refuge off the side of the narrow road, but didn't call out. Reports of soldiers, excisemen, and their paid blackguards being seen in the area demanded the utmost caution.

As the first wagon rolled into view, he breathed easier. His cousin Lachie urged the team of Shires onward, grinning like a fool as the enormous horses easily pulled the fully loaded wagon up the ever-steepening incline. "Ye're like a blister, Grant. Ye dinna show up until all the work is done."

Grant laughed as he rode alongside the wagon. "A wise laird knows when to trust his able men and let them alone. Any trouble?"

"None. That fog came in at the perfect time. Made it so we could load the wagons faster and head out afore anyone was the wiser. If ye prayed it in, ye best be thanking whichever saint ye asked for their help."

"I shall remember that when I say my bedtime prayers." Grant had a fair idea that Mairwen had called in the fog, but he wasn't about to share that with his cousin. He also wasn't entirely pleased to find himself beholden to the witch, who was most definitely not a saint. He twisted in the saddle and scowled at the swirling fog that appeared to be thickening by the minute. "I canna see a feckin' thing. Gordon watched the lads and ensured they loaded the crates proper, aye?"

Lachie shot him an insulted look. "I thought ye said a wise laird trusted his able men?"

"A wise laird also worries. This shipment will go a long way when it comes to adding to the coffers meant to get us through winter." He frowned and stretched forward, straining to better see something up ahead. A figure, a woman, stood in the middle of the road with the heavy fog swirling around her so only her head and shoulders were visible. Sudden recognition chilled him to the marrow of his bones. Her hair was the shade of dew-kissed pumpkins illuminated by the rising sun. Her abundance of curls was tousled, tumbling down her back and over her shoulders. Her smile plumped her cheeks and flashed in her eyes. "Feckin' hell," he muttered. It was the woman from his dreams. Had Mairwen been foolish enough to drop the lass out here in the middle of a smuggling run?

Then he noticed Lachie was not slowing the team. "Halt, man! Afore ye hit her. Halt, I say!" He spurred his mount forward, reached over, and grabbed the harness of one of the lead horses.

"What the devil!" Lachie yanked on the reins, struggling to stop the team. Once the wagon halted, he stood and shook his fist at Grant. "Have ye lost yer feckin' mind?"

"Me? Were ye damned and determined to kill her?" Grant jabbed a finger at the woman. Or, at least, where she had been. He stared at the spot, now empty except for the thinning fog.

"Her?" Lachie repeated. He leapt down from the wagon and trudged a good way up the path, then returned to stand beside Grant's horse. "Are ye mad with drink?"

Grant wished it were that simple. "Nay." He jerked his head at the wagon. "The fog played tricks on me. Let's be on with it, aye?"

"Not until ye tell me the truth."

Henry rode up, causing the silvery gray mist to swirl even more. "Since when do we *try* to get caught? The fog's lifted from the docks, and they're astir down there. 'Tis time to haul our arses out of here. Gordon and the lads have the other wagons headed this way."

"The truth, Grant," Lachie said, widening his stance as he folded his arms across his chest. "Who is this *her* ye thought ye saw?"

Grant gritted his teeth until his jaws cramped. He trusted Lachie as much as he trusted Henry. Both men were the brothers he had never had. Lachie was also a Defender of the Veil and *might* come close to understanding. "I thought I saw the woman from my dreams. The one Mairwen insists I must marry."

Lachie puckered a thoughtful scowl, then tipped a nod and climbed back into the driver's seat of the wagon. Kissing a clicking sound at the horses, he twitched the reins and got the team moving again, passing Grant and continuing up the road.

"And he's not going to say a bloody thing?" Grant asked Henry.

Henry laughed and shook his head as he nudged his horse to follow the wagon. "What's there to say? He knows what ye should do as well as I."

As Gordon and the lads came into view with the other two wagons, Grant urged his horse onward. "Why the hell does it matter if I marry again?" he muttered to himself. But he knew that answer, as if Mairwen floated alongside him and whispered it in his ear. Fated mates shared the strongest love of all, and that love strengthened the threads of the Highland Veil—the barrier that must be upheld at all costs.

CHAPTER 4

Jessa dashed into the pub with Emily on her heels. Laughing, she paused in the entryway, shaking the rain from her hair and brushing the water off her sleeves. "Sorry, Ems. I thought for sure we could make it before the sky opened up and dumped buckets on us."

"Ugh." Disgusted as a drenched cat, Emily pushed around her and headed for the restrooms. "I'm going to go dry off."

The mental picture of Emily crouching under the hot air hand dryer made Jessa snicker. "I'll get us a table."

"Did I not tell ye to go by Boyd's and get ye a pair of brollies?" Lilias, co-owner of the pub with her brother Lyal, called out from behind the bar. She shook her head as well as her finger, making the sheen of her sleek blonde pixie cut shimmer even brighter under the hanging lights that looked like golden starbursts. "Ye're in Scotland now, lass. Today's rain is tomorrow's whisky, and we love it. Ye must always be prepared."

Instead of choosing a table, Jessa opted to sit at the bar and chat with Lilias. Strangely enough, she already felt an unusual affinity to everyone she'd met at Seven Cairns. Kind of like long-lost friends she never realized she had and was just now getting reacquainted with. Well...except for Keeva and Evan. She was still trying to wrap her head around those two. They were nice enough, just a bit on the odd side. Not that anything was wrong with odd. She'd worn that label a few times herself.

"And what are my lovely Americans up to this fine day?" Lilias set a cup of coffee in front of Jessa, and a small teapot and an empty cup at the place beside her for when Emily finished drying off in the ladies' room.

"Emily *was* going to dunk me in the healing waters for good luck, but she might be rethinking that right about now. She hates getting wet and is probably sitting under the hot air hand dryer as we speak." Jessa laughed and then sipped the best coffee she'd ever had in her life, a rich, full-bodied blend with just a hint of vanilla and barely enough cream to lighten it. "This is the perfect cup. Do you always remember what every customer likes?"

"Most times." Lilias slanted a brow at Emily as she joined them. "I told ye to get yerself a brolly at Boyd's."

"Well, we can't go for an umbrella today. That man would triple the price and sell us all sorts of other stuff we don't need." Emily poured herself a steaming cup of tea, took a sip, then shook her head. "I have never met such a con man in my life, but you can't help but love him. That old guy is more entertaining than any reality show I've ever seen. The stories he comes up with to sell you something are amazing and impossible to resist."

"That's our Boyd. His father was the same. Trained him well, he did." Lilias cocked her head as if listening to something only she could hear. "Got a delivery in the back. Excuse me, ladies." She hopped down from the step that ran the length of the back of the bar and disappeared through the door to the side of the wide mirror lined with glass shelves loaded down with bottles of alcohol.

"You two were laughing about me hating to get wet, weren't you?" Emily glared at Jessa with mock sternness, but amusement flashed in her velvety brown eyes.

"We short people have to stick together," Jessa said. "She and I are the same height."

"You stood back to back to compare?"

Jessa laughed, then took another sip of her gorgeous coffee. "No. I told her I was five feet tall on a good day with good lighting, and she said she was the same." She dipped a piece of shortbread in her coffee, bit into it, and closed her eyes, reveling in the luscious, sweet butteriness melting on her tongue. "And we weren't laughing at you. She asked what we'd planned for today, and I told her that initially, you were going to dunk me in the springs for good luck, but you might rethink that because of the weather."

"I had definitely planned on you being the one to get soaked to the skin today, not me." Emily munched on a piece of shortbread, her eyes slowly narrowing as they always did whenever she was deep in thought. "Other than the healing waters and a massage, we've enjoyed most of what Seven Cairns has to offer. Been to the bookshop, the treat shop, and even took a tour of the bakery and the distillery. Maybe we need to widen our sphere of exploration. This is the Highlands. Even if we just travel along the coastline, I'm sure there's plenty to see."

Lightning flashed, lighting up the windows. A ground-shaking boom of thunder followed. "Wow." Jessa swiveled on the barstool and eyed the rain sluicing down the multiple squares of the old bubbly glass of the windows. Narrow strips of wood that must've taken a steady hand to paint that glossy black separated the small panes that, once put together, created a showcase of antique windows that filled the entire front wall. "I'm not so sure about driving in this. Especially while trying to stay on the wrong side of these narrow roads. Remember how interesting things got a time or two on the way up from Inverness?"

"I did not see all those sheep until we rounded the turn. At least I didn't hit any of them."

Jessa grinned. "I got an awesome picture of you in the middle of them, trying to herd them off the road."

"If you post that anywhere, you won't make it back to Jersey alive."

"And here Lilias assured me the two of ye were the best of friends," said a lilting voice from behind the bar.

Jessa turned back and faced the bar. "Uhm...Hi."

An older woman, dressed in a colorful shawl and dress and looking as though she belonged behind a crystal ball, smiled at her. "I am Mairwen. Sorry if I startled the two of ye. Lilias told me to come through and meet ye in person."

"Mairwen? As in the owner of the cottage who sends the nicest emails Mairwen?" Emily asked.

The lovely lady bowed her head and tugged her wrap, a dark blue, knobby weave splashed with rich burgundy flowers, closer around her narrow shoulders. "One and the same."

"I'm Emily, and this is Jessa."

Mairwen's startling blue eyes twinkled with what was surely a lively personality as she turned to Jessa. "And how are ye finding our fine Scottish summer?"

"I love the rain. Always have." Jessa shot a grin at Emily. "Ems is the one who hates getting wet. She was either a hen or a cat in a past life."

"Why a hen?" Mairwen asked, her puzzlement clear.

"I had a friend in college whose grandmother always said, *madder than a wet hen*. I took that to mean chickens don't like getting wet."

"Must be American chickens," Mairwen said with a laugh. "A Scottish chicken would be angry all the time were that the case."

"We'll have to research that, Jess," Emily said, sarcasm dripping from her tone.

Jessa grinned, knowing her friend's mood would improve once she had thoroughly dried out and finished her favorite tea that Lilias had blended just for her. "Maybe you could suggest something for us to do today," she said to Mairwen. "We were going for massages and to visit the healing springs, but Emily doesn't want to get soaked again, and we can't afford to go to Boyd's for umbrellas while it's raining."

"Aye, ye've the right of that. That man would skin ye of yer last pence if given half a chance." Mairwen resettled her colorful shawl again and seemed to grow thoughtful. "Some of the healing springs originate in the caves, ye ken? I could show ye the way to one of them after yer massages." She offered them a wily smile and lightly tapped her chest. "After all, I am the main massage therapist, and my sanctuary connects to the caves."

"Well, there you go then," Jessa told Emily. "After our nice relaxing massages, you can dunk me for luck, and then we'll head back to the cottage to enjoy the veggie stew I started in the slow cooker."

Mairwen gave Jessa a look she didn't quite understand. "Ye enjoy cooking, do ye?"

"I enjoy dabbling. Sometimes my experiments end up outside for the strays, and I eat peanut butter and jelly."

"Strays?"

"She feeds every cat, dog, raccoon, and any other creature that shows up hungry on her doorstep," Emily said before selecting another shortbread cookie and dipping it in her tea. She ducked her head. "And I should not have said that. Sorry."

"Why?" Mairwen asked.

"Because it makes me sad," Jessa said, her bright mood dipping with thoughts about the troubles back home. "The neighbors promised to feed everyone while I was in Scotland, but I don't think they'll do it after I move."

"They will," Emily said with a squeeze of her arm. "Mrs. Garducci always keeps her word."

"I know. I'm going to miss having her as a neighbor."

"People come into our lives and then leave once we've learned what we are meant to learn from them," Mairwen said, her tone gentle but firm. "All we can do is cherish the memories we make with them while they are with us."

"Brighten up now," Emily told Jessa. "It's your favorite sort of day, raining buckets. We're here in Scotland, and we're about to enjoy what I'm sure will be a phenomenal massage."

"That it will be." Mairwen nodded. "Phenomenal and then some."

"And then a dip in the healing waters for good luck and help in finding my Mr. MacSexy," Jessa said, determined to enjoy the day and not wallow in self-pity.

Mairwen laughed. "I dinna believe I am familiar with that clan. Are they reported to live in the Highlands?"

Jessa pulled out her phone, tapped on the app, then tapped again until her handsome, broody Highlander glowered at her. She showed him to Mairwen. "This is Mr. MacSexy, and I'm trying to find him because he keeps popping up as a match for me on this tarot dating app. You wouldn't happen to know him, would you?"

"Ahh." Mairwen nodded her approval. "Very bonnie indeed." Then she tilted her head and eyed Jessa. "And he listed his name as *Mr. MacSexy?*"

"No, that's the name Ems and I gave him because there was no name or profile for him." Jessa closed the app and tucked her phone back into the tiny crossbody bag she always used when she traveled. "Seriously, you wouldn't happen to know him, would you?" As soon as the question left her lips for the second time, she felt silly. Just because Mairwen lived in Scotland didn't mean she knew every person there. Jessa laughed away the notion. "Never mind. He's probably an AI image built into the app by Scotland's tourism board or something."

"A...I?"

"Artificial intelligence. These days, it's hard to tell what's real and what's not."

Mairwen laughed. "I leave those things to Keeva. She's better suited to them than I am." She nodded at the windows while motioning for them to follow her through the door behind the bar.

"Come. The rain has let up to a wee drizzle. Ye willna get too wet getting to my truck. I'm parked in the back alleyway."

"We need to pay Lilias." Jessa rooted through her tiny bag for a ten pound note as she hopped off the stool.

"She's already put it on yer accounts." Mairwen shooed them along like a mother duck keeping her ducklings in a row. "She had to pop into her office and settle up with the delivery lad from the distillery. She sent her best wishes that ye enjoy the waters."

They followed Mairwen through the narrow kitchen with its gleaming stainless steel counters, the dry goods pantry that was heady with the nose-tingling aroma of spices, and then on into the back storage room that held crates and barrels of spirits strategically stacked to the rafters.

"Wow," Jessa said. "I didn't realize this place was so big. It doesn't look like it from the outside."

"Looks can be deceiving," Mairwen said without slowing. "Here we are." She pushed open the back door and held it. A hard wind gusted against the door, making her brace and lean against it to keep it open. "Hurry, ladies."

Then the lively old woman muttered something so deep and low that Jessa couldn't make it out. It sounded like an ancient language, and yet it struck a chord, niggling at a memory just out of reach and making her feel as though she'd heard those words before. Chills rippled across her. Every hair stood on end. She shook off the feeling. It must be static electricity from the storm, and Mairwen was probably cursing at the wind and didn't want them to overhear any Scottish profanity.

"Hurry into the truck, ladies. The skies won't hold back long." Mairwen pointed them at a rusty red truck with a missing headlight. "And mind the door once ye're in. Ye have to slam it hard to make sure it catches."

Jessa climbed in first. As the shortest, it would be easiest for her to sit with her feet propped on the hump between the driver and passenger floorboards. Emily's long legs would hook over her ears if she had to sit in the middle. That mental image had Jessa snickering while Emily repeatedly slammed the door, trying to get it to stay shut.

"Put some ire into it, lass," Mairwen said as she climbed in behind the wheel and banged her door closed. "Think of it as the last person who crossed ye."

With a loud bang, the door caught and stayed shut. Emily grinned and waggled her eyebrows. "Thank you, Jack Ass Jeremy."

"Emily!" Jessa rolled her eyes but still laughed.

"And who is this Mr. Jack Ass?" Mairwen asked as she ground the gears, popped the clutch, then flinched as the truck lurched into motion.

"The man who dared to dump our Jessa," Emily told her while leaning forward to stress the statement with an indignant look. "Can you believe that?"

Mairwen clucked like an old hen. "I canna believe it. That man must be the greatest sort of fool."

"He's the greatest sort of something," Jessa said, struggling to take the high road and not blame everything that had gone wrong in the relationship on Jeremy. "But he's gone now, and I'm better off without him."

"That's the spirit, lass."

"And besides, we've got a month to find Mr. MacSexy." Emily caught hold of the door handle as they bounced through a pothole. "Or at least a reasonable facsimile."

With her eyes on the road, Mairwen bared her teeth as she ground the gears to climb the hill. Muttering more mysterious words, she looked ready to strangle the truck if it didn't cooperate. As the incline leveled out, she relaxed and returned to her usual state of serenity. "Ye know the legend says the waters are nay just for healing."

Jessa sensed where this was going. "You think they might help me find Mr. MacSexy?"

Mairwen's smile brightened even more. "I've no doubt about it, lass. No doubt at all."

⁓

"Oh, my goodness, you've made me feel boneless." Jessa exhaled, perfectly content to melt into the massage table. Her face rested in the padded hole, and her arms dangled off its sides. Eyes closed, she struggled to stay awake, which was odd, since she'd never been one to sleep on her stomach. "Mairwen, you are magical."

"I'm glad I've done ye some good, lass." Mairwen rubbed warmed oil onto Jessa's back and shoulders, down her arms, and on each of her fingers.

Jessa breathed in its scent and relaxed even more. It smelled of roses, with a soft note of lily of the valley and maybe even some sweet basil. "I hope Emily is enjoying her session as much as I'm enjoying mine."

"I'm sure she is. Ishbel is as talented as I."

Jessa had thought their massages would be in the same room, but in a way, maybe this was better. When she and Emily were together, they rarely stopped talking. With them separated, odds were better that they would soak in the benefits of the massage without distracting one another.

"Now then," Mairwen said, the gentle lilt in her voice almost as hypnotic and calming as the room softly lit by nothing but candles. "Behind the screen where ye left yer clothes, I've placed a linen shift and a pair of slippers. Put those things on, and then I'll take ye to the springs. Just ring the bell whenever ye're ready, and I'll return to show ye the way, aye?"

"Aye," Jessa mumbled through her drowsiness before realizing Mairwen had already left the room. She slowly pushed herself up to a sitting position and gathered the thick white towel around her, not really in a hurry to dispel the delicious laziness of being so relaxed. Letting her feet swing as she sat on the table, she idly studied the rough texture of the dark gray walls that looked like actual stone. She hopped down, went to the nearest one, and touched it. It was cool to the point of almost feeling damp and hard as granite. Maybe the room was a small chamber off the main cave that Mairwen had said was the origin point for one of the larger healing springs.

She padded barefoot across layers of worn tapestries tossed across the floor in such a haphazard way that it seemed like an intentional decorating choice. The rich patches of burgundies, blues, and golds matched Mairwen's shawl and skirt, which reminded her of a fortuneteller's costume she'd once seen at the Boardwalk in Atlantic City.

Behind the tall privacy screen of yellowed parchment framed with unpainted wood was a white, floor-length dress that would make a comfortable, old-fashioned nightgown. It was as soft as her favorite cotton shirts that had been washed so many times they were almost see-through. Plain with long, loose sleeves, it tied at the front of the gathered yoke neckline. Very much aware of her pantiless state, she debated slipping them on, then decided against it. If she went into the spring wearing her undies, they'd be soaking wet for the ride home. Besides, the *shift*, as Mairwen had called it, almost brushed the tops of her feet. It wasn't like she wasn't well covered. She returned her panties to the pile of her neatly folded clothes and eyed her phone, tempted to check it.

"No. There is nothing there that can't wait, and I don't want to ruin this gorgeous feeling of peacefulness." She shook a finger at the powered-down device as if putting it in its place. She hadn't felt this worry-free in a very long while.

The shoes Mairwen had left for her made her frown. She picked them up and examined them closely. They seemed to be real leather. Simple brown slip-ons with no heel, but soft as velvet, and even had a leathery smell. She didn't like wearing leather, but didn't want to wear her street shoes anywhere near the spring. They might have picked up some contaminants or something in their travels, and their dyes could pollute the area. She eyed the slippers again, running her thumb along what appeared to be their hand stitching. "I guess it won't hurt to wear these for a little while."

She slipped them on, determined to stop overthinking every little thing. The perfect fit of the shoes was surprising. She wiggled her toes and walked around the room, delighted with their comfort. It was a shame they were leather, or she might ask Mairwen if they were for sale.

A delicate silver bell inscribed with a phrase so worn it wasn't legible hung from a braided dark blue ribbon beside the door. As soon as she rang it, the entire room lurched with a deep, rumbling groan, knocking her off balance. She bounced against the wall, tumbled backward, then rolled to all fours, and tried to scramble back to the door. The harder she tried to claw her way to it, the more the floor tilted to a steeper incline, making her slide farther away.

"Mairwen! Help!" Was this a freaking earthquake? In Scotland? And here she was, trapped in a cave. Panic rising, she grabbed at the rugs that seemed to be caught in place and tried to drag herself up to the doorway, using them like ropes. "What the hell?" Hanging onto the worn tapestries, dangling with no foothold since the floor was nearly vertical by now, she looked from side to side. Disbelief shot a sudden rush of terror roaring through her ears, and her heart hammered so hard she struggled to breathe.

Nothing else in the room had toppled over, slid out of place, or collapsed. Nothing had moved but her and the floor. The entire room was intact, just merely tipped on its side.

Every tall pillar candle of the purest white still burned brightly on the tables and shelves, lending their golden glow to the now sideways room. The massage table and privacy screen remained in place, as if the floor hadn't suddenly become a wall. Mairwen's countertop was picture perfect with its colorful bottles, bowls of smooth black stones, and small towels rolled into neat bundles and stacked in a fluffy white pile.

"What hallucinogenics were in that massage oil?" Clinging to the rug, her only lifeline, she jerked at the sound of her voice echoing through the chamber as if it were a bottomless pit. "Mairwen!" she screamed, drawing it out until her throat felt raw. Hands cramping, she tried to drag herself higher and failed. She couldn't hold on like this much longer. Upper body strength was not one of her superpowers. In fact, she'd failed the rope climb in that despised phys-ed class she'd taken as an elective.

This had to be a nightmare. She'd gone to sleep during the massage and wandered into a bad dream. "Wake up, wake up, wake up," she muttered while bouncing her forehead against her throbbing forearms. "All you have to do is wake up, and everything will be okay."

She struggled to wrap her legs around her rope of rugs, swinging from side to side in her battle to hang on, but the long nightgown tangled around her and thwarted her efforts. "Maybe if I fall, I'll wake up," she said aloud. The disturbing echo of her voice was better than the suffocating silence and the creaking of the carpeting that would surely rip away at any moment. If talking out loud got her through this, then so be it.

The painful cramping of her fingers and hands traveled up into her arms. "All you have to do is let go." *Ain't no way*, she silently argued. Apparently, her logical side would speak aloud, and her belligerent self would only use thought to communicate. "I have lost my ever-loving mind. Let go and fall, so you'll wake up!" But she couldn't. She had always been afraid of heights, and even though the room had seemed nice and cozy when it was right side up, from this angle, it felt as if she was teetering off the side of a skyscraper.

"Emileeee!" As faint as a faraway whisper, Jessa heard an answer. It was Emily. She felt sure of it. "Emily! Ems! Help me!" She held her breath, praying to hear a reply, but nothing came. Nothing answered but silence.

"I can't do this." Jessa buried her face in her arms and sobbed. "I can't hang on like this much longer." If this was a dream, it was the most realistic nightmare she had ever experienced. The rug slid through her hands, burning her palms before she found the strength to tighten her hold again.

She twisted, peered downward, and immediately wished she hadn't. Below was blue-black nothingness spattered with stars. A midnight sky, the entire freaking universe, was just past her feet, and if she let go, she would fall for eternity.

Then the rug tore and sent her tumbling into free fall through the darkness. A shrill, desperate scream ripped free of her as she flailed and fought the fall. She was going to die. This was too real to be a dream.

"Lass! Woman!" A pair of large, powerful hands caught her by the shoulders and gently shook her. "Stop yer caterwauling and open yer eyes. Ye are safe."

A man's voice? She froze, held her breath, and kept her eyes shut.

"Aw, bloody hell, woman. Daren't ye die on me." He pressed his head to her chest. It was warm and heavy, making her panic even more until he lifted it away. "Thank the fates. Yer heart still beats."

A callused touch brushed her forehead and temple, pushing her hair away from her face. She kept her eyes shut, continuing to play dead or, at least, in a dead faint. If it worked for possums, it might work for her.

Wherever she was, it smelled...different. This place was no aroma candle and incense scented massage room. It reeked faintly of wood smoke and not so faintly of a man who didn't exactly stink but wasn't just out of the shower fresh, either. He possessed a natural, fragrance-free scent that was the pure, raw maleness of pinewoods, mountain air, and maybe a day's worth of sweat.

She risked easing in a deeper breath and strained to hear the slightest sound. The nose-tingling tang of whisky came to her. Or the fumes of some sort of alcohol faintly hung in the air. Beer maybe? No. It was ale. Just like the one Lilias had offered her at the pub. The only sound was gusting wind and maybe rain. Wherever she was had a window that was partially open because the damp air whispered across her, and she hadn't seen a ceiling fan since arriving in Scotland.

"I know ye're awake, lass. Yer wee nose is twitching like a cat's whiskers when it's tracking a mousie."

Whatever she was lying on shifted, and his warmth warned he had moved closer.

"Open yer eyes. I'll not harm ye."

What choice did she have? She was not only weaponless but also without her phone and couldn't call for help. She opened her eyes and choked on a sharp intake of air as she locked eyes with Mr. MacSexy. Coughing and wheezing, she rolled away from him, scrambling to escape. She hit the hardwood floor with a thud, spotted the door, and shot for it.

His arm snaked around her waist and yanked her back against a wall of muscle. "I said I'd not harm ye, but neither will I let ye run away."

She kicked, clawed, and tried to punch him. Twisting around, she tried to bite him. She tried anything she could think of to make him let her go. She had to get out of here—wherever *here* was—and find someone to help her.

He resettled his footing, blew out a heavy sigh, then tossed her back onto the bed and pointed at her. "Stay!"

"I am not a dog." Although she couldn't resist baring her teeth in case he doubted she would bite him if she could.

"Aye, and I am not a man with a great deal of patience. I said I wouldna hurt ye, and I always keep my word. Now, stop yer foolishness, and tell me yer name."

"You first." She didn't care that she sounded like a bratty child. Whatever had gotten her wherever this was gave her license to behave any way she wanted.

He glowered at her, then folded his arms across his chest, which looked much broader and more muscular than it had in the picture on that infernal app that had gotten her here. He was also a great deal taller than she had imagined. Mr. MacSexy possessed the height of a grizzly bear stretched up on its hind legs, the build of the biggest offensive lineman in the NFL, and the smug, drool-worthiness of a male model. His only flaw was a fresh scar that ran down his right cheek and damned if that didn't make him even more handsome.

She glowered back at him. This was a guy she could find all sorts of reasons to hate because if past experience had taught her anything, men who looked like him were jerks. And he already acted grouchy. She mimicked his posture, folding her arms across her chest even though she sat in the middle of what she assumed was his bed. Which was slightly disconcerting. Should she really push her luck with this guy? Especially since here of late, all her luck had been bad?

"Tell me your name, and I'll tell you mine," she said, trying to sound civil, calm, and not in the least bit afraid, which was a lie. She was a hair away from a hysterical nervous breakdown.

"Grant MacAlester, laird of Clan MacAlester, and since Mairwen probably already told ye, I am also the Earl of Suddie." He gave her a curt nod. "And ye are?"

He knew Mairwen. That meant Mairwen knew him and hadn't said a flipping word about it when she had shown her his picture. Resentment and a sense of betrayal filled her. She had trusted Mairwen, even thought they might end up being good friends. "I am Jessa Tamson. How long have you known Mairwen?"

"'Tis a pleasure to meet ye, Miss Tamson," he said with a grumpiness that called it out for the lie that it was. "And I have known that old witch for as far back as I can remember."

"I see." She glanced at the window and felt even more disoriented. It was night. How had she lost the entire day? When she'd powered off her phone in the massage room, it had only been ten in the morning. "What time is it?"

"Nigh on midnight, and afore ye ask, ye are in my bed, in my keep."

"*Keep.* That's the same thing as a castle, right?"

He studied her as if trying to decide what sort of animal she was. Eyes narrowing, he ambled closer to the foot of the bed. "Not exactly a castle. But MacAlester Keep is a fair-sized stronghold that the English left alone for reasons known only to themselves."

While she and Emily hadn't yet ventured any farther north than Seven Cairns, Jessa couldn't remember anyone mentioning MacAlester Keep. "How far is Seven Cairns from here?"

"Is that where ye're from? Ye dinna sound Highland born."

"I'm an American from New Jersey. How far are we from Seven Cairns? I have to get back there. My friend will be worried about me." Jessa scrubbed her fist against her breastbone, willing her heart to stop trying to hammer its way out of her chest. "How did I get here?" She wasn't about to share what she'd just been through. He'd think her crazy for sure.

With a heavy sigh, MacAlester lowered himself to sit on the foot of the bed. He rubbed his face with both hands, wincing when he hit the wound on his right cheek. "I dinna ken how ye got here, lass. I heard screams coming from my room, and when I got here, there ye were in my bed."

"You've made it bleed." She nodded at his cheek while gingerly scooting farther away from him. A calmer glance around revealed there was only one door in the room. Apparently, there was no en-suite bathroom connected to it. "You might want to go to the bathroom and see to it." She hugged her knees to her chest. "I'll wait here till you get back," she lied.

"Bathroom?" His perpetual scowl turned befuddled. "There is no one room in this keep for bathing. The tub is brought in here and placed in front of the hearth when I feel like washing in something other than the basin."

A knot of rising panic lodged in her throat, making it difficult to swallow. Why did he act like he had never heard of a bathroom? "You never said how far we were from Seven Cairns. I really need to get back there."

"A few hours, depending on the horse and the weather."

Depending on the horse and the weather? Was the keep in such a remote area that it couldn't be reached by car? And she still didn't know how she'd gotten here. "You swear you didn't see anyone bring me in here?"

He shook his head, his scowl turning fiercer and his dark brows knotting over his angry eyes. "No one enters my keep without my knowing it—except for that feckin' witch. This is Mairwen's doing. She had to have spirited ye here."

"That's impossible." Jessa swallowed hard, fighting the urge to throw up all the shortbread and coffee she'd enjoyed before her massage. She ran to the window, shoved the sash up higher, and sucked in great gulps of air. Oblivious to the increasingly hard rain, she hung farther out and stared. It was so very dark. As far as she could see, there were no lights anywhere. Of course, it was late, and this was the Scottish Highlands, remote and unpopulated. But wouldn't a building this size have some sort of security lights or something around it?

"Come back inside, lass. Ye're getting fair soaked and will catch yer death." He gently but firmly took her by the shoulders and led her over to the fireplace. "Stay here by the fire. I'll fetch ye a linen to dry yerself and a plaid to wrap in and stay warm."

"Why don't you call it blankets and towels?" she mumbled, numbed by the insanity of it all and struggling not to melt into a hysterical heap.

He fixed her with a stern look, but compassion flickered in the stormy gray depths of his eyes. "What does it matter what I call the things as long as ye're dry and warm?"

"I have to get back to Seven Cairns," she whispered, then dropped to the floor and stared into the hearth's dancing flames. Something deep inside told her she was much farther away from where she belonged than a few hours' ride by horse.

CHAPTER 5

Grant watched her curl into herself as she crouched in front of the fire like a homeless waif. *Damn ye, Mairwen.* What the devil had the old witch done to the lass? She'd not told her anything of her plans, of that, he was certain. But Miss Jessa Tamson had recognized him. How was that so? Had she dreamt of him as he had dreamt of her?

"Here, lass." He held out one of the linens from the stand beside the pitcher and washbasin. "To dry with."

She stared at it for a long moment, as if unsure whether or not to take it from him, then turned back to the fire as if he wasn't even there.

He shook out the folded cloth and carefully squeezed the water from her hair as he'd seen women do. She smelled of roses and a fair amount of fear. "I willna hurt ye, lass. I swear it."

"That's good to know, since Mairwen dumped me into your bed at midnight." She shied away from his help and ran her fingers through her hair, shaking and fluffing her luscious mane. "That's fine, thank you. I just need to—" She cut herself off and clenched her teeth, making her lovely jaw flex with the hardness of her fears.

"Ye just need to return to yer folk at Seven Cairns?"

She barely shook her head. "No. I need to get back to New Jersey and forget all about Scotland."

He had heard of a New Jersey over in the colonies, but couldn't recall meeting anyone from there. With the beginning of the Highland clearances, the families forced from their lands and sent across the seas never returned to share what had awaited them. He draped a plaid around her shoulders and grew even more concerned when she didn't move to hold it in place or cuddle deeper into its warmth. She had to be chilled after hanging out the window in the dead of the rainy night.

"How did ye come to be in Scotland?" He didn't add that she didn't seem to like it there. Or perhaps she had liked the place until old Mairwen had uprooted her and dropped her into his bed.

"An app," she said, keeping her gaze locked on the flames. She resettled herself on the floor, pulled the plaid around her, and rested her chin on her knees.

"What did ye say brought ye to Scotland?" Had she meant that an apple brought her here? Was Mairwen taken to poisoning apples now?

"A tarot card dating app on my phone."

Lore a'mighty, she might as well be speaking a different language. Frustration building, he resettled his stance, then backed up a step when he realized his towering over her might frighten her even more. Why the devil would Mairwen match him with a woman he couldn't understand?

"I dinna ken of what ye speak. I have heard tell of the tarot, but the rest—" He shook his head.

"If I had my phone, I'd show you." She twitched her shoulders in what was either a shrug or a shiver. "But I left it back in Mairwen's massage room with my clothes." She tipped her head, studying the burning logs from a different angle as if fighting to calm herself with the dance of the fire. "If you have your cell phone, I could probably find it in your app store and show you. Although what does it really matter? I'm here, and looking back won't change that." She huffed a soft laugh, sounding more upset than amused. "Take my advice—never listen to an app. It will only lead you to disaster."

"I dinna ken what an *app* is, Miss Tamson."

"You might as well call me Jessa. After all, I am here in your bedroom." Sarcasm dripped from her every word, giving him hope that she hadn't lost her will to fight. She closed her eyes and dropped her head into her hands. "And *app* is short for application. You download them onto your phone to do stuff with. Is that not what they call them here in Scotland?"

"I dinna ken what a *phone* might be, either."

She lifted her head and glared at him. "You're making fun of me? Really? After all—" She flipped her hand at the room in general. "—all *this*. Whatever *this* is?"

He settled into a nearby chair, since she seemed determined to sit her fine round arse on the floor. "If ye mean am I jesting or mocking ye, I would never do that to a woman as unsettled as ye appear to be." Were she not the mysterious temptation that had haunted his dreams for weeks now, he'd do what he normally did when a comely lass found her way to his bed. But whilst he wanted this one with a fury, a worrisome gnawing in his chest warned that Miss Jessa Tamson would be no casual dalliance. He shook his head at the irony. A desirable woman in his bedchamber, and he was afraid to touch her. "Now tell me, what is a *phone*?"

She rolled her eyes, ignoring him as she rubbed her knuckles against her temples. "Am I your captive?"

"Captive? Why would ye ask such a thing?"

"Oh, I don't know—maybe because you told me you weren't going to let me leave?" She paused in the massaging of her head and fixed him with a cutting glare. "Am I or not?"

"It's the middle of the night, ye're wearing nothing but yer shift, and ye've no idea where ye are, and I'd also wager, ye dinna ken the danger of a woman wandering alone in the Highlands." He leaned toward her and fixed her with a sneer just as cutting as her glare. "I am protecting ye, lass. Ye should be thanking me."

She narrowed her eyes, transforming her expression to anything but one of thankfulness. "Do you have anything for a headache? Aspirin? Ibuprofen? Acetaminophen?"

"I dinna ken what any of those things are, but I can rouse Mrs. Robeson and have her steep ye some tea. She uses willow bark and yarrow, among other things. Whatever else she brews always helps Henry with the aches he gets from that scar on his head."

She stared at him, blinking slowly as if waking from a daze. "Willow bark and yarrow tea," she repeated so softly he almost didn't catch it. "You only use natural remedies here?"

"I dinna ken about them being natural. Herbs and Mrs. Robeson's tisanes are the only remedies in this keep." He rose, went to the door, and yanked on the bellpull. It might take longer this time of night, but one of the servants would heed his call, eventually. A troubling suspicion filled him. If she was a slave to what had eventually killed his first wife, he'd put her out into the night and send her on her way at once. Never would he go through that misery again. "Were ye looking for laudanum?"

"What is that?"

"Tincture of opium."

Her mouth fell open, and her cheeks flared to an angry red. "Opium? I am not a druggie and do not appreciate that insinuation."

Her reaction enabled him to unclench his fists and call upon what little calm he had left under the circumstances. "It was nay an accusation. Merely a question. I dinna allow that vileness in my keep."

"I wouldn't think so," she said. "It's illegal—or at least it is where I come from. Is it not illegal here?"

"No. Not illegal in Scotland." The things she said befuddled him completely, but he shook it off. After all, she was from the colonies.

A knock on the door pulled him from his churning thoughts. He yanked it open just enough to see into the hallway and found Sawny, the kitchen lad, yawning and rubbing his eyes. "Rouse Mrs. Robeson and have her brew a tea for an ache in the head. A strong one, mind ye."

The boy straightened, immediately more alert, then bobbed a quick bow. "Aye, m'laird. 'Tis sorry I am that ye're feeling poorly. I'll make haste."

"Good lad." Grant shut the door before Sawny caught sight of Jessa, or she revealed herself by speaking. He wasn't ready to share her with everyone in the keep just yet, and especially not in her current state. That time would come soon enough. He turned back and motioned to one of the two wingback chairs angled in front of the hearth. "Would ye nay be more comfortable in the chair?"

With her bottom lip caught between her teeth, she hugged her knees tighter and barely rocked in place. She remained silent, looking distressed and fraught with worry.

"Lass? Miss Jessa?"

"If you don't know what a phone is, how do you communicate with anyone who doesn't live here at the keep?" she blurted out.

The phone thing seemed to mean so much to her. It must carry messages somehow. He joined her at the hearth but didn't sit. "I send a runner to places within a few hours' ride, and if the distance is greater, I send letters by coach or rider."

She stared up at him from her spot on the floor, then bent her head and rubbed her forehead between her eyebrows. Her pain must be worsening. "What about mail? The postal system?" Her voice was strained, vibrating with fear. The woman was on the verge of panic. "I think they call it the Royal Mail here."

"My runners and messengers are faster and more reliable than the king's, but I've been known to use the service when pushed to do so by the destination." He crouched in front of her and risked touching her arm. "Sit in the chair, lass, and I'll fetch ye more cushions. 'Tis much softer than the floor. Ye canna be comfortable here."

Tears welled, deepening the already vibrant green of her eyes. The fullness of her bottom lip quivered the slightest bit. *Lore a'mighty, dinna let her cry*, he silently prayed to any power that might be listening. He couldn't bear the vulnerability of a weeping lass. He scooped her up from the floor and gently deposited her into the chair, then tucked the plaid around her. "It will be all right, Jessa. Dinna fash yerself. Everything will be all right."

"It will not," she snapped, smacking him away as if he'd pinched her. She curled into a ball of misery, and her tears spilled over. "Everything is so effed up. So un-freakin'-believably effed up. I can't take it anymore." She shattered into a storm of uncontrollable sobs. "I don't know where the hell I am, can't call Emily for help, and you don't seem to understand anything I say." She paused long enough to suck in a deep breath, then unleashed a long, keening wail. "I'm jobless, broke, and tired of being a burden to my friends." Pounding her fist on the arm of the chair and kicking like a bairn having a tantrum, she screeched even louder. "And no matter what I do or what I try, things just get worse. I'm sick of this shit. Absolutely sick of it, and I never curse!"

Heaven help him, he couldn't bear her suffering. He yanked her up into his arms, sat in the chair, and settled her into his lap. "Shh... now. Ye're not alone, *sionnach beag*. I'm here, and I'll not let anything harm ye."

"What is a *shun-ukh beg*?" she asked, gasping through her tears. "Did you just call me an ugly name?"

Even though she sounded insulted, he noticed she curled tighter against him and tucked her head under his chin. He also noticed how very fine her soft, warm weight fit so perfectly in his lap. "*Sionnach beag* is Scots for *little fox*. Ye're as fearless and wily as those wee creatures, and yer red mane reminds me of their coloring."

"If I was wily, I wouldn't be here." She shuddered with another series of snuffling sobs, then fisted her hand in his shirt and pitifully tried to shake him. "I hate this," she said, hissing the words like an angry kitten. "Not knowing how I got here. You making fun of me by acting like you've never heard of a phone, a bathroom, or anything normal for a headache. How remote a place is this? The Highlands have paved roads, surely indoor plumbing and cell phone towers are here too. Or do you expect me to believe that civilization hasn't made it this far north in Great Britain?"

Paved roads? Was she speaking of the military roads constructed by General Wade? *Indoor plumbing*? There was the well house with the pumps that the servants used to draw water. Was that what she meant? And there was that *phone* word again. "What the bloody hell is a *cell phone tower*?" he asked. "The only towers we have are those at the corners of the skirting wall. I have watchmen there for security."

She pushed herself upright and stared at him. Fire flashed in her emerald eyes, and she looked ready to slap him. "Are you freaking serious?"

He slowly shook his head, hating that everything he said upset her even more. "Forgive me, lass. I dinna understand half of what ye say. *Bathroom. Phone.* Those words ye used when ye asked for something for yer head. This is the first time I have ever heard anyone say such things, and I speak French, Portuguese, English, and Scots." A groaning sigh escaped him. There went her lip again, quivering like a bairn about to squall to be fed. He touched her cheek. "Jessa—"

She slapped at his hand, fumbled out of his lap, and backed up one slow step at a time. Her finger shaking, she pointed at him, motioning up and down from his boots to his kilt to his shirt while opening and closing her mouth, but no sounds came out. Then she looked around the room, pointing at the candles and oil lamps. With a pitiful squeak, she covered her face with her hands and took refuge in the corner against the stonework of the hearth.

"Is this a reenactment?" Her desperation filled the air as she peeped at him through her fingers.

"A reenactment?" What the bloody hell was she asking him now?

She jerked with a quick nod, terror and confusion in her eyes. "Like a historical movie. Or a play or something. Or a really bad joke at my expense."

"This is no play or *something*, lass, and I dinna ken what a movie is either." His heart broke for her pain, for her fears, and for the sense of loss in her eyes. He held out a hand. "Come here, lass. Come and rest. Things will be better once ye've rested. Yer tea will be here soon, and then ye can lie down and have yerself a good long sleep."

She hugged herself tighter into the corner. Her stillness concerned him, and she'd gone so pale that her dusting of freckles had most nigh disappeared.

"What day is it?" she asked in a dull, hopeless whisper.

"Since we're well past midnight now, this is the summer solstice. June twenty-first."

"The year." She shuddered and touched the stonework of the hearth as if needing the support of something solid. "June twenty-first, what year?"

"1785."

She slumped to the floor and huddled in the corner like a wounded animal. "You lie."

"Why would I lie about what year it is?"

"I don't know—some twisted reason to make me think I'm crazy?" She was shaking, shaking so hard her teeth chattered. "It's 2025, and you know it. I don't know what's going on here or why, but I've had enough. If you don't take me back to Seven Cairns, I swear I'll make your life a living hell."

He sagged forward in the chair and dropped his head into his hands. That damned witch had pulled this poor unsuspecting woman back in time to be his wife. The legends had spoken of that happening before. Some such nonsense about joining fated mates across time so their love could maintain the strength of the barrier that protected the worlds. The Defenders had mentioned the practice as well. Some even said it would be an honor to support the Highland Veil in such a manner. Well, they could all feckin' go to the devil. The sheer terror in Jessa's eyes was pure torture, and there wasn't a damn thing he could do about it. All he could do was tell her the truth and pray she possessed the strength to come to terms with it.

"Mairwen is a witch of sorts. She brought ye back in time to be my wife."

※

With her head now pounding so hard that her heartbeat echoed in her ears, Jessa winced against the throbbing pain and pushed back tighter into the corner. Mr. MacSexy, aka Grant MacAlester, had to be nuts. And Mairwen must be crazy too, because she appeared to be helping him. The two of them must've somehow drugged her in the massage room, but for the life of her, she couldn't remember drinking anything while there. Whatever they'd used must have thrown her into that awful hallucination, and then he'd kidnapped her and brought her here. She almost laughed at that. Why in the world would anybody kidnap her? That explanation for this strange situation was ludicrous, but at the moment, it was the only logical explanation she could come up with.

She had to stop panicking, get a grip on reality, and figure out a way out of here. With a strength she never realized she had, she choked down her hysteria and swallowed hard. It was time to *woman up,* and *woman up,* she would.

Staring at Grant, she kept her gaze locked with his. He seemed so serious about everything. But then, he would. A crazy person believed their delusions were reality. But if this was a delusion, the guy must be rich, because he had fully bought into the wardrobe and location. His soft linen shirt was one laundering shy of being realistically threadbare. His kilt wasn't one of those neatly pleated styles she had seen in Inverness. It was belted and draped around him as if it were made of one large yardage of cloth he'd wrapped and folded into a garment. And the castle. No, he had called it a keep, not a castle. But from what she'd seen while hanging out the window, this stone structure was a freaking castle.

"Lass, did ye hear me?"

She swallowed hard again, trying to ignore the nausea sending the burn of bile to the back of her throat. "I am sitting three feet away. Why would I not hear you?"

His scowl darkened. He pulled in a deep breath and slowly released it, then dropped his head back into his hands. Jessa wondered if the man ever smiled. Maybe he should switch delusions because this one didn't seem to be making him very happy.

He lifted his head and eyed her as if trying to decide what to do with her. She took a little pride in that. At least she had succeeded in confusing him.

"Did Mairwen tell ye nothing of the Highland Veil or fated mates?" he asked with a weariness she completely felt, too.

"All Mairwen told me was how much her cottage cost for a month and that a massage and the healing springs would make me feel worlds better. Since she already hit mine and Emily's credit cards, I know the first part to be true. But so far, she lied about the massage and Seven Cairns' magical waters, because I do not feel better at all." Jessa rubbed her puffy eyes and vowed not to cry anymore. And her nose was running. She pinched the end of it and glared at him. "I don't suppose you know what a tissue is, either?"

He rose from the chair, strode over to a gorgeous antique dresser, and retrieved a handkerchief from the top drawer. His expression still grim, he returned and held it out to her. "Here—and no, I dinna ken what a feckin' *tissue* is, either."

"Thank you." She blew her nose and fisted the cloth to her chest, holding onto it as if it were a lifeline in this sea of madness.

"This is Mairwen's doing, lass. The legends say that she and her kind track down fated mates and unite them. The bond between two souls fated to be one is rumored to be the strongest love of all, and that love strengthens the weave of the Highland Veil that keeps the worlds and planes of time separated as they should be. If the Veil ever weakens or tears, chaos would rule, and entire worlds would be lost to the darkness."

"Chaos already rules this world. Have you not listened to the news or been on social media lately?"

"'Tis my understanding that if the Veil falls, the resulting chaos would be far worse than that which we have already experienced."

He had an answer for everything, but crazy people usually did. Or at least that's what Emily's mom had always said, and as a psychiatrist, she should know. "You said *Mairwen and her kind*. What *kind* is that? A witch? You've called her that a couple of times."

He pushed up from the chair and went to a cabinet on the other side of the room. "Shall ye have a whisky until Sawny decides to move his arse and bring up yer tea?"

"Just water, thank you. I'm not much on alcohol." Besides, she needed to keep a clear head. Everything was muddled enough without adding adult beverages to the mix. "Answer my question. What is Mairwen?"

"Henry calls her a Divine Weaver or some such nonsense." He paused, appearing to struggle with keeping his delusional facts straight. Then he nodded. "Aye. A Weaver. Henry could tell ye more. He's a sworn Defender. 'Tis his opinion that she is descended from the goddesses themselves."

"Goddesses?" This fairy tale kept getting more complicated. Jessa wished she had her tablet so she could take notes and keep everything straight. "Which goddesses?"

"Bride and Cerridwen." He handed her a glass of water before settling back into his chair with his whisky. "Benevolent goddesses until they decide to toy with ye, and then they can be a royal pain in the arse."

"So Mairwen is a goddess?" The older woman had possessed an air of agelessness and wisdom, but a goddess? Really? Jessa shook her head to clear it. She had to stay sane. This was his delusion. Not hers.

Grant sipped the golden liquid in his glass. "Nay. Not a goddess. At least not according to Henry, but a daughter of theirs and just as powerful."

"Of course." Jessa didn't attempt to veil her sarcasm. "She would have to be pretty powerful to rip me out of the twenty-first century and plop me into your time."

"Ye dinna believe me."

"I think you need help." Maybe if she approached this situation from that angle, she could talk him off the proverbial ledge, and he would return her to Seven Cairns.

He gave her a somewhat lazy frown while slowly nodding. "I see." After another sip, he asked, "And what sort of help might I be needing, lass?"

She wanted to say institutionalization, medication, and lots of therapy, but didn't think that would go over well. "I think you need help in realizing that legends are just stories. They are not real."

And then he finally smiled, making it impossible for her to breathe. How could something as simple as a smile completely transform a person? Her heart rate shifted into high gear, fluttering like the rapid beat of a hummingbird's wings. Something deep inside her clicked, and then she bottomed out with sadness. Why did her Mr. MacSexy have to be insane? *Her* Mr. MacSexy? Something indefinable within her nodded. Yes, Grant MacAlester would have been *hers* if he had been right in the head. She forced that disturbing revelation aside.

"Why does that make you smile?" she asked, struggling to sound nonchalant.

"*Some* legends are just stories, lass. Others are historical retellings, and a few are even warnings." He set his glass on the table between the chairs and stretched, exhibiting a spectacular wingspan.

Jessa cleared her throat. "And you believe the stories about the Highland Veil to be true?"

"I once doubted them."

"But not now?"

With a hint of amusement in his eyes, he slowly shook his head. "Here ye be, *sionnach beag*. A lass from the future. How can I deny them now?"

A knock on the door made her jump and shove as far back into the corner as she could get.

"Calm yerself. 'Tis more than likely yer tea." He went to the door and barely opened it.

"Sawny said ye're feeling poorly," an older woman said as she widened the opening with a bump of her ample hip and blustered her way inside. "'Tis dangerous on this day. Summer solstice. Did ye anger the wise one again?" She shook her head, clucking her tongue like a fretting hen. "What have I told ye, m'laird? Ye canna go against her. 'Tis for yer own good and the sake of the clan, it is. Ye must not vex her."

Jessa snapped her mouth shut after realizing she sat there with it hanging open. Had he gone to the trouble of hiring people to populate his delusion? His employee wore a period costume Jessa could only assume went with the year 1785. The elderly woman sported a full, long gray skirt, a white apron, and a white cap with wisps of her gray curls peeping out from under the ruffles. How much could all this be costing him? And why would he do it just to kidnap her? She was a penniless nobody. That was the troubling part and the glaring hole in her logic. There was no good reason for him to fake this being 1785. But if he wasn't faking it, she shied away from that thought. *No. That cannot be possible.*

"Mrs. Robeson," Grant said, "forgive me for getting ye out of yer bed at this hour, but it is my guest who is troubled with a terrible ache in her head. Not myself." He nodded at Jessa. "Allow me to introduce ye to Miss Jessa Tamson. Mairwen wished me to meet her, and it has not gone well at all."

Mrs. Robeson whirled around and squinted at her, then turned back to Grant with a scolding look. "What did ye say to the poor wee lamb?" Before he could answer, she set the tray bearing a small teapot and cup on the dresser, hurried over to Jessa, and tugged her up from the floor. "He is not always such an arse, lass. While he can be rough as a cob most days, the man has himself a good heart. Just ye wait and see. Give him a chance. Some lasses like him well enough, and I've never known him to treat any woman cruelly."

She herded Jessa over to the bed and had her propped against a pile of plumped pillows before she realized what was happening. "Here, ye poor lamb. Drink this. 'Twill stop that aching in yer pate. Ye must be jolted clear to the bone, what with the magic and all."

"Thank you." Jessa found herself at a loss for words in the whirlwind of the grandmotherly woman and the strange things she said. She sipped the tea and barely kept from spitting the bitter concoction back into the cup.

Grant rumbled with a low, deep laugh from where he stood at the foot of the bed. "Aye, the taste is wretched, but it will chase away the pain."

She blinked against the sting of tears and stared down into the cup. Why did he have to be crazy? When he smiled, when he laughed, when he acted *normal*, her heart did a little happy dance as if she had finally found her way home and everyone there loved her.

"There, there now, lass," Mrs. Robeson said softly. "'Twill be all right. Give it a bit of time. All will be well."

The old woman's gentle kindness made Jessa feel even worse. Before she lost control and started wailing again, she choked down more of the awful tea.

Mrs. Robeson ambled over to Grant. "Shall I have the maids sort the other room?"

"No," he said, while settling a determined look on Jessa. "I shall sleep in here to ensure the lass is safe."

"I'll be fine," Jessa said through clenched teeth. If he tried to get in this bed with her, he'd find himself neutered at her first opportunity.

"Safe?" Mrs. Robeson said to Grant. "How could she not be—"

"Mrs. Robeson."

The way his eyes narrowed on the old woman not only silenced her but made Jessa shiver. Neutering him might prove difficult.

"Hmpf." The matron stiffened and rested her folded hands on the shelf of her thick middle. "Dinna dishonor yer clan, m'laird, and remember how the goddesses view the disrespectful treatment of women." Then she threw her hands in the air and toddled out the door. "That's all I'll be saying about that," she said before closing the door behind her with an opinionated thump.

"That is not all she'll be saying about that. I guarantee it." Grant fetched the small ceramic teapot sitting on the tray and refilled Jessa's cup. "Try to drink all of it, lass. 'Twill help ye rest."

"Drugging me again?" She couldn't help saying that, even though the pain in his eyes made her immediately regret it.

He bowed his head with a formal nod, then moved one of the chairs out from in front of the hearth and placed it against the bedroom door. "I have done nothing to harm ye, lass, and would never do so. I may be *rough as a cob*, as my housekeeper said, but I am neither a cruel man nor do I take advantage of those deserving of my protection." He tipped her another nod. "And whether ye wish it or not, ye are deserving of my protection." Then he settled down into the chair, stretched out his long legs, and crossed them at the ankles. "Sleep, lass. 'Twill do us both a world of good."

"I want to go home," she said, not caring that she sounded like the whiny, homesick kid at a sleepover.

He eyed her for a long moment, the slow, steady rise and fall of his chest almost mesmerizing. "Ye are home, Jessa, and the sooner ye come to terms with that, the better off ye will be."

She downed the rest of the horrid tea and curled into a tight ball under the blankets. This couldn't be real. None of it. In the morning, she'd wake up back at the cottage and tell Emily all about this nightmare. She squinched her eyes shut, trying to shut off more tears, but they escaped and soon became a torrent. She wadded the handkerchief against the end of her drippy nose and willed herself to stop crying before she puked. This was all just a bad dream—and if it wasn't, she would figure it out. Somehow.

CHAPTER 6

It had taken forever for Jessa to cry herself to sleep. Now, even though she finally slumbered, Grant watched her, unable to look away and only blinking when his eyes burned with the need to do so. She huddled in a pitiful ball up in one corner of his bed, with the covers pulled so high that nothing but the top of her head showed. The wildness of her curls peeped out, splaying over the pillows like a fiery sunset. The faint shifting of the bedclothes with her relaxed breathing eased his mind somewhat, but his heart and soul still troubled him. He could think of nothing that would console her. Mairwen had ripped this poor woman from the world she knew and dropped her into his. All for the sake of the Highland Veil, with no thought to those affected by such an outrageous act.

He shifted in the chair, trying to move silently to avoid disturbing her. The night candle on the mantle sputtered, and the fire in the hearth occasionally popped and hissed. Other than that, the room was painfully silent, filled with the ominous weight of all that had gone wrong and all that could still go awry. He had not felt such a gnawing leeriness and uncertainty in a long while.

Mrs. Robeson's tea had likely helped the poor lass finally lose the battle against sleep. That made him feel even more guilty, especially since she had accused him of drugging her. She hated him, and damned if she didn't draw him in like a fresh bloom tempted a bee.

He pulled in a deep breath and eased it out in a heavy sigh. Lore a'mighty, she was even more stunning than in his dreams. He almost allowed himself a smile but stopped it before it twitched across his mouth. Nay, there was nothing to be pleased about when it came to this feckin' curfuffle.

The image of her eyes flashing with fire came to him unbidden, stirring him more than it should. Heaven help his sorry arse, but he had always loved a hot-tempered lass. More often than not, their tendency to fly into a rage hinted at the levels of passion they could attain. Sly old Mairwen had found him a woman she knew he could never resist. And now, thanks to the old witch, not only did that woman despise him, but thought him a liar or a babbling fool who had lost all reason. All of which could have been avoided if Mairwen had just told the lass what was what and given her the right to choose.

The pale gray haziness outside the window told him the sky was already growing lighter with the rising sun on the longest day of the year. He rubbed his tired, gritty eyes, remembering he had meant to catch up on his sleep since the night before had been spent seeing to a shipment. Ah, well, it was no matter. He could rest when he was dead.

He pushed himself to his feet and stretched, then rolled the sore stiffness from his shoulders. That chair had barely offered enough comfort for a wee nod, much less a few hours' sleep. Jessa never stirred, and from the continued slow, even rhythm of her breathing, he doubted if she was awake and trying to appear as though she still slept. The wily minx had attempted that once. He would not put it past her to try it again.

With the greatest of care, he set the chair aside and eased out into the hallway, quietly closing the bedroom door with a soft click.

When he turned, he nearly stepped on Sawny, who sat on the floor beside the door.

"What the devil are ye doing there?" he asked the boy in a loud whisper.

The lad yawned and clumsily stumbled to his feet. "Mrs. Robeson put me here. Said if ye needed something, ye would need it with haste, and there'd be no call for ye to have to ring the bell and wait for someone to answer if'n I was right here."

Grant knew that wasn't the only reason the nosy old housekeeper had planted one of her most trusted informants in the hallway. "'Tis a sorry thing to spy on yer laird. A crime worthy of banishment from the clan."

The youngling's eyes went round as basins. "Oh no, m'laird. I would never spy on ye. She told me to stay here in case ye needed something fetched. I swear it."

"Then fetch Henry. I have a task I want done before the sun rises much higher. Send him here and tell Mrs. Robeson I'll be breaking my fast in my solar with my guest."

"Aye, m'laird." The lad took off as if old Scratch himself chased after him.

Grant propped against the wall beside the door and closed his eyes. He'd not go back inside the room until he'd had a word with Henry out in the hallway. While he might not yet know his lovely wee fox all that well, he had a fair idea that she wouldn't appreciate waking to yet another strange man in the room with her.

After a while, the heavy thud of boots coming from the direction of the stairwell prompted him to open his eyes and meet Henry partway down the hall. The man had a booming voice and couldn't be quiet if his life depended on it.

"Aye?" Henry asked, looking as if he had just tumbled from his bed.

Grant nodded. "Fetch the witch. Fast as ye can get her here."

The man's ruddy brows shot up to his hairline. "Ye dinna fetch Mairwen. She comes and goes as she pleases."

"As a Defender, she will answer yer call. Ye made the mistake of telling me that once, remember?"

Henry winced, his regret at doing so clear. "Aye. But the call is not to be abused, or there'll be hell to pay."

"Hell can add it to my account. Fetch the witch."

His friend shuffled in place, raking his hands through his hair until it stood on end even more. "Grant—"

"She dumped a woman from the future into my bed last night, and that lass does not wish to be here. Fetch Mairwen. Now."

Henry's mouth sagged open. "From the future?" he whispered while sidling to one side to squint down the hallway at the bedroom door. "How far into the future?"

"2025."

"God's teeth."

"Exactly."

"Does she ken what year this is?"

Grant fisted his hands, fighting to keep his voice low. "Aye, she does, but doubts it. Haul yer arse to Seven Cairns, and get the old witch back here to make this right."

Henry nodded and backed away a few steps before spinning about and setting off at a faster stride.

Dragging a weary hand across his eyes, Grant returned to the bedroom door and eased back inside, holding his breath until his vision adjusted to the dimly lit room. Jessa hadn't moved. He released the breath he'd held. Of course, with him guarding the door and them being on the third floor, there was little chance of her escaping, but he wouldn't put it past the wily lass to use the bedclothes as ropes to climb out the window.

He stirred the fire, added a log to battle the dampness in the air, then sagged down into the nearest chair. It might be June, but the rain and the early morning hour lent a chill to the place. He didn't mind, but the lass would surely find it uncomfortable. The soft rustling of the bedclothes warned him she might be waking.

"Well, shit," came loud and clear from the bed. A dismal groan followed.

He scooted the chair, angling it away from the hearth, and faced it toward her. "Good morn to ye."

She pulled the covers over her head and ignored him.

"Mrs. Robeson will be up soon with a fine breakfast. I assumed ye would wish to eat in the privacy of my solar until we found ye some proper clothing, and ye felt a wee bit more settled."

"I am not hungry," came her muffled reply from under the blankets.

"If there is one thing ye should know about Mrs. Robeson, it's that she ensures everyone is fed, whether or not they wish to be. She'll not tolerate ye starving yerself to death to escape yer sentence of becoming my wife." His heart bolted to his innards and stirred them into a churning mass even though he'd just said it in jest. He rolled his shoulders and shook away the unnerving feeling. Nay, he did not want a wife—not even one as bonnie as the woman in his bed. "She'll probably bring along either Molly or Hester to tend to ye and yer needs."

"The only thing I need is to go home," she said while still under the covers, then mumbled something else he couldn't make out.

"What say ye, lass? Lore a'mighty, uncover yer head. It's not as though I dinna ken where ye are."

She flopped back the covers and glared at him. "I said I want to go home, want my coffee, and I really need to use the toilet. But I don't suppose you understand any of that, either."

He narrowed his eyes at her. "This is yer home now. I can have Mrs. Robeson send Sawny to the storage house for some of the coffee beans scheduled to shift to Edinburgh next week, and either Molly or Hester can help ye with yer toilette once they find ye some clothes."

She bared her clenched teeth at him. "Not *toilette*, as in washing and dressing me. *Toilet* as in I need to pee."

"Ah." He rose from the chair and pointed at the cabinet on the other side of the bed. "Ye'll find the chamberpot just in there."

She stared at him in disbelief. "Chamberpot?"

"Aye." He'd instinctively known she'd hate that, even though he had no idea what she was accustomed to in her time. "I'll step into the hallway to grant ye some privacy."

She dropped her head into her hands. "Lovely. Just freaking lovely."

He took that as her agreement to what he'd suggested, stepped out into the hall, and leaned back against the closed door. Bowing his head, he silently vowed to unleash the priest on the old witch at his earliest opportunity. Although, to be honest, it wouldn't be a fair battle. The priest would never stand a chance against Mairwen.

"Oh no, m'lord," Hester said as she and Molly rounded the corner. "Be yer lady unwell?" Both maids carried armloads of clothing and linens, and baskets of soaps and oils swung from the crooks of their elbows. Behind them followed Sawny, struggling to carry the large copper tub by himself.

"Ye're nay supposed to call him *lord*," Sawny said in an overly loud whisper. "He hates that."

"It's *laird*," Molly hurried to tell Hester, the newest maid to join MacAlester Keep.

Grant ignored the schooling of the new maid. She'd learn their ways soon enough, or she'd be sent back to whence she came. "Sawny—set the tub down, hie to the shipment headed for Edinburgh, and fetch back a bag of the coffee beans. Give them to Mrs. Robeson and ask her to prepare some coffee for Miss Jessa."

"Miss Jessa," Sawny repeated with a smile. "What a fine name for the laird's wife."

"She is not my wife. On wi' ye now and if ye dawdle, I'll have yer hide, ye ken?"

"Aye, m'laird." The lad turned and ran, then paused at the corner of the hallway and said, "I'll have the kitchen lads bring up the water for the lady's bath soon as it boils. Griselda's done ordered the fires stoked good and hot."

"Tell them to be quick about it," Molly said before Grant could respond. "The mistress needs a nice, long soak. Mrs. Robeson said so."

"And that's another thing," Grant said as he turned back to the maids. "The lady has been through a fearsome ordeal. She might speak of strange things or ask questions that dinna make sense to either of ye. Answer her truthfully and to the best of yer abilities, then keep her confidence and protect her, or I'll banish ye from this keep so fast yer head will spin off yer necks. Is that understood?" He would not have Jessa an object of ridicule. There would be enough gossip as it was, but there was no need for it to be made any worse.

Both young women gave him hurried nods and whispered, "Aye, m'laird."

Satisfied that he had instilled a healthy sense of fearful respect into the two of them, he gently rapped on the door, then barely cracked it open. "May I come in, lass? Have ye...have ye done what ye needed to do?"

"I'm done."

The hopeless dejection in her voice weighed heavily on his heart. With any luck, the bath might help her feel at least a little better. Women seemed to enjoy that sort of thing a great deal more than men. He ushered the maids inside, then hoisted the tub onto his shoulder, carried it in, and placed it in front of the hearth.

Jessa was back in the bed, sitting against the headboard, hugging her knees with her shift tucked around her feet. Her tumble of curls created a fiery curtain she occasionally peeped through. Saints help him and make him strong, but she entranced him—dangerously so. This woman was the Goddess Bride incarnate.

"She is so lovely," Hester whispered entirely too loudly, but Grant couldn't argue. Jessa Tamson was the bonniest lass his weary old soul had ever seen.

He shook himself free of her spell and pointed out the maids. "This here is Molly, and this is Hester. Mrs. Robeson sent them to help ye bathe and dress as soon as the water's brought up. I sent

Sawny for the coffee beans. Soon ye'll have a fine cup of that vile stuff to enjoy with yer breakfast."

Her eyes shimmered with emotions, but at least the sheen of tears was gone. Smudges of weariness beneath them somehow made her even more winsome.

"Thank you," she said quietly, then chewed on the corner of her lip, eyeing him as if debating whether or not to say what was on her mind. Nothing had stopped her earlier. What had changed?

"What is it, lass?"

Before she could answer, a knock rattled the door. "Got some water here, Molly," one of the kitchen lads called from the hallway.

"Let them in," Grant told the maid when she looked to him for permission.

Molly deposited her armload of goods onto the bench at the foot of the bed, hurried to the door, and waved them inside. "Did ye bring a full kettle for the fire so's I can keep the mistress's water good and warm for her?"

"Jasper's got two," Rob, the first lad entering the room, said. Before dumping his buckets of water into the tub, he paused and bowed in Jessa's direction and then at Grant. "Mornin' to ye, mistress. My laird."

Grant nodded at the lad, then studied Jessa, who seemed bewildered by the servant's manners. Moving to stand beside the bed, he leaned toward her to speak for her ears alone, dismayed when she shied away. "Lass?" How could she think he would ever harm her?

"Sorry." She backed up tighter against the headboard and rubbed her forehead. "Everything is still so messed up."

"Do ye need more tea for yer head?"

"No. It doesn't hurt anymore. I'm just—confused."

He could only imagine the depths of her confusion. Mayhap her coffee would help. Those he knew who liked that black swill sometimes claimed it settled their minds. "Hester—see about hurrying the mistress's coffee along, aye?"

"Aye, m'laird." The maid dipped a curtsy and rushed out.

Two more scullery lads showed up, bowed their *good mornings*, and dumped their buckets into the large copper tub that Molly had lined with linen. The maid turned, twisting a cloth between her hands. "Yer bath is ready, mistress."

Jessa's reddish blonde brows barely twitched higher, and she angled a wary glare his way. She didn't speak, but then, she didn't need to. Her expression spoke volumes.

"I shall retire to my solar to await ye," Grant said with a proper bow. "'Tis naught but across the hall. Molly will bring ye over when ye've finished here."

She didn't comment, merely hugged her knees tighter and narrowed her eyes as if drowning in her troubled thoughts.

"Well, then," he said. "I leave ye to it." After a curt nod, he strode out the door, methodically sorting through everything he had ever heard Henry and Lachie say about the Defenders and Mairwen. The witch had overstepped her bounds this time, and he fully intended to not only regain control of his own life but put Jessa's to rights as well. He'd not deny there was something about the woman that made him ache to know her better, but he'd be damned if he forced a lass who hated him to remain at his side.

CHAPTER 7

Jessa ran her tongue across her teeth. They felt fuzzy, and her mouth tasted of morning funk and the nasty tea she'd had last night. But in reality, needing to brush her teeth was the least of her worries. She eyed the maid, wondering if she could get the truth out of the girl who looked extremely young to work as a maid. "Molly, is it?"

"Aye, mistress. I be Molly, and Mrs. Robeson said ye could choose between me and Hester to be yer lady's maid." The thin brunette tilted her angular jaw higher and patted her chest. "I have the more experience, ye ken? Hester is nice enough, but she be the newest here at the keep." She cast a glance back at the tub. "Would ye care to enjoy yer bath now?"

While Jessa wasn't all that sure about stripping down in front of the maid, she wanted to wash since she hadn't showered since yesterday morning, which felt like eons ago. Remembering how she had grumbled about the cottage's poor water pressure, she wished she'd been more thankful for what she'd had at the time. Now, she was reduced to bathing in something better suited for watering livestock. Life had handed her quite the lesson in gratitude.

She clambered out of the bed, then skittered to one side as Molly hurried forward and reached for her.

"Forgive me, mistress." The maid backed up a step, wringing her hands. "I only meant to help ye with yer shift."

"It's all right. You didn't do anything wrong. I'm just a little jumpy."

"Himself said ye had survived a terrible ordeal."

"Himself?" Jessa had a pretty good idea who Molly was talking about, but it never hurt to be sure. Especially since she still hadn't figured out this alternate reality Mr. MacSexy had manufactured. She untied the nightgown and pushed it to the floor rather than slipping it over her head. She preferred to keep her line of sight clear at all times.

"The laird," Molly said while steadying Jessa to help her step into the high-sided tub. "Is the water warm enough, mistress? Ye want I should heat it a bit more? Jasper brought us two fine kettles that I've got warming over there on the fire. There's plenty."

"No, it's good, thank you." Jessa bundled her hair on top of her head, then was at a loss for how to get it to stay there. All her hair clips and ties were at the cottage or Mairwen's massage therapy room. "Do you have any clips or barrettes? Or a scrunchie would be awesome."

Sorting through one of the baskets, Molly paused in her digging and frowned. "Forgive me, mistress, but I dinna ken what ye need. If ye tell me what troubles ye, I am sure I can sort it out."

Well, of course, the maid wouldn't know about those things. Molly had been trained or brainwashed into living and believing all things 1785. "Something to hold my hair up so it doesn't get wet?"

The girl brightened and held up a length of ribbon and what looked like either wicked sharp chopsticks or meat skewers. "Aye, right here. I was just finding them for ye."

As Molly secured her hair, Jessa tried not to wince, then decided it was high time for some crafty fact-finding. Maybe the maid would accidentally spill the beans about what was really going on here. "How old are you, Molly?"

"I be ten and seven." The girl soused a cloth into the water and rubbed the bar of soap across it until it was frothy and the scent of roses filled the air. "Hester be only ten and five. That's why I've the more experience and would be a better lady's maid for ye."

Seventeen and fifteen-year-olds? What kind of guy was this Grant MacAlester? "Fifteen is pretty young to work as a maid. Aren't you both still in school?" Of course, it was summertime. Maybe this was summer work for them, like summer theater in the park or something.

Molly paused in her scrubbing of Jessa's back. "I dinna ken what ye mean, mistress. Both Hester and I can read already. I can even figure out some weights and measures. We've a pair of scullery maids that are naught but ten and eleven. They canna read nor do sums yet, but Mrs. Robeson and I are teaching them, so they might be a better help to Cook with her recipes one day. The MacAlester is a kind man who pays his servants more than most. The sculleries earn a whole ten pounds a year rather than the usual six or less. Our families would go hungry were it not for him paying us so good. Many from the village wish they could work here at the keep. 'Tis quite the honor." She lowered her voice to a whisper. "The MacAlester doesna trust easy."

"I bet he doesn't. Is your village Seven Cairns?" That was the only local name Jessa could remember.

"Nay, MacAlester Crag. Seven Cairns is to the west of here." She scrubbed Jessa's arms and smiled. "Yer skin is so fair, mistress, like fresh cream just poured into the pans."

Jessa wrinkled her nose, embarrassed by the girl's praise. "Ah, but I'm covered in freckles."

"That's just where the goddesses dusted ye with spices." Molly went to the tall metal pitcher beside the fire, added some water to it from the steaming kettle hanging from the rod over the coals, then returned and gently rinsed the soapiness away.

Jessa shivered beneath the torrent of heated water. Maybe washing in a livestock tub wasn't so bad after all.

"It's nay too hot, is it, mistress?" Molly clutched the metal pitcher to her middle, obviously afraid she'd done wrong.

"No. It's perfect."

The maid shifted in place with a worried frown. "I noticed ye already scrubbed the rest of yer parts. Does a lady's maid not wash ye all over? Am I doing this wrong?"

"You washed the parts I couldn't reach. That's what I look for in a lady's maid." Jessa gave up on tricking the devoted Molly into saying something she shouldn't. It would be like kicking a puppy. "I think you are a fine lady's maid." She didn't add that she had no idea what a lady's maid was supposed to do, but as long as Molly wasn't all that sure about it either, they'd get along just fine. "Maybe Hester can fill in for you whenever you take time off."

Molly went still and stared at her as if she'd just unhinged her jaw and revealed a set of fangs. "Take time off? No one shirks their duties unless they're dead." Then she shrugged. "Or so ailing that they canna rise from their sickbed. But ye best not let Mrs. Robeson discover 'tis more laziness than feeling poorly." She held up what looked like a large bedsheet. "I warmed the linen by the fire so ye willna take a chill. As cool as it is this morn, ye would hardly know 'tis June."

Jessa tried to remember every period drama she had ever streamed on her laptop so she'd know more about what was going on. Then she recalled all the chatter she'd read about Hollywood's historical inaccuracies. But if this was all an act—and it had to be since time travel was not possible—maybe they wouldn't notice whatever blunders she made. She stepped out of the tub and allowed Molly to wrap the toasty warm cloth around her. "Wow, this feels wonderful. Thank you for thinking of it, Molly."

The girl tipped her head to one side as though surprised, then she smiled. "Ye are verra welcome, mistress. 'Tis my duty to take the verra best care of ye." She led her over to a padded footstool in front of the hearth and helped her sit. "I'll fetch the oils and comb out yer hair. Then ye can choose what ye wish to wear."

"Choose?"

"Aye, mistress," Molly said while gathering items from the basket on the floor. "Mrs. Robeson has a good eye for that what fits and that what doesn't. She helped Hester and me gather some clothes for ye from the room. Once we see what ye like and what might need taking in or letting out, I'll put them to rights, and we'll fill the wardrobe with yer verra own things." She blossomed with a proud smile. "Mam always said I was quite the seamstress."

Jessa stared at her, slowly blinking as if it would help her understand what Molly had just divulged. "This *room* with the clothes. Is it some sort of thrift shop or something?" She tried not to think about the whole *a wardrobe holding her very own things* part. That implied she'd be staying a while, and she couldn't quite deal with that at the moment.

"I dinna ken what a thrift shop is." Molly gave her another puzzled look as she crouched in front of her and started rubbing a rose-scented oil on her feet and legs. "Is that a place where clothes are took when those that wore them canna wear them anymore?"

"Yes. That is what we call a thrift shop where I'm from." Jessa didn't mind second-hand clothing. Thrifting had saved her lots of money, and she'd scored several neat finds over the years.

"If ye dinna mind my asking, where are ye from, mistress?" Molly rubbed the oil onto Jessa's arms and smeared a generous dollop into her armpits.

Jessa tried not to shudder at the greasy feel when she lowered her arms. As slippery as she was, she could probably wiggle through a keyhole. "New Jersey, and I think that's plenty of oil for now."

"As ye wish." Molly set it aside and went to the articles piled in the other chair.

While she was turned the other way, Jessa dried the excess oil from her armpits. Mr. MacSexy would soon regret kidnapping her without her deodorant, toothbrush, and toothpaste.

Molly sorted through the pile of clothes like a squirrel hunting for a buried nut. She selected several items and held them up. "With yer eyes as green as a glen in springtime, these colors would suit ye. Do ye like the green or prefer the blue?"

"I usually wear black," Jessa said.

Molly's dark brows rose to her hairline. "Are ye in mourning, then?"

She might as well be honest with the maid. "No. Black makes me look taller and thinner."

The maid frowned. "Why would ye wish to look taller and thinner?"

"Because I'm short and plump." Jessa shrugged and tried to think of a way to explain it without sounding as if she was ashamed of her body—because she wasn't. Society just hadn't caught up with the notion that sizes other than tall and thin were beautiful, too. "I have a lot of jiggle to my wiggle, and from where I'm from, many men don't find that attractive."

"What a load of rubbish." Molly's eyes flared wide, and she clapped a hand over her mouth. "Forgive me, mistress. I should not have said that."

Jessa laughed. "Speak freely around me, Molly. It'll be our secret." She nodded at the clothing. "And pick whichever color. I trust you." It didn't matter what she wore, since she would be leaving at her earliest opportunity.

Molly bounced like a happy puppy. "Aye, mistress. First, a fresh sark. I'll have the one ye wore last night laundered."

Jessa could only assume that a *sark* was the same thing as a chemise, shift, or old-fashioned nightgown. If she was going to wear a dress, why did she need to put another nightgown on first? But she cooperated and shook the garment down into place. Surprisingly, the hemline fell to her shins. Usually, everything was too long.

"And now for the first of the petticoats." Molly bent and held the waist of the plain white skirt open wide so Jessa could step into it.

"More than one?" She stumbled to one side as the maid yanked the waistband snug and tied it.

"Of course, more than one. This one is to keep the finer ones clean when yer sark gets damp with sweat." Molly tugged on its folds and stepped back, eyeing the piece critically. "The length will do for now, but I'll hem it this evening. It's still a bit long. It'll be peeping out from under the others." While bending to select the next layer, she asked, "Do ye not wear more than one petticoat where ye're from?"

"Sometimes," Jessa lied. "Depends on the time of year."

"Ahh." Molly nodded and tied an item around Jessa's waist that looked like a neck pillow for naps while traveling.

"What is that?" Jessa angled from side to side, eyeing it.

"The bum roll holds yer skirts just so and makes them sway all lovely like. Draws a man's eyes to yer arse—I mean—yer bum. Ye dinna want to be all flat, do ye?"

"Apparently not."

"And now yer fancy petticoat. This one with the green stripes will set off yer overskirt just so. See it over there? It's green as an emerald."

"I'm sure it will be perfect." Jessa had no choice but to agree. No wonder she needed a lady's maid. These layers were ridiculous. "How exactly am I supposed to pee?"

"Do ye need the chamberpot, mistress? I can fetch it."

"Not at the moment, but when I do, I would prefer to be able to do it alone without needing someone to hold all my skirts out of the way."

"Did ye not wear clothes like these in yer New Jersey?"

Jessa had to admit Molly played the part of an eighteenth century maid well. "There were a lot fewer layers in New Jersey," she told the girl and left it at that.

"I see."

But she didn't. The girl was humoring her. Jessa could see it in her eyes. She waved to hurry her along. "Okay—what's next?"

Maybe once she was dressed, she could rinse her mouth with water. It wouldn't be as good as her sonic toothbrush and minty mouthwash, but it would be better than nothing at all. Or maybe they were done, but her bottom half seemed to have a great deal more coverage than her top, and the idea of bouncing around without the support of a bra was a little disconcerting.

"These fine stays." Molly proudly held up what appeared to be a very stiff, curvy vest made of panels of leather and a dark green plaid that matched the overskirt.

If it was meant to work like a corset or a bustier, wouldn't it go on the inside? Jessa eyed the garment. "Should we not have put that on first before the shift?"

"No, mistress. These stays are lovely and meant to be seen. They're quite proper for a lady of yer station." Molly helped her slip her arms through the straps, then tugged it closed in the front and started lacing. "Ye might wish to brace yerself, ye ken? It must be pulled tight."

The maid's strength as she yanked on the lacing surprised Jessa. "That's tight enough," she told her when her breasts bulged above the neckline. "Not only am I about to pop out, but I also need to breathe."

"I can pull it closer. Closer is always better, Mrs. Robeson says."

"No." Jessa tugged on the front and resettled the girls more comfortably in place. She'd wanted support, and now she had it. Apparently, she needed to be careful what she wished for. "What's next?"

"There's a jacket, but I dinna think ye'll need it today. All that's left are yer stockings, slippers, and then I'll dress yer hair."

"Dress my hair?"

"Aye, comb it out and put it up as befits a lady of yer status."

"What exactly is my status?" Jessa wondered what everyone had been told about her presence.

Molly went still, standing there with a pair of long ivory stockings in one hand and a pair of dark green ribbons in the other. "Are ye not here to wed Himself?" she asked, sounding as forlorn as a lost toddler.

"I have no intention of marrying anyone at the moment. Why would you think that?"

"I dinna ken," Molly hurried to say, her tone chilling with a distance that wasn't there before. "And besides, 'tis not my place to say." She nodded at the footstool again. "If ye'll be good enough to sit, I'll help ye with yer stockings."

Jessa lowered herself to the pillowed stool, determined to find out more. "You don't know or you won't say? What is it not your place to say? I told you to speak freely around me, remember?"

On her knees, Molly looked up with a pleading expression and whispered, "If Mistress Mairwen brought ye here to wed the MacAlester, it would be unwise of ye to refuse."

"I can handle Mistress Mairwen." In fact, Jessa had a few choice words to share with that conniving old woman who had turned out to be an accessory in kidnapping.

Molly glanced around as if someone was eavesdropping and taking notes. "Dinna say such things, mistress. It is nay wise."

Jessa wondered what Mairwen had done to put such fear into the young girl. Of course, if Molly was sticking to the eighteenth century mindset, then maybe she was playing the superstitious young Scot. Jessa wished the poor girl would just be honest with her, but she totally understood the situation where a paycheck was a paycheck. Choosing not to be difficult, she rubbed a finger across her teeth. "Do you have another washcloth I could use to clean my teeth? They feel icky."

Molly froze in the middle of tying a ribbon above Jessa's knee to keep her stocking in place. "Icky?"

"You know. Slimy. Gross. My mouth tastes bad."

The maid's mouth formed a small *o* of understanding. "I brought ye a freshly boiled toothbrush and some powder, but I thought ye'd nay need it till this evening."

"I like to brush my teeth in the mornings too," Jessa said slowly, wondering why the toothbrush had been boiled and what the powder was for.

"Here's yer slippers. While ye put them on, I'll fetch everything for ye, and then we shall do yer hair."

Molly seemed relieved that Mairwen was no longer the subject of their conversation. Jessa stored that away to think about later. If she found out that Mairwen or MacSexy was mean to this girl, she'd report them to whomever she could find and get Molly some help. Surely, Scotland had an equivalent to social services or resources for at risk women and children.

With a glass of water in one hand and what looked like a brush to scrub bathroom grout in the other, Molly glanced back at the pitcher and basin on the washstand. "I dinna have enough hands."

"I can stand at the washbasin and brush my teeth. You don't have to drag everything over here to me."

"Mrs. Robeson said I was to fetch everything ye need. A lady is nay supposed to be bothered with getting her own things."

"Yeah, well this lady is not helpless, and I don't mind doing some things for myself." Jessa took the grout brush from Molly and went to the basin. "So, this is the boiled toothbrush?"

"Aye, mistress. Brand new boar bristles and freshly boiled."

Jessa swallowed hard and stared down at the source of Molly's pride. They expected her to brush her teeth with pig hairs? "Alrighty then. Brand new. That's great." Gingerly, she started toward her mouth with it.

"Nay, mistress. Wet it first, so's the powder will cake on it." Molly prepared the toothbrush for her and handed it back. "Do ye not usually use powder?"

"No," Jessa said while eyeing the coated brush that now smelled like a pumpkin spice latte. "I'm used to a minty paste."

"I see." Molly opened the jar of powder and showed it to Jessa. "Mrs. Robeson uses cinnamon, nutmeg, and clove along with the eggshells and salt she grinds with her mortal and pestle. She says it's good for yer teeth and gums."

Eggshells and spices. Interesting. Determined to power through, play along, and not show weakness, Jessa scrubbed her teeth and tongue, surprised when it wasn't nearly as unpleasant as she'd expected. After rinsing her mouth, it felt a great deal better than before the brushing. "Thank you, Molly. Now my morning has been started right."

"Well done, mistress." Molly tugged her back to the footstool. "We'll finish yer hair, and then ye'll be ready to join Himself and see to yer breakfast. I'm sure Mrs. Robeson will have yer coffee ready by now or the MacAlester will be demanding to know why not."

"I can hardly wait." Jessa looked forward to seeing the rest of the keep and discovering the lengths the man had gone to all in the name of the eighteenth century.

CHAPTER 8

"If you don't take me to her, I'm contacting Interpol, Scotland Yard, the U.S. Embassy, and anyone else I can find who will listen to me." Emily charged across the meeting room toward Mairwen.

Ishbel and Reese, both of them Master Spell Weavers, blocked her way. The furious woman tried to shove around or through them, but they stayed in front of her.

"If you don't move, I will move you," Emily said to them, baring her teeth like a wild beast. "I put the fear of all that is me into my five brothers. Don't think I won't hesitate to put some fear into you."

"Let her pass," Mairwen said with a resigned sigh. It was always the same whenever the fated mates showed up at Seven Cairns with friends or family in tow. The one left behind struggled with accepting that which had been done not only for the sake of the mates but for that of the Highland Veil. "It is time she and I had our discussion."

"If acceptable," Ishbel said, "we shall stay since her energy is quite high and could become uncontrollable."

"What the hell is that supposed to mean?" Emily demanded.

When Ishbel remained silent, Emily stormed over to Mairwen, planted her hands on the table between them, and leaned forward until they were almost nose to nose. "I woke up this morning in that cave from yesterday's massage session after dreaming about Jessa screaming for help, and you think you're going to talk in code around me? I ain't having it!" She pounded the table with both fists, rattling Mairwen's notebook, pen, and teacup. "Where the hell is Jessa? What have you done with her, and what kind of drug did you slip me that made me lose an entire day of my life?"

"Sit and I will tell you everything you wish to know." Mairwen folded her hands and waited. Unstable energy rolled off Emily in waves. The lass needed to calm herself before discovering she was more powerful than she realized. Magical misfires were never a pretty sight.

"I shall put on more tea," Ishbel said with a pointed look at her husband.

Reese nodded and settled into a chair on Emily's side of the table.

"Just because you're a man, don't think I won't take you on," Emily told him. Fixing him with a glare that dared him to make a move, she jutted her chin higher. "Five brothers. Remember?"

Reese grinned. "Challenge accepted, lass, but let's hold off until ye hear what Mairwen has to say, aye?"

Mairwen settled more comfortably in her chair, hoping this time it would be easier to explain to the one left behind. After all, Emily was special. Mairwen even suspected there was Spell Weaver blood in her veins. She could almost smell it. "Yer Jessa is on her first date with her Mr. MacSexy, ye might say."

Emily's angry eyes narrowed even more. "You told her you didn't know him."

"Aye, well—I never exactly told her I didn't know him." Mairwen tipped an apologetic nod. "A lie of omission, I suppose ye might say."

"A lie is a lie, and why would it be necessary to lie about knowing the guy?"

"Because a first date with Grant MacAlester is not as simple as meeting him at Lilias's pub at an agreed upon hour, and it was verra important they meet and realize their fates are intertwined in the best possible way."

"Why is it that whenever you talk, you sound like the voice-over for some epic fantasy movie?"

Mairwen couldn't help but laugh. What a powerful personality this one had. She rather liked her. "It must be the Highlands. Magic runs deep here. Can ye not feel it?" She sent the faintest ripple of energy Emily's way, wondering if the lass would grant her a reaction or attempt to hide it.

Emily glared at her. "I don't believe in that stuff." But her eyes revealed her lie.

"I believe ye do, lass, at least, more than ye're willing to admit to me or yerself."

"Where is Jessa?" Emily straightened and resettled her stance, as if preparing to leap across the table and grab Mairwen by the throat. Reese edged forward, poised to stop her.

"She is with the laird of Clan MacAlester, the Earl of Suddie, at his keep just beyond the village of MacAlester Crag."

"She would never leave without telling me. What did you do? Drug her and carry her off?"

"She was not drugged. She was quite alert when she passed through the Veil to Scotland of 1785, where Grant MacAlester lives. That is why ye heard her call to ye in yer dreams."

With a disbelieving growl, Emily rounded the end of the table, yanked Mairwen's chair around to face her, and drew down until her nose was a hair's breadth from Mairwen's. "Enough of your games. Stop with the mystical bullshit you use on stupid tourists and take me to her."

Reese grabbed Emily by the shoulders and tried to drag her back. She popped her head back and butted him square in the face, then whirled around, planted her boot in his chest, and shoved, making him tumble back over a trio of chairs.

She turned back to Mairwen with dangerous fire flashing in her dark eyes. "Where is she?" she said, her voice a low guttural rumble.

Ishbel came running back into the room and hurried to set the tray on the end of the table. "*Quies!*"

Emily froze as if Ishbel had made time stand still.

"I told ye to watch her!" Ishbel told Reese, who was trying to stop the blood gushing from his nose.

"I was trying to be easy with her," he said, his words muffled by his bloody hands.

Ishbel rolled her eyes and turned back to Mairwen. "Forgive us for endangering you so."

"There is nothing to forgive." Mairwen shooed away the apology as she rose from her chair and slowly circled Emily. "I could have stopped her at any time. Ye know that." She concentrated on studying the lass, picking up and pulling in all the girl's strengths. A satisfied smile came to her when a familiar ripple of energy brushed across her senses. "I knew it. She is descended from Esme. Probably a great-great-granddaughter, if my calculations are accurate. Would it not be about that long ago that Esme was stripped of her longevity by the goddesses?"

"Aye, at her request to die after a life of love with her mortal." Ishbel came closer and tilted her head as she joined Mairwen to eye the inanimate lass. "She couldn't bear the thought of living on without him when he came to the end of his life's path." She pointed at Emily's face. "She has Esme's eyes. And her smile. I never noticed it before."

"Aye." Mairwen nodded, seeing the resemblance for the first time. "That she does. Esme would be so proud of this fiery lass descended from her love."

"It willna be easy convincing her of all that is a Weaver's world," Reese said while cleaning the blood from his face and hands. "She doesn't know that even though something might be difficult to believe, that doesn't make it impossible to be so."

"She belongs here," Mairwen said. "With us."

"But she has family in the United States," Ishbel said. "A loving family."

"That doesn't mean she canna live here and become all she is meant to be. I wish Esme were here to see her—to train her. What a powerful pair they would make." Mairwen smiled at the fury roiling in Emily's eyes. The chocolate richness of their color had taken on a reddish glow like that of hot coals. "She has heard all that we've said and is not pleased with her inability to respond. Release her, Ishbel. She is one with us, whether she likes it or not."

"*Libero*," Ishbel said.

"What the ever-loving hell was that?" Emily asked through clenched teeth.

"A calming spell, ye might say," Mairwen said. "We will not allow ye to harm yerself or others." She motioned to a seat at the table. "If ye will sit and maintain a calmness that I am sure ye are capable of, I will tell ye more of Jessa and her destiny."

Emily yanked out the chair and threw herself down into it. "And you will also explain how you know about my great-great-grandmother. What did you do? A background check on my family tree so you could mess with my head when you did whatever you've done to Jessa?"

"She is a suspicious one, I'll give ye that," Reese said. He gingerly touched his red, swollen nose. "I think she broke it."

"Go to the healer," Ishbel said in a disgusted tone. "Mairwen and I can handle this meeting."

"I believe I will." Reese hurried from the room, still gently patting at his face.

"Men can be such babies." Ishbel took a seat a few chairs down from Emily.

"He shouldn't have tried to handle me. I warned him." Emily folded her arms across her chest and squared her shoulders, still ready for a fight.

Ishbel grinned. "Ye did well. There is nothing wrong with setting the right impression and letting others know that ye are to be respected."

Emily shifted her glare back to Mairwen. "You expect me to believe that you sent Jessa back in time to eighteenth century Scotland? And you don't care that you did it without her knowledge or consent?"

"She gave her consent. Keeva and Killian included it in the fine print of the user's agreement in the app that brought her here to Seven Cairns." Mairwen settled into her seat, smiling as Ishbel refilled her teacup.

"Nobody reads all that stuff. If you want to use an app, you check the box and get on with it."

Mairwen enjoyed a sip of her refreshed tea, then nodded. "I am well aware of that, as are my apprentices who designed it. Nevertheless, legal consent from Jessa was obtained as soon as she opened the app the first time."

Emily stared at her, obviously stewing over all that had been revealed. She chewed on her bottom lip, the worry in her expression deepening her scowl. "She is the sister I never had. Family. I love her and need to know she is not only safe but happy. You have no idea all she has been through." She leaned forward and flattened her hands on the table. "So far, everything you've said is impossible for me to believe. I want the truth, Mairwen, or you're going to regret ever meeting me."

It was time for Emily to believe. "I will take you to her on the condition that you understand you cannot stay with her, nor can she return to this time with you, at least, not just yet. She and Grant must be given the opportunity to fully connect, time to *activate* their mate bond."

"Activate their mate bond? You make it sound like she is an animal about to go into heat."

"It has nothing to do with lust," Mairwen said with a solemn tip of her head. "Although that usually follows once the bond is acknowledged. Jessa and Grant are fated mates. Their souls belong together in each incarnation, and this time, they needed a little extra help to find one another because they were born into different centuries. That often happens with the strongest of mate bonds because the darker forces create obstacles to keep them apart."

"The darker forces." Emily's eyes narrowed. "What darker forces?"

"Those who would see the Highland Veil destroyed, and its protective barrier to all the worlds taken down. Unimaginable horrors would ensue if nothing prevented the planes of time and realities from mixing. All creation, as we know it, would perish in the battle between the various entities seeking to rule the chaotic infinite plane that would result."

"And how is keeping fated mates separated supposed to bring down the Veil?"

"The Highland Veil is a tapestry of time, energy, and mystical ether. Over the ages, it becomes worn and thins a bit here and there. Some beings, depending on their goddess given abilities, are sometimes able to slip through to other worlds or times and create havoc where they do not belong, giving birth to many of our myths and legends. There is but one thing powerful enough to keep the Veil's weave strong and intact enough to fully separate that which must be kept to itself for the good of all."

Emily rolled her eyes. "Let me guess—it is the love between fated mates."

Mairwen ignored the lass's sarcasm. She would prove it to her soon enough. "I canna take ye to Jessa until ye believe and agree to give her time to see just how wonderful her new life could be. I am sure she'll beg ye to help her find a way back, but ye must not do so. Not only does the Highland Veil need the connection between Jessa and Grant, but they need it as well. If one does not find one's fated mate, a lifetime of dissatisfaction and, often enough, misery follows. Then their lives end, and the only hope for their souls is that they have better luck finding each other in the next incarnation."

"How could living in the past be wonderful?" Frustration

shouted from Emily as she held up a hand and counted on her fingers. "No conveniences like air conditioning, electricity, or even the unnecessary hygiene stuff, not to mention the necessary things. No proper medical care. No antibiotics or birth control." She hopped up from her chair, unable to sit still. "And what about all those women who died in childbirth? And the babies? All the babies who died before they even reached their first birthday? That does not sound like a wonderful life to me." She shook her head. "That sounds more like a death sentence that Jessa doesn't deserve."

"Are ye telling me there are no dangers in this time? No inconveniences?"

"I knew you would go there." Emily flounced back into her chair with a disgruntled look. "I didn't say this time wasn't dangerous. It's just a more comfortable kind of dangerousness. Dangers we're trained to handle."

Mairwen laughed. "Only because these dangers are what ye have sadly become accustomed to. If ye were from two hundred and forty years into the future, ye would think this century as crude, uncivilized, and horrifying to adapt to as the eighteenth century." She tipped her chin higher, leaned forward, and laced her fingers together in front of her teacup. "Ye are a canny lass, and whether ye like it or not, ye are a part of this. Ye can help yer friend not only find the astounding love she was always meant to enjoy but also help protect this dangerous world and time that ye find so comfortable. So what will it be? As I said, I'll not take ye to her until ye agree to my terms." She angled a sterner look Emily's way. "And dinna think to deceive me, lass. At the first sign of treachery, ye will not only find yerself snatched back to this time, but if it pleases me to do so, I can send yer conniving wee arse back to New Jersey." She offered a curt nod. "Yet if ye comply and do as ye are told, Ishbel and I shall train ye in the ways of yer great-great-grandmother. I know ye can make her proud, if ye so choose."

Emily shifted with a deep breath, then hissed it out between her teeth. "Fine. I agree to your terms." Then she jabbed the air with a trembling finger. "But Jessa better be alive and well and headed for the biggest helping of happiness she has ever known."

∼

Last night, the sight of Jessa in her shift, with her hair all tousled and her curves teasing him through the material's thin weave, had set him ablaze. But now, this morning, dressed as a fine Highland lady, Grant forgot to breathe as she hesitantly entered his solar, looking around as if newly born to his world and seeing it for the very first time.

He went to her, easing across the room with his hand extended. She was a skittish colt he wished to caress, to tame. Even more, he longed to be burned by her fire. At the very least, he wanted to know her better, so he might discover if the stirrings she ignited within him were more than simple lust for a beautiful woman. He needed to know if those stirrings were truly a connection ordained by Fate itself.

"Ye are pure loveliness," he told her, awkwardly letting his hand fall to his side when she failed to take it. He shook off the sense of failure, knowing she had been so busy examining the room that she'd not noticed his offer.

"Thank you," she said softly, almost as an afterthought. She meandered behind his desk and its messy scattering of ledgers, logbooks, and correspondence. The delicate furrow between her feathery brows deepened as her gaze flitted across the mound of work he'd not yet had time to address. All her color drained away, and she awkwardly staggered back into his chair. She was even more pale than last night when he had first found her in his bed.

He hurried to her. "What is it, lass? Are ye in pain? Shall I fetch Mrs. Robeson?"

With her stare still locked on his desk, she jerked a nod at the pile of work. "Those dates. On those receipts and letters and all those books."

"Aye?"

"Why would you go to the trouble of writing the year 1785 on everything? Are you really that determined to play this off as the eighteenth century?"

It was then that he understood what ailed her. She still refused to believe she had traveled back in time.

"This *is* the year 1785," he told her with a gentleness he had never used with another. "I know ye dinna wish to believe it, and indeed it is a hard thing to swallow, but I swear it is true. I promise this is not some cruel jest brewed up by Mairwen or myself."

She slowly shook her head. "It can't be true. It cannot be." She finally looked him in the eyes. "I had trouble surviving my own century. How in the blue blazes am I supposed to survive here in yours?"

And that was the crux of it. Grant studied her, trying to puzzle her out. Here was a woman used to taking care of herself, and from the way she behaved, neither family nor lover had helped her in her era. The idea of a man in her life other than himself sent an angry tightness through his chest, a fierce possessiveness that both shocked and shook him. He'd had bouts of jealousy before, but never one this strong. Something deep within, something as hot and churning as a boiling cauldron, goaded him to find out more about her, about whether she had ever thought she belonged to anyone else.

He took her hand and gently coaxed her. "Come. Sit over here at the table. They've brought us a fine breakfast, and Mrs. Robeson brewed ye an entire kettle of yer coffee. As ye enjoy a cup, ye can help me understand why yer future was so difficult. Did ye leave behind no family? No man who cared for ye?"

Moving stiffly, she followed where he led, clinging tightly to his hand, but remained silent.

He helped her sit, then poured her a cup of the hot drink she had requested. "Do ye take anything in it, lass? I'm not one to partake of coffee, so I dinna ken what ye might wish to mix into it to make it worth swallowing." He flicked a hand at a ceramic pitcher on the table and a tall white cone standing on a plate beside it. "We've milk, and I can scrape the sugarloaf for ye if ye wish to sweeten it with sugar. Or there is honey as well. Just tell me how much ye need."

"No, thank you," she said, still sounding weak and lost. "I drink it black." Staring at something only she could see, she took a sip, then shuddered and shied away from the cup before placing it back on the table. "Wow. Maybe I'll add some milk, please."

"Is it not to yer liking, then? Shall I order it sent away?"

"No, I'll drink it, and I appreciate the efforts it took to get it to me." She licked her lips, then ran her tongue across her teeth. "The milk should mellow it enough so it doesn't dissolve the enamel off my teeth." She forced a smile that looked more pained than pleased. "It'll be fine. Really."

He wouldn't push her on it, but he'd be discussing the strength of the brew with Mrs. Robeson. Perhaps a bit more judicious use of the coffee beans was in order. It seemed the matron had ground too many for the inky black swill. He nodded at the many offerings on the table, an unusually large breakfast selection, since he seldom partook of anything more than a simple bowl of boiled oats. "We've scones, parritch, coddled eggs, blood sausage, and beans. Even some tatties and kippers. And Mrs. Robeson said she would send up some fried bread if that was to yer liking."

Jessa leaned back in the chair and hugged her cup to her chest. "I'm good for right now, thank you." Then she nodded at the food, not really frowning but not happy either. "Please don't hold back on my account. I'm just not sure about eating anything just yet."

"Ye should eat, lass. Keep up yer strength."

She eyed him, a faint spark flickering in her eyes, and he was glad of it. Her fire needed to return.

"What do you intend to do with me?" she asked, a hint of steel in her tone.

"Teach ye to not ignore me when I give ye advice ye should heed."

"Doubtful. Next option on your list?"

While he was glad her fight had returned, he was not in the mood to battle. He hadn't the stamina for it—at least not this morning. "I have summoned Mairwen."

"Good. I have a few choice words for that lady." She took another sip of her coffee and this time didn't grimace.

"Better?"

"What?"

"That vile tonic ye like."

The faintest smile tugged at the corner of her lovely mouth. A mouth he had already decided was made for kissing—slowly and as often as she would allow.

"I take it you don't like coffee?" she said.

"I do not."

"That brings us back to my original question that you failed to answer." She drew herself up as if calling on every ounce of courage she possessed. "What do you intend to do with me?"

There were many things he would like to do with her, but even with the numbing weariness of over a day and a half of no sleep, he had enough sense to know better than to tell her about them. "What do ye wish done with ye?"

"You already know the answer to that."

"Aye, and I already told ye that was not possible. I dinna have the ability to return ye to yer time."

She took another sip of coffee, a longer one this time, then set her cup on the table and stared down at it. "I didn't even get a chance to say goodbye to Emily." Her voice quivered with emotion.

Gads alive, dinna let her cry again. Her teariness broke his heart. "Who is Emily?" he hurried to ask, hoping it would distract her.

With her focus still trained on her cup, she barely smiled, then tipped the slightest shrug. "The only person in this world who has ever understood me. Sister. Friend. Confidante. Emily is just—Emily."

"So ye do have family, then?"

"She is my sister by choice, not by blood." She jerked another shrug, but this time, it revealed anger instead of nonchalance or uncertainty. "I was taken from my biological mother because she preferred drugs and alcohol over motherhood. The people who fostered and then adopted me did it for the *look-at-what-a-wonderful-thing-we-did* perks rather than because they wanted to help a child." She finally lifted her gaze and leveled it with his. "Emily and her family always loved me no matter what. They've also done everything they could to help me. I owe my sanity to them. They are my family—and I have no earthly idea why I am telling you all this. You didn't exactly request a life history, did you?"

At least she was talking. He would hear whatever she had to say. "Yer family with Emily. They helped ye survive in yer time?"

Her jaw tightened. "I am an adult. I should be able to take care of myself with no one's charity."

Such a proud woman. Maybe there was a wee bit of Scotland running through her veins after all. "And ye had no husband? No man to help ye?" He had to know, even if his asking angered her even more.

"Yeah, well, that didn't work out either. He stuck a pin in that a couple of weeks before I left for this trip to Scotland."

"I dinna ken what that means, lass."

"It means he dumped me before I had the chance to dump him. I should've beat him to the punch, but I kept thinking things would get better."

Dumped. Grant had a pretty good idea of what she meant. "That man was obviously a fool."

She snorted a bitter laugh. "Once you get to know me better, you might agree with him. That's the way my luck's been running lately. Then I'll really be up an eighteenth century creek without a paddle." She rubbed her eyes while shaking her head. "Sorry. This situation has made me ridiculous. I'm better than this. At least—I used to think I was." She dropped her hands back to her lap, then leaned forward, refilled her cup, and drank it without adding any more milk.

He shook his head, understanding everything except for the eighteenth century creek part. "No matter what happens, no matter what the witch says, ye'll not be without protection or refuge in this time. Mairwen brought ye here on account of me. I consider myself responsible for ye."

"You make me sound like a puppy she left on your doorstep."

"I like puppies."

She sidled another glance his way while once more hugging her cup to her chest. "Let's say you're telling me the truth. Why is it you're not surprised to suddenly find yourself in possession of a twenty-first century American?"

"I've known the witch for as far back as I can remember, and two of my most trusted friends are Defenders. They've told me tales of fated mates being united across the centuries. The women travel to the men because they are the life bringers—or so I am told. Men are born where they are meant to stay."

"Defenders?"

"Members of an order sworn to defend the Highland Veil, and I have, on occasion, helped them when the need arose."

"But you're not a Defender?"

"I am not." While he didn't like being interrogated, the lass did have the right to know and was actually speaking to him in a somewhat civil tone, so he would tolerate it.

"Why not?"

"Why not what?"

"Why aren't you a Defender if you're willing to help them?"

"Because I believe in doing that which is right for the sake of it, not because I've sworn an oath for someone to hold over my head." He took a long draught from the tankard of ale he always had with his morning parritch, then angled a nod her way. "After all that ye've seen since ye arrived, why do ye still think me a liar or a madman?"

Her emerald eyes widened in surprise, making it impossible for him not to smile. "I can't help it," she said softly, "and I really don't want you to be a madman."

"Ye would rather I were a liar?" He found that hard to believe, especially coming from a woman.

"I'd rather you were the twenty-first century Highlander that the tarot card app said I needed to meet." She huffed, then squirmed from side to side. "I also wish Molly hadn't pulled these ties so tight. Standing, this vest wasn't so bad, but sitting, it's digging into me."

"It's nay a vest, lass. Those are yer stays." His mouth started watering as he eyed the laces threaded through the front of the garment that displayed her very fine form in the best way possible. "Ye could always loosen them. If Molly is to be yer lady's maid, ye will need to train her properly. Make sure she understands yer orders and correct her when needed."

"She is not my slave."

"No. But she is yer servant and a servant of this keep. Unclear orders not only do her a disservice but yerself as well. If she understands what ye wish, she will do her best to see it done, and then ye'll both not only be pleased, but she'll also know the satisfaction and pride of a job well done."

"She spoke highly of you," Jessa said, but her scowl didn't match her words.

"As she should. I am her laird." The back of his neck tingled, making the hairs twitch. "What is it, lass? Something's astir in yer eyes. Ye might as well spit it out and be free of it."

"You said Mairwen brought me here to be your wife, and you've mentioned fated mates more than once. Do you really believe in all that?"

A cageyness swept over him, a need to protect himself from whatever her question intended. "Do ye believe in it, lass?"

She stilled and went thoughtful while slowly running the tip of her finger around the rim of her cup. Then she fluttered her long lashes as though waking from a dream. "I think it is a delightful fairy tale." She looked up and locked eyes with him. "But I asked what you believed."

"I dinna ken what to believe. Not yet, anyway."

Her shoulders slumped the slightest bit, making her seem to wilt in front of his very eyes. Was she disappointed that he refused to say whether he thought her his fated mate, or if he even believed such a thing might be possible? His jaded heart gave a dangerous shudder at the prospect and softened toward her even more than it already had.

"Would ye rather I lied, lass?"

"No. Of course not." She straightened in the chair, casting off a quick shrug. His opinion was obviously irrelevant to her. Or was it? Shadows flitted in the green depths of her eyes, nudging his heart in a direction a wise man would avoid at all costs.

"Eat some breakfast, lass." He poked at the parritch he'd spooned into his bowl. If they failed to eat any of this food, he would never hear the end of it from Mrs. Robeson. "At least a scone or something if ye dinna wish a lecture the likes of which ye have never heard before."

"I would not recommend that you lecture me." The daring in her tone stirred his blood.

"Not me, lass. Mrs. Robeson. She can be more worrisome than a swarm of midges."

"I don't recommend *anyone* lecturing me." Jessa refilled her cup yet again. "In my current mindset and fueled with caffeine, I'm more dangerous than I look."

She was dangerous all right. More dangerous than she realized.

CHAPTER 9

"Do ye need more tea for yer head, mistress? Or a tonic, perhaps?" Mrs. Robeson hovered around Jessa like a wee bird that couldn't decide where to light.

"No, thank you." Jessa didn't look up from the book she was slowly paging through.

Grant smiled to himself, risking a glance at her from where he stood at the window, watching for Henry and that infernal witch. He had warned the lass about the motherly housekeeper. She would do well to learn that he was only trying to help when he offered advice.

"But ye ate nothing," Mrs. Robeson said while fussing with her apron, smoothing it back in place, then wringing it around her hands all over again. "Was none of it to yer liking? Cook was shocked at the untouched plates the lads carried back to the kitchen. She's frettin' something fierce. Afraid she's displeased ye."

"I am sure everything was wonderful," Jessa said, still not looking Mrs. Robeson's way. "I would love another pot of coffee if she has time." Jessa closed the book and shoved it back on the shelf between the others. "Other than that, I'm fine. If I get hungry later and there's nothing to be had, then it will be no one's fault but my own."

The housekeeper drew herself up and hissed like an angry cat. "If the mistress of this house be hungry at any time, day or night, there will always be something to be had, I'll grant ye that."

"I am not the mistress of this house," Jessa said quietly, but her tone rang with determination and the tiniest bit of hopelessness.

Grant allowed himself a heavy sigh. Damn that Mairwen for dropping them both into this unnecessary tempest. "Mrs. Robeson, leave the lass be. When she's hungry, I'm sure she will tell ye."

"But—"

"Mrs. Robeson."

The kindly old woman bowed her head, but her displeasure showed in the hardened set of her jaw. "Aye, my laird *and* my lady." She flounced out of the solar and thumped the door shut behind her.

"So, does that mean I don't get my second pot of coffee?"

"Soon as she calms down, she'll remember yer request and send it up."

Jessa nodded, then meandered around the room. She seemed even more unsettled than when she'd first arrived. But he supposed that made sense. After all, she now knew more about this strange situation in which she found herself.

"So what do you do?" she asked after her third lap around the room, where she'd lightly run her fingers across every book, bauble, and piece of furniture.

"Do?"

"As a laird. If I weren't here. What would you be doing?"

"Sleeping." It came out before he could catch it, but at least it was the truth.

"Sorry."

"My lack of rest is not entirely yer fault. A necessary venture night before last kept me from my bed, and then last night, I was concerned about ye."

"I'm fine," she spat out so fast that it painted the words as the lie that they were. "Or I will be. Once I figure everything out." She went to the window and scowled outside. "I don't think it rained this much in the future."

"Today's rain is—"

"Tomorrow's whisky," she finished, then snorted an unhappy laugh. "I know. Lilias at the pub in Seven Cairns taught me that the day I was caught without my *brolly*."

"*Brolly*?" he repeated slowly.

"Scottish slang for umbrella. Or maybe British slang for it? I don't know. All I know is that I'd never heard the word before until I came to Scotland." She propped her shoulder against the window's inset alcove of stone. "So if you'd caught up on your sleep last night, what would you do today? As a laird?"

His usual leeriness reared its head, the leeriness of a successful smuggler. "Survey the grounds. Ensure all is secure and well. Provide for those in need and settle any grievances among my people."

She cut a sideways glance his way. "You don't trust me."

"Why would ye say such a thing?" He almost smiled at her craftiness but held it back. This sly lady was indeed a delightful challenge.

"Because that answer was vague. You made some noise but told me absolutely nothing."

"Each day is a new challenge," he said. "My duties are rarely the same."

"Then you should consider yourself a lucky man. At least you'll never be bored." She returned her attention to the view out the window. "When do you think Mairwen will grace us with her presence?"

"That I canna say because the old witch does as she damn well pleases." He tapped on the pane, pointing toward the west. "See that rise? The one wearing the haar like a shawl around its shoulders?"

"You mean the one almost hidden by fog?"

"Aye, that be the one. Seven Cairns lies within that mist that always rolls in off the sea. We call it the haar. Henry's gone there to fetch her."

She squinted at the spot and drew closer to the rain spattered glass. "How far is that from here? It looks like a long way."

"A few hours' ride because of the treacherous nature of the land between here and there." He'd told her that before, but after all she'd been through, he didn't blame her for not remembering. "But the length of that journey only limits Henry."

"What's that supposed to mean?"

"Mairwen does not ride. Or at least I have never seen her ride. And yet she travels from here to there in the blink of an eye. She is not constrained by time or distance."

Jessa turned and studied him, so very close that it would only take a little effort to sample the sweetness of her mouth. Her warmth teased him, daring him to move in closer and breathe her in to fully intoxicate himself with her scent of roses and a woman who didn't realize how desirable she was. The tip of her tongue raced across her barely parted lips, tempting him to show her.

He almost groaned but caught it in time. With more control than he realized he possessed, he eased back a step, increasing the distance between them. "We could find Mairwen at our door at any minute—or never. I fear we are at her mercy."

"Well, that is complete horse shit." Jessa bowed her head and growled, making him struggle not to smile. "You know, I hardly ever swear, but this century brings out the worst in me."

"Ye are merely a lady expressing herself according to what the situation demands." Grant prided himself on his diplomacy.

She snorted. "Yeah. Right." She fidgeted away from the window and paced around the room again. Her agitation filled the air, while her spirit silently wailed its need for relief from these circumstances.

"Would ye like to go up to the tower? From there, ye can see a good bit of MacAlester land." Shielding her by keeping her in his private solar was not going well. While he wished to protect her, this was no timid lass satisfied to hide away until the world decided to be kind to her. Nay, she was a caged beast, gnashing its teeth to be freed. "I can take ye around the keep so ye can roam wherever ye like." His smuggler's sense of survival nudged him, reminding him that might not be wise. "Within reason," he added.

She eyed the door to the hallway, then looked back at him while nervously chewing the corner of her bottom lip. He waited for her to decide. Only she knew what served her best. Mayhap she preferred Molly take her around and show her the things the lady of the keep might wish to see. A rumble of irritation escaped him. Gads alive, now *he* was calling her the mistress of the house. What the devil was wrong with him?

"Don't growl at me. I'm thinking, all right? Wouldn't you be a little nervous if you landed in my century, and I offered to walk you around like the prize pooch at the dog show?"

"The noise I made was not directed at ye." He almost did it again. "I believe I have been patient, considering the circumstances."

"What is that supposed to mean?" Indignance flashed in her eyes, honing her glare.

"What?"

"*Considering the circumstances,*" she repeated. "I did not come here of my own free will. I was dumped in your bed. Remember?"

He lifted his hands in surrender, something he had never done before and wasn't all that keen on doing now. "I meant no disrespect or impatience with ye, aye? And I nay asked Mairwen to snatch ye up out of yer time and send ye here to be my wife. The feckin' witch took it upon herself to do so after I told her plainly I never wished to marry again."

Jessa's scowl darkened even more, and the parting of her sumptuous lips slowly opened wider as her jaw dropped. "Again? You've been married before?" She took a step toward him, her hands slowly closing into fists. "Or are you married now, and if so, where is she?"

Feckin' hell. He resettled his stance and clasped his hands to the small of his back as if preparing to be executed, and execution didn't seem like all that bad of a choice at the moment. "I am widowed."

She didn't believe him. He could see it in her eyes.

"My late wife grew to like laudanum more than anything else. She consumed it until it finally consumed her."

"Is that why you asked if I was looking for laudanum when I wanted something for a headache?" Her eyes narrowed with watchfulness.

"Aye. If I thought ye bound to the opium, I would have put ye out immediately."

"At midnight. In the rain. Out here in the middle of nowhere."

He jutted his chin higher. This woman had no idea what that poison made people do. "Aye. Better to put ye out and let the Highlands deal with ye rather than bring that danger back into my clan once again."

She shut her mouth, flattening her supple lips into a cold, hard line. Then she surprised him with a curt nod. "I can't say as I blame you. I know firsthand what drug addicts are capable of. By the time I was eight years old, I had experienced it all in its horrible glory. Thankfully, social services rescued me, and the legal system cut the tie to my mother once and for all."

Taken from her mother at a young age and fostered by a family who did little to care for her. That explained her independence and pride. It also bespoke an amazing strength. She considered herself a survivor, not a victim. She was so much more than a bonnie wee lass that pleased the eye.

He offered her a formal bow. "I admire ye, my lady. Not everyone could rise from those ashes and become the glorious phoenix ye are today."

"Thank you," she said, sounding almost confused by the compliment, confused and perhaps even a little hopeful.

"Why do ye look at me that way, lass?"

She barely shook her head. "I don't know. Just trying to figure you out, I guess. You tell me Mairwen sent me here to be your wife, but you make it quite clear you don't want one. And yet—."

"And yet?"

Her jaw flexed the slightest bit as if she wanted to say more but thought better of it. Then she looked away and moved to stand beside the door. "It's not important. You mentioned a tour of the keep?"

Both mesmerized and perplexed by this complicated yet glorious woman, he held the door open and offered his arm. "M'lady."

She eyed his extended arm, then lifted her gaze to his. "Are you mocking me, or are you serious?"

"Mocking ye?"

"In my time, a man only offered a woman his arm in a formal setting. Like walking the red carpet or as part of a wedding party. Is it common practice in this century for me to hang onto you for something as simple as walking around your keep?"

What the devil had happened in the future to the way a man treated a woman? "'Tis a show of respect, lass. Of my protection of ye. With ye on my left arm, my sword arm is free to defend ye. All who see us will know that I will give no quarter to anyone who dares insult or harm ye in any way."

"Oh." She slid her arm through his and offered him a smile that actually reached her eyes. Thank the fates, she appeared to be pleased. "That's kind of nice."

"Aye, lass. It is at that." He led her to the stairwell. "Which way shall it be first? Up to the watch house or down to the great room and out into the bailey if the rain's lifted for a while?"

She leaned into the stairwell and looked up, then looked down at the stone steps. "What floor are we on?"

"This be the third level."

"Those are some seriously wicked spiral steps. And narrow too. Like a corkscrew. How in the world did those boys carry buckets of water up three flights of that with no problems?" She turned and stared at him in amazement. "That's inhumane to have them do that."

"It's the only way, lass, if ye wish to bathe in something other than a basin." Her concern for the servants warmed his heart. This was no spoiled lady who thought only of herself.

Her expression darkened with the storminess of a mother about to scold a thoughtless child. "There has to be an easier way for them to carry water to all the floors. Devise a pulley system or something." She shook her head and shot another critical look up and down the stairs. "Until we figure out a solution, maybe Mrs. Robeson can curtain off a corner of the kitchen or something, and I'll just bathe down there."

"Like hell ye will. I'll not have ye washing yer bare arse in the kitchen among the servants, and that issue is not up for debate." He pointed at the stairs. "Now, which way shall it be? Up to the watch house or down to the bailey?"

She glared at him. "Take me to wherever they fill their buckets. I want to see the starting point so I can think of a better way to get the job done. Work smart. Not hard. Right?"

"They do as they're told. That's a smart enough servant." He nodded at the stairs. "I shall go first to keep ye steady until ye become more accustomed to the footing. The well house is off the kitchens."

"See? Even you think they're unsafe."

The victorious crow in her tone made him clench his teeth. Where the feckin' hell was Henry with that witch? Before his control slipped, and he said something he shouldn't, he entered the stairwell, descended a few steps, then turned back and held out his hand for her to take.

"You really should have handrails installed." She took his hand while wrangling the fullness of her skirts. "I can't see where I'm stepping with all this yardage. How am I supposed to stay away from the narrow edge?"

He'd traveled these stairs so many times that he'd never really thought about how difficult it might be for a woman. "Keep to the left. They're wider on the outside rather than the center, where they lock into the column. Feel for them. We'll take it slow."

"I don't like this," she grumbled under her breath with every downward motion. After progressing no more than a few steps down, she halted and pulled her hand out of his. "Wait a minute."

He leaned against the curve of the center column and waited. What did the lovely wee fox hope to do now? The tower stairs were what they were. They couldn't be helped. And then he nearly lost his own footing, as she bent, gathered the length of her outer skirt, petticoats, and shift up above her knees, and hugged them into the crook of her arm. When she reached for him with her free hand, he stared at her, unable to speak.

"Now I can see where I'm stepping." She did a little hop, tapping both feet as if the sight of her shapely legs encased in stockings didn't already hold him prisoner. With unbelievable innocence, she smiled and swayed from side to side, proud of her handiwork. When he didn't take her hand, her smile slowly faded. "I still need to hold your hand, though, since there's no railing."

"Lass." He didn't know what else to say. All sense had left him.

"What?" She looked down at her feet and tapped her toes again. "It's safer this way."

"Aye, but—"

"No one will see but you. We're the only ones here."

"And ye dinna care if I see yer legs?"

"All you're seeing are my plump little calves and my knees dressed up in stockings. It's no worse than if I had on my leggings."

His mouth had gone so dry that he struggled to speak. "Women dinna wear leggings." He finally managed to dip a nod at her comely knees. "Nor do they show themselves in such a way to just any man. Only their husbands see them in this state of undress."

Her shoulders sagged in disappointment as she lumbered down another step toward him. "Thank you for the eighteenth century survival tip. This is why I really hoped you were lying about time travel. I'll never fit in here, and your people will probably try to burn me at the stake for witchcraft or something. Do they do that in this century?"

"I would never let them do that to ye," he said, unable to pull his focus from her legs. What he wouldn't give to run his hands along them, higher and higher still, until—

"Lovely. Now I've got yet another thing to worry about," she said in a sharp, grumbling tone, yanking him from his fantasy. "Can I at least hold up my skirts this one time since we're alone? I'm really nervous about these stairs."

"Nay, lass." He refused to give over on this. "Shake yer skirts back down where they belong. We could meet a maid or one of the lads carrying wood at any moment. I dinna wish them to think ill of ye."

"Fine." She dumped them from the crook of her arm and stomped them down in place. "If I break my neck, my death is on you."

"Well, I canna have that." He scooped her up into his arms and cradled her to his chest like a wee babe. "I'll have ye downstairs in no time. Whole and unscathed."

She squeaked, making him wonder what other delicious noises she might make if he pleased her into the notion. She tightened an arm around his neck as he plodded down the narrow, winding steps. Tensing against him, she thumped him on the chest. "What do you think you're doing?"

"Carrying ye." He struggled to concentrate on his footing rather than her warm softness against his chest.

"Why?" she asked, growling the word through clenched teeth.

"I dinna wish ye to break yer lovely wee neck."

"I'm going to break your lovely wee neck."

He laughed, moving slower because his cock had stiffened to a merciless hardness. Lore a'mighty, what he wouldn't give to take her right here on the stairs. He hitched her higher against his chest, making her squeak again with the wee toss. "Why would ye wish to break my neck when I've been nothing but the most thoughtful of hosts?"

"How much farther?" she asked with another lovely wee growl that thrilled him.

"Nearly there, lass," he answered, slowing even more.

"You're stretching this out on purpose." Accusation flashed like lightning in her eyes. "You think this is funny."

"Actually, I do find this quite enjoyable." He halted just before rounding the final curve. As soon as he descended the last few steps, he would have to set her on her feet, and he was nay yet ready to deny himself the feel of her in his arms. Whether it was his weariness, the irresistibility of this fine woman, or another of Mairwen's spells, he sensed his control was slipping and didn't give a damn if it did. He leaned to one side, propped against the wall, and tipped his mouth closer to hers. "Do ye not find this enjoyable, Jessa?" he asked soft and low.

She scowled at him as if trying to destroy him with the ferocity of her glare.

He nuzzled closer and touched his forehead to hers. "Have ye no answer for me, my lovely wee fox?"

"I do not want to find this enjoyable."

"And why is that?" He barely brushed his lips across hers, killing himself with the teasing. Lore, he needed to taste her soon or die in the trying.

"Because you're—complicated," she whispered, then fisted her hand in his hair and pulled him in, kissing him hard and deep, devouring him heart and soul. A fiery shudder tore through him like an uncontrollable inferno. He tightened his hold on her and sank to the steps to keep from dropping her. She broke the connection, squirming as she turned her face away. "Let me go. Now."

He released her and helped her stand. "Jessa—"

Chest heaving, she pressed the back of her hand to her mouth while pointing at him with the other. "Do not say it. I can only handle a certain amount of weirdness at a time, and I have reached critical mass."

"Jessa—"

"No." She shook a finger at him, forbidding him to say another word. "Shut it. Right now."

Shut it? No woman told him to shut it. "I will damn well speak whenever I wish." He rose to his feet, gathered her back into his arms, and kissed her again, showing her exactly what he thought about her ordering him to *shut it*. Aye, this intimate connection was the same. The searing burn, the raging sense that every tiny piece of his soul was falling into its proper place and settling into a perfect wholeness.

She clung to him, kissing him back as if starved for the taste of him, then she jerked and pushed away again. "Set me down. Now."

"Lore a'mighty, woman, are ye trying to kill me? How can I let ye go when ye make me feel so—"

"Stop it. Please." Her words didn't get through to him, but the fear in her eyes did.

He immediately steadied her safely back onto her feet and backed up until several steps separated them. "No matter how badly I need ye, never would I ever force myself upon ye, Jessa. Never."

She fisted a hand to her heart. "I never thought you would. I was just afraid. That kiss. It was unlike anything I've ever felt before." She shook her head, or maybe she shuddered. He couldn't tell. "That was not a..." She blew out a shaky breath and pressed a hand to her forehead. "That wasn't normal." She turned and plopped down on the step, sitting with her elbows propped on her knees and her head in her hands. "That was strange," she whispered, then shivered again.

Her words concerned him. "Ye found it unpleasant?" The way she had responded—surely, she had felt the same passionate wave that had coursed through him. "Are ye saying it was intolerable?"

She gave him a disbelieving look. "That is not what I meant. I found it entirely too *tolerable* for a first kiss with someone I've just met, whom I'm not entirely sure about." She wrinkled her nose. "Of course, I don't usually make it a habit of kissing people I'm not sure about, but you don't exactly fit into any of the neat little boxes I pigeon-hole people into when I meet them. You're shockingly different. In more ways than I am presently able to describe." Twisting to look at him, she caught her bottom lip between her teeth and hugged herself. "Was it—really different—for you too?"

"Aye, lass." He sat on the steps, keeping a bit of distance between them for both their sakes. "Fiery. Raging. Yet peaceful and complete. As if I'd finally found that which I'd been missing all along." He knew what he was describing, but couldn't bring himself to call it what it was. Breath held, he waited to see what she would say.

"Two halves finally snapping together to create the whole they were always meant to be." She hugged herself tighter, as if suddenly cold. "Fated mates," she whispered, then huffed and gave him a sour look. "But you don't believe in that, do you?"

"I said I dinna ken what to believe. Not that I did not believe. There is a difference, lass."

"I don't know what to believe, either. About any of this."

As she dropped her head back into her hands, he ached to console her, to hold her again, but he was afraid. The intensity of everything she stirred within him shook him to the marrow of his bones. What she'd said about his people harming her because she was different came back to him with a vengeance, tempting him to lock her away and protect her like the priceless treasure she was. He slowly shook his head. Nay, he could never do that. She was indeed the glorious phoenix and the flame-haired fox combined—a sly wee beastie, risen from the ashes, in need of her freedom.

"Jessa?" He pushed himself to his feet and descended the steps until he stood one step behind her. When she didn't answer, he bent, trailed his fingers down her arm, and scooped her hand into his. "Come, lass. Between the two of us, we'll sort this out. Above all else, know that ye are not alone here. I will always be at yer side."

She didn't lift her gaze to his, but she squeezed his hand and rose to her feet. After a long moment that made him wonder what was going on in her lovely head, she turned and looked up at him. "If it was my destiny to go through this craziness, I'm glad you're the one helping me survive it."

The insatiable urge to pick her up and carry her to his bed raged through him, but he fought it. Struggling for control, he kissed her hand. "Not only will ye survive, my lovely one, ye will thrive. I shall see to it."

CHAPTER 10

Grant escorted Jessa through the main floor of the keep into what looked like a massive dining hall filled with rows of trestle tables. Its whitewashed walls were covered in tartans, tapestries, ancient weapons, and an astonishingly large hearth that could probably burn entire tree trunks. She tightened her grip on his arm. Everything looked so real, so chillingly authentic.

It even smelled real. Not that she was an expert on how the eighteenth century should smell, but she felt like she was quickly becoming one. She swallowed hard and tried not to shudder. Admittedly, she was a chronic worrier, an over-planner, and an overthinker, but she never panicked. Until now. This introduction to time travel and kisses that triggered so much more than simple lust overwhelmed her, and Emily wasn't here to talk her off the ledge. She gulped another hard swallow to keep from throwing up the coffee Mrs. Robeson had worked so hard to make for her. If she didn't calm down, control her breathing, and slow her erratically pounding heart, she was going to pass out. That's what Emily would say if she were here. A sad wave of homesickness made her bite her lip.

"And this is the main kitchen," Grant said, oblivious to her internal war, as they passed through a stone archway and came to a halt. "The outside kitchen is just beyond that door. There, ye will find the firepits and cauldrons where meat is put by for the winter and roasted for summer meals."

Bundles of dried herbs, pots, pans, and flat disks of weathered iron hung from massive wooden rafters that crossed the low-ceilinged area. A haze of smoke beyond the tiny windows on the far wall revealed that the outdoor firepits were already in use. Enormous cauldrons and kettles, their surfaces seasoned to a gleaming black, hissed and bubbled from iron bars hung across the large hearth that took up one end of the room. Heat waves shimmered in the air over a large stone box that jutted out from one end of the hearth. Deep-sided skillets rested on the grid of metal bars that topped it. Hunks of meat sizzled and popped in the pans, making the air almost greasy with the aroma of highly seasoned beef and pork frying.

Jessa tried to ignore the stares of the two young girls at the long worktable under the windows on the other side of the room. Even though they attempted to hide behind the piles of vegetables they were peeling and chopping, she felt their curious glances pinging off her like mosquitoes trying to get through a window screen.

An older girl entered the kitchen from a side room. As soon as she noticed them, she jerked to attention, then hurried over to Grant and curtsied low while still hugging a basket overflowing with some type of leafy greens. "Cook's outside starting the venison, m'laird. Ye want I should fetch her?"

"Nay, Alison. We'll go outside presently." He tipped a nod at Jessa. "This is Mistress Jessa. She is our honored guest and is to be treated as such, ye ken?"

"Aye, m'laird." The girl offered Jessa a hesitant smile and another deep curtsy.

Jessa nodded and returned the maid's smile as she'd done with everyone else she'd met, hoping that was the correct response. So far, Grant had only advised her against hiking her skirts above her knees, and that had led to those kisses that had shattered all her preconceived notions about the ridiculousness of fated mates being fictional rather than real. She pulled in a deep breath, forcing herself to concentrate on the present moment rather than the memory of those kisses.

Grant turned them toward a stone arch to the left of the one that had led them into the kitchen. "The well house is this way. Ye wished to see it, aye?"

"Yes." Maybe if she kept her mind occupied with devising an easier way to get water from Point A to Point B in this place, it would help her maintain a firm grasp on reality. The first thing she noticed as she stepped down the three stone steps to the dirt floor of the windowless room was the temperature change. Not only was it a great deal cooler than the kitchen, an earthy dampness hung in the air. Iron-caged sconces lined the walls, their sputtering candles making shadows dance throughout the cavelike space. The well was at the center of the room, its stone block walls approximately three feet high. A heavy wooden rack with a handle to turn the beam straddled it. Two heavy ropes attached to the beam descended into the well's unfathomable darkness.

Jessa rested her hands on the ledge of the well, leaned over, and peered down into it. That turned out to be futile. Without a better source of light, all she saw after a foot or two was total darkness. She squinted up at the low ceiling and discovered it was stone. "So the well house isn't part of the original structure?"

"No." Grant eyed her with an unreadable expression. "The well has always been here, but it was not connected to the kitchen until several years ago. This fortification was built around it at that time to keep our water source safe from attack. How did ye know that?"

She pointed upward. "The stone ceiling. The kitchen and the main meeting hall both had wood ceilings with beams running across them for support." She slowly turned in a circle, eyeing the room's every angle. "That makes things more complicated, since the pulley system can't come directly from the well. It would have to be built in another area so that it could be brought up through the wooden floors."

She envisioned what she had in mind, placing herself in the position of the poor servant charged with hauling water up those steps. She'd always been able to *see* things and then create them. Usually, they worked, and whenever they didn't, she kept at it until they did. It was fun. Kind of like solving a puzzle. "You could install a waterproof tank or barrel of some sort on each floor. Fix it in a closet or somewhere out of the way. Then a series of buckets attached to a pulley system could draw the water up to them without it having to be carried up those steps."

"And ye'd not heat it until it got to where it was going? Seems like that would take longer due to the size of the hearths."

She groaned. No water heaters, and she didn't have a clue how to build one. She'd studied a lot of things in college and also via the University of the Internet, but building an efficient water heater was not one of the things she'd taught herself to keep that creepy building superintendent out of her apartment whenever something broke. "Does the kitchen heat the water now?"

"The laundress."

"Is the place where they boil the water part of the original structure?"

"Nay. Outside in the lean-to. The fires for the boiling cauldrons keep that bit of cover warm enough in the winter to dry the clothes and keep the laundress and the lasses who help her warm."

She blew out a frustrated huff. This was more complicated than she'd thought it would be. "So, they haul the water from the well to the laundress's pots, and she stokes the fires under them until the water boils?"

"Aye. The lads are charged with filling the cauldrons, however often Griselda wishes."

"Can I see the lean-to?" If there were windows from each floor above it, maybe they could work some sort of pulley system up from the laundress's area. Although whenever the weather was cold, the hot water would cool a great deal faster going up a pulley system attached to the outer wall than being carried up the inside stairs.

Grant made an odd grumbling sound, as if not really wanting to, but he offered his arm again. "Ye can, but I must warn ye, Griselda gets along with no one."

"She has a hard job," Jessa said, envisioning the poor woman toiling over boiling cauldrons. "Passing heavy, wet clothes from a top load washer into the dryer always made me grouchy because I'm so short." She threw up a hand and turned away from him. "Don't say it. I know you don't know what a top load washer and dryer are." She ignored the offer of his arm and led the way back up the kitchen steps, a heavy sigh escaping her. "I know I'm going to have to start self-editing before I open my mouth, or someone's going to burn me at the stake. It's just going to take me some time to adjust."

A powerful hand closed around her arm and pulled her to a stop. A great rumbling sound filled the small space, a rumbling that could pass for the low, irritated growl of a caged lion. He spun her to face him. "No one will ever harm ye. Not whilst I live and breathe. Know that, woman, and know it well. I protect my own."

The flash of lightning and something much more in those silvery gray eyes of his made her forget to breathe. She couldn't look away. Couldn't argue. All she could do was wet her lips and hope he would kiss her again. When she realized she had reached up and touched his strong jawline, she blinked several times and pulled her hand away, curling it to her chest. This was utter madness. She needed to maintain control at all costs. After all, as soon as she straightened Mairwen out, she'd be returning to her time. "Uhm...on to the laundress?"

He blinked as though dragging himself from a daze. "What say ye?" he asked gruffly, yet in the softest voice.

"You were going to take me to the laundress's lean-to?"

He barely jerked his head, clearly battling his own inner demons. "Aye. To the laundress. So ye can spoil the servants."

She hesitated to loop her arm through his, but the broodiness of his glare convinced her to just go with it. This century was exhausting. "It is not spoiling them. It's making their task more efficient. If they're not having to haul water, they can do something else. And it will also decrease the risk of injury."

"Injury?"

"Has anyone ever slipped while carrying water up those steps?"

"Aye, we had a poor maid break her arm once."

"There you go." Jessa allowed herself a victorious little skip that made her skirts bounce. "A pulley system would lessen the risk of another such accident." She sashayed outside with a smile.

"Be gone with ye afore I clout ye again!" a woman shouted in the distance. "Be gone I say. Leave her be! She be mine, and ye know it."

"What the devil?" Grant took off like a shot.

Not about to be left behind, Jessa gathered up her skirts and ran after him. She skidded to a halt in front of a three-sided shed tucked into the corner between the keep and the tall outer wall that enclosed the courtyard. Steam, or maybe smoke, roiled out its front and curled out around the boards of the lean-to's sides.

An angry man, grubby with something that smelled a great deal worse than plain dirt, stood in front of the place, with his hand raised to strike an old woman who was threatening him with a wooden paddle that was the size of an oar for a large boat.

"That be my bitch and pups, Griselda! Everything is mine, and ye know it. If I wish to kill the useless mongrels, 'tis my right!"

"Dubhglas," Grant said with a ground-shaking roar. "Ye best lower yer hand or—"

Enraged that anyone would not only strike a helpless old woman but threaten to hurt an animal, Jessa scuttled around Grant, grabbed another oar propped beside a boiling cauldron, and took her place beside Griselda. "I'll smack you right between the eyes if you take another step toward her," she told the man. "Nobody hurts women or animals on my watch."

"Him's always been a cruel, hard man," Griselda said. "I seen him kick my poor wee dog with me own eyes when I tried to feed her more because of her pups. My lasses fetched her for me and brought her and the pups here so's I could protect them."

Jessa resettled her grip on the oar, choking up on it like it was a baseball bat. "Get the hell out of here and never come back," she told the man while stepping between him and his wife. Out of the corner of her eye, she noticed Grant had stepped back, folded his arms across his chest, and was smiling. Was he serious? An irritated hiss escaped her. She'd deal with him later. When Dubhglas just stood there glaring at her, she took another step toward him, brandishing the wooden paddle. "Did you hear me? I said leave!"

"That be my wife." He pointed at Griselda. "I can do whatever I wish with her and anything else what lives in me house."

Jessa glanced back at the old laundress who had lowered her wooden oar and leaned wearily against it. "Is he out of here or not? It's your choice."

Using the paddle like a cane, Griselda hitched her way closer and peered at Jessa. "Be ye the Goddess Bride come to us in the flesh?" she whispered, her bloodshot eyes filling with tears.

"No. I'm Jessa. But I'll not stand idly by and let anyone be mistreated." She pointed her oar at Grant. "These are your people? Do you back me up on this?"

Grant gave a formal nod. "I do, m'lady. It appears we have discovered a situation I was not aware of and will not tolerate any more than ye will. No one mistreats women, children, *or* animals in my clan. Name the man's sentence and it shall be done."

Dubhglas growled and charged forward, sputtering, "That be my wife. I own her."

"Bullshit!" Jessa swung as hard as she could, landing a blow to his chin that backed him up a step. "You don't *own* people." She glared at Grant. "Make him behave while I talk to Griselda and see if the dog and her puppies are all right."

Grant nodded. "He'll not move again. Will ye, Dubhglas?" His tone left no question about what he would do if the man failed to agree.

Dubhglas dropped to one knee and bowed his head. "Nay, m'laird. I shall stay here till ye bid me do otherwise."

Jessa gently took hold of Griselda's arm and led her inside the lean-to so they could talk in private. This situation reminded her of how her biological mother had never been able to find the strength to send her abusers packing, no matter how bad it got. Even as young as Jessa had been when social services rescued her, she could still remember her mother always saying, *Any man is better than no man at all,* because she needed their money for drugs and alcohol.

"Now is your chance to be rid of him," she told the laundress, " but you have to decide what you want."

"The pup and her wee ones are over there." Griselda pointed at the corner, as if Jessa hadn't spoken.

Jessa eased forward and found the small brown dog huddling on a pile of rags, baring its teeth and growling to protect the three tiny puppies behind her. "I know you've been treated badly," she said softly to the poor furry mother. "It's going to be all right now, though. I'll never let anyone hurt you ever again."

The dog stopped growling, lifted its head, and perked its ragged ears as if it understood every word.

"Can I pet you?" Jessa crouched and held out her hand, still easing forward and ready to stop if the poor thing was too upset. An ugly gash on its head and an odd lump in the middle of its visible ribs made her blood boil. Not only had the animal been beaten, but it had also been starved. Who knew how long it would take for the mama dog to trust her? Jessa sat on the ground. She had all the time in the world. Maybe it was time to see what these servants were willing to do for someone they thought was the mistress of the house. After all, that's what they kept calling her. "She needs food," she told the washerwoman. "Tell Grant I said so."

"Tell the laird ye said so?" Griselda repeated, her scraggly white brows arching to her hairline.

"Yes. And tell him I said to get rid of Dubhglas. Your husband is not welcome here anymore."

"Ye mean to kill him, then? Make me a widow?"

Jessa refused to let this play out the way her mother's scenarios always had. She was no longer a helpless eight-year-old whom no one listened to. "I want him gone. Whether that means he leaves and never returns, or he's beaten to death like he beat this dog, is up to you. Either way, I will not tolerate his presence at this keep any longer. You don't need him, Griselda. Will you stay here and enjoy your freedom from his hell, or will you join him? From what I know about Grant, at least so far, what I know about him, you'll be safe here and not go hungry."

The old woman shook her head. "Nay, the laird would never let me go hungry. He is a good and fine man."

"Then why didn't you go to him about Dubhglas?"

Griselda stared at the ground and rocked back and forth in place. "I dinna ken, m'lady. I was ashamed, I suppose."

"You have nothing to be ashamed of, Griselda. Dubhglas is responsible for his behavior. Not you." Jessa gave the woman the most reassuring smile she possessed. "And I'm proud of you for fighting for this mama dog and her babies. Now go ask Grant to send for some food, and then tell him what you want done with Dubhglas—choosing one of my options, of course. Those are the only choices I will allow."

The gray-haired matron managed a deep curtsy. "Thank ye, m'lady—my honored goddess."

"I am not a goddess," Jessa called after her, then shrugged when the laundress ignored her and continued on her way toward the men. She turned back to the leery canine. "We're going to get you some food, and then we'll see about making you a more comfortable bed."

Its big brown eyes shone with yearning; then she gave a pitiful whine and barely twitched her tail.

"I'm going to scoot a little closer," Jessa said softly as she moved. She held out her hand with her knuckles up so the dog could sniff them. "I'll protect you as long as I'm here, and maybe, when I go back, you and your babies could come with me. Em's family loves dogs." A subtle ache took root in her chest. Her feelings were so twisted. She missed Emily and her family with a vengeance, but everyone here had been so nice to her, and then there was Grant. She swallowed hard at the thought of never seeing him again, which was freaking ridiculous since she'd only just met the man. Her eyes burned with the need to cry as the dog licked her knuckles. "I'm so confused. But I'll take care of you and the puppies. I promise."

The dog scrambled back and growled, looking at something behind her.

"What are ye confused about, lass?" Grant's deep voice washed across her, making her shiver.

"You scared her." Without looking at him, she waved him away. "Don't come any closer. That bastard hurt her, so now she's afraid of men."

"Like yerself?"

"I am not afraid of men." And she wasn't. She just wasn't all that sure about time travel or fated mates. After all, both defied logic. "So, did you drop that asshole off a cliff or send him packing?"

Grant rumbled with a low chuckle as he crouched beside her. "Which did you prefer?"

"A slow, painful death by beating, actually. Isn't that what he planned for his poor dog?" Jessa held out her hand to the canine again. "Grant won't hurt you. He's a good guy."

The sweet dog settled down again in the rags but kept her frightened focus locked on Grant.

"Lachie is escorting Dubhglas off MacAlester lands and convincing him never to return. Griselda is fetching food for yer wee friend here and informing Cook that the beastie is to be given the choicest scraps and treated with the care befitting an animal under the protection of the goddess."

Jessa rolled her eyes but concentrated on inching closer to soothe the dog rather than turning to glare at Grant. "I am not a goddess."

The canine whined again and lowered her head, finally allowing Jessa to rub her ears.

"You're such a sweet girl," she crooned. "Everything's going to be all right. I promise." Her heart warmed, and a strange sense of calm flowed through her as she petted the precious animal that was too large for a lap dog but too small to defend itself or others. She already loved the mistreated cur. How could she not after seeing a flicker of trust and hope in the creature's beautiful brown eyes? "I love you too, Brownie."

"Blessed be," Grant whispered, his voice filled with awe. "Look, lass. The cut on her wee head, the broken rib, her wounds are going away. She is healing."

Brownie wiggled closer, wagging her tail and snuggling her way into Jessa's lap. Her three puppies, small as large potatoes and their eyes still closed, grunted and squeaked with irate little puppy yips at the loss of their mother's warmth.

"How could she heal like that?" Jessa hugged the dog, smiling and laughing as the canine transformed from a terrified, abused animal into a healthy, happy dog. When Grant didn't answer, she turned to find him staring at her with a look she couldn't quite decipher. "Does that mean Mairwen is close? You called her a witch. Did she heal her?"

"Mairwen is not here, lass," he said with a quietness that made her shiver. "No one is here except yerself and me."

"Maybe you're the witch, then." Jessa leaned over and patted the dog's nest of rags. "Come on, girl. Back over here by your babies. They're looking for you." Without risking a glance at Grant and being forced to consider what he suggested, she tossed her words back to him, "Could we find her some nicer bedding? Griselda's done the best she could under the circumstances, but Brownie and the puppies need something softer."

"Aye," he said, still sounding distracted, "I'll have Jasper fetch some hay and fix her a bed here in the corner rather than the stable. She'll be well out of the weather and close to the kitchens, so we can make sure she's properly fed. I'll charge him with seeing that she gets her supper each evening and breakfast every morning, as well. Will that do?"

"And snacks too. She's a nursing mama. She needs extra food." Jessa risked turning to meet his gaze. "Thank you. She needs to know she's safe now—and loved."

"How did ye heal her, lass?" He eyed her, something akin to fear and so much more flickering in his eyes. "Can ye heal me?" He leaned forward and angled his right cheek toward her, the one with the angry-looking cut.

"I can't magically heal anyone." She fisted her hands, trying to forget what she'd felt moments ago just as the dog took a rapid turn for the better.

"Try," he prompted in a rasping whisper, making that single word echo through her entire being.

"I don't know what to do," she said just as quietly while gingerly reaching for him and resting her fingertips on his face.

"Ye told the dog ye loved her while ye rubbed her ears."

She jerked her hand away and tucked it back against her chest. "I didn't heal her. Something else must have happened. If this place is some kind of time travel bus stop, then maybe other impossible to believe things happen here too."

"What are ye afraid of, lass? Why are ye scairt to even try?" He trapped her in his gaze, pulling her in like a powerful tide that threatened to drown her.

She glared at him. "I told her I loved her because she needed me, and I saw unconditional love in her eyes. I have yet to see that in any man's eyes."

His eyes flexed, narrowing as if she had slapped him. He nodded. "I understand."

She doubted that he did. "Have you ever loved anyone unconditionally?"

"I could ask ye the same." His jaw flexed, then hardened, revealing she'd hit a nerve.

"If you did, I would tell you that the only people I have ever loved unconditionally are Emily and her family. They have always loved me, even on my worst days. I owe them the same. And animals, I always love animals unconditionally."

"So ye've never loved a man unconditionally?"

"No. I've never felt that close to any man."

"What about that man ye said ye wished ye had—" He frowned, suddenly befuddled. "Ye said ye wished to be rid of him first, but I dinna remember what ye called it."

"Dumped?"

"Aye, dumped."

"Trust me. I never loved Jeremy unconditionally. I would label the feelings I had for him as hoping for the best because I was too tired to keep looking for someone to love me."

"I have her food, my goddess," Griselda said as she hurried into the shelter, moving with a spryness she hadn't shown before. "Do ye wish to feed her, or shall I?"

Relief filled Jessa. Thank goodness for the interruption. She pushed up from the ground and dusted off the backside of her skirts as she moved to one side. "You feed her. That way, she'll know you fought to save her."

The laundress curtsied, then bowed her head. "Thank ye, my goddess. Thank ye for the life of my wee pup and for freeing me."

"I am not your—"

Grant cut her off by stepping forward and pulling her arm through his. "I am thankful to her as well, Griselda, for opening my eyes to something I should have seen long ago. Forgive me."

The washerwoman curtsied again. "All is well now, m'laird. Thanks to the goddess and yerself."

"I am not—"

"Come, m'lady. Let us leave Griselda to her wee beasties." Grant nearly propelled her out of the laundry lean-to and across the cobblestoned area surrounded by the amazingly high stone wall.

"She needs to know I am not a goddess." Jessa tried to turn back, but he stopped her. "I am just an average, chunky redhead."

He turned her to face him. "There is nothing average about ye, lass, and while yer hair is indeed red, I disagree that ye are *chunky*." He shook his head. "I dinna like that word." He tucked a finger under her chin and lifted her face to his. "Ye are damn near perfect by my reckoning. As perfect as anyone I have ever known. And I have known many in my day."

She wished he wouldn't look at her that way. It made her all melty inside, and if her heart beat any faster...She swallowed hard. Was this nothing more than lust, or was the legend about fated mates fact rather than fiction?

"What are we going to do, Grant?" she finally whispered.

Still cupping her chin, he slowly grazed the heel of his thumb back and forth across her bottom lip, then arched one of his dark brows. "I fear we are doomed, lass."

"Doomed?" she repeated in a squeaky whisper that made her cringe. "Doomed for what?"

"Doomed to love one another with a fearsomeness we have never known before." A heavy sigh left him before he added, "Eventually."

CHAPTER 11

Grant needed to kiss her. Again and again. As many times as she would allow, but she drew away from him, a heady combination of fear and yearning in her eyes.

"Jessa," he whispered while reaching for her, not a bit ashamed about begging her to return to his touch. "I am just as fearful, lass," he said softly, "and I never admit to being afraid. Not ever."

She remained rooted to the spot, an arm's length away, but her longing was slowly overcoming her fear. He could sense it.

"But what happens when I leave?" she asked.

"Leave?"

"When I go back." She barely shook her head. "I don't belong here. You know that."

"Ye belong wherever ye wish to belong."

"You don't want a wife. Isn't that what you told me? Isn't that what you told Mairwen?"

"Have ye never had a change of heart, lass? Never changed yer mind?"

"What changed your mind?" A defensiveness came over her. She jutted her chin higher, challenging him to answer.

He would much rather sweep her into his arms, haul her up to his bedchamber, and spend the rest of the day convincing her to stay and make a life with him. The thought surprised him, but then again, it didn't. His heart had known it all along. 'Twas his mind that had to catch up with the realization that he needed to make her his—permanently.

"What changed your mind?" she repeated.

He closed the distance between them. If she wouldn't come to him, he would go to her. "Yer stubbornness changed my mind." Pulling her into his arms, he locked eyes with her, daring her to move away from him again. "Yer fire. The way ye fought to protect Griselda and her wee dog." He slid his fingers along the curve of her cheek and deeper into her hair. "How cold and empty I feel whenever ye are not in my arms."

"That is just lust," she said, attempting to seem defiant, but the quiver in her voice gave her away.

He shook his head. "Nay..." Then he shrugged and offered her a faint smile. "Well, mayhap a wee bit of lust, but this is different. A far sight stronger than the mere need to bed a comely lass. This feeling is more like I finally found my way home, and I never wish to leave the warmth of this elusive hearthstone ever again."

"Home." She licked her lips as if hungry for the feeling. "That word kept coming to mind when we kissed."

"Could be because we both yearn to be where we belong."

Recognition flickered across her before she hid it. "This is your keep. You already belong."

"Nay, love. That is not the belonging of which I speak, and ye know it. This attachment between us is something a great deal rarer, a precious thing few ever find." He longed to cover her mouth with his, but instinct warned it was not yet the time. "Do ye not feel it at all? Not even a wee bit? Or are ye simply afraid to admit it?"

"I am not afraid."

He bit the inside of his cheek to keep from smiling. He had asked her that purposely, knowing she would hate being accused of being fearful. "Then ye dinna feel that of which I speak? Are ye telling me this powerful connection is one-sided?"

"I didn't say that." Her reddish blonde brows knotted in a worried frown over her troubled eyes. "I feel everything you have described, but I can't imagine staying here in the past. It's so...so..."

"What, lass?" He had no idea what she would be giving up, but surely the future could not be so grand as to wish to live there alone and leave behind this connection. This thing between them was addictive. The longer he was around her, the more time he needed with her. "This age is really no different from your own."

She stared at him as if he were mad. "How can you possibly say that? The first hour I was here, you couldn't figure out half of what I said."

"And yet, here we are." He tightened his arm around her waist and continued stroking her cheek with his thumb. "What does your future possess that ye canna possibly live without?" He held his breath, praying she wouldn't gush out a long list of things, or worse, another man's name.

She opened her mouth and then closed it three times, reminding him of a fish pulled from the sea. Finally, she clamped it shut and gave him a pitiful frown. "I miss Emily."

Ah, yes. The sister by choice and not by blood. A strong connection, indeed. "Leaving kin behind, losing them, is a hard and ugly business. For that part of yer coming here, I am sorry. But I am also a selfish man, m'love, and an honest one. I will not lie and tell ye I wish ye had never come, so ye would not have lost yer Emily. At first, I wanted to help ye find yer way back because I never wished to live a life with someone who hated me at my side. But I dinna think ye hate me so much now, and I damn sure know I dinna hate ye."

"So now you want a wife."

"Nay, love. Now, I want ye. No one else. I want the other half of my soul to traverse this life's treacherous path, a partner, a friend, a lover, and, aye, a wife if that is what ye wish to name it, but that one word hardly seems apt to describe all ye would be to me."

"Even if it means I have to sacrifice everything I've ever known to stay here?"

His heart shifted, sagging with a heaviness that felt as if the bottom had fallen out of his world. "If ye dinna think me worth the sacrifice, then no, I dinna want ye to stay. As I said, I dinna wish to go through this life with someone who hates me." He released her, dropping his arms to his sides as he stepped back.

"I do not hate you," she said, her voice quivering with the tears that gleamed in her eyes. "I think…"

He waited, bracing himself and holding his breath.

"Jessa!"

He whirled toward the excited shriek, then turned back again as Jessa squealed just as loudly.

"Emily!"

He shifted again and scowled at the two walking toward them. It was that damned witch with the one Jessa cherished as a sister. Mairwen silently greeted him with a smug nod and a knowing smile.

Before turning his full attention to Jessa and her Emily, dancing and squawking like a pair of feckin' geese, he shot a narrow-eyed glare at Mairwen, knowing she would get the gist of his displeasure at her timing.

"I never thought I would see you again," Jessa told the tall, dark-haired woman who reminded Grant of his allies in the east, the royal merchants native to the lands that his nemesis, the East India Trading Company, exploited for coffee and spices. The lasses caught each other up in another hug and continued spinning in a dizzying circle.

"One would think they had been separated a lifetime," Mairwen observed as she joined him.

"Those two are bound by something much stronger than blood." Grant resettled his stance and folded his arms across his chest. The women's greeting and excited talking over one another could last quite a while. He nodded at Jessa's Emily. "That woman is the sole reason the lass refuses to remain in this time."

"Refuses?" Mairwen said so sharply that it made him smile. "What do ye mean—refuses?"

"What does *refuses* usually mean?"

The old witch wrinkled her upper lip as if about to gnash her teeth at him. "Dinna test me, laird. Until ye are fully and happily bound with yer mate, I have enough to say grace over."

"What the devil does that mean? Are ye telling me the priest converted ye?"

"I am telling ye there is evil afoot. Evil not of this world. One of my Tranquility Weavers sensed a dark energy lurking around the lass before she came to ye."

A protectiveness shot through him with the heat of a raging inferno. "What dark energy?"

"One that would benefit from the fall of the Veil and thrive upon the chaos that would ensue. Yer Jessa and yerself possess an unusually strong connection. They dinna wish ye united. They fear the strength of yer bond."

"Aye, well, the strength of our bond may not be strong enough for Jessa to choose to remain in this time and become my wife." He nodded at the women still holding tightly to one another. "The bond she shares with that one pulls at her, strengthens her reluctance to leave her old life behind."

"I have spoken to Emily about that. It is my hope she will help Jessa open her mind to all the possibilities a life here offers. She has promised to do so to the best of her abilities."

"All the possibilities a life here offers?" Had the old witch told the woman that the only way he kept his clan's body and soul together was by funding his people's needs through smuggling?

"She does not know ye are a smuggler, and stop calling me an *old witch*. I have told Emily little about ye. I thought it better that Jessa fill her in so Emily might encourage her. Enough of their ridiculous chattering. We have a union to safeguard." She charged forward and pushed her way between the lasses, then looked back and summoned Grant with a pointed glare.

He glared right back at her and narrowed his eyes. They would be having a word about her eavesdropping on his thoughts. They had addressed that invasion before. Gritting his teeth, he strode across the way, took his place at Jessa's side, then gave Emily a gallant bow. "Welcome to MacAlester Keep. I am the laird, Grant MacAlester, at yer service."

"Good to meet you. I am Emily Mithers, but then you probably already figured that out." The woman smiled and held out her hand, acting as though she wished him to take it as if she were a tradesman, and they had just struck a deal.

Odd, indeed, but mayhap that was a quirk from the future. He shook her hand, impressed by the firmness of her grip, and wondered if she was handy with a sword. When he noticed Jessa watching him, as if afraid he wouldn't accept her friend, he did his best to charm the woman who Mairwen had said was going to help him win his Jessa's heart. "It is glad that I am that ye have come to visit, Mistress Emily. Jessa and I were just discussing how much she missed you."

With tears in her eyes, Emily turned to Jessa. "I had to come. I was so worried about her." She shot an irritated look Mairwen's way. "Her departure was very abrupt." Her tone clarified that she and the old witch were not on good terms.

Interesting, indeed. Grant smiled. If he could win Emily's trust, she could prove to be a valuable ally. He wondered if she would consider staying in this time with himself and Jessa.

"That is not her fate," Mairwen snapped.

"Stay out of my mind, witch," he retorted with a growl.

"Good," Emily said. "He's on our side."

"He's on *his* side," Jessa corrected, then gave him an apologetic nod. "But he's been very kind and sort of patient, for which I am very grateful."

"Sort of patient? I have given ye free rein to spoil my servants, allowed ye to banish a clansman, and dipped into my supply of coffee beans, which I intended to sell in Edinburgh for enough to feed my kinsman for a few months this winter."

"That clansman was a wife beater and an animal abuser. The pulley system for the well will increase efficiency and decrease injuries, and I never said you had to dip into your precious coffee beans. I would've just as gladly drank tea for breakfast."

"Wow." Emily appeared impressed. "You two sound like you've already been married for like fifty years."

He jabbed the air, pointing first at Jessa and then at her. "She'll not agree to marry me because she refuses to leave yer side." *Feckin' hell.* The words had burst free of him before he could stop himself. He snorted and bowed his head. "Forgive me. I should not have said that.'Twas quite rude."

"Yes, it was," Jessa said, but followed the accusation with a sigh. "But what he said is true. Grant is many things, but he is not a liar." She resettled her footing like a hen scratching for bugs, then surprised him by hesitantly looping her arm through his. "He is a good man, Em. Nothing like any of the others."

"Others? What others do ye speak of?" He glared down at her, ready for an immediate explanation.

"Women sometimes go out with several men before settling down," she explained.

"Go out with?"

Jessa shook her head. "Never mind. I'll explain later. Or Mairwen can explain it after she and I have had a nice long chat."

"Come then," Mairwen said in acceptance of the unspoken dare. "Walk with me. I feel sure Lord Suddie will not mind entertaining yer Emily."

"Who is Lord Suddie?" Emily wrinkled her nose as if the name had an odor to it.

"I am, but it is not the title I prefer, and the witch knows it. Call me Grant, the MacAlester, laird, or arsehole, if ye wish, but dinna call me the feckin' Earl of Suddie."

Jessa and Emily snorted in unison, then clapped their hands over their mouths, failing to hide their merriment.

Mairwen rolled her eyes, shook her head, and took off across the courtyard, pausing only long enough for Jessa to catch up with her.

"So, why do you hate that name so?" Emily asked once they were alone.

"I feel it, but one more way for the English to distance me from the blood of my ancestors."

"It is important to remember your ancestors. It took my parents a while to retrace our lineage because it hit so many places: the Caribbean, India, Spain, and South America, to name a few. But now that we know it, we feel we're richer for it." The way her dark eyes narrowed made him brace himself for whatever she was about to say. "So, do you believe in this fated mate stuff Mairwen is trying to sell us?"

"I canna say that I did at first."

"But now?"

He would not lie to Mistress Emily. He owed Jessa that much. "Never have I felt what I feel with Jessa."

"*With* Jessa," Emily said, "not *for* her."

"I shall describe it to ye the same as I told her. 'Tis as though I have been adrift all my life, lost and searching. When I am with Jessa, I feel as though I have finally found home." He slowly shook his head. "It defies everything I ever believed myself capable of—an insatiable hunger I never knew I could possess."

Emily fixed him with an unblinking stare. "You told her that. In those words?"

"Aye."

The lass shook her head as though reeling. "Damn. And she hasn't jumped at the chance to marry you?"

He clenched his teeth, sucked in a deep breath, and refrained from reminding the woman that he'd already told her about that particular matter. It was *her* fault Jessa had yet to accept him.

"Have you slept with her yet?" Emily asked before he could answer.

"She slept in my bed when she arrived. I slept in the chair."

The lass wrinkled her nose as she stepped closer. "I wasn't exactly asking about *sleeping* sleeping." She twitched a brow with a meaningful look. "I was asking about *sleeping*—you know."

"Is this something from the future of which I am unaware?"

"Have the two of you had sex yet?" She scowled at him.

"That is a private matter between myself and Jessa and none of yer damn concern."

Emily shrugged. "Fine. She'll tell me."

Realizing that the cocksure minx was probably right, he bared his teeth. "We have kissed. Nothing more. It would not be fair of me to try anything more whilst she was still so confused."

"Wow."

"And what is that supposed to mean?"

"It means you are a rare find, Mr. MacAlester."

"Dinna call me that either."

"I could call you what Jessa and I named you when your photo popped up on that app."

A heavy groan escaped him. He couldn't help it. There was that feckin' word again, *app*.

"What?" Emily frowned. "Did Jessa already tell you we named you Mr. MacSexy? Surely you didn't find that offensive."

"Mr. MacSexy, eh?" As a matter of fact, he did not take offense at that name. He grinned. "Whilst I find it verra flattering, perhaps it would be best if ye called me Grant, aye? Do ye not think Jessa would prefer that?"

"Probably." Emily went quiet and fixed her attention on Jessa and Mairwen across the way, where they were carrying on quite a robust conversation. "You know I don't want her to stay in this time, right?"

"I nay thought ye would, but would ye mind telling me yer reasons other than missing her in yer time?"

"Of course, that's the main reason." Emily shifted with a heavy sigh, then shook her head. "I just feel like if she stays here, chances are she'll die long before she would die in our time."

"Are ye a seer, then?"

She tore her worried frown from Jessa and fixed a scowl on him. "Well, no. But you know what I mean. In the future, we've improved upon a lot of things that kill people right now."

"So, there are no dangers at all in the future? None that might take her from the world long before anyone is prepared to see her go?"

"Maybe I will call you *arsehole,* after all."

"Ye know what I am saying, lass, and ye ken well enough that it be true. We die when we are meant to die. No matter what century in which we find ourselves."

"Predestination as opposed to free will?" she said. "No matter what choices we make, whatever Fate says will be—will be. That's what you believe?"

"Aye. The only thing free will affects is how miserable or happy we are during the days between birth and death."

"Interesting viewpoint." Emily kicked a small clod of dirt across the cobblestone courtyard. "I still don't want her to stay."

"So, Mairwen lied to me yet again?" He had known it all along, felt the truth of it searing a hole through the pit of his stomach.

"I promised Mairwen I wouldn't talk Jessa into coming back to the future without giving you a chance," she said, "and I never go back on a promise." She slowly shook her head while eyeing Jessa, who stood shaking a finger at the old witch. "I just wish it were different." She sniffed, then turned away so he couldn't see her face. "I can't imagine life without Jess."

"Neither can I, lass. Neither can I."

∽

"I trusted you." Jessa was so angry with Mairwen that she couldn't think of anything else to say. "I trusted you!" she repeated even louder, hating the shrillness of her tone. The old witch, as Grant so aptly called the woman, had turned her into a snarky bundle of nerves.

"I had yer best interests at heart, lass," Mairwen said quietly.

"Bullshit! All you care about is your Highland Veil mumbo jumbo. Grant told me so himself."

"So ye feel nothing toward him, then?" The irritatingly calm elder arched a silvery brow. "And afore ye lie, remember two things: I am quite adept at reading minds, and ye have a tell."

"A what?"

"A tell," Mairwen said. "Ye would be a horrid card player. Whenever ye feel uncertain of yerself, not only do ye chew on yer bottom lip, but yer fair skin takes on the heady blush of the reddest rose. Telling lies is not one of yer strengths."

"I do not belong here."

"That is not what I asked ye. The question was: do ye feel nothing toward him?"

"I am afraid," Jessa admitted softly, trying to ignore the shame churning through her. If a love wasn't strong enough to overcome fear, then was it really a love worth fighting for, a love worth leaving everything behind and leaping into the unknown? "I barely passed the history class required for my degree."

Mairwen chuckled. "Some things ye canna learn from books or online. Some things can only be learned by being lived." She nodded in Grant's direction. "And he'll not be grading ye, lass, or testing ye on yer knowledge. This is life. Ye are the judge and jury of yerself—as ye have always been. Do ye not think it high time ye stopped being so quick to condemn yerself with a less than satisfactory grade? Look at all ye have survived, lass. Look how brightly ye shine."

"I do not need a therapy session on self-esteem."

"I disagree. Ye dinna believe in yerself enough to face yer fears and embrace a life worth living—a life much more than a mere existence."

Jessa glanced back at Emily and Grant and gave up on trying not to cry. The hot droplets of pure frustration burned their way down her cheeks, and her nose immediately started running. "Dammit." She sniffed and patted her outer skirt, searching for the opening in the seam that Molly had shown her. Somewhere under all those layers was the small cloth sack the maid had tied around her waist to carry *necessaries,* as she had phrased it. "When are real freaking pockets invented?"

"Did yer maid not tuck ye a bit of linen behind yer stays?" Mairwen tipped a nod at Jessa's chest. "A circa 1785 handkerchief? In the winter, ye can keep it tucked inside the sleeve of yer jacket. Much easier to get to that way."

"I don't know what she tucked where while trussing me up like a turducken for Thanksgiving."

Mairwen stepped closer and angled an ear toward her. "Trussed ye like a what?"

"A turducken." Jessa fished down into the front of her tightly bound stays and found the handkerchief. "You stuff a deboned chicken filled with dressing inside a deboned duck layered with more dressing and herbs, and then you stuff all of that inside a deboned turkey, sew it shut, slather it in butter, wrap it in caul fat, then bake it."

"Interesting." The silvery-haired matron brightened. "Ye must show Cook. I am sure the clan would enjoy a dish like that."

"I don't make it a habit of eating meat," Jessa said with an overwhelming sense of guilt at betraying her animal friends. "I love animals alive. Not on my plate."

"Then how do ye know how to prepare such an extravagant dish?"

"I dated a chef once."

"I take it that did not last long once ye told him ye preferred yer meals animal-free?"

"Pretty much." Jessa dipped a curt nod. "See? Yet another reason I can't stay here. These folks would never tolerate a vegetarian."

"They will tolerate whatever Grant orders them to tolerate."

Jessa snorted. "Like the social worker telling the other kids to be nice to me while she met with my fosters. As soon as she left the room, they morphed into demons."

Mairwen bowed her head and pinched the bridge of her nose. A sternness settled over her as her hand dropped to her side, and she fixed Jessa with a look that made her shiver. "If ye dinna choose a life with yer fated mate, ye will never be whole. Never truly happy. Ye will always feel as if ye are watching life pass ye by. As if ye are standing on the sidelines while everyone else dances. Is that the life ye want? Because the choice is yers. If ye so choose, we will return to the twenty-first century immediately. But know this—whatever you decide, you condemn Grant to that same fate."

"That isn't fair."

With a bitter laugh, Mairwen shook her head. "And who was it that lied to ye, lass, and told ye life was ever fair?"

As Jessa turned and looked at Grant, he looked her way as well. When their eyes met, something indescribable passed between them. Whatever this fated mate fairy tale connection was, it was real and growing stronger by the minute. She could almost hear his deep whisper, "*Stay with me, Jessa. Please.*"

"What happens to Emily?" she said to Mairwen without breaking the connection with Grant.

"Yer Emily has a fated mate as well, but he is not in this time."

"So, when I say goodbye to her, it will be forever?" The hot tears overflowed again, and Jessa didn't care.

"For a little while. At least, at first." Mairwen lightly touched her arm. "But I offer ye this solemn promise. When I speak with the goddesses, I shall ask that the two of ye be granted the power to pass through the Highland Veil to visit one another whenever ye like. At Seven Cairns. Such a gift of power is rarely given, but I feel the love between the two of ye could benefit the blessed weave just as much as the love between fated mates. Love is a powerful healing energy, no matter its form. Love is love."

That wasn't much, but it was something, she supposed. Jessa fisted her hands to her middle and gave Emily a sad smile. When

Emily smiled back at her, she knew then and there that Emily already knew everything Mairwen had just told her. But that was dear, sweet Em to a tee. She was a selfless friend who would do anything to keep Jessa safe and happy. While looking in that direction, a movement in the sky, a shadow much larger than any bird, caught her notice in the clouds. "What is that?"

"What, lass?" Mairwen turned and looked in that direction.

"There is something in those clouds. Something really dark." A strangely familiar fear, a primeval urge to either fight or flee, nearly choked off her air. "I don't know what that is, but we need to get inside. All of us. Now. I feel it."

"*Protego!*" Mairwen said, in a voice so powerful the cobblestones shuddered beneath their feet.

Jessa ran to Grant and Emily and started pulling them toward the laundress's shelter. "We have to take cover. Something is coming."

"Go. The both of ye. I dinna run. I fight." Unsheathing his sword, Grant crossed the courtyard in long, fearless strides and took a defensive stance beside Mairwen.

A fear worse than any Jessa had ever known, an aching worry for his safety, paralyzed her. She could lose him. That thing could kill him before they ever discovered what they could become. From deep within her, a raging *NO* burst free and boiled her blood to battle readiness.

"What is it, Jess?" Emily stared up at the strangely swirling cloud, its murky, dark center an unmistakable shadow of a person—an enormous person with arms outspread like great, ratty wings.

"Something bad, like in a horror movie bad, where just as the car starts and you think you're home free, the monster rips off the roof and grabs you." Jessa pushed Emily toward the washhouse lean-to. "Go in there. Huddle against the back wall with Griselda and her dog."

"Where are you going?"

Jessa locked eyes with Emily. "I can't let him die defending me. I can't let him die—period." She pointed at the lean-to. "Now, go. I don't want you hurt, either."

Emily huffed. "You're not the boss of me. Come on. We'll fight the cloud monster together."

Jessa didn't like it, but also didn't have time to argue. "Come on, then. Let's do this."

Emily caught her by the shoulder. "One question—what are we going to use as weapons?"

"Not sure. We'll make it up as we go along."

CHAPTER 12

"What is that feckin' thing?" Grant asked Mairwen when he reached her. The wind picked up, and more dark clouds rolled in, as though summoned to join the war and blot out the sun.

"It is not a *what*." Mairwen kept her focus locked on the sky while flexing her long, bony fingers. "It is a verra dangerous *who*."

"Now is not the time to dance with words, witch." A flicker of movement to his right made him turn. He nearly choked with an overwhelming surge of rage, fear, and panic. "Get inside, woman! I'll not have ye out here. 'Tis too dangerous."

Green eyes flashing like brilliant emeralds, Jessa pointed at the cloud and shouted, "I spotted it first. It's mine."

"And I'm helping her," Emily said, squinting against the stinging whip of the wind.

"No!" he roared above the howling furor of the rising storm.

Jessa ignored him, infuriating him even more as she shoved her way in front of him and ridiculously tried to shield him with her outspread arms.

He picked her up and set her behind him, then bared his teeth at Mairwen. "Get her out of this! Take her back to her time!"

"I cannot," Mairwen said. "It is too dangerous during an attack."

Lightning splintered the sky into a thousand dancing pieces, and deafening thunder shook the earth.

"My goddess!" Screeching like a banshee, Griselda, the laundress, hobbled toward them as quickly as her bent body allowed, dragging along an armload of wooden paddles with her. Her small dog raced ahead and took a protective stance in front of Jessa, staring up at the roiling storm with its hackles raised and teeth bared.

If the danger were not so great, Grant would laugh at this army of women and the newly healed dog. Then he went still, remembering how Jessa had made the dog strong and healthy, even though she had denied it. If she possessed the power to heal, might she also possess other powers? "Mairwen—Jessa healed that dog. Made it whole again. Do ye ken she can do more? Could she repel that thing?"

"I did not heal the dog!" Jessa shouted over the wind, but her denial lacked conviction.

Mairwen shook her head, curling away against the gale and shielding her face with her arms. "The Morrigan is too powerful for any of ye. Go inside. The dark one and I have old scores to settle. I shall deal with her myself."

Grant's blood ran cold. "The Morrigan?" Fear rooted deep in his heart, not for himself, his clan, or his keep, but a heart-clenching terror for his precious Jessa. He caught her wrist and pulled her close. "Ye must go inside. I beg ye."

With her teeth clenched in a fierce scowl, she stared up at him as if about to refuse. Then she lunged forward and pulled him down for a kiss, clinging to him with a fury. Nothing else mattered. If they died this day, at least they died together. He dropped his sword and crushed her to him, tangling his fingers in her hair and delving ever deeper into the wondrous taste of her. A force as powerful as lightning crackled through him. When he lifted his head, he lost himself in her eyes.

"I need ye safe," he rasped, "because I have discovered I love ye just as much as I loved ye in all our past lives."

She defiantly jutted her chin higher. "And because I love you, I will not leave you here to die alone."

An ear-splitting wail whipped around them, unleashing the storm's anger and stinging them with torrential rain and debris.

Grant didn't care. He had his beloved in his arms, and she had not only admitted she loved him but sworn she would not leave. Filled with joyous defiance, he caught her closer and locked his glare with hers. "So, ye'll be marrying me then, aye?" When she didn't answer, he jostled her. "Aye?"

Blinking through the blinding rain, she gave him a curt nod. "Yes."

He threw back his head and unleashed a victorious roar.

Lightning splintered the world again and struck the courtyard with a powerful explosion that burnt the air and sent the cobblestones flying. All went deadly quiet. Even the rain disappeared like morning mist burned away by a blazing sun.

"Is it over?" Emily whispered through the eerily heavy silence.

"No," Mairwen answered. "It has only just begun. The dark one is merely taking a deep breath before she shows us her displeasure that Jessa and Grant have discovered their bond."

An unholy roar rumbled from deep below their feet as if the earth was about to open its great maw and swallow them whole. The ground trembled and rolled, making them stagger. An eerie groan came from the keep, dust shaking free of its stones and rolling down its sides. The watchtowers jutting up from the corners of the skirting wall swayed like trees in the wind.

"*Tenete!*" Mairwen shouted, dropping to her knees and digging her fingers into the ground.

Emily ran toward the open kitchen windows, screaming, "Don't come out! It's an earthquake. Take cover under something sturdy."

"The puppies!" Jessa tore out of Grant's arms and dashed for the laundress's lean-to.

"No," he bellowed, charging after her. "Jessa!" As he dove into the shack to drag her back out, the earth shuddered harder, making the ramshackle structure shake with a deathly rattle. "Damn ye, woman! Listen to me!"

"I am not leaving those puppies to die."

In the choking dustiness of the darkness lit only by the hot coals beneath the wash cauldrons, Grant barely made out Jessa crawling toward the dog's nest of rags and hay, searching for the wee mongrels.

"I can't find them." Panic filled her voice, and he knew without even seeing her that tears streamed down her face.

Her sorrow killed him, forcing him to drop to his knees beside her and run his hands along the ground. "The wee ones are afraid and hiding."

The timbers above them popped and crackled, warning of what was to come. They had to find the pups before everything collapsed and caught fire in the cauldrons' coals.

"They're here! All three." She gathered the tiny things into a fold in her skirt and went to stand, but the roof gave way, knocking her into his arms.

Just as he had feared, the coals got a taste of the wood, burst into flames, and crackled and popped with a greedy hunger, eating up the wreckage and trapping them with a blazing wall that would not yield.

Dust and smoke choked them. The heat threatened to sear their lungs. Coughing, Jessa sidled along the wall, moving as far from the flames as possible. "This way," she called out, shouting above the roar of the fire.

"Jessa!" He caught her arm and shook his head while pointing. "We canna escape that way because of the skirting wall." Lor a'mighty, if they didn't escape soon, the thick air would take them before the fire could.

In the smoky darkness of the fiery hell, her panic reached out to him. Her desperation screamed for him to save them, her and those damn pups she loved like they were her bairns. That thought strengthened him. They would live through this and fill the keep with so many sons and daughters that their laughter would shake the foundation stones to dust.

"Hold tight to the wee dogs," he shouted into her face, "up close to yer chest."

"Why?"

"Just do it. There's nay time to explain."

She gathered the folds of her skirts around the puppies and curled herself around them.

He had to save them. No matter what. Jessa had to be safe. He shook out the extra length of his great kilt over her head to shield her, then swept her up into his arms. Ducking, he charged into the wall of fire, aiming for a patch of lightness that he prayed was the sun fighting against the clouds. The acrid stench of burning hair filled his nostrils along with its hissing crackle filling his ears. His flesh sizzled, but he didn't care. He would save his Jessa. As he lowered his shoulder to break through a blazing timber, another one snapped and caught him across the back, then raked its fiery shards across his ribs, nearly causing him to drop his precious bundle.

"Grant!"

"I have ye, lass, I have ye." Excruciating pain thrummed through him, but he refused to yield. All he had to do was make it into the clear. He only had to hold fast that long. As he stumbled free of the last of the raging fire, Emily and Mairwen rushed to him.

Erratic flashes of light and dark blurred his vision, then blinded him completely. He dropped to his knees and ever so gently lowered Jessa to the ground. Wheezing in agonizing breaths, he collapsed forward but caught himself on his forearms to keep from going face first into the mud.

"Take care of her," he said, the raw growl burning his throat. "Keep her safe." He couldn't see, nor could he tell if the roaring in his ears was the continued raging of the storm or his own blood bellowing for relief. "Take care of her," he repeated.

A soft touch to his face turned his head. Something softer still brushed against his ear. The sweetness of his dear one's mouth, perhaps? That notion granted him what little ease there was to be had. "I am safe, Grant. I am safe."

"Aye," he whispered. Or he thought he did. With his head swimming and the demons raking their talons across his body, 'twas difficult to be certain of anything. "Safe. My love is safe."

"Don't you dare die on me!"

That made him smile. She sounded so far away that he feared his soul had already started its journey to the next place.

"Bind yerself to him, lass," another voice said. "Rejoin yer soul to his. Lend him yer strength."

The witch, maybe? He tried to blink his eyes open wider, but it did no good. Only darkness filled his vision, and the wind howled louder in his ears.

"Bind myself to him? I don't understand."

Ah, now he knew that voice, and he heard it as if she were within his mind rather than beside him. It was his precious Jessa. He reached for her, but the demons flexed their talons in his flesh and made him roar with the pain instead.

"Ye must say the words to him. Say them as I tell ye. Quickly now, afore the Morrigan returns and carries him off to the land of the dead. Bind him to ye and hold tight to his spirit so she canna rip him away."

He fought to push himself upright. If the Morrigan was returning, he had to rise, had to protect his Jessa.

Then a sweetness of roses wafted into his awareness, chasing away the stench of burnt flesh, smoke, and singed hair. A velvety soft mouth kissed him, and in his mind, clear as the bell ringing in the kirk's tower, he heard his dear one say the words:

Heart of my heart,
Soul of my soul,

We reunite,
To never let go.
Blood of my blood,
Bone of my bone,
We two are now one,
Our halves are now whole.
For the good of all,
With harm to none,
So let it be spoken,
So let it be done,
So mote it be.

"So mote it be," he whispered, breathing easier as a familiar warmth, a comforting serenity washed across him like a soothing balm. Darkness and the suffocating pain no longer blinded him. Instead, a golden glow of ethereal light buoyed him, filling his awareness. "I love ye, my Jessa, my precious wee fox."

"I love you, too," she said and gave him another tender kiss. "Heaven help us both."

~

JESSA WAS ABOUT to shatter into a hysterical mess. Maybe if she kept whispering, *So mote it be*, Grant would be all right. The oath had calmed him, and with any luck, it would send that dark monster straight to the deepest pit in hell. An earsplitting boom made her jump and clutch him tighter, sheltering him as best she could with his head in her lap. She struggled to keep him on his uninjured side. The last thing his ragged, bloody back needed was a roll in the mud. He had to live. She couldn't bear it if he died because he had followed her into that fiery death trap.

A hiccuping sob escaped her as she gently rocked with her cheek pressed against his charred, matted hair. His thick, dark mane, once shoulder-length, had burned off in jagged patches, leaving him raggedly shorn and smoldering with faint wisps of smoke still rising from the longer sections. The wound on his cheek was even angrier than before, encrusted with blisters as though his raw flesh had boiled in the heat.

"I am so very sorry," she whispered against his closed eyes before looking up at Mairwen. "Can we not take him to the twenty-first century to heal and then bring him back?"

"I am sorry, lass." The elder shook her head. "That is not how it works. The Veil would allow ye to pass since ye are a woman, but being a male, it is doubtful he would survive it. Especially in his condition."

"Can we not go back, get some medicine, maybe even a doctor, and bring it all here?" Emily asked.

"No. We dare not overly muddle history. We trouble it enough by our very presence." Mairwen tipped a nod at those emerging from the keep to join them. "Ye are their mistress now, Jessa. Tell them what ye wish done."

"What I wish done?" Had the meddling old woman lost her mind? Jessa stared at the men, women, and children. All of them stared back at her with expectant expressions. What was she supposed to tell them? She didn't know what they needed to do. "I have no idea what to say." Too much had just happened—and Grant, the man she had finally admitted she loved—was dying because of her.

"A good leader reassures the people and assigns them tasks so they not only feel useful but keep their minds occupied with beneficial thoughts rather than worries." Mairwen knelt beside her and nodded at Grant. "What do ye believe he would say to them?"

Before Jessa could reply, three men she hadn't yet met pushed free of the crowd and knelt in front of her.

"Mrs. Robeson has gone to her apothecary for healing poultices," the largest of the trio said, before thumping his fist to his chest and bowing his head. "Forgive me, mistress. I be Henry Skelper. Close as a brother to the laird, I am."

"I am Jessa," she told the red-haired giant, then eyed the other two men.

"I be Lachie," said the muscular blond who could pass for a battle-scarred Viking. "Close as a brother to him, as well."

The last of the three, short and wiry, and somehow reminiscent of a ferret, offered her a gallant bow. "I be Gordon. If ye need a lock picked or some gold pinched, I be yer man. I can get whatever Himself might need. Daren't ye worry about that."

Henry shook his head. "I feel sure the mistress finds comfort in yer adeptness at thievery at a time such as this." He bowed to her again. "We can carry him to the bedchamber, m'lady. If'n ye wish it done. What would ye have us do?"

Jessa couldn't bear the thought of letting go of Grant, but she supposed he'd be better off in his bed instead of here in the mud. She shuddered at the thought of what needed to be done to the torn flesh on his back to keep the infection at bay. "I guess that would be best. But be careful. Try not to hurt him any more than has already been done. He saved me. We have to save him."

"Aye, mistress," Lachie said with a calmness that told her no matter how careful they were, the journey to the bedroom would cause Grant hellacious pain.

Lachie and Henry placed themselves on either side of their unconscious laird, hooked their arms under his, and lifted.

"Nay!" Grant came to life, growling and thrashing like an enraged beast. He knotted his fists in her skirts and yanked her closer. "I'll not let ye take her! Never!"

"Let him go." Jessa swatted them away, then hugged Grant and resumed her gentle rocking. "Shh...I am here. No one is taking me anywhere. I will never leave you. I promise."

Distant thunder rumbled sorrowfully in the distance, and a respectfully shushing rain pattered in the mud, gradually increasing to a steady downpour.

"M'lady—" Henry shuffled with uneasiness. "Ye must let us move him. 'Tis for the best."

She glared up at the man and decided that now was the time to set the tone for how they would treat her. Never again would she just go along and settle when she knew it wasn't what was best for her or those she cared about. She deserved better. She deserved respect. "Leave us for a while. Let me get him calm while you see if anyone else is hurt or needs rescuing. Others could be trapped if anything else collapsed. You know he would want them seen to first. I'll take care of Grant." She swiped the rain off his face and kissed his forehead. She would sit here in the mud with him for eternity if need be. Something deep inside told her he did not need to be moved. Keeping her cheek against him, she said, "Make them go away, Mairwen, because I am not moving him. It would be wrong. I feel it. He needs me to hold him until he is ready."

Before Mairwen could respond, Griselda spoke up, raising her shrill voice for all to hear. "Her be the goddess. Do as she says for the good of our laird."

"The goddess?" Henry repeated, his tone equal parts awe and horror. "Forgive us, divine one." He dropped to his knees and bowed his head. Lachie and Gordon did the same.

Griselda's dog moved to Jessa's side, threw back her head, and howled as if singing her goddess's praises.

"Help the others," Jessa told them through clenched teeth, grateful for the rain because it hid her tears. She'd clear up the confusion about the goddess thing later. If it made them listen to her now, she would use it to her advantage. She didn't want Grant moved. It just *felt* wrong.

As everyone except Mairwen, Griselda, and Emily moved away to assess the damages and help anyone who might be injured, Grant relaxed, slumping against her. Alarmed, she pressed her lips to his temple and concentrated on detecting the faint tapping of his heart. To make sure she hadn't imagined it, she worked her fingers under what was left of his neckcloth and pressed them to his throat. A slow, faint pulse barely tapped against her touch.

"You cannot die," she said in a desperate whisper, then closed her eyes and pressed her cheek tighter against him, envisioning the healthy, sexy grump who had thrown her back onto the bed the first time she had tried to escape him. The coolness of his skin and his slower breathing both terrified and enraged her. "You will not die. I will not allow it!"

The unexplainable, loving heat that had surged through her when she had healed Griselda's dog returned, lifting her heart and filling her with hope. Fearing she would scare the feeling away, she closed her eyes tighter and added the memory of the breathtaking fire of their first kiss to the vision of his healthiness. The soothing flow of the eerie tingling hummed through her even stronger. On impulse, she gently flattened her hands on his wounds, instinctively spreading her fingers as wide as she could. Eyes closed, she pressed her mouth to his temple and held the kiss, willing the loving energy to flow out of her and into him. Even if it didn't heal him, at least he would know she loved him.

"Believe," Mairwen quietly ordered, as she laid a hand on Jessa's shoulder and squeezed. "Believe, child, and it will be so."

"You are capable of anything you set your mind to," Emily told her as she laid both hands on her other shoulder. "Anything is possible, Jess. Absolutely anything."

Their touch steadied her. Their words gave her strength and clarity. "You are healed," she whispered against Grant's forehead, concentrating on believing every word. "You are whole." Intuition from the very depths of her soul nudged her to add, "So mote it be."

He shuddered with a sudden, deep intake of air, then turned and pulled her down for a kiss. He tasted of hope, of happiness, but most of all, he tasted of life. She sobbed and clutched him tighter. An overload of joy hurtled through her, exploding her senses.

"Lore a'mighty, woman," he whispered between rapid fire kisses. "Ye've made me as strong and mighty as a Highland stag."

She cradled his face between her hands and smiled. "I was so afraid you were going to die."

He reached up and brushed his thumb across her tear-soaked

cheek. "I just needed a wee rest to catch my breath, and yer loving touch to awaken me."

"Thank you."

The bewilderment in his eyes made her smile.

"For what are ye thanking me, love?"

"For being you." She didn't know how to explain it. They had only just met, and yet, now that she had fully embraced all the magical intricacies of the Highland Veil, fated mates, and whatever Mairwen and the people of Seven Cairns were, it was as though a fog had lifted. She finally saw everything clearly and remembered it as though she had known it all her life. And it was as though she knew Grant almost as well as she knew herself. She shrugged. "Thank you for being you."

With a smugness that somehow made him endearing rather than infuriating, he pushed himself up to his feet and helped her stand. "And where are yer wee pups, m'lady?"

"Pups?" He'd just escaped death's door and was asking her about the puppies? "I-I don't know," she stammered with a shake of her head. "I was worried about you."

"With their mama," Emily said, pointing out the dog sitting beside a basket, washing her babies. "And they're all fine. Mama dog is grateful to both of you."

"Are you really all right?" Jessa touched his cheek. The angry wound was gone, replaced by a silvery thread of a scar that made him even more handsome.

He caught her close and held her as if fearing she might disappear. "I am better than all right, my love, and I am grateful, as well." His embrace tightened around her. "My spirit tried to leave here, but ye held fast, and then ye healed me."

Emily cleared her throat. "Mairwen and Griselda, is there not someplace else we can be? Like helping with cleanup or something?"

"We need to hie ourselves to the kitchens and set some water to boiling," Griselda said. "Himself and the goddess be wanting a fine hot bath, I'm thinking."

Even though a bath sounded wonderful, especially one with Grant, Jessa felt guilty about even thinking of such a luxury while everyone else was busy putting everything back together. "Everyone has enough to do right now. A bath is too much to worry with. All we need is a pitcher or two of hot water and a basin."

"It shall be done," Griselda said, "and I shall settle the pups and Brownie-dog in a corner of the pantry if that be all right with ye, my goddess?"

"That's fine, Griselda. Thank you." Jessa heaved a great sigh at the woman's insistence on addressing her as a divine being, but didn't correct her. She'd been called worse, and now that Grant was alive and well, a bone-aching weariness had settled over her.

Grant pulled her arm through his and tucked her to his side. "Come, m'love. Let us survey the Morrigan's destruction whilst Griselda tends to our water. She'll send Mrs. Robeson or Molly to find us once it's ready."

Jessa paused long enough to wave at Emily. "We'll talk later. Okay?"

Emily gave her a smile that settled heavily on her heart. Soon, she would never see dear Em again—or at least—not for a while. Not until the goddesses granted Mairwen's request. If they granted it. She tried not to think about it. Head suddenly swimming, she stumbled to one side and caught hold of Grant to keep from falling.

"Jessa?" He caught her by the shoulders. "Are ye injured? Ye healed me, but what about yerself?"

"I'm just really tired. My adrenaline must be bottoming out." She pulled in a deep breath and looped her arm through his once more. "I'm fine. Come on. Let's make sure no one else is hurt and see how badly the keep was damaged. Has anything like that ever happened before?"

"No. But I am worried about ye. Ye've gone peely-wally."

"I was accused of that in Glasgow. What exactly does that mean?"

"Sickly. Pale."

An apt description because she felt sickly and pale but wasn't about to admit it. It had to be the drop in adrenaline after so much terror. Inhaling all that smoke probably hadn't helped either, but if she kept busy and powered through, everything would reset, and she would be fine. "We'll check the kitchen first. A lot of heavy stuff could've fallen from the rafters."

He glared at her in a growly yet protective way that sent a surge of contentment through her. She patted his arm and laughed, her weariness already lifting.

"Ye laugh when I look at ye with a sternness that means ye should do as I ask?"

"You make me happy when you look at me that way. It makes me feel loved."

His sternness melted away, replaced with a soulfulness that stole the air from her lungs. "As long as my soul exists," he said softly, "I will love ye with a fury that burns hotter than any fire that exists in this world or any other."

She threw herself into his arms, hugging him tightly while burying her face in his chest. "I love you so much it almost hurts," she whispered. "I never knew it could be like this."

He held her right there in the middle of the outside kitchens as if no one else in the world existed. His heartbeat thumped a strong, reassuring beat beneath her cheek. "We are going upstairs," he said with quiet firmness, then bellowed, "Sawny!"

She cringed and pulled back, unable to resist scolding him. "I am now deaf in one ear."

"Forgive me, but I nay wished to miss the lad when I saw him pass by."

Jessa tried not to smile as Sawny slowly approached, his eyes wide and his mouth hanging open. Apparently, word about the laird being at death's door had already spread through the keep.

The boy dropped to one knee and bowed his head. "My laird —'tis glad I am to see ye so braw and filled with life."

"Thank ye. Now, I need ye to find Henry and Lachie. Tell them to care for the clan jointly, using their best judgment until my lady and I have recovered from our ordeal. They can update me on any damages at that time. Not before. Have Mrs. Robeson send food and drink to my chambers. Griselda is seeing to the hot water for our wash. It needs to be delivered to us as well. Can ye remember all that, lad? Can I trust ye to see those things carried out with no issue?"

Sawny lifted his head and nodded, reverence in his eyes. "Aye, my laird."

"Off wi' ye, then."

As Jessa watched the boy go, a niggling worry, a concern that refused to be ignored, gnawed at her. "What are your people going to think about today? About your healing? About Griselda calling me a goddess? When word spreads, there is bound to be trouble. Don't you think?"

He scooped her up into his arms and carried her like a babe. "I think those are worries for another time. Now is our time for thankfulness, joy, and love."

CHAPTER 13

"Carrying me up three floors on that winding staircase was very impressive."

"'Tis my hope to impress ye in many ways, m'love." Grant shouldered open the door to their bedchamber and lowered Jessa's feet to the floor, watching her closely for any additional signs of weakness. She still had a paleness about her, and while it was rightly so after all she had been through, it worried him. The wily lass could be injured somehow and determined to hide it.

"How in the world?" She turned in a slow arc, pointing at the turned-down bed, the table laid with an assortment of fruits, cheeses, breads, and bottles of wine, and the long, low dresser piled high with fresh linens, a quartet of basins, and their wide-bellied, steaming pitchers. "How did they do all this so quickly? And not only that—how did we not pass them in the stairwell?"

"I have often thought the women of this keep in league with the Fae. What with the way they make things appear—and disappear if they so wish it. And I feel sure Mairwen lent her magic to their aid this day." He gently brought her closer and lifted her face to his. "I dinna care how they did it. What I care about is ye. I find yer coloring worrying."

"I'm fine." But her eyelids drooped as if she could barely keep them open. Then she wrinkled her nose. "The smell of smoke is making my stomach churn, though. Would they be upset if we stripped down and tossed our clothes out in the hall?"

Her suggestion nearly undid him. The perfection of her in his arms, as he carried her to the bedchamber, had hardened him to the readiness of a rutting stag. "I shall be upset if we dinna strip down."

With a coy look and keeping her gaze locked with his, she tugged on her stays' front lacings. Then she tugged again and growled. "Seriously?" Glaring down at the front of her corset and using both hands, she picked at the knotted ties. "Did she mean for me to wear this thing until it rotted off?"

"Here, now. Let me." He wouldn't tell her he was quite experienced with removing a lady's underpinnings. *Feckin' hell.* The front ties refused to yield. "Let me try the back ones. Surely they're not so knotted. 'Tis as though the wetness and filth bound them and made them one."

Jessa laughed as she turned. "Kind of like us."

"Aye, lass." He swallowed hard, finding this newfound sense of completeness, the strong contentment centering his very core, both strange and wonderful. He resettled his stance, aching with the lusty need to complete the spiritual binding with a physical joining as well. "Bloody hell—enough!" He pulled his *sgian dubh* from his right boot and severed the ties that refused to give.

"Well, that was effective." Jessa peeled off the grubby thing, held it by two fingers, and carried it to the door. "I don't want to nasty up the rug, so I'm starting our pile one thing at a time." She nodded at his boots. "You might want to do those first."

"Ye are a rare woman, m'lady." He started to sit on the bench at the end of the bed to remove his boots but halted when she made the same sound his mother used to make when warning him he had better stop whatever he was doing or she would tan his wee arse for him. "How am I supposed to remove my boots if I canna sit?"

"Lean on a wall or hold on to something," she said. "Your backside is even filthier than your front." She tugged her overskirt around, unfastened it, then stepped out of it and added it to the pile in the hallway. "And why am I a rare woman? Is that good or bad?"

"Most women would not consider this a verra romantic path to their first loving with their new husband."

She went still, and both her brows arched high behind the curtain of messy curls she kept shoving out of her eyes. "Husband?"

"Aye." Her tone and expression worried him. "We married in the old way, lass. With the binding oath." He held to the bedpost, toed the heel of his boot, and worked it off his foot. "Ye knew ye were marrying me, aye? Ye told me ye were willing."

She avoided his gaze by concentrating on untying her bum roll and petticoats. She tipped a nervous shrug without looking up. "I knew it—I guess. Hearing it out loud for the first time kind of startled me."

He carried his boots to the door, set them in the hall, then returned to her and took her by the shoulders, forcing her to look up at him. "Are ye already regretting it?" he asked softly, dreading her answer.

Her sad smile worried him even more, but then she barely shook her head and touched his cheek. "No. I do not regret it. But it is a change. A ginormous change. And I have never handled change well."

He wasn't familiar with the word *ginormous*, but he caught the gist of all it encompassed. "I dinna wish ye to change yer mind or regret choosing me over everything ye have ever known." He wiped at a smudge of soot high on her cheek and made it worse with grime from his thumb. "Know that I am aware of yer sacrifice, m'love. Know that I am not only honored but touched beyond words and will spend the rest of my days showing ye."

"I know it," she barely whispered, then patted him on the chest. "Now let me go so I can shed the rest of these smelly layers."

He leaned closer and nibbled at the salty sweetness of her throat. "I could always kiss ye out of them."

A humming purr escaped her as she unbuckled his belt and let it drop. His kilt followed. "As long as we don't get too carried away before we wash. We can't get in bed like this."

"More room on the floor, anyway," he said as he slipped a hand down the front of her chemise and palmed the bountiful fullness of her breast.

"I smell like a smoked ham." She ripped away what was left of his tattered shirt and tossed it aside.

"I love smoked ham." He took hold of her chemise by the neckline, rent it in two, and threw it down.

"Grant!"

"Ye tore mine off—lore a'mighty, lass." The lusciousness of her curves robbed him of the ability to speak. All he could think of, all he could fathom, was sinking into her and never leaving again. Her skin shone like cream, freckled as if the gods had dusted her with sweet spices to lead his gaze from her face to her dusky pink nipples and lower still to the delicate vee of reddish curls at the juncture of her thighs. He wet his lips, starving for the taste of her, but when he reached to pull her close, she shook a finger and backed away.

"We should wash first. You don't want to get soot and mud all over your nice rug, the bed, or any of your cushions, do you? We're filthy."

"I'm filthy with need, woman. I dinna give a rat's arse about the furnishings."

And the way she kept trying to cover herself with her hands and arms as she backed away from him inflamed him even more.

"I can bear this no longer." He closed in on her, backed her to the wall, then lifted her and pinned her against it. With her wrists in one hand above her head, he cupped her fine round arse in the other and set to the task of sampling her wondrous breasts. With the tip of his tongue, he teased a trail around her nipple before suckling it deep and hard. Easily keeping her pinned between him and the wall and keeping her wrists held firmly above her head, he adjusted his cupping of her delectable arse so his fingertips grazed back and forth across the sweet wetness awaiting him between her thighs.

He knew he should take his time and meant to do so—truly, he did. But a greediness took him over. Silently, he swore he would worship her body all the rest of his days as he shifted his hold to her legs and buried himself inside her with a shuddering groan.

"Yes," she hissed through clenched teeth, digging her nails into his shoulders.

"Forgive me, love, but I had to have ye." He drew out, then rammed in again, her wet heat daring him to pound into her until they both were senseless. Another shudder rippled through him as he struggled for control. Heaven help him. He didn't want to spill himself like a lad with his first woman. His precious Jessa would find her pleasure first, or he would die in the trying.

"Give it to me," she ordered, tightening her legs around him. "We'll take our time next time. I'm on the edge. Just push me over it before I die."

Grant had heard the stories about the intensity of the claiming. He'd laughed and dismissed it as a myth or exaggeration on the part of the Defenders, hoping to find their fated mates. This was no feckin' myth or an exaggeration. This was an all-consuming hunger, an insatiable need to hear her delighted cries in harmony with his roars as they reached inexplicable bliss. He pounded harder, rocking into her with the primeval urgency of an ancient being marking his mate as his own.

She screamed and arched against him, her ecstasy clenching around him, pulling him in deeper to join her.

He gladly joined, unleashing a tremendous growl as he buried himself and held fast, exploding with a power that shook through him with even more strength than the tremor of the earth during the earlier attack.

Still pinned between him and the wall, Jessa let her head fall back while gasping to catch her breath. "I have never..."

He kissed the curve of her shoulder and nibbled his way up the side of her neck. "Have never what, m'love?"

Combing her fingers into his hair and guiding his kisses along her neck, she hummed a purring sigh. "No word comes to mind to describe what I just felt."

"Good."

She giggled, making the ripple of her hot wetness encourage his cock to harden again as soon as possible. "Now we smell like microwaved smoked ham."

"What is *microwaved*?"

"Reheated."

He rocked into her, flexing as he quickly recovered and was ready to go again. "I like that word. Reheated."

"Me too," she said, then pulled him in for a slow, deep kiss. When she gently freed him of it, she delighted him with a loving smile. "This is—perfect."

"I am right where I belong, m'love. With ye. Inside ye. Beside ye." He kept his thrusts slow and steady while holding her gaze with his. "Always and forever."

"Always and forever," she repeated softly while closing her eyes.

He increased his pace, moving faster, harder. "Lore a'mighty—I may knock this wall down this time."

She flexed her hands, then dug her fingers into his shoulders again. "Do it, now. I dare you."

He hooked her legs over his arms and pounded, careening them both toward rapture once again. His muscles knotted with the fervor, burning with excitement and expectancy. He hammered harder, melding their bodies into one.

She cried out even louder than the first time, clutching two handfuls of what was left of his singed hair and pulling as she rocked with wave after wave of pleasure.

"Mine!" he bellowed with a last thrust that emptied him. With her legs still hooked over his arms, he locked his knees to keep from collapsing and rested his forehead against the wall above her shoulder. "Griselda is right," he said between gasps to catch his breath.

"About what?" Jessa asked, her voice hoarse from her shouts of delight.

"Ye are a goddess."

She hummed a lazy chuckle, vibrating with amusement. "We really do need to convince her otherwise."

"A problem for another time." He kissed her shoulder, pushed them both away from the wall, then carried her over to the long dresser and set her on it beside the basins. "But for now, I shall wash ye and worship ye for the goddess that ye are."

She leaned back, barely propped herself upright, then cast a glance back over her shoulder. "Grant."

"Aye?" He wet a cloth and rubbed a fresh bar of Mrs. Robeson's best rose petal soap until the suds boiled over his hands. But when he went to lather his lady love, her scowl stopped him. "What is it?"

"This window is open."

"Aye. Fresh air is good for a body."

She narrowed her eyes at him. "There are quite a few people gathered down there. All smiles and staring up at the window."

"Good. That means there must be little damage to the keep, and no one injured."

"It also means they probably heard us. You were loud."

He couldn't resist a grin. "Ye were nay too quiet yourself, m'love."

"You know what I mean."

With a slow, seductive walking of his fingers down her leg, he lifted her foot and started washing her toes. "A clan is most happy when their laird is happy. Would ye deny them that pleasure?" He ran the sudsy cloth up her calf, massaging her fine, thick legs that weren't the spindly sticks of a prim woman afraid to enjoy a stroll through the glen. Nay, Jessa was perfect, and she was his.

"I can't carry on a logical argument when you're doing that." She shifted in place as he rinsed the cloth in the basin and wiped the suds from her silky leg.

"Good. I shall store that for future reference. And now for the other leg." After washing her arms and legs, he changed out the water, dumping the old water into a bucket beside the dresser and filling the basin with fresh. He wet another cloth and ever so gently washed her face, moving in close and standing between her knees to pepper a trail of kisses along her jawline and throat as he washed her. "They say ye can tell when a fair woman has enjoyed her loving by the richness of her blush."

"Then I should be fire engine red." She rested her arms on his shoulders and cradled him, leaning forward and purring like a happy wee beastie as he embraced her and washed her back.

He would try to remember to ask what a fire engine was later. "And now I shall place ye on the bed and wash the best of ye that I saved for last."

"But I haven't washed you yet. You're still all sooty."

"I'll not be getting on the bed with ye, m'love. I intend to worship my goddess fully and then tend to my own washing afterward." He pulled her into his arms, thrilled when she wrapped her legs around his waist and locked her heels at the small of his back. Moving over to the bed, he gently lowered her onto it, placing her crossways of the large, overstuffed tick made up with fresh linens. After fetching the basin and a pitcher of water, he stood there at the side of the bed and stared. "Ye are a goddess, Jessa," he said. "Not just because of yer loveliness but because of the way ye've touched my heart."

She swiped a hand across her eyes as tears overflowed. "You've done the same for me," she whispered, then reached for him. "I don't care about the sheets. Come here."

"Nay, my love. Not until I've worshiped ye as ye deserve." Not that he didn't long to lower himself into her embrace and never rise again—but he wished to do this for her, to worship her.

The brilliance of her red hair was splayed across the bedclothes, and her eyes were even greener with her tears. Her fair skin was flushed with a mouth-watering rosiness that renewed his hunger. With a cloth in each hand, he washed her breasts until they gleamed with a tempting slipperiness. After wiping them clean of suds, he tasted her nipples, laving them with his tongue and treating them to sucking pulls until she squirmed and arched beneath him.

"I'm clean," she said. "Come here."

"Not yet, my precious one." While keeping his gaze locked with hers, he ran the rinsing cloth down between her legs and slowly massaged her, loving how her breath quickened and she bucked into his touch. "I'll not use soap here, for I want to taste yer true essence."

"You are a cruel man, Mr. MacAlester." Her breathlessness fueled his need to give her even more. "You know what I need," she said, fixing him with a look that nearly undid him.

He went to his knees, hooked her legs over his shoulders, and feasted, licking and sucking, until the level of her moans encouraged him to grant her relief with his fingers. He'd promised not to join her in the bed until he washed, and he meant to keep his word—even though it was about to kill him.

"And now I will wash," he said, his voice sounding strained even to him, as he returned to the cabinet and added water to the second basin.

"No," she said from behind him. "Now, I will wash you." She cleaned his face, shoulders, arms, and back, torturing him by trailing her nipples and the warm softness of her lush curves against him while sprinkling kisses across the dampness of his clean skin. When she dropped to her knees and washed his legs, he held his breath and stared straight ahead, knowing she intended to torment him with the same deliciousness that he had tormented her. He groaned and curled his toes as she washed his length, then took it into her mouth while palming his bollocks. The harder she sucked, the tighter he clenched his fists to keep from burying his hands in her hair and using her mouth with abandon.

"I must have ye!" He caught her up, tossed her onto the bed, then covered her with his body. Her wicked smile not only gave him pause, but dared him to take her and make her cries of pleasure echo through the entirety of the keep. "Lore, woman, I will never get enough of ye."

"Good. Now, show me."

He drove into her, determined to prove to the lady that he meant every word.

~

Jessa sat on the wide windowsill, hugging her knees and staring into the darkness. With no light other than the moon and the lone candle on the mantel, she hadn't been able to find any clothes of her own, so she'd settled for one of Grant's shirts she'd come across in the wardrobe. With its sleeves rolled up past her elbows and its length hitting her below the knees, it served the purpose just as well as one of those old-fashioned nightgowns—no, not nightgowns, but shifts. She had to get this century's language straight.

This century. She nearly choked on that. Here she was, barely twenty-four hours into the eighteenth century and already married and more perfectly *consummated* than she had ever been in her life, and without the protection of a condom or any other means of birth control. Allowing herself a dismal sigh, she tried to calculate exactly where she was in her cycle. Raised as a *go-to-church-on-Christmas-and-Easter-only* Catholic, she had a vague understanding of the rhythm method but understood quite clearly its unreliability. That's just what she needed. To get pregnant immediately in a time when giving birth was as dangerous as playing with an armed hand grenade, maybe even more so.

A low, mumbling groan from the bed pulled her from her muddled thoughts. She glanced over at the shadowy form of the massive Highlander sprawled across the tangled sheets. Damn, she loved him even though she didn't understand how it could be possible to love someone this hard after just a day.

Fated mates, several had said. According to Mairwen, the mates met, joined, and loved each other in every incarnation. Maybe that was why love had happened so hard and fast. Their souls had recognized one another, known each other throughout eternity. She'd also said that those who didn't find each other in any particular incarnation were doomed to a lifetime of feeling as though something was missing.

She chewed on her bottom lip as her inner demons pelted her with insecurities. Was this new love strong enough to endure the eighteenth century? Was it strong enough to last through all that this era threatened? What if Morrigan returned? Better yet, what the hell *was* Morrigan? Would that thing eventually go after Emily, too?

"Jessa?" His voice rasped with an endearingly soft sleepiness, calling to her on an unfathomable level. It was as though her heart heard him before her ears did.

"Over here," she said, wishing he had stayed asleep. She couldn't even make sense to herself. How could she make sense to him?

"Come back to bed, love. I miss ye."

Propping her chin on her arms, she turned her attention back to the dark, velvety blue of the night sky. "I'll be there in a minute. Try to go back to sleep. You said you needed to catch up, remember?"

The bedclothes rustled, making her close her eyes and listen for his feet thudding on the floor. A moment later, he gently touched her shoulder. "Dinna leave, Jessa," he said with a quiet earnestness. "Please."

She turned to deny that she would do such a thing, but the words caught in her throat. Even though she had not admitted it to herself, he had said exactly what she was subconsciously considering. Her heart shifted with a decisive thump. No matter what century she found herself in, she couldn't survive without him. "I won't leave, but I also won't promise that I'll be easy to live with while I try to adjust to this time in history."

He gave her a lopsided grin. "And ye think I shall be easy to live with?"

She returned his grin. "Probably not."

"Yer Emily is still here." He moved through the room, his body a large, shimmering ghostliness in the moonlight. The deep, hollow pop of a cork told her he'd gone to the table for wine. "While ye slept, I slipped out and discovered Sawny at his post in the hallway. He said Mairwen promised they wouldna leave until ye had time to settle things with Mistress Emily."

While she found that somewhat reassuring, she also wondered about the *servant at his post* comment. "And where exactly is Sawny's post?"

"Mrs. Robeson has him sleep beside our bedchamber door in case we need anything with haste."

"That is terrible." Not only because the boy would overhear everything, but also because it couldn't be comfortable on the floor. "You need to tell Mrs. Robeson not to do that to that poor kid."

He shook his head as he offered her a glass of wine. "She'll not listen. Mrs. Robeson does as she pleases."

"She's the housekeeper, right?" Jessa tried a small sip of the wine and decided it was bearable.

"Aye."

"And you're the laird, right?"

He blew out a huffing sigh. "Aye."

"You see where I'm going here?"

"I see I shall be speaking with Mrs. Robeson about Sawny ever sleeping in the hallway again."

"Not only is it creepy, it's not fair to Sawny." Jessa took a deeper sip, then set the glass aside. "Was there not any drinking water left in the pitcher?"

"Water is water, lass. It all comes from the wellhouse."

"Right." She hugged her knees tighter and rested her head on her arms.

A moment later, he nudged her. "Yer water, m'lady. Shall I tell Sawny to fetch ye some coffee?"

"Is he still out there?"

"Aye, the lad knows better than to cross Mrs. Robeson."

Jessa rolled her eyes and made a mental note to have a word with the well-meaning housekeeper. She accepted the glass of water. "Thank you. And no, don't bother anyone about coffee. I'm sure they need their rest after the attack."

"No one was injured. Henry confirmed it. The only damage was minor between the west watchtower and the skirting wall. The MacAlester ancestors built this keep to last." He dragged a chair over and poured his nakedness into it with the self-assuredness of an elite cover model who commanded nothing less than seven figures per photo shoot.

"Were you naked when you walked out of here?" She had to ask, since he seemed so comfortable in his bare state.

He snorted. "I covered m'self, wife. I am not a beast." Then he suggestively waggled a brow. "Unless ye wish me to be?"

She couldn't believe she was saying this, but she made a *T* sign with her hands. "Time out for a little while. My mind goes into overdrive late at night, and I have to sort through things, or I have nightmares—no matter how wonderfully exhausted you make me."

"Overdrive?" he repeated carefully.

"I have a whole bunch of thoughts and worries all at once, and they tangle up in knots until I work them out and shut them away in their neat little boxes."

"I see."

He didn't, but she didn't expect him to, not when she didn't fully understand it about herself. Emily's psychiatrist mother had told her it was from childhood trauma. Spending her first eight years of life in a household where her drug-addict mother ran through men like water ran through a sieve had scarred her. Her nightly thought sorting was a coping mechanism she had never quite learned how to let go of, even after years of free therapy from Emily's mom.

"What's happening in Scotland in 1785? Current events?" she asked to change the subject.

"Happening?"

She nodded. "I don't remember my history classes as well as I should, considering how much that degree cost me in student loans." Now, there was a silver lining to time travel. She was now debt free. "I remember a war where England did unspeakable things to Scotland."

Grant's expression hardened. "The last Jacobite uprising in '45. Bonnie Prince Charlie failed."

"So that was forty years ago." She rubbed her forehead, wishing that would help her remember. "The Clearances. I remember a little bit about the Clearances because I had to do a paper on how so many lost their land. That's when hordes of Scots emigrated to the United States, Canada, Australia, and New Zealand to survive. That happens soon. Entire clans were forcibly removed from the Highlands and the surrounding islands so greedy landlords could make more money off sheep and whatever other commerce." A shudder of dread rippled across her. Holy crap—what if Clan MacAlester lost its land? "That's not going to happen to us, is it?"

"I am the Earl of Suddie. The landlord of these lands." His voice had become a low, rumbling growl, and his hands tightened into fists. "As long as I pay our taxes, we are safe. What else do ye know of what is coming?"

"About Scotland's history? Nothing, I'm afraid. I only remembered the part about the Clearances because if I didn't do well on that paper, I would've failed the class." She hated that she knew nothing more. History no longer seemed a bunch of dry, meaningless names and dates that needed to be memorized to pass a course. It was people. People who loved, laughed, and died. People who suffered and fought to survive. "I'm sorry." She felt as if she had failed him.

He pushed up from the chair and held out his hand. "Do not apologize, my love. Together, we will conquer whatever is ahead. I swear it. Now, come to bed. I need to hold ye."

She slid her hand into his, very much needing that too. Once safely nestled in the crook of his arm, her head pillowed in the dip of his shoulder, a calmness filled her, a sense that somehow, everything would be all right. What a strange sensation, but she gladly accepted it and held on tight. She would worry about tomorrow's problems tomorrow. Not a usual course of action for her, but during this great upheaval in her life, maybe it was time to make some changes for the better.

CHAPTER 14

"So, you're positive this is what you want to do? You are sure?" Jessa snorted as they climbed through the split in the skirting wall—a disturbing reminder of Morrigan's visit. Emily knew her far too well. "When have I ever been positive about anything? You know I am always the one foot in, one foot out sort. Your mom always blamed it on childhood trauma, but I think it's because it never fails, once I commit to one thing, something better comes along."

Emily wrapped an arm around her and gave her an affectionate shake. "But there's a difference about you now, Jess. I can't remember ever seeing you this...this..."

"This...what?" All sorts of varying adjectives sprang to mind, but Jessa couldn't wait to hear which ones Emily chose.

Emily shrugged. "It's hard to explain. For lack of a better word, you're not as *twitchy* as usual. And I mean that in a good way."

And Jessa took it in a good way because she understood exactly what her friend meant. "I'm connected to Grant. A connection I never dreamed could exist." The warm contentment that had taken up residence within her, always simmering just below the surface, rippled with her acknowledgment of it and sent a stronger surge through her. "I love him, Em. It's as if I've known him forever. I love him so much it's scary. The only thing I'm still *twitchy* about is taking up residence in this time." She held onto the front of her stays and fished deep into her cleavage for the square of linen that would have a hard time holding up to the onslaught of tears the upcoming separation from her friend was sure to trigger, no matter how stoic and dry-eyed she was determined to be. "Well, that's not the only thing I'm twitchy about. I'm twitchy about losing my best friend, my real sister, and the only genuine family I've ever had."

"Mairwen thinks the goddesses will allow us to visit at Seven Cairns," Emily said. "From what I understand about all this mystical stuff so far, it's sort of a way station for all the eras of time and what we used to consider the mythical planes that the Highland Veil keeps in place." Emily hugged her again. "But when I asked her if Mama, Papa, and the fearsome five could visit…"

The heaviness of the silence between them as they walked through the tangled grass spoke volumes.

"I take it she said no?" Jessa wondered if Emily realized that meant she would eventually lose her family, too. After all, Mairwen had said Emily had a fated mate waiting somewhere or *sometime* for her."

"And yeah, I know what that means," Emily whispered. "I can't even begin to wrap my head around never seeing them again." She attempted a cocky wink, but her voice faltered. "But you know me. I always find a way around the rules I don't like. We'll see them again. Just you wait and see."

Now it was Jessa's turn to hold tightly to Emily. For all her friend's fussing about how her parents and brothers meddled in her life, Jessa knew Emily would be lost without her close-knit family. Maybe it was better to change the subject. "I wonder why everyone doesn't get a fated mate? Or is it that Mairwen and her army of matchmakers just don't have the manpower to snap that many souls back together?"

"I asked her about that," Emily said as they meandered over to the cliff's edge and seated themselves on the bench overlooking the sea. "It took her a while to come to the point and admit that it is exactly that."

"Exactly what?"

"The auld ways are dying. When people stop believing, that which they no longer believe in ceases to exist. Scotland and the Highland Veil are one of the last strongholds because superstition is alive and well in this part of the world. Mairwen says there used to be several veils located all over the earth—but not any longer, and when those veils fell, the dark forces destroyed the Defenders and Weavers of those veils. Why do you think there's already so much chaos and suffering in the world?" Emily bumped shoulders with her. "That is why you have to believe with all your heart and soul that you belong here, belong with Grant. Any doubt about any of it gives the dark ones a dangerous toehold."

A pair of terns, white as fluttering ribbons, floated on the updrafts above the churning, frothy waters below. Their shrill keening as they circled in their gracefully spinning flight joined the symphony of the waves crashing against the base of the cliff, the shush of the wind rustling the tall clusters of grasses, and the faint noises of cleanup from the keep behind them. Jessa smiled at the peacefulness of the eighteenth century's natural music.

Sitting in companionable silence, she mulled over what Emily had said. "I know I belong with Grant," she said almost more to herself than to Emily. "It's the *when* of it I'm none too sure about. This isn't exactly the safest place for a digital creator and wannabe engineer. Everything I say makes them look at me as if they're sizing me up for the stake and bonfire it would take to roast me." And she was only partially joking. Grant's clan had been more than kind and welcoming, but ever since she had healed him and with Griselda crowning her as one of the divine, everyone treated her differently. They were afraid of her. She could see it in their eyes, hear it in their voices, and sense it by the way they immediately went quiet whenever she walked into a room.

"You have to commit," Emily said. "One way or the other. All in or all out. If you don't…"

"I know." A chill raced across Jessa, making her rub her arms and look up for any sign of the sun. "It's clouding up again. I guess we need to get back inside the safety of the walls. Clouds make me nervous now."

"Not a good thing, considering how often it rains in Scotland."

"No kidding."

A sudden rise in the wind gusted against them, strong and hard, shoving with amazing force, as if trying to push them over the edge of the cliff. Jessa stumbled, her feet tangled in her skirts and the long grass matted into knobby piles of treacherous hillocks.

Emily grabbed her by the arm, half dragging her to regain her footing. "I don't like this," Emily shouted, bowing against the gale as they fought to return to the keep.

"Go ahead!" Jessa told her. An eerie tingling at the base of her skull warned this was no natural storm kicking up without warning. "You are a tall target for the wind. Stay low and scuttle fast. I'll be right behind you." She dropped to all fours, waving Emily onward, knowing if she told her what was really going on, Emily would stay. This *felt* the same as before. Apparently, the Morrigan, whatever it was, did not give up easily.

Bent double by the wind, Emily squinted at her, eyeing her for a long moment that told Jessa her friend knew exactly what was happening. But Emily needed to go. Jessa couldn't bear it if anything happened to her. She pointed at the keep. "Go! Warn the others! I'll be fine. I can hold on until you return with Mairwen."

Squinting against the gale, Emily's dark eyes flashed as she bared her teeth. "Don't you dare die on me!" she shouted. "I'll be back with reinforcements!"

Jessa nodded and waved her onward. "Go!"

And then the ground beneath her fell away, and everything went dark.

~

Jessa opened her eyes. Or, at least, they felt like they were open. Nothing but blackness filled her vision. Panic surged through her hard and fast, making her blink rapidly. Maybe she had somehow been blinded by a blow to the head or something, or the collapse of the cliff had stolen her eyesight. *Stop it,* she silently ordered. Spiraling out of control helped nothing. She needed to calm down and think, not give in to hysteria. It was just dark wherever this was. Dark as the inside of a freaking cow. Or like she was buried alive. *Great.* Because that possibility was so much better than being blinded—right? But it could be true. After all, the ground had fallen away when the cliff had separated and slid into the sea. She sucked in a deep breath to convince herself she had enough air. Damp, cool, and maybe a little earthy, wherever this was smelled like the potting soil she had helped Mrs. Garducci add to her windowsill garden. Maybe this was some kind of air pocket created by the landslide. That made her swallow hard and press a hand to her pounding heart.

Must. Not. Panic. She needed to see if she was hurt, then figure a way out of here. She tried to inventory all her parts without moving too much in case she was injured or maybe even perched on a narrow ledge in this strange pit of despair. That gave her pause. *Pit of despair?* Where had that come from? She didn't usually *talk* like that —not even to herself. Mairwen must be rubbing off on her.

The silence of the darkness deafened her. She couldn't even hear her own breathing or the beating of her heart. She could feel it hammering in her chest, but couldn't hear it. At least, she thought she felt it. She tried to find a pulse at her wrist and, failing that, tried to confirm life by feeling for her jugular. She clamped her hand to her chest again. The pounding was gone. Had she died? Was this death?

"Ye are not dead. Yet," a powerful voice, a woman's voice, told her.

"Where is this, and who are you?" Jessa flinched at the quiver in her voice. Something deep inside, an old childhood instinct she had never left behind, told her now was not the time to reveal any weakness. No answer came from the disembodied voice. Just more suffocating silence. "Are you Morrigan?" she hazarded to ask.

"I am."

Jessa pushed herself up to a sitting position and squinted all around, trying to make out anything in the darkness. It was impossible. Never had she been in a place so lacking in any light whatsoever. She reached down and felt the surrounding ground. Where she sat was stone. Damp, hard, and kind of crumbly. Like shale, maybe? She reached to the left and discovered a wall that was more of the same but less crumbly. To the right was a nothingness that could be anything. Unknown nothingness lurked behind her and in front of her as well. But there was that wall to the left, a solid wall. Safety. Maybe this was the back of a cave of some sort.

Pit of despair whispered its way through her thoughts again. *Stop it,* she told herself again.

"I really do love Grant," she announced, proud that her voice was loud and strong this time, the words echoing over and over like a war chant across the pit. "We are connected, he and I. Our souls reunited. You are too late."

"Am I?"

Jessa gritted her teeth, biting back a frustrated and borderline hysterical growl. Apparently, this Morrigan demon enjoyed mind games. "This is extremely boring," Jessa taunted. Maybe she could goad the *thing* into saying more. "At least before, there was some excitement in your attack. What do you want? What are you trying to prove here?"

Thunder rumbled through the darkness, and the distinct sound of shifting earth, maybe rocks tumbling down the wall, followed in its wake. "I am war, sovereignty, and prophecy. I have to prove nothing. Death and Fate do as I bid them." In the distance, so very far away that Jessa barely heard it, came a cacophony of guttural croaking, the chatty cawing of ravens or crows, definitely large birds. They sounded like a choir, giving the Morrigan a hearty *amen*.

What a drama queen. Anger leveled out Jessa's adrenaline fueled panic, and she welcomed the shift in power within her, the settling, the strength. She shoved herself to her feet while keeping her hand on the wall to her left. Who knew what awaited her in the darkness? Caves had bottomless cracks and fissures, didn't they?

"What do you want?" she asked again, determined to sound as powerful as possible. A personal trainer had once told her that fifty percent of success was bravado. The other fifty was believing in yourself. Time to lock into that mindset for real. "What do you want, Morrigan?" she repeated.

"Many things. As do you."

"What I want right now is some light, so I can see what I am dealing with here."

"Are you certain about that?"

Squaring her shoulders, Jessa braced herself while fighting off the ancient childhood memory of being locked inside the dark, stuffy bathroom cabinet for hours on end while her mother *entertained*. "I am positive."

The surrounding darkness softened to a dismal gray that sifted down like a strange waterfall of colorless dreariness. But at least she could see now. The wall to her left was black slate or maybe coal. It was scarred with chisel marks and scratches, as if some ancient being had either mined for whatever mineral it was or tried to claw its way to freedom. The narrow ledge on which she stood was the same material. It was about four feet wide, seemed to run on forever in front of her and behind her, but disappeared into an eerie black nothingness to the right.

"I recommend keeping to the left," said the tall figure cloaked in black that stood in the center of the path several yards ahead of her. "At least, for now."

Jessa blinked and opened her mouth to speak, but the being shapeshifted into a swelling column of large black birds that swirled upward like a building storm, then exploded outward. With her hand still on the wall, she crouched, cowering from the ominous fowl with their snapping beaks and eyes that flashed with an unholy light. They circled overhead, occasionally dipping low to snatch at her hair with their gleaming black talons.

If she got out of this alive, she would never own a birdfeeder or birdbath again. Birds could fend for themselves.

"I thought you liked animals," one of them cackled and screeched as it came at her.

She ducked and tried to knock it away. "You're not an animal. You're a nightmare of unexplainable weirdness."

The relentless army of birds evaporated into ribbons of black smoke rising through the grayness in narrow, curling tendrils.

Jessa exhaled and slumped back against the wall. She could hear her heart pounding now. But then, a subtle clicking drew her attention back to the path.

A silver wolf of unbelievably large proportions ambled toward her, baring its dripping fangs and growling, "I am not unexplainable."

Backed against the wall, Jessa locked her legs to keep from slumping to the ground. She had to fight. Make a show of bravado. She refused to leave this world without a fight. She had survived too much to turn soft now. "If you're not unexplainable, explain yourself. As you've probably figured out by now, I'm not exactly an expert when it comes to this business of the Highland Veil, the Defenders, or fated mates." She resettled her footing, wishing some of the loose rocks around her were big enough to be worth throwing. "And when you're finished educating me, tell me what the hell you want."

The horrendous beast tipped its head to one side and flicked an ear. Its long red tongue lolled out of its mouth as it cracked a hideous grin. It lifted its muzzle, its gleaming black nostrils twitching. "The air reeks with yer fear."

"I never said I wasn't afraid. I asked, 'What the hell do you want?'" Jessa wished she had her pepper spray. Dark being or not, she doubted that Morrigan the wolf would like a snoot full of cayenne and jalapeño.

"Retribution," said the animal in a rumbling growl.

"What did I ever do to you?" Maybe if she could keep the thing talking, Grant, Mairwen, and Emily would rescue her. "Grant is my fated mate. He will come for me, and you know it." Jessa knew it, too. She felt it in her heart, and that feeling strengthened her.

The wolf snapped, baring its long, lethal fangs. "Ye will be my weapon to destroy the Veil."

"I will not."

"Ye care not for it. Dinna even believe in it. All ye care about is the time ye came from and that friend ye left behind."

Jessa swallowed hard. Sweat peppered across her forehead, burning as it trickled into her eyes. "If I didn't believe in it, I wouldn't still be here. Mairwen gave me the chance to go back and forget about everything. I stayed with Grant."

"Aye, but ye're still not certain, are ye?" The wolf reared up on its hind legs and took the form of a haggard old woman wearing a ragged cloak of black feathers. She pointed at Jessa with a crooked finger, knobby and bent with age. "Ye didna go back because of yer lust for him. That does not mean ye believe. Ye dinna feel the truth of the ways in yer heart."

"Just because I have never been the decisive sort does not mean I don't believe." Jessa angled her chin higher. "It just means I like to keep my options open. Can you honestly say you've never done that?" Her fosters had always hated how she would argue with them and try to turn the tables. Maybe that technique would buy her some time. At the very least, it should irritate whatever this thing was that couldn't decide what form it wanted to take. She pointed at the crone. "Just look at you. When you first appeared, you were some kind of shadow figure, like the Grim Reaper or something. Then you changed into a flock of buzzards, a wolf, and now an old hag. You can't even settle on what you want to be, and yet you criticize me, saying that just because I can't make up my mind, I don't believe."

"They were ravens, ye insolent wee chit! Not buzzards. And I am the Morrigan. The Phantom Queen. Goddess of War and Fate, and when I bring down the Highland Veil, all will bow to me. Even Mairwen, with whom I shall finally have my full revenge." The old one threw back her grizzled head and laughed. "She has no idea how I intend to use him."

"How you intend to use who? Grant?" Jessa strode forward. The only fear she possessed now was fear for Grant's safety. "You stay away from him."

The old one laughed. "Or what?"

"Or I will become a royal pain in your nonexistent ass."

The hag shooed away the threat as if it were an annoying fly. "Ye have no idea of what ye speak. One as weak as yerself would stand no chance against me."

"When people stop believing in something, that which they once believed in ceases to exist. Is that not true?"

Iron bars shot up from the path in a circle around her just as a large black slab fell from above and landed atop them with a deafening clang. Balled up on the floor, her eyes shut and ears covered, Jessa braced to be crushed. After a long, terrifying moment of expecting to die, nothing happened. She opened her eyes, and once again, all she could see was impenetrable darkness. Gingerly patting the floor, she felt around to find the wall but couldn't reach it. The iron cage, her tiny prison, had her corralled in the center of the path.

Holding tight to the bars, she tried to shift them, even tried to squeeze through them, then gave up. If she somehow escaped, where would she go? "Anywhere but here," she told the darkness. She slid to the ground and hugged herself against the ever-increasing chill creeping into her bones. Maybe the eighteenth century wasn't so frightening after all. It had to be safer than being trapped in the darkness, in a cage, in some evil goddess's playroom.

"If you're still here, you just proved I'm right," she taunted. "You know it's really easy to get people to believe in something new and chalk their old beliefs up to myths and legends—fairytales to tell their children. Nothing more than pretend stories that are totally and completely powerless."

A wave of icy water slammed into her, choking her with its force and knocking her hard against the iron bars. The briny deluge burned her eyes and her lungs. She coughed and wheezed to get air. Hanging on to the bars, she dragged herself back to her feet and braced herself, waiting for another soaking, but it never came. She almost laughed as she coughed and spat more water. Damn, she'd hit a nerve that time. She had also discovered the Morrigan's greatest fear: to be forgotten and cease to exist.

∽

GRANT SHOVED another pistol into his belt, then added two more daggers to each of his boots. He would strap on every weapon in the keep, if need be, to get his precious Jessa back.

"Those will do ye no good against the dark one," Mairwen said from behind him.

"Aye, well, having them makes me feel a damn sight better prepared." He should never have allowed Jessa to go beyond the wall. Why the hell hadn't he told her to stay within the safety of the keep? Why the hell hadn't he kept her at his side?

"The Morrigan would have stolen her no matter where she roamed," Mairwen told him, as if he had spoken his misgivings aloud. "She seems to fear yer match more than she has feared the others. Yer binding oath should have sent her on her way. I dinna understand it."

"Stay the feckin' hell out of my mind, witch!" He advanced on the old woman, pointing at her with his blade. "I canna live without my

Jessa. If anything happens to her, know that I will come for ye first. Ye will be the last life I take afore I take my own, so I can join my precious love."

Mairwen backed up a step, seeming more fragile than usual. Almost human. Her regret and worry were impossible to miss. "We will get her back. The Defenders and Weavers await yer orders." She went to the door but stopped, looked back, and locked eyes with him. "But ye should know, ye may be the only one able to save her."

"As it should be." He trusted no one else with his precious lady love. "Keep them the hell out of my way." He lashed short swords under each arm rather than the usual wearing of the one sheathed under his left. As he turned, Lachie and Henry stepped into the room. "Report?"

Henry nodded. "The *cleugh* echoed with the cries of birds for a while. Sounded like a battlefield when ravens come to feast upon the dead. The blackness of the cracked earth lightened for a bit, but the mist never fully cleared to enable us to see more than a wee bit. Then it went dark again and growled like thunder."

"Take heart with this news," Lachie said. "It means she has not given up. She is fighting the evil."

"I take heart in nothing. None of this should have ever happened to her." Grant passed between them and exited the weaponry hold, unquenchable rage coursing through him. The closer he drew to the part of the cliff that had turned into an unholy, gaping maw to the earth's bowels, the hotter his fury boiled.

The oldest of his MacAlester kin still walking this earth sometimes whispered that Grant possessed berserker blood, reminding anyone who would listen about the elite warriors from his father's ancient line. For the first time in a long while, he hoped the whisperings of his ancestry were true. He could use a touch of invulnerable savagery today.

As he trod toward the strange ravine that was more like a crack between this reality and the next, a call went up from the watchtowers, announcing the approach of more Defenders on horseback.

Word had spread fast. He had Henry and Lachie to thank for that. But he would just as soon do this himself. The Morrigan needed to learn once and for all that he was not the one she should toy with.

Emily stood at the edge of the abyss, peering down into it, her cheeks wet with tears.

"Move back, lass. Take safety within the walls of the keep. My Jessa would never forgive me if the dark one hurt ye."

"I never should have convinced her to come to Scotland. We should've ignored that fucking app!"

He understood the woman's pain. Her regret. But she couldn't blame herself for anything that had happened. "The Weavers would have still found a way to coax ye into coming here. Trust me. I know their relentlessness firsthand." When she didn't answer, he sidled closer and leaned in to force her to look him in the eyes. "This is not yer fault, Emily, and Jessa would be the first to tell ye that."

She made a hard nod at the swirling darkness below. "What are you going to do? How are you going to save her when you don't even know what's down in there? Where she might be? Or, God forbid, if she is even—"

He caught her by the arm and jerked her around to fully face him. "Ye will not say it! My Jessa is alive, and I will find her." He gently shook her, baring his teeth. "Ye must believe. Has Mairwen taught ye nothing? *Belief* is often the strongest weaponry we mere mortals possess. When we believe, we see it in our minds, and it becomes so. Hold her in yer mind. See her healthy. Laughing. Happy. See her back among us. Do ye ken what I am saying?"

She flinched as though losing the battle with her own demons. "I'll try," she said in a hitching whisper. "I'm just…afraid."

He couldn't allay her fears, nor did he have the time or the inclination to try. His spirit burned to save Jessa. "Go back to the keep or join Mairwen and those from Seven Cairns. I canna bear to delay any longer."

"Save her." After a hard squeeze of his arm, she caught up her skirts and ran back to the keep.

Lachie joined him at the edge of the eerie pit. "Orders?"

Grant tossed a hard look back at the keep. "If I dinna survive, take care of them, aye?"

The brawny Highlander agreed with a single nod. "How long afore we join ye in the abyss? I assume ye wish to go alone at first."

"Dinna follow at all. That could be her plot. Destroy the Defenders and Weavers both to clear a path to the Veil. And if I canna save my Jessa—no one can. I feel it to the marrow of my bones. Even the old witch hinted at such."

Lachie stared at him long and hard, then thumped his fist to his chest in their age-old salute. "God be with ye, brother."

"If I dinna see ye again in this life, I shall look for ye in the next."

With another curt nod, Lachie turned and strode away, but Grant felt better for the conversation. Brothers-in-arms didn't need words when the time to battle came.

Grant moved to the edge of the dark, gaping seam and squinted down into it while flexing his fingers. The swirling blackness revealed nothing, not even any sounds. He lowered himself to the edge and dangled his legs off into it, thumping with his heels to test the earthen wall behind his calves. But it wasn't earthen—it was solid stone. He reached down and felt it. It was slick and cold, like the finest marble. To use a rope to lower himself into the unknown didn't sit right with his gut. There was just something wrong about that. He envisioned the Morrigan swatting at him like a cat toying with a mouse on a string. The sly shapeshifter loved her wicked games. To jump could mean certain death, but somehow, he found that choice more appealing. But the longer he ran his fingers along the refined smoothness of the wall behind his calves, the more he was certain. This was a riddle, and the vile harpy had purposely done it that way. This was a test.

He tore off a chunk of earth from the uppermost portion of the edge and stared at it there in his palm. A rocky mix held together by roots, and yet the wall behind his heels was nothing like that. If anything, it felt made by man rather than nature. Holding the dirt in one hand, he felt the edge with the other, digging his fingers into the softness of the loamy soil the seaside grasses loved. That soft, pebbly earth wasn't even as deep as his longest finger. The gods had slathered but a thin layer of the natural covering atop their walled pit of marble. On a whim, he let the handful of dirt and pebbles dribble through his fingers into the darkness just past the edge. The clear clicking of the wee rocks as they bounced not too far below surprised him. The dark mist hid a level closer to the surface.

Unsheathing his sword, he rolled to his stomach and reached down into the unseen with the overly long blade that had been forged to fit his height. The tip struck something solid, not too far down, about the distance from his heel to his hip. Concentrating on the sound, he tapped the blade as far out as he could stretch his arm, discovering the length of whatever it was to be about as wide as he was from shoulder to shoulder. He brought his arm back and tapped his blade parallel to the marble wall.

"It's a feckin' step." Either that or a ledge. Whatever the devil it was, it got him that much closer to Jessa. He sheathed his sword, drew two daggers, then rolled to his belly again and stabbed them into the ground. They wouldn't be much of a handhold in the shallow soil as he lowered himself over the edge, but they would be something in case he needed to dig his way back up.

As soon as his toes hit the ledge, he eased down into the darkness and sat, feeling for what he prayed was another step below that one. Could he be so fortunate as to have found a stairway into the depths of this inky hell? His boots thunked solidly on the next step down. Hope flared strong and sure. He was another step closer.

It might not be manly to hug the wall to his right and feel his way downward with his feet while he slid on his arse across the steps, but it was safe, and if he was safe, he was whole and could fight for his precious Jessa.

The deeper he descended, the colder it became. Morrigan's hell lacked warmth, and that nay surprised him. A low, hollow sound filled the void, the wind moaning as it rushed through the unholy space. The steady crash of waves came to him, gnawing at him with a new, worrisome fear. What if the briny deep had swallowed his sweet Jessa?

He bowed his head and shook away the terrible thought. "No," he told the darkness. "She lives. I know it."

"Are ye certain of that, warrior?" a voice of pure evil quietly asked.

CHAPTER 15

"She lives," Grant said, pouring all his rage into the darkness. "Show yerself, coward." He scooted down the steps faster. He had to reach Jessa. Had to find her. Now.

"Coward?" A low, deep chuckle made the suffocating darkness ripple across his flesh. "And why would ye think me a coward, foolish mortal?"

"Because ye dinna fight me face to face. Ye hide yerself in storms or blinding mists, shielding the truth and making it look a lie."

"That is not cowardice, warrior, but good battle strategy, ye ken?"

The wind changed, hitting him full in the chest and shoving him back. The crash of waves sounded closer now, and he instinctively knew he had reached the last step. His boot tip confirmed there was not a next one. He stood and unsheathed his sword but remained in place. There was no way to know if the solidity of the ground ran throughout or if he stood on a small landing amid dangerous nothingness.

"Ye are too late, ye ken?" The void repeated the goddess's words over and over in a taunting echo. The wind caught hold of them and swirled them around him in an icy caress.

He would not show fear. Instinct told him the wicked one fed on the fears of mortals. "Have ye grown so lazy and vain as to think I would accept whatever ye said without question?" he asked, shouting the words up into the darkness. He snorted with forced laughter that he hoped would enrage the goddess even more than his words. "Ye are nothing to me. I know my loved one lives."

The ground beneath his feet trembled. Deafening thunder made him squint against the harshness of the sound. "I am the Morrigan," the thunder said, "the Phantom Queen. Goddess of War and Fate."

"Aye, well, the only war I fight at the moment is keeping my clan fed with the spoils from my smuggling, and my fate is to see them thrive. Ye will have to pardon me for being less than impressed with yer title, Yer Majesty. As far as I am concerned, ye are an old myth, a legend better off forgotten." As he talked, he slid the tip of his sword back and forth in front of him, carefully guiding his steps and ensuring he remained on solid ground. Jessa was near. And she lived. He *felt* her.

"I could take yer soul to the other side at this verra moment, Defender, and there would be nothing ye could do about it."

He laughed again. "Ye are slipping, old one. I am nay a Defender nor a warrior. I am a smuggler. A laird. A feckin' earl. And a man blessed to be husband to the most precious woman who ever graced the face of this world or any other."

Thunder crashed again, almost shaking his footing. "Ye are a Defender! Ye have helped them and aided the Weavers, as well. I have witnessed it myself."

"Henry and Lachie are my kin. Members of my clan. Why would I not help them if they are in need?" He bared his forearms and extended them even though the inky blackness prevailed. He knew the Morrigan could see him as if the hell were lit as brightly as a sunny day. "I dinna bear the mark of a Defender not only because I have never taken the oath, but because I dinna plan to."

"Ye lie."

"When necessary, but not at the moment." He resumed his slow, forward progress, then halted, and strained to locate the slightest sound the wind had carried to him—a soft, whispery moan, like the faint cooing of an injured dove. *Call to me, my love*, he silently pleaded. *Reach out to me again.*

"Do ye deny ye help those of Seven Cairns?" A hint of desperation, a tinge of frustration filled the darkness, somehow making the cloyingness of it ebb and flow like the tide.

Grant smiled. The Morrigan was questioning her actions, wondering if all this was worth the effort. From what he knew of the immortals and their ways, this slice of hell she had manifested had to require a great deal of energy for her to maintain on this particular side of the Veil. Perhaps she had finally realized this might not benefit her nearly as much as she had hoped.

"I dinna help them," he told her. "I sell them goods, as any good smuggler would." Now, that was somewhat of a lie. More often than not, he offered Mairwen tea, wine, and spices, so she and her Weavers would leave him the hell alone. But it was still a business arrangement. It wasn't like he offered supplies and expected nothing in return.

The vile one didn't respond, and neither did the darkness. The feel of it had reflected the Morrigan's emotions up to this point, but now? Nothing. And that concerned him no small amount. Something was building. It was her turn in this horrible game, and he had no doubt she would take it.

Something shifted not too far in front of him. He resettled his grip on his sword, torn between sheathing it and falling to all fours to crawl faster and search for Jessa or maintain battle readiness. The raw urgency to save his lady love pounded through him ever harder.

A weak cough broke the silence.

That decided him. He sheathed his sword, dropped to his belly, and scrambled along the rocky ledge, feeling with his forearms. This was most definitely a ledge. If he veered too far to the left, he would help no one, and he doubted they would ever find his body in that abyss. To his right was another wall, but it was layers of stone, shale that flaked and crumbled at the merest touch, unlike the wall of polished marble beside the steps. "Jessa—find the strength to make another sound so I can find ye. Try, my love, I beg ye."

No sound came. The silence knifed through him, twisting in his gut. He belly crawled faster, writhing through the darkness like a mighty snake.

"Jessa!" he called out. "I am coming, my love. Hold fast."

"Please be real," said the sweetest voice he had feared he would never hear again. "Please."

He hit the metal bars and reached through them, patting around in the darkness. "Jessa! I am here. Where are ye in this damnable pen?" His fingertips brushed cloth, soaking wet and almost frozen stiff, but cloth just the same. He stretched as far as the bars allowed, jamming his arm between them up to his shoulder. "Jessa—lore a'mighty. Can ye move at all or are ye frozen to that spot?"

A featherlight touch ran across the back of his hand. "Grant? Is it really you, or is this just another cruel trick?"

He caught hold of her fingers and squeezed. "I am here, love. It is truly me." The iciness of her flesh filled him with a fear the likes of which he had never known. He could not lose his Jessa. Never would he allow that.

An eerie glow, soft and golden, enveloped their hands, barely beating back the darkness.

"I knew you would come," she whispered and gave his hand a weak squeeze. "I knew you wouldn't let me die alone."

Her words jarred him. "I will nay let ye die at all, wife. Daren't ye speak of such again."

"I am so glad you came," she said so quietly that he strained to hear her. She sounded finished, resigned to her fate.

"Jessa! Move closer so I can lend ye some warmth." When she didn't answer, and the golden glow around their hands seemed to dim, he yanked on her, trying to shake her. "Jessa! Move this way. Now."

"I am so tired. Can we not just rest for a minute? I know I'm safe now that you're here, and I am so very tired."

"No. Ye must stay awake. Swear ye will."

"I will try."

The raspy weakness of her reply spurred him to his feet. Holding onto the bars, he tried to make his way around the cage in search of a gate and almost lost his footing. The unholy thing was perched too close to the abyss. He went back the other way, but the space between it and the wall was too narrow. He daren't attempt to squeeze through. Feckin' Morrigan would probably release the cage so that he would shove it off into the darkness and be responsible for his dear one's death. The roof of the enclosure felt like the same crumbly limestone as the wall. If he attempted to hoist himself up onto the slab, he risked bringing it down on Jessa's head.

"Quite the puzzle. Isn't it, warrior?" Morrigan said with a taunting laugh. "It took quite a few soakings to teach yer lady love some proper manners and to quiet her tongue. Now that her clothes are frozen as hard as the rocks that imprison her, she has become quite docile."

"How do our deaths benefit ye? Ye should realize by now that neither the Defenders nor the Weavers are coming. They are nay so stupid as to take yer bait." He wasn't about to die, but it served him to keep the hag distracted as he worked out the puzzle of the cage. He crouched and reached through the bars again to touch Jessa's hand. "Awake, my love?"

"I am awake," she whispered, but the glow that appeared when they touched was not nearly as bright.

"Ye nay answered me, Morrigan!" he shouted into the darkness. "Ye ken as well as I that if we die, ye have gained nothing."

"That is not true!"

"Name a benefit, then," he dared the hag as he tried to shove the roof off the cage.

"The Highland Veil is not yet strengthened by yer bond."

"Our bond already strengthened it," he argued, straining to push the thick stone slab up and off into the abyss. "Have ye forgotten the rules, old one? As soon as the mate bond connects, the energy joins the weave of the Veil."

Silence followed, but it wouldn't last. The suffocating darkness vibrated with the Morrigan's anger, pounding like an enraged heart.

"Grant," Jessa whispered.

He crouched again and reached through the bars, elated when he found she had moved closer. But when he touched her cheek, his heart fell, and he nearly roared in agony. No warmth at all remained in her flesh. His precious Jessa felt lifeless. He hurried to remove his great kilt and shoved it through the bars. "Cover yourself, love. Soak in my warmth."

"Grant?"

"Aye?" He could barely see her sweet face illuminated by the golden glow.

"Don't die."

He tightened the wrap around her and tried to warm her face between his hands. "Neither of us will die this day, m'love."

"Ye will both die!" the Morrigan thundered. "Mairwen took what was mine. I shall take what was hers."

"We dinna belong to Mairwen, ye bloody demoness," Grant bellowed. "Jessa and I belong to each other—no one else."

"Mairwen favors the two of ye. I have seen it!" Lightning splintered the darkness, forcing Grant to shield his eyes. "She especially likes ye, Earl of Suddie, because ye remind her of her son!"

"And yet I am human, and she knows I shall die long before she moves on from Seven Cairns. If she loved me as much as ye say, why would she not offer me immortality?"

"No one can offer immortality other than Bride and Cerridwen."

Grant allowed himself a smile. The doubt had returned to Morrigan's voice. "And who is Mairwen the daughter of, foolish one? Who are her mothers?" He prayed the rumors were true because, if they were, Morrigan would know them as well. She would not, however, expect him to be aware of them.

Silence fell again. The wind ceased to blow, and the crash of the waves disappeared. For the first time since entering the unholy bowels, Grant felt as if the evil writhing through the darkness had somehow lessened. Maybe even disappeared.

"She's gone," Jessa said, her voice breathy as though the mere act of speaking exhausted her. "I can't feel her anymore."

"Neither can I." He didn't add that he knew she would return. The legends sang of the Morrigan's vindictiveness and jealousy. She never relinquished a battle without a fight. "Stay close. The roof of this feckin' birdcage is a brittle rock. 'Tis my hope to shatter it so I can move the bars and free ye."

"I'll rest while you work on that."

"No. Ye must stay awake. Do ye hear me, woman?"

"Just let me close my eyes for a minute."

He crouched and reached for her with both arms, silently cursing the damnable bars that separated them. "Jessa, my love. Please stay awake. If ye give in to the weariness, ye may never open yer eyes again, and I canna bear the thought of that."

When she worked her arms through the bars and tried to hug him, his heart soared.

"I'll do my best," she told him with a heavy sigh.

He tightened his plaid around her, then kissed her icy hands. "Talk to me while I work, aye? That will keep ye awake."

She released another bone weary sigh into the darkness.

"Tell me of the first thing ye intend to do when we step into the sunlight," he prompted as he stood once more, leveraged both hands under the rim of the roof, and lunged upward.

"Take a nap in a sunny spot on the grass."

"A fine choice." He gritted his teeth, locked his legs, and shoved again, lifting with everything in him. He had to take care to lift rather than shove lest the entire wee cage slide off the ledge. The shelf of stone crackled and groaned, but more importantly, it moved the barest bit. As he resettled his footing, with one braced on the wall beside the path, he asked, "And what will ye do once ye have had yer nap? Ask Mrs. Robeson for a cup of that vile coffee?"

She didn't answer.

"Jessa!"

"What?" The snappishness in her tone pleased him. Irritation would not only keep her awake but also help keep her warm.

"I asked what ye would do after yer nap? Drink some of that black swill?"

"I don't know."

"Dinna get sullen on me, woman. Talk to me. Berate me. Curse at me or shout. I dinna care which ye choose, just keep talking and stay awake."

"I don't want to stay awake."

"I am well aware of that, but ye dinna have a choice. What shall we name the puppies? What shall we name our children?" He set his hands on the roof of her prison again and shoved upward, using the wall behind him as leverage.

"We'll name them all *hey you,* so we'll never be wrong when we call them to come inside."

The roof didn't shift this time, but the wall behind him did. In fact, the shale crumbled, swallowing his foot to the ankle. "Feckin' hell." Thrown off balance, he fell forward and caught himself against the bars.

"Grant!"

"I am all right. I broke the wall, and now my foot is stuck in the mountain."

"Bio mom once dated a guy who broke walls, but he always used his fists."

"What the hell is a *bio mom?*" While he lauded her for staying awake and babbling, he needed to understand what she said so he could respond.

"The woman who gave birth to me."

The coldness of her tone reminded him of all she had shared

about her early life. "Forgive me, love. I allowed all that to slip from my mind."

"Well, you are a little preoccupied with a very important job. Can I please close my eyes now? Just for a little while?"

"Ye may not! Do as I tell ye, woman. Yer life depends on it this time, and ye ken that as well as I. Once I get loose, I'll start again to free ye from yer wee cage. Now, keep talking—and I'll nay allow ye to name my sons and daughters, *hey ye*." He pushed himself upright, backed against the wall, and tried to twist free of the weak spot he'd found with his boot. "What will ye name our first daughter and first son?"

"First?"

He held to the bars and stamped on the wall with his other foot, trying to break away more layers of the shale and enlarge the crack where his boot was wedged. "Aye, first daughter, first son. Names?"

"How many children do you have in mind?"

She still sounded bone weary, and that worried him as he finally wrenched his foot free. He had to anger her again. "At least a dozen each. I love bairns. We need to fill the keep with them."

When she didn't answer, he slid downward and reached for her. "Jessa?"

She reached through the bars and touched him; her face filled with fear. "Where is that light coming from? I can see you now."

In the strange illumination, her eyes were round and dark. She possessed the eerie pallor of a specter. He looked at his hands. The blue white glow had turned him ghostly as well.

"There." She pointed at the break he'd made in the wall. "It's coming from that hole."

He drew his dagger and edged closer, taking care to place himself between whatever that was and Jessa. "Stay back. It could be one of Morrigan's tricks."

"Then leave it alone. I don't want you hurt any more than you want me hurt."

"I have to see what it is, lass. It also could be something to help us."

"Like what? Bionic glowworms or something?"

He refused to grace that with an answer, especially since he wasn't quite sure about what she had said. At least, she appeared to be a great deal more awake. "Keep to the side of the cage in case something springs out. Away from the edge closest to the abyss."

As he drew closer, a soft humming filled the air. The strange light appeared to have its own song.

"Holy crap. It's a bomb." Jessa reached through the bars, snagged hold of his shirt, and tried to pull him back. "Get back. It sounds like it's going to go off."

"What?"

"It could be a bomb. Explosion. Rocks flying. A powerful force blows everything to bits. Little pieces of us flying through the air."

"And ye think my scooting an arm's length away will deter that?"

"Don't be an ass about it."

Lore a'mighty, he loved this woman. "Sit there and pray for my protection while I dig."

Her only response was an unintelligible grumble that made him laugh.

The more shale he broke away with his blade, the brighter the light and the louder the humming. Whatever was buried was ready to come out. He shielded his eyes and kept digging. Metal hit metal, and the blade of his dagger curled to one side as if soft as newly churned butter.

"What the devil?" He leaned in close and brushed the debris away from what appeared to be the haft of an ancient longsword. When he slid it free of its tomb, the steel rang out, and its powerful whitish blue light beat back the darkness of the great ravine. "Caladbolg," he whispered. Never in all his life would he have expected this. He had always believed the ancient sword to be a myth.

"It's like a lightsaber." Jessa stared at the amazing blade.

"I never believed it to be real." He stood and reverently ran his fingers down the shimmering blade, covered in markings he was far too human to read. "It is the sword of Leite from the elf mounds. Its name is Caladbolg."

"A few days ago, I never would've believed in glowing Elven swords, but after all I've been through..." She shrugged and shook her head. "Is it a good sword or a bad sword?"

"Weapons are not good or bad, lass. The intent within the hearts of those who wield them decides that." He tested the sharpness of the blade, impressed with the feel of it against his thumb.

"Well, at least if Morrigan comes back, maybe she'll be more afraid of a glowing sword than a regular one." Jessa slumped back to the ground and leaned against the bars while holding her head in her hands.

"Jessa?"

"What?" She spoke as though it took more strength than she possessed. Her burst of energy that had given him hope had left her. She didn't lift her head, just curled into a tighter ball and clutched at the folds of his plaid with trembling hands. She was dying, freezing to death.

He resettled both his hands on the exquisitely crafted haft of the sword. "Shield yer face, love."

When she didn't even question why, he knew he had to make haste.

Moving to the edge of the path overlooking the abyss, Grant extended the sword and swept its light back and forth, trying to see what lay below. The action proved useless. The void beyond the ledge appeared bottomless. It was just as well. As soon as he freed Jessa, he'd carry her back to the stairs.

He swung the long blade, testing its balance and weight. If the legends were true, the mighty Caladbolg had once lopped the caps off mountains. Known for its hardness and strength, the sword was said to be indestructible and able to sever anything. Grant prayed the legend was as true as the steel's ability to shine like a star from the heavens. He touched it to the prison's bars on the side closest to the bottomless abyss. If he sliced low, cut them away like felling a mighty tree, the roof of the cage should slide off into the darkness without causing Jessa harm.

"Shield yer eyes, m'love," he told Jessa, praying she had the strength to do so. Then he drew back the heavy blade and swung it. It cut through the base of the bars as though they were butter. He hurried to cut them again, making a low wedge on that side that would cause the section next to the abyss to collapse. With a deafening crash, the roof slid that way, but then it cracked in the middle and rocked toward the inside of the cage toward Jessa.

"No!" He dove under the stone, slicing through the rest of the bars and shielding Jessa with his body. The slab hit and settled its weight on his shoulders, but he locked his legs and braced himself, refusing to give way. The sword glowed brighter, and its hum grew deafening as he reversed the blade and shoved it under his arm, thrusting it deep into the thick shale trying to crush him. A thunderous boom rattled him as the slice of rock shattered into a cloud of shards.

Shoulders throbbing with pain, he set the sword aside, then dropped to his knees beside Jessa and gathered her into his arms. Cradling her close, he held her tight, raining kisses upon her while rocking as if she were a babe. "I have ye, m'love. Ye truly are safe now."

Trembling, she burrowed closer, clutching at him as if afraid he would let her go. "I knew you'd save me," she whispered. "I knew you would."

"And now we shall be leaving this hell," he rasped, then pressed another kiss to her icy forehead.

"Funny," she mumbled, "I always thought hell would be hot."

"Aye, love. So did I." Thankfully, he had worn his trews, waistcoat, and jacket along with his kilt, so he was plenty warm. But soaked and frozen as she was by Morrigan's malicious waves, Jessa was in danger—badly so. "I am going to set ye down so I can give ye my coat and wrap ye in my kilt, aye? Then I'll carry ye out of here and get ye to a fire."

"Ye truly believe I mean to let ye leave here alive? That I will allow ye to take yer mate out of here?" Morrigan said.

"Shit," Jessa whispered, curling tighter against him. "I knew she'd be back."

"Stay behind me," he told her quietly as he set her on the ground, took up the humming sword, and faced the hooded figure slowly moving toward them.

"Give me the sword," Morrigan said, stretching out her hand, her bony fingers long and pale, curling like talons. "It is mine."

A ripple of blinding light shot up from the haft of the sword to its tip. It warmed and molded itself more comfortably in Grant's grip, as if settling in and readying for battle. "It appears Caladbolg means to remain with me."

"I told ye, ye were a Defender."

Lightning flashed and thunder rumbled in the distance. Grant wondered if it was the sword or Morrigan, since the steel was also known as the Blade of Lightning.

"I defend my wife, my future children, and my kin," he said, widening his stance and resettling the weapon in his hands. "Ye have lost this day, Morrigan. I dinna give a damn what shape ye take. This blade will find ye."

"Ye canna kill the likes of me." She shoved her hood back and shook out her raven mane, assuming the form of a breathtakingly beautiful woman clad in armor. "Have ye forgotten yer teachings?"

"Aye, just as I intend to forget ye and order my clan to do the same. We will wipe yer name from every book and every tale we tell our children. Nor will it be spoken anywhere on MacAlester lands—just as it is forbidden to be uttered in Seven Cairns."

Her dark eyes narrowed, then flared wide as if he had struck her in the face. "But ye will remember me." She jerked a nod at Jessa. "And so will she. That will be enough. I will live in yer minds long enough to destroy the Highland Veil."

"But that's the thing about humans, or have ye forgotten?" Grant gave her a grin he knew would enrage her as he swept the sword back and forth, readying for attack. "As we age, we forget. Our minds dim with the fog of time." He sliced the air, flashing the blade's light across her as if splitting her in two. "And if ye kill us this day, Mairwen and my men will see yer name wiped from my clan and all their descendants. She gave me her word that she would do so."

Morrigan screeched with rage, then lunged for him in the shape of the enormous wolf.

He brought the sword down with a hard slash, cleaving her skull and then her body. The grizzly halves fell to the ground, twitching and gushing blood before exploding into a cloud of ravens and swirling upward out of sight.

Grant held his breath, crouching, waiting to unleash the lethal Caladbolg again. He might not be able to kill Morrigan this day, but he could damn sure swear that she would be forgotten and thereby weakened. A forgotten goddess was a powerless goddess. Immortals only thrived when they were remembered.

The surrounding darkness exploded, knocking him off his feet. As the earth itself roared and shook, he rolled and crouched over Jessa, holding her tight in one arm while keeping the Elven sword held above them for protection. Bits of shale, chunks of rock, and debris rained down on them as the world shuddered with fearsome violence.

Jessa wrapped her arms around his neck and cried out, her lips brushing his ear, "I love you."

He closed his eyes and tightened his embrace, acknowledging nothing but the connection with this precious woman. "I love ye, my own. Love ye 'til time ceases to be."

CHAPTER 16

The stone ledge around them fell away, leaving nothing but a small platform to crouch upon atop the jagged spire. The wall of shale at their backs crumbled, becoming a waterfall of oily black shards showering down into the abyss. Grant held Jessa tighter, shielding her as much as he could from the stinging debris.

The shuddering upward thrust of their dangerous perch halted with a violent stop. As Grant lifted his head to look around, bony fingers closed around his throat, tearing him away from Jessa as they squeezed off his air. He fought to free himself, baring his teeth at the dark, empty eyes of the skull staring at him from the depths of Morrigan's hooded cloak.

"Ye will remember me always," she said, her voice a deadly hiss as she crushed his throat. "Ye will tell yer children of the benevolent goddess who spared ye this day because ye possess the heart and soul of a truly courageous warrior. Ye will teach them my name until they chant it in their dreams." She shook him, nearly snapping his neck with the strength of her bony grip. The warm trickle of blood where her sharp fingertips pierced his flesh turned into a steady stream. "Tell Mairwen I'm coming for her. Our mothers canna protect her forever. When I take down the Veil, she will join Lùnastal and Valan in their crystal prison for all the rest of her days."

Vision failing, lungs burning for air, Grant grappled a dagger out of his boot and stabbed it deep into the bony specter's eye socket. She burst into a whirling mass of ravens that shot up into the sky, leaving him coughing and wheezing on the grassy knoll.

Must get to Jessa. He shook his head, fighting to clear his vision while wheezing in great gulps of air. He dragged himself back to her, pulled her close, and rolled to his back. The sudden brightness of the sky blinded him as he sank into the softness of the heavy sea grasses covering the top of the cliff. For that was where they were. Somehow, the cliff overlooking the sea had been restored.

Morrigan's dark chasm, her icy hell, was gone.

Something dug into his back, right between his shoulder blades, vibrating as if trying to shove him away. He found the strength to shift, reach underneath him, and free the gently glowing sword. He laid it at his side, keeping his fingers on its haft in case the dark one returned.

"Jessa," he whispered, his raspy voice breaking. Ignoring the pain, he turned his head and kissed her forehead. Lore a'mighty, his dear one was icy as death.

And she didn't answer. Nor did she move. She lay in the curve of his arm, her head on his shoulder. Her stillness was not that of sleep or a lady caught in a swoon. His precious one's soul hovered at death's threshold. Struggling, he forced himself to his knees, gathered her up, then staggered to his feet. He had to get her to the keep. To a fire. To a dry bed and shelter.

"Let me carry her, brother," said a strangely muffled voice to his left.

Grant slowly turned, fighting to remain upright. Henry looked at him with pity and resignation, filling him with raging determination. "Fetch the witch," he croaked to the man. "My Jessa must be saved."

"I shall fetch Mairwen," Lachie said from his other side, his voice just as muffled.

Grant swallowed hard and shook his head, trying to clear his ears without dropping his precious wife. "Nay. Walk with me," he told them, reluctantly acknowledging he might not make it to the keep. "Help me save her."

Flanking him, they stayed close, joining him in one painful step at a time. The skirting wall seemed so very far away.

His feet caught in the long, matted grass, making him stumble and fall to his knees more than once. Each time, with Henry and Lachie steadying him, he rose and whispered to Jessa, "Nearly there, my own. Hold on."

By the time they reached the split in the skirting wall, swirling spots of blackness filled his vision, making him stumble to lean against the ancient barrier built by his ancestors. His shoulders throbbed with a pain so powerful he couldn't draw a full breath.

Henry caught hold of him. "Ye brought her home. Now let us serve ye as we are meant to. Give her over, man. I'll carry her to yer chambers, and Lachie will lend ye his strength and get ye there as well." He squeezed Grant's arm and leaned in, forcing Grant to look him in the eyes. "Dinna let yer stubbornness and pride kill the both of ye, aye?"

As much as Grant hated giving in to the weariness and pain, Henry was right—although Grant would never admit it out loud. Grudgingly, he dipped a weak nod. "Take her—but mind her head. She is weak as a blade of brittle grass in a windstorm." As Henry gently took her, Grant sagged back against the wall and almost went to the ground.

Lachie caught him, pulled his arm across his shoulders, and helped Grant stand. "Lean against me, brother. I'll nay let ye fall."

Grant locked his gaze ahead on Henry's back, watching the man as if doing so was the same as carrying Jessa in his own arms.

"Make way for our laird! Make way for our lady!" The cry went up again and again as they crossed the courtyard and entered the keep.

Grant was barely aware of his people. He had to focus on Jessa. If he kept his eyes locked on her head resting on Henry's shoulder, her soul wouldn't slip away and leave him all alone.

"Mrs. Robeson!" Mairwen shouted from somewhere nearby as they crossed the length of the main hall. "Every tonic and herb ye have. Boiling water. Plenty of linens. To the master's chambers. Now."

At least, that was what he thought the old witch said. Every sound was still so feckin' muffled. He stumbled and went down to one knee again, nearly pulling Lachie down with him.

"Ye will never make it up the stairs," his friend told him while helping me rise. "And we're too broad to climb them side by side. Give me yer arms."

"Why?" Grant squinted at the man, fighting to clear his failing vision.

"Because I mean to drag ye up the stairs while ye lean on my back because yer arse is too big to carry. Now give me yer arms. Put them over my shoulders so's I can hold them to keep ye from sliding back down."

"This is feckin' humiliating."

"Do it, man. It's either this, a battlefield litter, or I leave yer stubborn arse at the bottom of these steps. Now what shall it be?"

Lachie always did have a way with words and no patience whatsoever when times demanded action. Deciding not to spend what little strength he had on arguing, Grant wrapped his arms around Lachie's neck as if about to choke him from behind. And then they entered the stairwell and climbed, one slow step at a time. Grant helped as much as he could. With his forehead shoved against Lachie's shoulders, he concentrated on lifting his feet and supporting his own weight at least a little. *Feckin' hell.* Climbing the stairway was like plowing a hard-packed field, and he was the ox lashed to the plow.

"Nearly there," Lachie told him, grunting as he tugged him up another series of steps. "What is that unholy humming?"

"The sword shoved through my belt." Grant dragged his foot up to the next step, then fought to find the strength to lift the other. "It is Caladbolg."

When Lachie didn't answer, Grant knew his kinsman thought he had gone mad from all that had happened. He would've thought the same if he'd not seen the blade's power. "If aught happens to me, guard it well. Only yerself or Henry should carry it, ye ken?"

"*Aught* is not going to happen to ye. Get that through yer thick skull, aye?"

Head swimming, Grant closed his eyes and swallowed hard. He had to make it to his chambers. "Can ye see Henry? Has he got her to our rooms yet?"

"He is out of the stairwell. I am sure Lady Jessa be in the hands of the women by now. Take heart, man. The Weavers and Defenders plan to surround the keep. Probably already have."

"Morrigan will not return. At least not here." A knowing filled Grant. The dark one had as much as given her word that she would threaten them no more. He and Jessa were safe, but God help Mairwen, the Veil's protectors, and the other fated mates. "Tell them to stand down."

"They surround the keep to join auras and bathe the place with healing." Lachie sagged against the wall and drew in several deep, ragged breaths. "Why the devil did ye put yer chambers on the third floor?"

"Because it suited me." Although Grant didn't disagree. He presently wished he had made his rooms on the ground floor. "And what do ye mean *bathe the place with healing*?"

"I canna tell ye," Lachie said, as he resumed climbing. "Ye've not taken the oath, ye ken?"

"Now is a hell of a time for ye to get so high and mighty about Defender rules. My not taking yer damned oath didna give ye pause whenever ye needed my help."

With a mighty growl, Lachie dragged him up the last few steps, swung him into the third floor hallway, and dropped his arse to the floor. Doubled over, his hands propped on his knees, he bared his teeth and looked ready to spit. "Once ye've healed, and yer fine wife is doing well, we will continue this discussion. It would not be fair for me to thrash yer arse in yer current condition."

Henry joined them, impatiently waving for them to follow. "Mairwen said to make haste."

Fear jolted through Grant, forcing him to his feet. "Jessa!" His vision failed, trapping him in frustrating darkness. He hit the wall but kept moving in the direction he knew he needed to go. "Get me to her! My sight has left me."

Strong hands caught hold of his arms and dragged him along. A solid thud and then a loud bang told him that either Lachie or Henry had kicked open the bedchamber door so hard it had bounced off the wall.

"She needs your heat," Mairwen said from somewhere to the left. "The mate bond will help her heal—and help you too."

Grant pulled the mighty, humming sword out of his belt and held it out. "Guard this, Lachie," he said. As soon as his kinsman took the sword, Grant felt around for the chair that was usually on the side of the bed closest to the door. Once he found it, he sat, stripped off his boots, then teetered back to his feet and stripped off the rest of his clothes.

"Yer back," Mairwen said from behind him. "Yer throat. Morrigan's work?"

"Aye." Grant didn't care that Mairwen or anyone else would see his nakedness. The need to get to Jessa consumed him. Nothing else mattered. He bumped into the bed, fumbled his way under the coverings, and pulled himself around his lady love. "Lore a'mighty, she is as cold as the bottom of the loch."

"Too much time in the Morrigan's domain poisoned the both of ye," Mairwen said. "Mortals canna tolerate her overlong or the darkness she breeds. Give me yer hand."

With Jessa wrapped in his arms, Grant was reluctant to turn loose of her long enough to do what the old witch said, especially when he couldn't see anything other than swirling darkness. "Will it help her?"

"It will help ye both. Put yer hand out of the covers now. Time is of the essence."

Gritting his teeth, he slid his left hand out from under the covers and waited. A strong yet feminine touch grasped his wrist.

"Keeva, hand me the crystal athame, then hold her right hand steady alongside his left," Mairwen instructed. "Emily, be ready with the bindings, aye? Our hands must be joined for no less than three full breaths."

"How many are in here with ye?" he asked.

"As many as needed," Mairwen said. "Now quiet yourself. If this doesna work, I canna save either of ye."

Something cold and hard dragged across his palm so quickly that it took a moment for him to realize his flesh had been sliced. Then a hand gripped his, clasping tight and pressing their palms together.

"The binding, Emily. Now."

It was then he realized it was Mairwen's surprisingly strong grasp holding his. A cloth wrapped around their hands and wrists, lashing them tighter together.

"*Unum Sumus*," Mairwen intoned, the depth of her voice mysterious and powerful.

"We are one," said Emily. Keeva echoed the same.

"We are one," Henry repeated in his booming voice.

"We are one," Lachie said even louder, not about to be outdone.

A blinding blast of the purest white light exploded in Grant's mind—or maybe it was in his sight. He couldn't tell because its power consumed him. There was no pain. Merely a sense of completeness. Of belonging. It reminded him of the sense of rightness he had felt when he and Jessa had acknowledged their bond and melded as one.

Then a wave of the quietest silence, the serenest peace, washed across him and closed his mind.

~

"When will we know if they will be all right?" Emily asked as she smoothed a healing balm across the cuts on Mairwen's palms.

Mairwen kept her attention focused on the pair in the bed, closely monitoring not only Jessa's breathing but Grant's as well. "I dinna ken, child. Morrigan tainted them both with her darkness. The mating bond protected them somewhat, but not enough. By filling them with my light and surrounding them with the devotion of not only the Defenders and Weavers but also those who care about them, it is my hope that we healed wherever she touched."

Emily held out her hand, showing Mairwen her palm. "My cut is already gone. Why?"

That pleased Mairwen greatly. If there had ever been any doubt about Emily's Spell Weaver ancestry, the speed of her healing cast it aside. "Yer bloodline, child. That of a Weaver. See?" Mairwen opened her hands, revealing hers to be healed, and the balm glistening on fresh new skin. "Go see to Henry and Lachie. They added their blood to the bond. See to their wounds."

As the girl left to attend to the men, Mairwen allowed herself a deep sigh. The ancient ceremony had taken much from her. If not for the others adding their blood to the bindings as she mixed her blood with Grant's and Jessa's, she wasn't certain she could've completed the draining ritual. Morrigan's darkness was strong, and the cruel goddess had laced it with painful images. Mairwen blinked them away, refusing to give them power over her. After all, Bride and Cerridwen had given her their promise, and they never lied.

Grant stirred, rumbling with a soft growl, as he tightened his hold on Jessa without opening his eyes.

Mairwen smiled and relaxed deeper into the worn cushions of the chair, envisioning many generations of strong MacAlesters bearing not only Defender blood but Time Weaver blood in their veins. It felt good to have more kin again and gave her even more reason to watch over Grant and Jessa throughout their time on this plane. She swallowed hard against the knot of emotions threatening to overcome her. Valan and Grant would have made good brothers, and Lùnastal would have been so proud to have two such sons.

"Someday, my loves," she whispered, her voice cracking. "Someday, I shall win yer freedom and bring ye home."

∽

Wherever this was, it was so very nice and warm. So much better than the pit. Maybe it was a dream, or maybe she was dead and finally out of the Morrigan's reach. Jessa didn't know. All she *felt* was safety.

She drew in a deep breath, and a wave of contentment washed across her. Grant was here with her. That was all that mattered, and that, in and of itself, relaxed her even more. She breathed him in again, reveling in his scent of raw alpha maleness—pinewoods, mountain air, and the clean, briny tang of the sea that could also be pure, unadulterated hero sweat from pulling her out of that dark hell. Yes. He had saved her. She remembered it clearly now. He had ordered her to stay awake while he battled the cage, the Morrigan, and everything in between.

She burrowed deeper into his embrace, tucking herself up under his chin. "I knew you would save me," she whispered without opening her eyes. "I never doubted you would come."

His arms flexed, then tightened around her. "Praise God Almighty," he said, his voice broken and rasping.

She pushed herself up and studied him in the soft glow of the lamp burning on the bedside table. His bruised face, covered in cuts and scrapes, squeezed her heart and made her catch her breath. "How badly are you hurt? Your voice..."

"The dark one crushed my throat." He gave her a loving smile and reached up to touch her cheek. "It will heal in time—I am already much better than I was. By the time Lachie got me here to our bed, I was blind and nearly deaf as well."

Guilt crashed through her, sending her heart to her gut. "This was all my fault. I am so sorry."

Confusion filled his eyes. "What?"

"If I hadn't held back, had second thoughts about this century, the Morrigan never would have gotten a toehold here and been able to create that...that...horrible place." Before he could speak, she pressed a finger across his lips. "I did not have second thoughts about us. I was worried about living in this time. Surviving in the eighteenth century." She gingerly touched his ravaged face, silently begging him to understand and find a way to forgive her. "But now I know all that matters is that I am with you. Everything else will fall into place, and I'll figure it out. I am so sorry for doubting."

He pulled her down into a kiss so tender she nearly wept. "Much has happened in a verra short time, m'love. Even though we be fated mates, we know verra little about one another. Doubt is natural—especially with ye coming from the future." He flinched with a hard swallow. "And the Morrigan wouldha come for us no matter what. Did ye not sense that about her?"

"It felt like she was more after you. Or maybe Mairwen." Jessa couldn't explain it, but the entire time she'd been trapped in that dark, icy hell, she had never really felt that the dark one's wrath was directly aimed at her. "I think I was more of a tool for her to torture others. Don't get me wrong. I think she would've snuffed me out in a heartbeat, but it was almost like I served a purpose. Gave her a way to get back at someone else."

He pulled her in for another kiss, then held her close and pillowed her head on his shoulder. "Whatever her vile reasons, she'll not be back for us. Rest now, love. We are safe and where we belong, in each other's arms."

"You're sure she won't be back for us?" she whispered, giving in to the bone-aching weariness still plaguing her.

"She swore she would leave us in peace," he rasped, then nudged a kiss to her forehead. "I wish I had the strength to make love to ye, but I fear I've a bit more healing to do before I can do right by ye."

Eyes already closed, she smiled and tightened her arm across his chest. "Raincheck. If I weren't so weak, I'd heal you, but I'm afraid to even try it right now."

"*Raincheck?* What does it matter if it's raining? This is feckin' Scotland."

She huffed a laugh. Heaven help her with this infuriating man who made her feel more alive than she had ever felt before. "A *raincheck* is like a promise, an I.O.U., a voucher for payment later. We are giving each other a raincheck to make love when we've both fully healed."

"Hmphf."

"And what does that mean?" she asked, still not adept at interpreting all his grunts, growls, and groans.

"'Tis an odd word. Is it from the colonies?"

If her eyes had been open, she would've rolled them. "Probably." She patted his chest. "Go to sleep."

"I love ye, lass," he said in a soft, croaking whisper.

"I love you more."

CHAPTER 17

Jessa slowly backed up as Grant walked the enormous reddish brown horse with the white, hairy feet toward her. "Are there not any smaller ones?"

He rumbled with a low chuckle, then motioned for her to come closer. "Jock here is a fine lad with infinite patience. His temper is so even that all the bairns love him. He is perfect for yer first time on a horse."

Emily walked up and gave her a playful nudge. "If I can do it, you can do it, and you promised to join me on the trip back to Seven Cairns so we can have that last little bit of extra time together before I return to the future. That's why I told Mairwen to let us travel the mortal way, rather than the Weaver way."

"But that is not a normal-sized horse." When Grant had agreed they would escort Mairwen and Emily back to Seven Cairns the old fashioned mortal way, she had envisioned an animal like the ones she'd seen on television. This one looked bigger than those Clydesdales from the beer commercial. "He is the size of an elephant."

"It would be wise for ye to learn to ride, lass," Mairwen said as she joined them, her own mount docile as a lamb, following along behind her. "Besides, ye love animals. Horses can sense such things and will take good care of ye."

"Ye dinna wish to hurt old Jock's feelings, now do ye?" Grant patted the horse, then motioned her closer still. "Come. Introduce yerself to him. We're losing daylight and need to ride while the weather is fair."

He had a point about not riding in the rain, but it also made her wonder if horses hydroplaned on wet grass like her car had on wet pavement. But then again, she supposed that was a tire tread thing. Jock's feet looked pretty big and sturdy.

She eased closer to the monstrous beast and hesitantly held out her knuckles so the horse could take a sniff. The stiff whiskers on his velvety nose tickled across the back of her hand and made her giggle.

"Pleasure to meet you, Jock." She scratched his muzzle and then on up to the white blaze on his forehead. "I've never even sat on a horse. Be patient with me. Okay?"

He made a deep grumbling sound, not an angry one, but more like the fussing of a harmless old man, then nudged her with his head as if urging her to mount up.

"I thought you said he was patient?" she asked Grant.

Before she realized what was happening, he swept her up onto the horse's back and steadied her in the saddle. "He is like me," he said with a wink. "Patient up to a point."

She made the mistake of looking down. "Holy crap. If I fall off, I'll break my neck."

"Then dinna fall off." Grant launched himself up behind her, curled an arm around her waist, and settled her back against him. "I decided yer first time riding alone should nay be the trip to Seven Cairns. Parts of the land would challenge ye."

"As long as those parts don't challenge you, I'm good with that." She hugged the arm he held around her, feeling a great deal better about this adventure already. The distinct sound of snickering made her turn and point at Emily. "Not a word. You know I've never been athletic. You were made to ride with those long legs of yours. I'm like an ant trying to straddle a cow."

Grant's poorly suppressed amusement vibrated against her back, making her elbow him. "You better remember whose side you're on."

He nuzzled a kiss to the curve of her neck, triggering a series of delicious ripples through her.

"That is not fair. You know I can't be stern when you do that."

"I know, love. Why do ye think I do it?"

Before she could comment, the horse took off, settling into a steady trot.

"Pull yer claws back in, lass. I'll not let ye fall."

Without realizing it, she had clutched Grant's arm so tightly that her fingernails dug into him. She rubbed at the bloody little half moons along his arm. "Sorry! I'll try to relax."

"Feel the sway of the beast and listen to the creak of the leather." Grant kissed her neck again and hugged her tighter. "Once ye set into the rhythm of the ride, ye will be fine. Just ye wait and see."

She withheld judgment on that until they were deeper into the journey.

Jessa noticed the formation they easily fell into as their group exited the gate. She and Grant, with Mairwen riding alongside them, were at the back while Emily took the lead, and Henry and Lachie rode on either side of her. The men tossed conversation back and forth to each other, and Emily joined their banter. The sight both pleased and saddened Jessa. Even with the promise of occasionally visiting with Emily at Seven Cairns, it wouldn't be the same as being able to talk or text her best friend any time she wanted. But watching them, she noticed something. Henry and Lachie were competing for Emily's attention.

"They like her," she said, probably louder than she should have.

"Aye, they do." He shifted against her, huffing a deep sigh.

"What? What am I missing?"

"Her fated mate is not in this time," Mairwen said, inserting herself into the conversation. "I have seen it, and so has Ishbel." She shot a pointed look at Jessa. "Do ye not wish yer Emily to know the same contentment ye found with yer husband?"

"Well, yes, that goes without saying." But Jessa acknowledged and fully owned her selfish side. "I just thought it would have been nice if one of them was her fated mate. Then I wouldn't lose her."

"Ye're nay losing her, love," Grant gently reminded. "The two of ye will always have Seven Cairns as common ground, remember? A rare gift from the goddesses."

"Why aren't more fated mates offered that gift?" Jessa fixed Mairwen with a pointed look of her own. "You said Emily and I were allowed that because of our sisterly love. We can't be the only pair of friends or relatives separated by a rogue mate bond from a different century. Wouldn't it help the Highland Veil if more were given the same opportunity of meeting at Seven Cairns?"

From her pale, almost silvery horse that came amazingly close to matching the shade of her hair, Mairwen stared back at Jessa as if she had never seen her before. "Unlimited access to Seven Cairns? A meeting place for those separated by the planes of time and reality?"

"Wouldn't that make your job easier?" Jessa shifted in the saddle and adjusted an uncomfortable wad of petticoat that had wedged against her right hip and was rubbing it raw. "And can I have my leggings back for when I ride?"

"No," Grant said before Mairwen could answer. "I dinna ken what leggings from yer time might look like, but I know well enough what the ones from now show, and I will not have ye wearing them. Perhaps Mrs. Robeson and Molly can help ye design a *modest* yet comfortable skirt for whenever ye ride."

"As I was saying before we were so rudely interrupted by male insecurity," Jessa said to Mairwen, "wouldn't everyone being allowed to meet at Seven Cairns make your job easier?"

"What are we talking about?" Emily asked as she rounded back and brought her mount up alongside them on the other side.

"All fated mates being allowed to meet with their closest friends and family at Seven Cairns," Jessa told her.

"That would risk revealing the true nature of Seven Cairns." Mairwen slowly shook her head. "Discretion and secrecy are some of our greatest protections."

"Well, how have you been explaining when people disappear?" Jessa couldn't believe that Scotland Yard or Interpol or whoever ruled that part of the world hadn't picked Seven Cairns to pieces because of missing persons' cases.

Mairwen shrugged. "We make them forget."

"You make who forget what?" Emily asked.

"The families and friends looking for their loved ones are made to forget they exist."

"That's terrible." Jessa looked at Emily for support on this. Her friend nodded in agreement. "It's cold-hearted, selfish, and uncaring. Do you make the fated mates forget, too?"

"At times. It depends on the situation. The good of the all is far more important than the good of the one." Mairwen's tone had become snappish and defensive.

"Then why didn't you do that with me and Emily? Make us forget each other?" Jessa wished their horses were close enough so she could reach over and shake that old woman. While she now fully understood the importance of stopping the Morrigan and those who fought with her, that didn't excuse what Mairwen had just confessed that she and the Weavers did with people's minds.

"The two of ye were…are…different." Mairwen frowned as she stared off into the distance, idly fidgeting with the reins that appeared to be useless because the horse knew where to go. She slowly shook her head. "Ishbel noticed yer gifts right away." A faint smile danced across her pale pink mouth. "Then I sensed Emily's Weaver blood. The two of ye possess an ancient greatness, and ye dinna even realize it. I am not so certain we possessed the power to erase yer memories."

Grant's arm tightened around Jessa's middle and hugged her closer. "And ye're mine. Daren't ye ever forget that."

"I would never forget that." She patted his arm but was determined to convince Mairwen that wiping people's memories was wrong. "When you make a person forget, you realize you're changing who they are?"

"How so?" Mairwen tossed her head, obviously ready to be done with that subject.

"Our memories, the way we process them and either learn from them or learn how to escape them, make us who we are. Erasing those memories takes that way. While I have a lot of memories I'd like to forget, I can't deny that I learned things from them. Some of what I learned wasn't pleasant, but I learned it just the same and use it like backfill to keep my foundation solid, keep me aware of just how far I've come, and all I have survived."

Mairwen snorted. "I have seen memories cripple some. Many a mortal has thanked me for freeing them from their past's prison."

Henry and Lachie halted their mounts and drew their weapons.

Grant drew his sword—the mighty Caladbolg already hummed and shone with a blue-white glow.

"What do they see?" Jessa scrubbed her arms. Every hair stood on end, and a nauseatingly familiar eeriness washed across her. "She's here. I thought she told you she was going to leave us alone?"

"Not in so many words," Grant said quietly. "It was more implied than stated."

"Lovely." Jessa motioned at Emily. "Get behind us. I don't know if it will help or not, but it can't hurt, and she's sure to go for you next."

"But I don't see anything," Emily argued. "There is nothing up ahead."

"Yes, there is," Jessa told her without shifting her gaze from a point up ahead that shimmered as though extreme heat rose from the ground. "Get behind us, Em. Please?" Morrigan might go after Emily next since she had yet to find and connect with her fated mate.

A raven appeared in the middle of the path at the base of the shimmering heat waves. It shape-shifted into a wolf, then changed again into an all too familiar cloaked figure. Morrigan lifted her bony hand and clicked her long, lethal black nails. "*Induciae.* I would speak with Mairwen and Grant's mate. Alone."

"My name is *Jessa*, and what does *induciae* mean?"

"Suspension of hostilities." Morrigan pushed back her hood, revealing her form of the armored warrioress who was almost too beautiful to look upon. She bowed her sleek head, making the ebony gemstone in her silver circlet glint in the sunlight. "And forgive me, *Jessa*."

"When ye speak to one of us, ye speak to us all," Grant said.

Morrigan twitched a shrug, then shifted her gaze to Mairwen. "Is that what ye wish, sister?"

"Sister?" Jessa repeated in a squeaking whisper. Why had Mairwen not told them that little tidbit of information?

Grant gave her a subtle squeeze meant to make her be quiet.

Mairwen drew herself up, sitting taller in the saddle. She gave the barest dip of her chin. "Say what ye will, Morrigan."

"Our sons are dead."

Mairwen's hands tightened on the reins, and her horse shifted from side to side, displaying the agitation of its rider. "That is not possible. Bride and Cerridwen promised—as did the ancient one, the mighty Danu."

Morrigan's pained scowl almost softened as she lowered her gaze. "Carman's sons destroyed Valor and Valan's vaults in a bid for power. They scattered the crystal shards across eternity."

"The jars," Mairwen said, her voice ragged. "The jars housing their essence crystals?"

"That is why I am here."

When Morrigan's focus slid to her, Jessa instinctively backed up against Grant's chest. "What?"

"Ye dinna realize it yet because mortals are oblivious to such things until their bodies bellow with the proof of it, but ye carry twin sons in yer womb. Mine and Mairwen's sons. The sons fathered by Lùnastal when he could not choose between Mairwen and me."

Jessa swallowed hard, struggling to wrap her mind around what the dark one had just shared. "If I am pregnant—and that is very big if—then I'm barely pregnant and Grant's the father. Not someone named Lùnastal."

"There is no such thing as *barely* pregnant," the Morrigan said. "Did you not once utter those exact words to an acquaintance? Either ye are with child or ye are not. And ye are. Two of them, as a matter of fact."

"How do you know what I've uttered to anyone?" Jessa asked, trying to ignore Grant's ever-tightening embrace. His excitement at the prospect of fatherhood pulsed through her. "And like I said, Grant would be the father."

"Aye, Grant is the father of the wee bairns," Mairwen said, "but their souls—" She bowed her head and covered her face with her hands, her shoulders trembling with her grief. "The goddesses promised. How could they let this happen to my son?"

"When I opened their jars," Morrigan told Mairwen, "their essence crystals were gone. The ancient one granted me a rare audience because she felt my sorrow as a mother. She assured me they had kept their promise that our sons would not die for their mistakes—" She drew in a deep breath and lifted her chin higher, then shifted her focus back to Jessa. "After Dub, Dother, and Dain razed the crystal vaults, the mighty Danu, Bride, and Cerridwen gathered what was left of Valor and Valan's souls and intertwined them with Jessa's children."

"Intertwined?" Jessa repeated. "My babies aren't even born yet, and you're telling me they're going to have multiple personality problems?"

Morrigan frowned, visibly confused. "No. They will merely grow to be extraordinary males, powerful, and possess the same lifespan as Mairwen and I, rather than you weak, insignificant mortals."

"You're not getting them," Jessa said, already seeing where this was going. She shook her head at Mairwen too. "These babies are mine, and no one is taking them away."

The Morrigan smiled, sending a chill through Jessa that made her shudder. "I am glad ye will keep them safe. Once I bring down the Veil, I will come for them."

"The Veil will remain strong," Mairwen said, her voice like thunder, "and once the goddesses allow, I will come for my Lùnastal. We all know ye assumed my form when ye seduced him." She jutted her chin higher, her face wet with the tears of her loss. "He does still live, aye?"

"Aye," the Morrigan said. "*My* beloved still lives. Angry and handsome as ever in his crystal cell. Even Carman's wicked sons are not so foolhardy as to meddle with the god of light while he repents in the mighty Danu's prison."

Jessa fisted her hands to keep from digging her nails into Grant's arm again. Here she was, caught in the middle of a love triangle of immortals, and if there was one thing she despised, it was being manipulated for someone else's gain. She had spent her formative years enduring that despicable abuse. She'd be damned if she went through it again.

"I am not a pawn in your stupid little games," she said, bouncing in the saddle to get the horse to step forward and take a more dominant stance. "Or at least I am finished being a pawn in your selfish games." She laid her hand on Grant's, taking hold of the sword that had banished the darkness when she needed it most. As soon as she touched its haft, the blade's light became blinding and shot a powerful beam of pure white brightness into the heavens and held it. "You will stay away from me and mine—and that includes Emily and the mate she has yet to claim. I might be mortal, but I will fight like hell for those I love. My children will never know you." She turned and glared at Mairwen. "Either of you. Keep me and mine out of your petty fight over some stupid man with fidelity issues. I can get behind protecting the Highland Veil because of what I have seen so far. But I will be damned if I get caught up in two jealous women fighting over a man who apparently thinks with nothing but his cock."

"Ye dinna understand," Mairwen said. "Ye—"

"I don't have to understand!" Jessa gripped the sword tightly, increasing the strength of its light. "You have lied to me. Repeatedly. You mishandled and manipulated me. You and your Weavers need to do better, Mairwen. Bringing fated mates together should be an honorable act both for them and for the protection of the Veil. It should not be one of kidnapping and treachery."

Morrigan tossed her head back and laughed. "Yer pet has grown claws, sister! See what happens when ye dinna properly train them?"

Jessa aimed the sword's arc light at the snarky goddess, trying to slice her in two.

The Morrigan exploded into a cloud of ravens, then morphed back into her warrioress form. She shook a cautionary finger at Jessa. "Careful, little one. Ye canna defeat me. Not even with the Elven sword." She sauntered back and forth in front of them, as if walking some sort of invisible line. "I came here to tell ye of the sons ye carry." She tossed a nod at Grant. "I already gave yer mate my word that I would not trouble the MacAlesters again—the bairns merely strengthen my oath." Her eyes narrowed. "But I mean to take down the Highland Veil and rule over the chaos with Lùnastal at my side." She angled a dark look at Mairwen. "He chose me afore Danu imprisoned him. Ye know that as well as I."

Mairwen sat taller in the saddle and remained silent.

Sympathy for Mairwen twitched at Jessa's heart and made her a little more forgiving of the manipulative woman. A little. Mairwen needed to work on her method of uniting fated mates. But poor Mairwen had been wronged. Possibly by her fated mate, definitely by her *sister*, and yet she still fought for the greater good of the Veil. That, in and of itself, convinced Jessa that she and Grant were on the right side of things.

"You have said your piece," Jessa said. "If that's all, go."

Morrigan went still, eyeing her with an unreadable expression. The longer she stared at her, the harder Jessa fought to stare right back at her without blinking.

"One more thing," the dark one finally said, her voice returning to its dangerous, purring tone. The faintest smile, an evil smirk, tugged at the corner of her mouth as she nodded at Emily. "I am not the only one trying to destroy the Veil and rule chaos. The light has many enemies other than my particular form of darkness." Once again, she burst into a swirling mass of screeching ebony birds and disappeared into the clouds.

"What did she mean by that?" Emily asked, drawing her mount closer to Jessa and Grant.

Jessa turned to Mairwen. "What *did* she mean?"

"The Veil has many enemies, and we must remain vigilant even though here, at this point in history, and this place in Scotland, Morrigan has agreed to honor the rules governing warfare on holy ground. Much as she does at Seven Cairns. But that does not mean others will do so. We must watch for the others."

"Who are the *others*?" Jessa asked.

Mairwen released a heavy sigh and suddenly looked much older than she ever had before. "Too many to name, child." She nudged her horse into motion. "Come. It is past time that Emily and I returned to the Seven Cairns of the future."

Henry and Lachie glanced back at them, then moved as one to flank Mairwen on the path.

"Are you all right?" Emily asked Jessa.

"Lots to process." And that was the biggest understatement she had ever made in her life.

"I am going on ahead." Emily tipped a thoughtful nod at Mairwen's retreating figure. "I'm sure you two have a lot to discuss. We'll have our time before I pass through the curtain."

Jessa had no idea what curtain Emily was talking about, but was certain she would eventually find out. After all, Seven Cairns was her way station, her connection to the life she had left behind. Who would have thought she'd be sitting on a monstrosity of a horse in the eighteenth century with a man she couldn't imagine living without?

"Jessa?"

"Can we get down and walk a while? I need to see your eyes when we have this conversation."

Without a word, Grant slid to the ground, then gently took her by the waist and set her down in front of him. "Tell me yer thoughts, m'love," he said quietly, his tone deep and worry in his eyes. "I would know them. Good or bad."

Instead of walking as she had requested, she hugged him close and rested her head on his chest. "Have you ever seen a tangled knot of yarn made up of a bunch of different colored strands?"

"Aye." He tenderly stroked her hair and kissed the top of her head.

"Those are my thoughts."

"What is in yer heart, then?" His arms tightened around her.

"Love for you. Worry. Fear. Protectiveness. Dread."

"Worry, fear, and dread?" He kissed the top of her head again, gently swaying as though soothing a crying child. "Give those to me, m'love. Allow me to slay those beasts for ye because they canna withstand me."

"Those goddesses had no right to mess with our children just because of some promise they made to Mairwen." Still unable to believe she was really pregnant, the thought of anyone taking advantage of an innocent for any reason absolutely infuriated her. "They had no right."

Grant tipped up her chin and smiled down at her. "We will love and protect our bairns. Prepare them to face any obstacle and nurture them with kith and kin. Those goddesses underestimate the stubbornness and strength of MacAlester blood."

"I cannot believe I'm pregnant." She flinched at her unrealistic whininess. Of course, she could be pregnant. It only takes one time of unprotected sex, and they'd been going at it like rabbits whenever they weren't teetering on the brink of death. "I never thought about becoming a mother. I'm not so sure I'll know how."

"With every bairn and every mother being different, I'm not so sure anyone is an expert on wee ones. Some just have more experience than most. The women of the keep will help ye any way they can. As will I."

"What do you know about babies?" She couldn't wait to hear what an eighteenth century Highland smuggler laird had to say on that subject.

"When they cry, ye do yer best to figure out if they're hungry, soiled, or just after a good cuddle." He twitched a quick shrug. "I remember my mam with my brother. Whenever he cried, she patted his wee arse until he passed a good bit of wind to make his belly feel better."

Grant had never spoken about a brother before. She almost hated to pry. "What happened to him?"

After a long look upward, as though seeking the right words from the heavens, Grant gave a sad shake of his head. "With so little to eat that winter and all of us weak from nothing more than a bit of parritch each day, he and Mam took ill. Da, the laird, did as well. The fever took them all 'cept for me. Henry's family took me in. Lachie's family shared what little they had, too." He stared off into the distance, his jaw flexing. "I was their only hope for leading the clan someday, so they often went without to feed me first."

Jessa swallowed hard and blinked fast, trying not to cry. "I am so sorry." The tears overflowed. She couldn't help it. He had been through so much. Suffered so much loss.

He drew her close again and held her. "It was a long time ago, lass," he said quietly, "and they're with me still. I carry everyone I have ever loved in my memories and my heart."

"I'm afraid, Grant," she whispered, trying to sort her churning mess of emotions into neat little boxes that she could label and store away for when she felt like dealing with them.

He tipped her face to his again. "What do ye fear, m'love?"

She stared up at him, despondent yet finding comfort in losing herself in his gaze. "Everything. Bringing babies into this cruel world. Those *others* Mairwen hinted at. Being a decent mother. I'm worried about every freaking thing under the sun, and there's not a damn thing I can do about it."

"There is where ye are wrong, my own."

"What?"

"Ye can love me. Know that I will always do my damnedest to protect ye. Cherish every precious moment we are given in this life. Dinna let the dark ones steal yer joy, for when ye do, they also steal yer light. Nothing in this life is guaranteed, no matter the time in which ye live. If ye live yer life in fear, ye dinna live it at all."

He was so right—and wise, but she wasn't all that sure she should tell him. After all, he was pretty smug as it was. "If Mairwen and Morrigan are right about our pending parenthood—"

He silenced her with a long, slow kiss, then lifted his head and smiled. "I pray they are right. Remember, I told ye we needed at least a dozen bairns? The keep is large. It will take a good-sized herd of children to fill it with laughter. If ye bring them in two at a time, the keep will fill even faster."

"You are being ridiculous."

"Nay, my dear one. I am a man wise enough to know when I am truly blessed, and I love ye more than life, more than I ever dreamed I could love anyone—and it scares the blazes out of me as much as it thrills me."

"I love you." Somehow, those three little words didn't begin to describe all she felt for him. She reached up and touched his face, wondering how she had ever managed without him. "I guess we should catch up with the others."

"Aye." He lifted her back into the saddle and hoisted himself up behind her. "On to Seven Cairns."

CHAPTER 18

As they drew closer to Seven Cairns, Jessa caught herself staring at it with her mouth ajar. Amazement and a healthy dose of eeriness shot through her. The eighteenth century Seven Cairns was identical to the one in the future. Well, almost identical. Rather than electric lights brightening the shop windows, oil lamps and candles burned. Instead of cars and trucks parked beside the sidewalks, horses, carts, and wagons waited. And the sidewalks weren't poured concrete. Flagstones paved the ground, providing dry walkways for the villagers. But then again, maybe the walkways had been the same in the future. She couldn't recall. The main road was the same. She remembered how she and Emily had admired the beauty of the cobblestone road even though all its bumps had made their little rental car vibrate like a windup toy.

Grant lifted her down from the saddle and gave her an encouraging smile. "I'll be here with old Jock if ye need me."

He understood she needed alone time with Emily.

"Thank you." She squeezed his hand, then joined Emily in front of the pub. "It's the same but not," she told her.

"I know. It takes some adjustment." Emily nodded at the doorway. "Same people too. Lilias and her brother are probably behind the bar waiting on customers right now. Only their apparel changes to fit whatever century they decide it is. It's all one grand illusion."

"How do the inhabitants of the village collectively decide which century it is? Not everyone who lives here is a Weaver." Jessa weakly waved at Nonie, the bookshop owner she'd met in the future. The woman was dressed as a sedate, gray-haired eighteenth century shopkeeper, yet in the future, she'd been a pink-haired, middle-aged woman who loved dressing in flamboyant styles. This was all so confusing.

"You'll have to ask Mairwen how they decide what year it is," Emily said. "I'm not that far into my training."

"Training?"

Emily took Jessa by the arm and led her to the bench beneath the wide antique windows of the pub. Except now, they were no longer antique. They were probably the latest invention in window panes. "You remember me telling you about my great-great-grandmother from Scotland?"

"Vaguely."

"Well…as it turns out…she was a Spell Weaver."

Jessa shifted on the bench and fully faced Emily. "I'm almost afraid to ask, but I'll bite. What is a *Spell Weaver*?"

"A Mairwen person with an aptitude for magic."

Pulling together everything she knew of the Weavers and Mairwen so far, Jessa found herself thoroughly confused. "But…your great-great-grandmother isn't…if she was like Mairwen…Is she still here? Somewhere?"

"She had the goddesses strip her of her longevity because she fell in love with a mortal and couldn't bear the thought of living on without him. She chose to die the same day my great-great-grandfather did." Emily stared down at her folded hands in her lap. "They were a rare combination of fated mates—a Weaver and a mortal. Mairwen said it doesn't happen very often."

"But you inherited her magic?"

"Yes."

"Do you feel magical?" Jessa eyed her friend. She didn't look any different.

"I'm not sure *magical* is the word. You know I've always driven Mama insane with my intuition. Maybe that's part of it. Only time will tell." Emily shrugged. "Maybe whatever I'm capable of is latent—like your ability to heal. That's why I agreed to train with Ishbel. I'm curious."

"I wish I could train with someone and figure out that healing thing. I never know when it's going to work, and when it's not."

Emily reached over and squeezed her hand. "I wish you could come with me and train too, but riding a few hours here and a few hours back every day would be quite the commute in this century." She nodded at Jessa's flat middle. "And soon, it won't be recommended."

"I don't feel pregnant." Jessa clung to Emily's hand with both of hers. "If the goddesses only allow us to visit in Seven Cairns, I may not be able to see you when I need you the most."

"Don't invite another day's worries into today. Mama would give you *the look* right now. Remember?" A sheen of tears made Emily's dark eyes glisten a deeper shade of brown. "At least we can still visit. Not everyone has that option."

"I'm going to work on that with Mairwen," Jessa said. "If this is a way station for us, it should be a way station for all the fated mates. I would think such harmony would not only make the Weaver's matchmaking go smoother, but it would also give the Veil an extra boost of good *ju ju*."

"And from what little I've seen, we don't want that Veil to fall." Emily patted Jessa's hand as she stared off into the distance. "Who would have thought? All this?"

"No kidding." Jessa could feel time slowing, feel it dragging across her and snagging like a hangnail in a sweater. The Weavers were silently telling them it was time for Emily to go. "Where is the curtain you have to walk through to go back through time?"

"The one I used before was in the pub's back room, but from what Ishbel's told me, portals are scattered throughout the village."

"Isn't that dangerous? What if some unsuspecting visitor wanders through one?" Jessa envisioned a delivery person accidentally passing through to another time.

"A Weaver has to activate them—kind of unlock them and aim them."

"Then you'll always have to be the one to come back here, and I won't be able to travel forward?" That seemed like a recipe for missed visits. What if Jessa needed to see Emily or Mairwen for some unknown reason but couldn't move past the eighteenth century?

"All you have to do is ask one of the shopkeepers for help," Emily said. "They'll open a portal for you, or get a message to me. Whatever you need. You already know them. They're the same ones you met in the future."

"Everyone living in the village is a Weaver?"

"Most everyone, from what I understand. Several Defenders live here too. But it depends on the century, which Defender lives where, because they are mortal."

Jessa held Emily's hand tighter, *feeling* their time together slipping away. "I hate this, Em."

"I do too, Jess." Emily coughed and swiped her fingers across her eyes, trying to hide her tears. "I have to go now. The portal is pulling at me." She rose and fisted her hands against her middle.

Jessa stood, too, then pulled Emily into a fierce hug. "I love you bunches, Em."

"I love you more," Emily said, choking out the words in a hiccuping sob.

"I'm going to stay out here—to make it easier." Jessa hugged her again, then stepped back. "I'll see you before too long. Learn some spells to show me." She didn't bother trying to dry her tears, knowing it was futile. The way she felt right now, she would never stop crying. "Learn how to conjure up a magic mirror or something so we can FaceTime."

Tears streaming, Emily gave a quick nod as she backed toward the door to the pub. "I will." She lifted her hand. "Bye, Jess. See you soon."

Jessa held her breath and blinked fast and furiously against the onslaught of tears as Emily disappeared into the pub. She slowly lowered herself to the bench, covered her face with her hands, and sobbed. Her friend was gone. She hadn't felt this lost and abandoned since she was eight years old and hiding in the bathroom cabinet.

Strong arms gathered her up and held her close, gently swaying and shushing but wisely not telling her not to cry. Grant seated himself on the bench and settled her in his lap. But he didn't speak. He was simply *there*, silently giving his strength, his support, and his love.

With Emily gone, and Mairwen probably hiding, Jessa's impossible to imagine emigration to eighteenth century Scotland suddenly seemed startlingly real. And she was married. And pregnant. And who knew how long it would be before she talked to Emily again? She unleashed a desperate, keening wail that startled the dog sleeping on the steps of the bakery.

The shaggy canine joined in with a heartfelt howl.

Grant never said a word. He held her, gently stroked her hair, and occasionally pressed a kiss to the top of her head.

The longer they sat there, the more she *felt* the depth of his patience, support, and undeniable love. Few other men would give her free rein to cry buckets, wail until the village dogs howled, and snot all over them like a toddler. This was most assuredly the definition of true love.

She fished in her cleavage for the ever-illusive square of linen that would never effectively take the place of a gorgeous cardboard box of facial tissues—or at least as far as she was concerned, it wouldn't. She wiped her eyes, blew her nose, and silently told herself to get it together before she cried herself into a case of the hiccups that would rapidly devolve into a puking session. That was too much to ask of anyone, no matter how much Grant said he loved her.

After another loud blowing of her nose, she pushed herself out of his lap, shook out her skirts, and squared her shoulders. "I am sorry."

With an endearing tip of his head to one side, he studied her. "For what, my love?"

She arched a brow at him. "You know *for what*."

He rose from the bench, wrapped an arm around her waist, and hugged her to his side. "While ye might find this difficult to believe, I would say ye've handled these past few days with courage and grace." He brought her around to face him and tipped her face up to his. "Ye are a rare woman, Jessa MacAlester, and I am proud to call ye mine."

"I have always felt like I was missing something," she said. "But I don't feel that way anymore." She rested her hand on his heart, its steady thump against her palm, calming her jumbled emotions into a manageable bundle of chaos. "Em told me her great-great-grand-mother gave up her Weaver lifespan because she couldn't bear the thought of living without her fated mate, who only had the short lifespan of a mortal. Once upon a time, I never would have understood why, but now I do."

He covered her hand with his, then lifted it to his mouth and kissed each of her fingertips. "Are ye ready to go home, my own?"

"Aye."

∽

Mairwen watched Jessa and Grant from the window of one of the upstairs rooms of the pub. A sense of completeness settled over her, and in the ether, she picked up on the joyful, humming glow of the Highland Veil. "We did well," she told Keeva. "Even though this time was fraught with challenges."

"Are ye all right, Mairwen?" the apprentice gently asked. "The goddesses spoke to us through the knowing. They told us of yer son."

"Was it Cerridwen or Bride's voice traveling through the collective mind?" Mairwen had hoped to mourn Valan privately for a while before having to deal with the other Weavers' pity.

"It was Danu," Keeva whispered. "It is the first time I have ever heard the mighty one's voice."

"Life goes on, Keeva. Always remember that. Life goes on, and our duty to the Highland Veil never ends." Mairwen didn't have the emotional strength to explain about Jessa and Grant's twins, Morrigan's loss of her son, or the need for them to consider all Jessa had suggested when it came to making Seven Cairns a meeting place for the estranged friends and loved ones of the fated mates across the realms of time and realities.

She was weary. Morrigan, the vile sister whom she had never quite found the strength to love, had come close to winning this time. That could never be allowed. And in her usual backhanded way, Morrigan had warned them of the others: Beira, Carman, and her sons, and many more. Mairwen closed her eyes and tried to shut out the names of all those from the darkness, those who sought to destroy the Veil.

"Did Emily pass through the curtain with no issue?" she asked Keeva to force herself to think of other things. "Has she returned to her appropriate time?"

"Aye, Mairwen." Keeva leaned closer to the window, smiling down at Grant and Jessa. "Ishbel said she was a quick one. She'll make a braw Spell Weaver."

"Has Bedelia found Emily's mate yet?"

"No. But she feels he is close."

"Very well." Mairwen shooed the girl away from the window and pointed at the door. "On wi' ye, aye? Go help Lilias with her latest delivery or find Ishbel and see if she needs any help with Emily. I am going to stay in this time a bit. And rest."

Keeva gave her an understanding nod. "Peace to ye, Mairwen."

"Peace to ye as well, my child."

EPILOGUE

MacAlester Keep
Spring 1786
Scottish Highlands

"She is asking for ye," Mrs. Robeson said from the doorway of the solar. The worry in her voice and the way she kept wringing her hands in her apron deepened the terror already simmering in Grant's gut.

He shot a tortured look at Henry and Lachie, who paced alongside him. "I have heard no cries. Did ye hear any cries?"

Henry avoided his gaze, then shook his head. "Nay. No cries."

"Lachie?" Grant willed the man to give him hope.

Lachie turned away and stared at the floor. "No, my brother. No cries."

Old Griselda burst into the room, shaking her bony fist. "The goddess wants ye at her side. Are ye such a coward that ye would refuse her when she fights to bring forth yer bairns?"

Ashamed that he had hesitated in Jessa's time of need, Grant charged out of the room, crossed the hall, and entered the suffocating darkness of the bedchamber. "Jessa—I am here."

"Will you please make them leave that freaking window open? I cannot breathe with it shut, and they're fighting me on everything!"

"Do as she says," he told the shadowy figure by the window, who could either be Molly, Jessa's personal maid, or some other servant. The room was too dark to tell. "'Tis hotter than the seventh level of hell in here and too feckin' dark. Ye know yer mistress hates the darkness." He was none too fond of it himself. Neither of them tolerated a darkened room all that well ever since their time in Morrigan's ravine.

"Too much air and brightness are bad for the babes, my laird," Mrs. Robeson said. "The wind still has a bite of winter's touch to it."

"I'll open the damn window myself, then. Again." Jessa snarled and hissed like a cornered animal fighting to escape a snare as she floundered across the bed. Huge with the children she had yet to bring forth, she roared with frustration.

"Nay, love. I shall open it." Grant sprang across the room, ripped open the heavy curtains, and pushed the panes open wide. A hearty gust of sweet, damp air whooshed into the room along with the blessed softness of light from the rising sun. He turned from the window and pointed at each of the wide-eyed women who had refused to listen to his beloved wife. "Ye will always obey her. Always. Is that understood?"

Mrs. Robeson, Griselda, Molly, and the MacAlester Crag midwife bowed their heads and shifted in place like bairns caught misbehaving. The midwife inched forward and dared to settle a glare on him. "We ken well enough what to do for the safety of the mother and the wee ones. We protect them, my laird. Would ye have us do that which we know to be wrong?"

Jessa wallowed her way off the bed, holding her swollen middle with one hand and her lower back with the other. "I know what my body tells me is right. You will listen to what I know is best for me and mine, or you can haul your ass out of this room and never return. Got it?"

Grant caught her and steadied her as she doubled over and groaned. "Lore a'mighty, love. Should ye be out of the bed?"

"Don't you start. Walking makes me feel better, and I think it moves things along." She curled against him, burying her face in his chest with another loud groan. "And for the record, we are never having sex again."

He glared at the gloating women across the room while praying his overwrought wife would change her mind about that once she had healed from having the wee ones.

"Light more candles," he told them, barking the orders so loud they jumped. "Ye know she hates the shadows."

They hurried to light every lamp and candle in the room as he helped Jessa slowly walk back and forth beside the bed.

"I don't know how long this is going to work," Jessa told him as she halted for another pain and dug her fingernails even deeper into his arm. "I feel like they're hanging down to my knees."

"Aye, well—" He didn't know what to say. Men did not belong in this sort of chaos. "If one comes out, I'll be sure to catch it."

She stopped walking, leaned against him, and laughed. "Good. I may take you up on that."

Lore a'mighty, he hoped not. While he'd helped deliver foals, calves, and lambs, the complicated process of a bairn coming into the world was better left to the women. But he didn't tell her that. She needed him here, and by heavens, here he would stay. He nodded at Molly. "Fetch a cool cloth for yer mistress's face. 'Twill give her some ease."

"I cannot stand this much longer," Jessa said, leaning heavier against him and breathing harder. "These babies have got to come out soon." She shoved at the damp curls stuck to her face and started to cry. "I would kill for an epidural."

He had no idea what an *epidural* was and wasn't about to ask.

"We put a knife under the bed to cut the pain," Mrs. Robeson said. "It canna help ye if ye walk, m'lady."

"And I told you that was superstitious bullshit!" Jessa growled through her clenched teeth, hanging onto Grant while leaning forward. After a long, pained groan, she jerked on his arms. "Are you ready to catch one?"

"What?"

She squatted lower. "A baby is coming out. Catch it. Now!"

He dropped to her feet, rent her shift in two, and caught the squirming, dark-haired being in his trembling hands. "Lore a'mighty. Lore a'mighty." It was all he could say, awestruck by the slippery, red-faced babe. "Why is he not crying? What is wrong?"

"Is he all right?" Jessa clutched the side of the bed, twisting to see the child.

"Give him to me," the midwife said, lifting the wee one out of his grasp. The wriggling mite squalled with rage, making the old woman laugh. "Aye, his wee lordship doesna like my cold hands. None of them do. They always cry good for me and clear their bodies of the fluids."

Jessa groaned and pressed her forehead against the side of the bed. "Grant! Another one's coming."

Better prepared this time, Grant deftly caught his second son, laughing when the tiny wriggling beast fussed at him. "Aye, my wee lad. Tell me all about it."

"Hand this one to me," Mrs. Robeson said, a linen held between her hands. "I'll tend to our angry wee laddie whilst ye help our lady into the bed so we can see to her needs and make her more comfortable."

Bursting with joy, he rose and laid his hands on the beloved woman who had just blessed him with two healthy sons. "Come, m'love. Let me help ye into the bed. Ye've battled hard and heavy. Time to rest."

With her fists knotted in the bedclothes and her face still pressed against the bed's edge, she shook her head. "No. I don't think we're done. Another one's coming."

Awestruck, Grant stared at her as she bore down as she'd done twice before, then turned to the midwife for an answer.

The old woman waved away the words and whispered, "'Tis the afterbirth, my laird. They sometimes think it's another because their body works to push it out."

"Grant!" Jessa squatted even more, reached down, then steadied herself as she carefully pulled the babe from its birth into her arms. "I knew you were there," she told the precious child, holding the baby to her chest as she rocked to her haunches and leaned against the bed. She looked up and narrowed her eyes at all in the room. "Never ignore what I say ever again unless you want to be banished." She focused her anger on Grant. "That especially goes for you."

"But the goddesses said there were only two." He cringed at the weakness of his excuse for not listening to her. "I am sorry, Jessa. Never again will I ever take anyone's word over yers. Please forgive me." He crouched beside her and risked caressing her cheek. "Please?"

Her glare softened, as did the hard line of her jaw. "Always believe me. Okay?"

"Always," he promised, then cupped the babe's tiny head. "I canna believe we have three sons."

Jessa grinned. "We don't. We have two sons and a daughter."

"A wee lassie?"

"A wee lassie to make sure her brothers toe the line." Jessa reluctantly handed the baby girl off to Molly, then accepted Grant's hand and allowed him to help her back into the bed.

He noted she didn't seem at all surprised about their third child. "Ye knew about her."

As she sagged back into the pillows, she gave him a wan smile. "I had a feeling but didn't know for sure, and I had no idea whether number three was a boy or a girl."

He sat on the bed beside her, his heart so full he couldn't speak.

She arched a brow at him. "What?"

"I canna begin to tell ye how relieved I am that all of ye are well. I am blessed beyond my wildest imaginings." He smoothed her damp hair back from her face and kissed her. "Thank ye, my own. For staying with me. Loving me. Putting up with me and giving me three braw children."

She rested a hand on his cheek and gave him a weary smile that made her eyes sparkle. "Thank you for the same."

"M'lady?" Molly said with understandable wariness.

Jessa looked her way.

"If it be to yer liking for the laird to step out, we'll be making ye more comfortable so ye can put the wee ones to yer breast." The maid glanced back at Mrs. Robison, Griselda, and the midwife as if they had chosen her as the unlucky one to speak. "And with three, we'll need to be sending for a wet nurse, ye ken? To help make sure the wee ones have all the milk they need."

Grant hoped Jessa would agree to the help of a wet nurse, but he wasn't about to push her on it. Not after his grave error from earlier. He leaned forward and kissed her again. "Let them care for ye, my love. I'll be in the solar, telling Henry and Lachie the news."

"You remember the names we picked for the boys?"

"Lucian for the firstborn. Kiran for his brother. But what about our daughter? We nay had Emily search her inter—world for a girl's name that means light."

"*Internet*," Jessa said with an indulgent giggle, "and I had her search for one just in case. Meira means bringer of light."

"*Internet*," Grant repeated, trying to commit the term to memory. He would never remember Jessa's strange words. He shook away the unimportant thought and tried the name, "Lady Meira MacAlester, daughter of the Earl of Suddie." He nodded. "A fine name. So be it." He cradled her face and kissed her again. "And ye'll let them fetch the wet nurse to help ye? Please? I fear if ye dinna accept help that weariness will make ye fall ill."

"As long as the wet nurse is a loving woman. I will have no unkindness around my babies."

"That goes without saying, love." He tipped a nod at Molly.

She gave him what appeared to be a very grateful curtsy, then hurried out to send for the woman.

He held tight to Jessa's hand, unwilling to leave her side. "Ye are the greatest warrior that ever was, m'love. What ye went through to bring our children into this world." He slowly shook his head, his throat closing off with the fullness of his emotions.

Her cheeks flared a brighter shade of red. "I'm not the first woman to give birth."

"Ye are the first and only woman to give my bairns life."

From the foot of the bed, Mrs. Robeson cleared her throat. "Off wi' ye, my laird. Our lady needs cleaning up, and yer children need her to feed them."

"You better go," Jessa told him softly with a gentle squeeze of his hand. "Go tell Henry and Lachie they've got three little warriors to train."

"Three?" Grant sat taller. "No daughter of mine will ever have to fight."

"We will discuss that later," Jessa said with a look that told him he had already lost that battle.

Ah, well. He didn't care. Much. He rose and leaned over for another kiss. "I love ye, my own."

"I love you more."

GLOSSARY
PERTINENT STUFF TO KNOW

Auld Ways, The - Earth religions, Paganism, belief in the gods and goddesses

Bride - the goddess of healing symbolised by the element of water, goddess of the alchemical force of fire, and goddess of poetry

Caladbolg - the sword of Leite from the elf mounds

Cerridwen - a figure of significant importance in Welsh and Celtic mythology, often revered as a goddess of wisdom, inspiration, and rebirth

Crystal Athame - Ceremonial knife used for spell work, healing, and sometimes, binding ceremonies

Crystal Prison, aka Danu's Prison - where the mighty Goddess Danu imprisons immortals unwise enough to cross her

GLOSSARY

Danu - a central figure in Celtic mythology, specifically Irish lore, regarded as a primordial mother goddess associated with water, fertility, and wisdom

Goddess's Ledger of Infinity - used to report the Council's meeting minutes to the goddesses

Highland Veil - a tapestry of time, energy, and mystical ether. Over the ages, it becomes worn and thins a bit here and there. Some beings, depending on their goddess given abilities, are sometimes able to slip through to other worlds or times and create havoc where they do not belong, giving birth to many of our myths and legends. There is but one thing powerful enough to keep the Veil's weave strong and intact enough to fully separate that which must be kept to itself for the good of all: Love.

Induciae - a spell or request for the suspension of hostilities

Knowing, The - the way the goddesses speak to the Weavers as a whole. Their minds connect, and knowledge is shared.

Libero - a spell to release a subject from the effects of another spell

MacAlester Craig - village nearest to MacAlester Keep

Order of the Defenders of the Veil - mortals sworn to defend the Highland Veil and work with the Weavers. They also possess a few special powers and a longer than usual lifespan...but they are still mortal and eventually die.

Portal Bell - when an unsuspecting mortal rings it, they travel to another time; the time chosen for them by a Weaver.

GLOSSARY

Quies - a spell to freeze someone in place and time to prevent them from harming themselves or others

Seven Cairns - a quaint Highland village that is so very much more ;)

Talam - the Weavers' word for the earth realm. Earth = Talam

Tarot Card Dating App - an irresistible phone application that helps the Weavers lure fated mate prospects to Seven Cairns

Tenete - a spell for strength to hold fast and stay together

Unum Sumus - a healing spell that unites the powers of others

Weavers - the ten immortals charged with the protection and rejuvenation of the Highland Veil

SNEAK PEEK INTO: A FINE SCOTTISH SPELL

Modern Day - Autumn
   Scottish Highlands
   Village of Seven Cairns

"Mama...Mama..." Emily Mithers gave up. She snapped her mouth shut and nodded in all the right places of her mother's long diatribe about missing her, missing Jessa, and wanting to hold Jessa and Grant's babies rather than coo at them over video calls. What her mother didn't realize was that it had taken a battle of epic proportions to convince the goddesses and the Weavers to back down off their stance of erasing the memories of family and friends to protect the secrecy of fated mates brought together through time travel and magic so their loving bonds strengthened the weave of the Highland Veil—a mystical shield of sorts that separated all the worlds, realities, and timelines in existence.

Emily and Jessa were the first outsiders able to convince the goddesses that they should be allowed to maintain contact with their loved ones as long as they handled it delicately and protected the secrets of the Highland Veil, its Order of Defenders, and the Divine Weavers who cared for it.

"If you're not going to listen, we might as well end this call—even though it's long overdue." Her mother sniffed and assumed the aloofness of a parent more than willing to hand out a generous helping of guilt. "But I'm not complaining. I'm just thankful you spared a few moments out of your busy schedule for a brief chat with your mother."

"Passive aggressiveness is beneath you, Mama. Save it for the fearsome five. It always works on them."

Her mother just jutted her chin even higher. "At least your brothers adore me."

"I adore you, too, and you know it." Emily rested her fingertips on the computer screen, wishing she could reach through it and touch her mother's soft cheek. As the youngest of six and the only girl, her parents had lovingly spoiled her rotten, and she missed them with a fury. "You and Papa are still coming to Seven Cairns in the spring. Right?"

"Are you coming home for the holidays?"

"I'll be there for Christmas. You already extracted that promise. Remember?"

"And what about our Jessa? And the babies? We consider her family too. I never want her to forget that."

"Jessa and Grant aren't brave enough to make an almost eleven hour flight with seven month old triplets." Emily couldn't add that by the goddesses' order, eighteenth century Grant MacAlester's forays into the twenty-first century were limited to the boundaries of Seven Cairns, the way station sanctioned by the goddesses for the use of fated mates and the Weavers.

"I suppose that would be a bit much. I'll simply ship their gifts to them. I assume I'll have to send them to your cottage there in Seven Cairns, since Royal Mail still hasn't figured out where their castle is?"

"It's a keep, Mama. Remember?" And she couldn't very well tell her mother that twenty-first century Royal Mail didn't deliver to the eighteenth century. "If you don't want to ship them, I can always bring them back when I return after Christmas." Emily braced herself. That particular subject was still a raw nerve with her mother. Her parents couldn't understand why she had decided to stay in Seven Cairns indefinitely, and she'd given up on trying to explain it in vague yet convincing terms.

"That won't work. I doubt the airline's weight limits would allow it." The self-ordained grandmother wasn't the least bit ashamed that she might have overdone it a bit in purchasing gifts for the babies.

Emily couldn't very well tell her mother that, depending on the gifts, they might not be allowed into the eighteenth century. That was another rule from the goddesses, and this one, she understood completely. They had to be cautious about fouling history's timeline with knowledge or items from the future. The results could be disastrous. The babies would have to enjoy their presents in Seven Cairns and leave them there whenever they went home. She gave her mother a stern look she knew would be ignored. "Remember Papa's back. Don't pack the boxes too heavy."

Her mother rolled her eyes. "Don't get me started on your father's aging insecurities and determination to prove he's still as fit as a twenty year old."

The video on the laptop froze before Emily could comment. A sure sign that Ishbel, Master of the Spell Weavers, was tired of waiting for Emily to show up for their daily work in spell casting. With a resigned sigh, Emily pulled out her phone and texted: *Sorry! Lost the signal. Love you!*

Her mother responded with a long string of heart emojis and *Love you too!*

Emily tucked her phone back into the thigh pocket of her black, fleece-lined leggings, then pulled on her favorite creamy white cable knit sweater over her sleek black workout tank. She had learned early on that layers were the best defense against the damp chill of Scotland in late November. Thick wool socks. Waterproof hiking boots. Wool gloves. All the accoutrements she never thought she would wear for anything other than climbing a mountain on a cold, windy day had become everyday garments here. She tied back her mane of long black braids into a neat twist that would keep them out of the way and pulled on a chunky knit beanie. A backpack with a change of clothes completed her preparations for her magical workout. Even though it was a short walk from her cottage to the Weaver's meeting house, and she and Ishbel always practiced inside, past experience with the unpredictability of Seven Cairns had taught her to be as prepared as possible.

"Ye should never call yer mother when ye know ye're due to be somewhere," Ishbel said as Emily entered the practice hall. "It makes ye tardy every time."

Emily gritted her teeth against telling the Master Spell Weaver that it was none of her business. Wasn't it enough that she had put her life on hold and remained in Seven Cairns to get in touch with her Spell Weaver ancestry as the Weavers had requested? Of course, she had also stayed because of Jessa, but the more she saw how happy and settled Jessa was, the more restless she felt. Not that she wasn't happy for Jessa—but...well...it was complicated, and she wasn't in the mood to get into it with Ishbel.

She dropped her backpack onto the bench against the wall and started stretching as if about to lift weights or run a marathon. Sometimes, magic turned physical, and she had the bruises to prove it. "So, what are we working on today? Same old stuff?"

When Ishbel remained silent, she turned to find the Weaver studying her with a worried scowl. Emily tensed, or more aptly, her already tensed muscles ratcheted into even tighter knots. Of late, she stayed so overwound it was a wonder she wasn't a cramped bundle of misery. "What?"

"We have talked of how yer emotions feed into the magic, ye ken?" Ishbel moved closer, her long, silky robes of purple and red splashes fluttering around her as if she were a colorful butterfly. She had released her gray hair from its usual messy bun, and the silvery curls cascaded down well past her waist. "Yer aura is full of chaos, child. Murky with troubled shades. Perhaps ye best spend yer day elsewhere and leave the energies be. They dinna take kindly to those who poke at them with negativity. Mayhap Mairwen could give ye a massage."

"I am not negative." Emily huffed at her own snappishness. She sounded like a brat even to herself. "Or at least I wasn't until you accused me of it."

"What is wrong, child? What has ye so upset?"

"I am not your child, and I'm not upset."

Ishbel spread her hands and offered an apologetic bow.

The Weaver's placating dramatics and faint smirk made Emily even pricklier. She plopped onto the bench and dropped her head into her hands. She was upset, had felt that way for days, and was sick and tired of it. "I don't know what's wrong with me, and nothing I try helps."

"What about meditation? Seeking the problem and working it out the way I showed ye?"

"No luck." Emily stared at the toes of her boots and noticed some of the stitching had torn free. Great. She had spent a bundle on those and even sang their praises to her bazillion followers on her influencer channel. Looks like she would have to go back online and tell everyone she'd been wrong. And that was just it. She'd been wrong about so many things. "I'm tired of being wrong, Ishbel. Tired of screwing myself over by making the wrong choices." She snorted a sad laugh. "And I have no one to blame for my misery but myself."

Ishbel settled down beside her and wrapped an arm around her shoulders. "I have never seen ye like this, child...er...Emily. Ye worry me when ye are so troubled. Is part of it because we've not yet found yer fated mate?"

Every frustration churning within her roared even louder, making Emily twitch to shake Ishbel away, then immediately feel guilty about even thinking that. "I didn't come here looking for a fated mate and don't expect to find one."

"Why did ye come here, lass?"

SNEAK PEEK INTO: A FINE SCOTTISH SPELL

"To help Jessa find happiness. She deserved it."

"And ye dinna believe ye deserve that same happiness as well?"

"I didn't say that."

"Ye nay had to." The determined glint in the Spell Weaver's pale green eyes warned she was not yet finished. She shook a finger as if winding up for one hell of a sermon. "Why do ye not believe ye have every right to be as happy as yer friend?"

"Why do you believe I can't be happy without the complication of a relationship?"

"The *complication* of a relationship?" Ishbel nodded. "I see now. Ye have been burnt by that fire before and still feel a bit singed, I reckon. Is that not what ye worked so hard to help yer Jessa overcome? The *complication* of a relationship that had soured?"

"Enough therapy, Ishbel. Shall we get started?" Emily jumped up from the bench, strode to the center of the room, and bounced in place while flexing her fingers. "What spell are we working on today? Same one as yesterday?"

Ishbel's eyes narrowed with a displeased glare. "I doubt verra much ye can manage the serenity spell today any better than ye managed it yesterday. The thatching on Innis's cottage is still smoking."

Emily rolled her shoulders and stretched her tensed neck muscles by tipping her head from side to side. "I apologized for that and even made it rain to put out the fire."

"I was the one who made it rain, lass, and shielded the rest of the village from the lightning ye conjured with yer weather spell."

"I'll do better today." And she would. She would concentrate. Clear her mind and her heart, and swim with the energies as if she were a magical dolphin. She forced a smile she didn't feel. "I promise."

Ishbel did not appear convinced, but she nodded for Emily to proceed.

Pulling in a deep cleansing breath, Emily closed her eyes and struggled to calm her thoughts—never an easy task, even on a good day. She had always considered it a strength, the way her mind jumbled with limitless possibilities, and prided herself on the ability to juggle any number of ideas while handling whatever needed to be handled in the forefront. It was simply a matter of channeling all her lively internal wiring into successfully firing on all cylinders at the same time.

Unfortunately, magic was a greedy energy that demanded her full focus, or at least her version of focus. As a child, her teachers had labeled her with all the usuals: ADHD, hyperactive, dyslexic, neurodiverse, or just plain difficult. Thankfully, her psychiatrist mother and internal medicine physician father had lovingly embraced her unique way of thinking and refused to allow the education system make her feel ashamed or ostracized. But even though she had thrived and amazed them with her brilliance, as her father had always said, she still struggled when it came to focusing on one finite thought and blocking out all the others. Magic was hard, and hard frustrated her. How dare that energy not cooperate with her way of thinking!

"Yer aura is flaring red, Emily. Rage will poison yer power. Go to yer vision and rid yerself of it."

"My vision," Emily repeated calmly, even though she wanted to tell Ishbel to be quiet and let her work this out for herself. That would be rude, and Ishbel didn't deserve rude. The Weaver had always been patient and kind. Emily counted her breaths, concentrating on slowing them while bringing forth the memory of a pristine white beach she had enjoyed while visiting the island of Saint John in the U.S. Virgin Islands. She returned to the waters that had been bluer than the bluest crayon in the jumbo crayon box she had always prized as a child. The gentle shush of the waves stroked the shore like a devoted lover. A gentle breeze tickled across her as she basked in the warmth of the tropical sun after a nice, long swim. Her heart rate slowed, and breathing came easier. The impossible to explain feeling she needed, the relaxing fluidity of centering herself, flowed through her.

"*Tranquillitas*," she whispered, envisioning herself as a serene being floating among the clouds.

"Emily!"

Ishbel's panicked cry exploded through her like an electrical jolt. Emily hit the ground hard. The spell turned on her and attacked with a fury. She thrashed to be free of the painful energy searing through her. If she didn't release it, she'd surely burst into flames. "Stop it! Leave me!"

"Feckin' hell!"

Clods of dirt and grass showered her as a monstrous horse leapt over her. Instinctively, she curled into a ball and covered her head. Thankfully, the fiery barbs of mystical energy nipping at her bones had eased, but now she was in the middle of a field somewhere. And she had dropped herself in the path of somebody riding a horse. Damn, magic! She tried to push herself to her feet, but agony knifed through her hip and knocked her back down. "Shit!"

Head pillowed on her arms, she pulled in several deep breaths, fighting the horrendous pain and trying not to give in to the nausea it stirred. Then she opened her eyes. Whatever damage she had done to her hip was the least of her worries.

A very large, angry man had alighted from the horse and was headed her way. She didn't know him, and that meant she had spelled herself somewhere away from Seven Cairns. Wasn't that just freaking wonderful? Then she noticed his clothing and clenched her teeth even tighter. From his manner of dress, the twenty-first century was not his time. The *where* of her landing was no longer the larger problem—the *when* was.

"Shit, shit, shit," she hissed under her breath. Now what was she going to do?

His worn leather boots rose to his knees, and with every forceful step, his kilt molded itself across the muscular powerhouse of his long legs. His impressively broad shoulders were encased in a black wool coat that didn't come close to matching the sooty darkness of his shoulder length hair and the short beard that enhanced the angular lines of his face. The coldness living in his flinty stare made her wonder if he was going to kill her. This man made the mountains look small. She might've held her own when it came to tussles with her five older brothers, but she would never stand a chance against this guy.

"I'm sorry," she blurted out, instinctively raising an arm as if that would somehow protect her from his wrath. "I didn't mean to land in your way. I didn't mean to land here at all."

Silent and grim as death, he stopped, then crouched in front of her, eyes narrowing as he raked his gaze across her.

Maybe he didn't speak English? He looked like a Scot. An eighteenth century Scot, in fact. His clothing reminded her of what Jessa's husband, Grant, always wore. Had she sent herself back in time? If she had, she prayed she'd hit Jessa and Grant's 1786 timeline. "Uhm...I'm Emily. And again, I'm really sorry. Is your horse okay?"

The man's baleful expression darkened even more. He tipped his head to the side as if struggling to decide what species she was. "My horse is Avric—not *Okay*."

"Sorry." She chewed on her bottom lip. Jessa had told her about the problem of using modern words in a different time and the confusion they caused. She'd have to filter herself more carefully. "I'm Emily," she said again as if he might've missed that, even though he was kneeling within a foot of her. "Would you mind telling me the date?"

"The date?"

His hard eyes reminded her of onyx, or black quicksilver, if there was such a thing, or maybe some sort of dark molten ore. A sudden shiver stole through her along with an unmistakable certainty that he meant her no harm. In fact, she felt as if she had met him before. That was pure crazy. She didn't know this guy. How could she *know* on the deepest level imaginable that he wouldn't hurt her?

"Today's date," she said, flinching at the quiver in her voice. She cleared her throat and tried to push herself to a sitting position, only to cry out as pain burned through her hip.

"Ye are injured." His deep voice washed across her, making her catch her breath. "Where are ye hurt?"

"The date?" She had to know the date. He couldn't possibly understand how important that was—way more important than whatever was wrong with her backside.

"Late November, I think. I dinna ken for certain the day." He leaned closer. "Where are ye hurt?" he repeated with a gentle sternness that clearly said he wanted an answer.

"My pride. I landed on it." She gingerly rested her hand on the joint of her left hip. "And the year is?"

"1786." He tipped his chin higher, as if daring her to lie. "What of it?"

"Thank goodness. 1786. You don't happen to know Grant MacAlester, do you?" The lack of recognition in his eyes disappointed her immensely. Where the devil had she landed? "The village of Seven Cairns? MacAlester Craig?"

Still scowling, but maybe he was one of those who always scowled, he shook his head. "Is Grant MacAlester yer husband, then? Are ye running from him?" The growling ferocity rumbling through his voice surprised her.

"No. He's my friend's husband. I thought you might know him." She shifted on the cold, hard ground, hoping she could convince her rear end to let her sit upright this time. It did not. "Shit!"

The glowering Highlander's expression softened somewhat, but he still didn't smile. "Ye'll not be able to ride with that injury."

"Can you just help me stand? I don't like being lower while I'm trying to have a conversation with someone. It's like I'm a rabbit in a trap or something."

He didn't move. Just studied her, sweeping his gaze from the top of her head to her feet once again.

"Is that a *no*, then?"

"I think I should carry ye. Yer arse may be out of joint."

She bit her tongue to keep from firing off a smart remark. Her entire life had been *out of joint* for a while now. "Just help me stand, and we'll go from there, Mr...?"

"MacStrath—Chieftain Gryffe MacStrath of the Midlands. Ye may call me *Gryffe*." He caught her by the shoulders and swept her to her feet as if she weighed no more than a blade of grass.

Her hip raged against the move, punishing her with a dangerous slap of nausea. Dots of blackness swirled through her vision, making her head swim. She fell forward and fisted his shirt in both hands while breathing deep to keep from losing the pot of tea and toast she'd had for breakfast. Eyes closed, forehead braced against his chest, she prayed she wouldn't throw up all over his boots. "I apologize in advance if I puke on you," she whispered, then swallowed hard and willed herself not to vomit. This first impression was not going well at all, and she needed it to. She'd need his help getting back to Seven Cairns, since her freaking magic had turned on her.

He held her with a gentleness that helped her catch her breath and reconsider pulling away. This man was a total stranger—and yet, he wasn't. His nearness, his warmth, the reassuring hardness of his muscular chest against her face both calmed and confused her. She should pull away. Stand on her own. But—she couldn't and wasn't all that mad about being mesmerized into breathing him in and resting in the moment. He smelled of an exciting wildness, cold crisp air warmed by a smoky fire that made you want to curl up and enjoy it. Stroking her hair, he softly murmured a string of words she didn't understand, but she *felt* them. What the devil was happening here?

"What are you saying?" she whispered without opening her eyes.

"Just words, lass. Dinna fash yerself."

Breathing him in yet again, she found the strength to lift her head and look up at him. He was so tall. At just a whisper shy of six feet in height herself, he was a full head and shoulders taller than her. "I'm better now. Thank you." Her hip still throbbed, but it wasn't as bad as it had been. She could bear it as long as she didn't put any weight on her left leg—which would be a problem. "I need

SNEAK PEEK INTO: A FINE SCOTTISH SPELL

to get back to Seven Cairns. What part of Scotland is this, so I can get my bearings?"

He studied her for a long moment, looking deep into her eyes as if walking into her soul and wandering through the shelves of her innermost thoughts to learn more about her. "Seven Cairns is several days' ride from here. Due north. It could take ye nigh on a sennight, depending on the weather, and how hard ye push yer mount. This is my land. Edinburgh is a wee bit to the south of us. Not far from here at all."

"Edinburgh?" Her heart fell. Seven Cairns was north of Inverness, about an hour by rental car—not horse, and it was well over a four hour drive from Edinburgh, depending on how many sheep blocked the road in various places. How had she managed to shoot herself so far south and into another century with what was supposed to be a simple serenity spell? Then it hit her that he knew of Seven Cairns when earlier, he'd shaken his head that he didn't. "I thought you said you didn't know about Seven Cairns?"

With his arms still around her, he twitched a shrug. "I never said that."

"You shook your head when I asked about Seven Cairns and MacAlester Craig."

"I shook my head because I dinna ken MacAlester Craig nor the name of yer friend's husband." His expression darkened again. "Or was that a lie?"

She tried to shove out of his embrace, hobbling her weight onto her right leg and nearly falling. "Shit!"

Baring his teeth, he caught her arm and steadied her. "So it was a lie then, was it?"

"Grant MacAlester is the husband of my friend, Jessa, who is more like a sister to me than a friend. In fact, my parents even think of her as family, and I consider myself an auntie to their three babies. Their favorite auntie, I might add!" She thumped his chest with both fists, then almost fell before grabbing hold of his arms. Why was she telling him all this? He obviously didn't care.

"If you don't want to help me, then don't, but nobody calls me a liar."

"I dinna make it a habit of leaving the injured to fend for themselves until the wolves end their misery."

"Wolves?" Mairwen had told her that Scotland had hunted wolves to extinction by the seventeenth century. "Wolves survive on your land?" She loved wolves, had even gone so far as to sponsor several sanctuaries and raise donations for them on her influencer channel.

A leeriness settled across him as he slowly pulled one of his arms free of her hold and only allowed her to steady herself with the one. "Wolves roam the vastness of the United Kingdom of Scotland. King Roric IV respects their right to survive alongside the rest of us."

"King Roric IV?" While she had never been a history buff, she'd never heard of a King Roric or known Scotland to ever be called the United Kingdom of Scotland.

"Aye. Roric rules this land."

"He rules Scotland."

"Aye. He rules all Britannia."

All Britannia? "Scotland rules England? They not only won their independence but also overcame England's rule?"

"Aye. The English made a poor attempt at an uprising in 1746, but we convinced them of the error of their ways. Both them and the French."

The leeriness in his eyes seemed to shift to concern. Maybe. She'd never really been that good at reading people. "What about England's royals? Their peerage? The dukes and earls and stuff?"

"They all pay fealty to Roric. In return, they're allowed seats in parliament. Some say our king is a wise and fair ruler for doing such, hearing the opinions of those who once opposed him. Some say otherwise." His scowl tightened with a narrowing of his eyes. "Where are ye from, lass? Ye dinna speak like anyone I have ever known, and the questions ye ask are worrisome. I am thinking Seven Cairns is nay the home of yer birth."

"I'm from..." She didn't know how to finish that sentence and wished she had paid more attention to her history lessons. Or maybe she was better off because she hadn't paid that much attention to them. This eighteenth century defied what little history she happened to remember. Almost like it was flipped. Scotland over England. An entirely different reality. What had Mairwen said about alternate realities? Emily's throat closed up, making her gasp for air as the dark spots returned to her vision, spinning at a dizzying pace this time until everything went black.

Tentative Release Date: August 12, 2025

If you enjoyed this story, please consider leaving a review on the site where you purchased your copy, or a reader site such as Goodreads, or BookBub.

Visit my website at maevegreyson.com to sign up for my newsletter and stay up to date on new releases, sales, and all sorts of whatnot. (There are some freebies too!)

I would be nothing without my readers. You make it possible for me to do what I love. Thank you SO much!

Sending you big hugs and hoping you always have a great story to enjoy!

Maeve

About the Author

maevegreyson.com

Maeve Greyson is a USA TODAY bestselling author, Amazon Top 100 bestseller, Amazon All Star, multiple RONE Award winner, and a multiple HOLT Medallion Finalist.

Maeve Greyson's mantra is this: No one has the power to shatter your dreams unless you give it to them.

She and her husband of over forty-five years traveled around the world while in the U.S. Air Force. Now they're settled in rural Kentucky where Maeve writes about her courageous heroes and the fearless women who tame them. Sometimes her stories are historical romances, time travel romances, or escapist romantasies, but the one thing they always have in common is a satisfying happily ever after. When she's not plotting the perfect snare, she can be found herding cats, grandchildren, and her husband—not necessarily in that order.

Also by Maeve Greyson

THE MAGICAL MATCHMAKERS OF SEVEN CAIRNS

A Fine Scottish Time

A Fine Scottish Spell

A Fine Scottish Dream

A Fine Scottish Love

A Fine Scottish Harmony

A Fine Scottish Curse

A Fine Scottish Keeper

SEVEN UNSUITABLE SISTERS SERIES

Blessing's Baron

Fortuity's Arrangement

Grace's Saving

Joy's Willful Wager

Felicity's Eloquent Earl

A less Than Merry Marquess

Serendipity's Suitor

The Making of a Duke

HIGHLAND HEROES SERIES

The Chieftain - Prequel

The Guardian

The Warrior

The Judge

The Dreamer

The Bard

The Ghost

A Yuletide Yearning

Love's Charity

TIME TO LOVE A HIGHLANDER SERIES

Loving Her Highland Thief

Taming Her Highland Legend

Winning Her Highland Warrior

Capturing Her Highland Keeper

Saving Her Highland Traitor

Loving Her Lonely Highlander

Delighting Her Highland Devil

ONCE UPON A SCOT SERIES

A Scot of Her Own

A Scot to Have and to Hold

A Scot to Love and Protect

HIGHLAND PROTECTOR SERIES

Sadie's Highlander

Joanna's Highlander

Katie's Highlander

HIGHLAND HEARTS SERIES

My Highland Lover

My Highland Bride

My Tempting Highlander

My Seductive Highlander

THE MACKAY CLAN

Blessed by a Highland Curse

A Heartsong Back to the Highlands

Beyond A Highland Whisper

The Highlander's Fury

A Highlander In Her Past

OTHER BOOKS BY MAEVE GREYSON

Stone Guardian

Eternity's Mark

Guardian of Midnight Manor

When the Midnight Bell Tolls

Once Upon a Haunted Highland Mist

Loving the Lady of Skye

THE SISTERHOOD OF INDEPENDENT LADIES

To Steal a Duke

To Steal a Marquess

To Steal an Earl

Printed in Great Britain
by Amazon